RESET

RESET

BENSON SECURITY
BOOK 7

JANET ELIZABETH HENDERSON

Can't Buy Me Love

And more on my website
Janet Elizabeth Henderson

CHAPTER ONE

Present day
Location unknown

For the second time in two years, Ryan Granger woke in a strange place with no recollection of how he got there.

"Not again," he groaned.

Blinking, he tried to focus his blurred vision on his surroundings. The light was low and flickering, and he spotted a candle placed on a rocky protrusion.

Rock?

Dirt?

What the hell?

He angled his head to look around him, and pain made him grit his teeth until it passed. Gingerly, he felt for signs of head trauma. The last thing he needed was another concussion. His brain was still Swiss cheese from the bullet that'd skimmed his skull.

Skim—it was such a wimpy word. It did nothing to

describe the bullet's impact on his head or the way it'd made his brain slam against the inside of his skull. And it definitely wasn't a word that sounded like it would cause him to spend seven months in a coma healing from the damage.

To his relief, there were no signs of injury to his head, this time, but the side of his neck ached. There was no mistaking the circular wound his fingertips found. It was an injection site, which meant he'd been drugged.

"Just what I need," he muttered. "Like my brain isn't foggy enough."

Fighting against the weight of his own limbs, Ryan sat up and looked around properly. There was sandy-colored dirt beneath him and hewn limestone walls around him. Hewn. Not natural. So, not a cave. A mine? Maybe?

The walls were rough, although there'd been clear intent in the design of the chamber. A raised stone platform against one wall must have been meant for a bed. And there were nooks carved out for belongings. A miner's accommodation? If it was, it hadn't been used for years, which meant old mine.

An old abandoned mine, then.

Great...

The air was musty. The dust coated his lungs with every breath, leaving him with a dry cotton feeling in his mouth. Instinct made him look for water, although he didn't expect to find any. To his surprise, he spotted a large bottle in a nook high in the wall. It looked full.

"What the hell have I fallen into?"

The walls seemed to shift around him as he struggled to his feet. The ground undulated beneath him. If he didn't believe his eyes, he'd think he was on a boat instead of in a cavern.

"Damn drugs."

Slowly, he made his way to the water. The top of his head skimmed the stone above him, making him aware of the weight of the rock overhead. The bottle was still sealed and cool to the touch, which meant it hadn't been there long. Someone had left it for him. Training made him to check for needle marks or tampering before he cracked it open. There was nothing obvious, and he was desperate for a drink, so he unscrewed the cap.

Years of army experience meant he only sipped at the water, instead of draining the bottle as he wanted. Even foggy, he knew he had to ration. There was no way to tell where he was or how long he'd be there. That bottle could be the last water he saw for a while.

Leaning against the wall, he pulled out his phone and switched it on.

No signal.

No surprise.

It did tell him that it'd been ten hours since he'd walked out of the Department of Neurology after his appointment with his head doc, and that his battery was still pretty much full. He switched the phone off to conserve it and closed his eyes while he tried to remember what'd happened.

The last thing he recalled was opening the door to a hackney cab and telling the driver to take him to Benson Security's office in Victoria. He'd wanted to get in some last-minute practice at the gun range before taking his firearms proficiency test again. Someone had bumped into him—making Ryan apologize, for some reason—and then the world had faded. Next thing he knew, he'd woken up in a cavern.

Fantastic...

He'd been drugged *and* abducted.

His team were never going to let him live this down.

Assuming he managed to get back to them.

The kidnapping made no sense. It wasn't like he had a rich family that'd fork out a ransom for him. And he hadn't been involved in any of Benson Security's recent cases either. In the six months since he'd woken from a coma, he'd worked on building up his muscle mass, regaining control of his body, and trying to put together the parts of his past that he remembered. There were still gaps. Some that'd never fill. Including the month or so before he'd been shot. According to his doc, that was gone forever, which meant it was possible he'd pissed someone off enough to kidnap him, and equally possible he couldn't remember who.

It wasn't like he didn't have enemies. He'd been in the military and then he'd worked all over the world with a specialist security team. They'd taken on the South American cartels, Russian mafia, and London gangs, leaving him with a pretty long suspect list.

Running a hand down his face, he sighed. There was no point in trying to figure out the why and who of the situation. His priority was getting out of there. He'd work out the rest later.

Taking a couple of steps, he tested his equilibrium. Better. At least the room wasn't moving anymore. Time to explore.

As he reached for the candle nearest to him, a faint noise made him freeze. It sounded like a moan. Cocking his head, as though that would help him hear better, he waited.

There it was again.

He spun, regretting the action instantly, as the room kept spinning after he'd stopped. Closing his eyes tight against the moving walls, he fought the nausea that assailed him and strained to listen.

Another moan.

Louder this time.

And it was coming from the far corner.

Ryan's eyes snapped open while everything within him became laser focused. Instantly the nausea disappeared, or maybe he just wasn't aware of it anymore, as he willed his gaze to penetrate the darkness beyond the platform bed.

Movement. Slight but definite.

He grabbed the nearest candle stub and inched his way across the room. With each stiff step, the dim glow of the candle shifted, illuminating the hidden corner in agonizingly small increments. His breath hitched when he realized what he was seeing.

A shoe.

A leg.

A skirt.

A woman.

"Crap!" He slapped the candle down onto the platform and bent over the crumpled form. She was breathing steadily and her pulse was strong. "Okay, okay. That's good..."

He let out a shaky breath as he reached for his phone, needing something brighter than candlelight to check her for injuries. The sharp white beam of the flashlight app was startling after the faint glow from the candles, but it easily illuminated the woman at his feet.

No blood.

No obvious injury.

Except a telltale circular mark on her neck that told him she'd been drugged and taken, just like him. Automatically, he cataloged everything about her that he could see: average height, dark bronze hair in a tight bun at her nape, large round glasses, conservative pale blue blouse, straight navy skirt, sensible heels. And curves. The kind of curves women called fat, but men called lush.

There was something familiar about her, but he couldn't place where he'd seen her or how he knew her. Tearing his eyes from his mystery companion, he spotted a discarded handbag sitting beside her hip.

As she moaned again, fighting off the effects of the drug in her system, Ryan reached for the bag. It was navy leather, good quality, and obviously expensive. A sensible work bag for a businesswoman. The interior was neat and organized, not the jumble he'd seen fall out of other women's bags, making her wallet easy to locate.

"Time to find out who my fellow victim is," he muttered.

The wallet held her driver's license, the photo showing wide hazel eyes and full lips on a heart-shaped face. She'd obviously posed on a workday because she was buttoned-up with tied-back hair. The clothes did nothing for her. This was a woman who should have been wearing diamanté-encrusted jeans and a glitter top. Sarah Jean Davidson was a fifties' pinup girl hiding in drab work clothes.

Another glance at the license told him she was twenty-seven years old, an organ donor, and didn't have any penalties for reckless driving. A gym card told him that she either worked or lived in South London, and a work ID revealed she was an actuary with Steele-Shepherd Insurance.

"Actuary?"

He cocked his head as he considered her. Something to do with birds, maybe? His dentist had a massive aquarium in the waiting room, so it wasn't a stretch to think an insurance company would have an aviary. Still, the job didn't seem to fit her.

Ryan tossed her bag onto the floor beside her and

turned his attention to Ms. Davidson. It didn't seem right to leave her lying on the ground. And even though the platform was made from the same dusty rock, he felt it would be more respectful to put her on it. He took off his brown cord jacket, folded it to make a pillow and placed it on the platform, before turning back and bending to lift her.

There wasn't a lot of space in the corner, but he managed to get his arms under her. She was a soft bundle and she smelled of strawberries, which made his mouth water and his belly rumble. Straightening, he turned toward the platform again. Only to be pulled up short.

Holding her firmly, he twisted to see what her clothes were caught on—and stilled.

"What the hell?" he hissed.

A wave of adrenaline flooded his system, washing away the last of the drug that'd left him foggy. Something clicked into place within him, and the calm clarity he experienced before every mission slid over him like a well-worn coat.

His jaw clenched as he studied the problem.

There was a manacle.

Around her wrist.

She was chained to the wall.

Fury was a blade, barely sheathed, as he examined the restraint. This wasn't something left behind by the miners who'd carved out the space. It was rust free and custom made. Recently poured concrete had been used to anchor the chain to the wall. This had been done just for them.

Slowly, so as not to jar Sarah, he managed to place her on the stone bed and untangle the chain so her arm lay naturally at her side. The restraint around her wrist was an abomination against the pale perfection of her skin. A screaming neon sign flashing "ESCAPE NOW" to anyone who saw it.

"This situation is totally fucked up." His words echoed around the hollow space.

Their kidnapper hadn't bothered to take their belongings from them. Ryan still had his phone, wallet, and Swiss Army knife. Sarah still had her handbag full of stuff. That told him nobody expected them to use those things to get out of the cavern. Their captor had deemed their belongings useless.

Sarah groaned loudly, and her thick, dark eyelashes fluttered.

Ryan was at her side in an instant, trying to appear unthreatening—like that's possible when you're over six foot tall and built like a bruiser.

"Hey," he said softly. "You're okay."

He started to pat her arm, in reassurance, but quickly drew back. They were strangers and he wasn't shackled, which meant there was a good chance she'd think he was her captor.

"Don't get hysterical," he told her. "Everything is going to be okay."

She moaned again, her head turning toward him while she blinked.

Ryan smiled, in what he hoped was a reassuring manner but feared might come across as sociopathic. "I'm not going to harm you. We're in this together." Why did everything he say sound deeply creepy?

Sarah blinked several times as her eyes began to focus. The cutest little frown furrowed her brow, right between her eyebrows, while she stared up at his face with puzzlement.

"It's okay," he cooed. "Don't be scared. I won't hurt you. I woke up here too. I don't know what's going on yet, but we're in this together."

She opened and shut her mouth several times, as though she wasn't sure what to say.

Ryan had a lot of sympathy for her confused state. "You've been drugged, but don't worry, it will pass. I was drugged too. It's natural to feel foggy when you first wake up. I'm still feeling a little dazed as well. Gimme a sec and I'll get you some water. That'll help."

He stepped away to retrieve the water, and her voice stopped him dead.

"Ryan?" she said, sounding confused.

He jerked back to face her. "You know me?"

The frown deepened as she glared at him with a piercing intensity that made it clear any fog she had was gone. "Ryan? Is that really you? Are you real or am I dreaming?"

Okay. Now they were both confused. "You aren't dreaming, I'm real. Do we know each other?"

"Do we know each other?" Her voice rose with every word until she was almost screeching. "Do we know each other?"

Without warning, she swung her free arm straight at his face. Her fist connected with his nose, and he toppled to the floor. Where he lay, staring at the roughly carved ceiling as his nose bled and his thoughts spun wildly.

CHAPTER TWO

Sarah was disgusted with herself. She stared at Ryan in horror as blood trickled from his nose. How could she have lost control like that? There was no excuse for it. None. The first time she'd seen him in over a year and she turned rabid. Mortified did *not* go anywhere near describing how she felt.

"Ryan." She tried to salvage a sliver of dignity. "I shouldn't have hit you. I'm very sorry. I don't know what came over me."

"Anger?" he asked dryly.

"That's no excuse. I...you surprised me, and well, I wasn't expecting to see you again after...well, last time, and here you are..." She frowned as the "here" part of the sentence began to register. "Um... exactly where are we?"

Carefully, she swung her legs over the edge of the stone platform she found herself lying on and took in her surroundings. And what she saw made her heart race and her mouth become suddenly dry.

She'd been in a cafe, meeting a client, and now...

She was in a cave?

With Ryan?

How was she supposed to process this?

As her hands began to tremble, she sucked in some much-needed air, only to find it musty and dry. She licked her lips as she tried to figure out what was happening. It was useless. Literally no logical explanation came to mind.

Dread seeped into her bones, making her feel heavy and cold. She attempted to wrap her arms around herself for warmth and comfort, but her arm felt weighted and restrained. There was a thick metal cuff, fastened tightly around her wrist.

A low scream started to build in the back of her mind as the horrors of the situation sank in.

"Ryan?" Her voice sounded like it was coming from far away as she stared at the restraint. "What's going on?"

"It's going to be okay," he said as he got up from the floor. "Don't panic."

Sarah never panicked. But then, she was never in a situation that merited panic—at least not since she'd been a child. Did wanting to scream and claw at the cuff mean she was panicked?

"I just want to know what's going on." Her voice sounded tinny and tight.

"Listen to me." Ryan didn't sound panicked. He sounded calm and reasonable. "We've been abducted. I'm not sure where we are or who's behind this. All I know is we were drugged. I woke up a few minutes ago and my head is still foggy. You have to be feeling disoriented too, but it's going to be okay. I'll get us out of here."

Nope. That didn't clear anything up. "I don't understand. I was in a cafe, meeting a new client, and now..."

"You're shivering. Here, this will help."

Something wrapped around her shoulders, and warmth seeped into her. Ryan's concerned face peered down at her.

Which begged the questions, where had he been and why was he suddenly back? He was just standing there, staring at her. This huge, hunky apparition from her past, acting as though nothing had happened between them. Surely it wasn't a coincidence that he turned up at the exact same time she ended up cuffed to the wall of a cave? Which meant...

"Why did you bring me here?" It amazed her that she sounded so calm.

He reeled back. "Wait a minute, you think I did this?"

Sarah held up her restrained hand. "I don't see one of these on you and there's nobody else here to blame it on. The logical conclusion is that you brought me to your... dungeon." It became harder to breathe as that scream in the back of her mind grew louder. "Why do you have a dungeon? And why am I chained to the wall? What are you going to do with me?"

The scream in her head became too loud to contain. Sarah opened her mouth, sucked in air, and—

A hand gently, but firmly, covered her lips.

"Please don't, my head is pounding and I'm pretty sure you're only going to attract the attention of whoever dumped us here. You have to believe me, I had nothing to do with this. I've been abducted the same as you have."

If she'd been braver, she'd have chomped a chunk out of his palm. But—blood. And germs. Instead, she glared at him.

"If that's true, why am I the only one who's chained up?" she demanded. It came out muffled.

"I only got part of that. If I let go, do you promise not to scream?"

Okay, that made her pause. A kidnapper who'd take her at her word? Either he was very dumb or just plain optimistic. It was probably the latter. The Ryan she'd known had been smart as a whip.

Trying to appear innocent, Sarah nodded to tell him she wouldn't scream.

Looking relieved, Ryan removed his hand.

Idiot.

Sarah sucked in a deep breath, but before she could shout at the top of her lungs, the hand was back.

"You promised," he accused.

She couldn't help rolling her eyes. "Take your hand from my mouth, or I'll bite it."

"I only got 'bite' from that." With a sigh, Ryan removed his hand again but kept it close to her face, just in case she showed signs of screaming again. "Look, I don't know who you are, I don't know how we got here; all I know is we need to get out before whoever took us comes back. It'd be better if we worked together to do that, but I'm not beyond carrying you out of here kicking and screaming if I have to."

Her right hand tingled, itching to curl into a fist all over again. In her mind's eye, his face turned into a giant bull's-eye, his nose dead center. "Stop saying you don't know me. It's rude."

"I'm not being rude, I'm being honest. First time I laid eyes on you was when I found you lying in that corner." He pointed to the spot beside the platform.

"Are you kidding me?" Now, she was shaking from anger instead of fear. She narrowed her eyes at him. "We dated. Over a year ago. Before you ghosted me."

Honestly, his acting skills were superb, because she almost believed it was news to him. "I don't remember."

"Seriously?" She shrugged off the jacket he'd placed over her shoulders because she was plenty warm now.

He backed away a step. "I have amnesia. There are chunks of my past that I don't remember."

"By any chance, do all the missing parts contain women you've dated?"

"No!" He heaved a sigh. "I'm not playing you here, I'm telling the truth."

"You expect me to believe you have amnesia? That the reason you stopped calling and didn't answer any of my messages was because you couldn't remember me? Is this a daytime soap? Next, you'll tell me you have a twin and I've confused him with you."

Obviously irritated, he put his hands on his hips. "I don't have a twin. I do have amnesia."

"You know I'm too smart to fall for this, right? I'm an actuary. We spend years studying, collecting data, calculating the chance of random things happening, and I can tell you right now, the odds of you having amnesia are about the same as me having a lunch date with the Queen."

"Huh. I thought you looked after birds." He pointed at her handbag. "I went through your wallet while you were out cold and saw your work badge."

Oh, this wasn't amusing at all. "You know exactly what I do for a living. We talked about it—at length—during our many phone conversations."

"I keep telling you. I suffered a head injury. My memory is Swiss cheese."

There was a rumbling noise and, if she wasn't mistaken, it came from his stomach. *Typical.* The man had a Pavlovian reaction to even the slightest mention of food.

It was her turn to point. Which she did, straight at his stomach. "Stop thinking about cheese, we're arguing here."

"How did you know what I was thinking?"

Oh, now she was really beginning to lose her patience.

"Because I know you. And you know me. Stop pretending otherwise."

"Listen, lady—"

"Sarah. My name is Sarah Davidson, as you well know, *Ryan McKay.*"

"McKay?" That shocked him. "My name isn't McKay, it's Granger. McKay is my boss Callum's name."

Why was she even surprised?

"Of course it is. Was anything about you real? I thought I was getting to know this nice, safe, stable guy who installed alarms for a living. Instead, he ghosted me, only to turn up a year later and kidnap me for his freaky dungeon."

Ryan stalked over to her and pushed his unruly, overgrown hair up on the right side of his head. A long, white scar appeared, running about an inch above his temple. "A bullet skimmed my head. The impact turned my skull into a pinball machine, my brain being the ball. Trust me, if your brain smashes against bone enough, you lose some normal physical function and you can kiss goodbye to a whole bunch of memories."

Anger rushed out of Sarah in a long, silent whoosh. *That* definitely hadn't been there the last time she'd seen him. Stomach clenching, she hesitantly reached for the scar.

A strong hand wrapped around her wrist. "No hitting."

"I told you. I don't usually hit."

He stared at her, waiting while he held her in place.

"I'll be gentle," she promised.

As soon as he let her go, she traced the scar with trembling fingertips. An inch lower and it would have shattered his temple. An inch to the right and he would have died. Her throat tightened as she frantically blinked back tears.

"How?" she whispered; her voice rough.

He let his hair drop to cover the scar. "I don't remember,

although I've been told I was protecting a friend in a bad situation when I was shot. Took a couple to the chest too, but the head injury was the worst."

A memory from the weeks following their first—and last—in-person date smacked her in the face. "Did it happen in London?"

When he nodded, she felt bile rise in her throat and forced herself to swallow it down.

"There were news stories." Her hand fluttered anxiously to her throat. "A security company had been attacked and blown up. Then there was a shootout in the center of London involving organized crime and a team of bodyguards. A crime lord's daughter was kidnapped. People died and a bodyguard was critically injured..."

No.

It couldn't be...

"That was me," he said, making her feel light-headed. "I spent seven months in a coma, and the past six months trying to build up muscle mass and regain some of the dexterity I lost while I was out of it. I'm almost back to where I was before I was shot, but the neurologist says I'll stumble over holes in my memory for years to come." He shuffled awkwardly. "I guess you fell through a hole."

This was a nightmare.

All those times she'd cursed him for being a creep and he'd been lying in a coma.

He could have died...

"I watched the news and didn't know it was about you," she whispered, horrified she hadn't made the connection. "You told me you fitted alarm systems."

"I do that too."

"As well as bodyguard work?" Like he'd been doing when he was shot.

"And hostage retrieval, company espionage, covert operations—whatever is needed. At least I did before the injury. Until I'm cleared for weapons handling, driving, and physical activities, I can't work with my team. But I'm slowly sitting the tests I need to retake. I should have been sitting my firearms proficiency today."

"And you really had nothing to with this?" She indicated the cavern.

"No. I really didn't," he said firmly.

There was silence for a moment as Ryan's revelations sank in. Her heart literally ached for him and everything he'd gone through. And it ached for what they could have been if he hadn't been shot. Mostly, she ached because she wished she'd been there beside him, helping him heal.

"If I'd known, I would have been there for you when you were injured."

"I wouldn't have noticed, so don't beat yourself up about it."

"Right. Coma." She nodded.

"Anyway, there would have been no way to contact you to tell you what happened. My phone was destroyed in the attack. Otherwise my friends would have found your details and told you about the injury." His beautiful eyes, although filled with understanding, showed no recognition at all when he looked at her.

"You really don't remember me, do you?" A deep sadness welled within her at the realization.

He ran a hand through his hair. "I wish I did." It sounded like he meant it. "How well did we know each other, exactly?"

Sarah took a shaky breath. "We met on Tinder. We messaged and talked for weeks before we went on a date—we were taking things slow."

"That doesn't sound like me." He looked so bewildered that a chuckle erupted from her, surprising both of them.

"You told me you'd made mistakes in the past and didn't want to rush in again. We spent weeks talking about everything, being really open with each other." Now that the last vestiges of anger had dissipated, she felt like a deflated balloon. A guilt-ridden piece of useless rubber. "At least, I thought we were. I guess that wasn't the case if I didn't even have your real name. It does explain why I couldn't find you though."

He shifted uncomfortably. "I have a vague memory of thinking I needed a different name for dating because my dates kept ripping me off. It's harder to clear out somebody's bank account, or their house, if you don't know their name and address."

Um, what? "Your dates stole from you?"

"All the time. I was cursed." He held up a hand before she could ask any more questions. "Don't worry, it broke before I met you."

"You remember *that* but don't remember me?"

"I remember the night the curse broke. I was having a talk with a friend about making the effort to get to know someone before jumping into bed with them. Then...nothing. You must have been the woman I was planning on getting to know before we took the next step."

"We slept together on our first date, Ryan."

"Yeah, but it sounds like we talked a lot beforehand."

The man was impossible. "We obviously have a different idea of what taking it slow means. Anyway, our second date was scheduled for the following Saturday, but you texted me to tell me that you were up to your ears in work and would contact me when it was over. I never heard from you again. I tried texting and messaging, but there was no reply. When I called, your number had been disconnected. You disappeared from Tinder too. I thought..."

"You thought I'd manipulated you into bed and then moved on to my next mark."

She winced. "Do I have to apologize again?"

"No." His smile was devastating, especially as there was no recognition in his eyes. As far as Ryan was concerned, they were meeting for the first time. "I'm sorry, Sarah. I would never have done something like that to you. I'm not that kind of guy. And, for the record, it doesn't take me a month to get a woman into bed." His sparkling eyes made it clear he was mocking himself. Something he'd often done. Before.

"Got it. Big stud. Little effort. Honestly, I didn't think you that kind of player either, but then I couldn't think of another reason why you'd just disappear." She gave him a wry smile. "Coma and amnesia never even entered into my thinking. I mean, statistically, they weren't even worth considering."

His lip quirked. "Statistically?"

"It's my thing." Pretty much her only thing. Although, she couldn't complain. Knowing the data, and making decisions based on it, had kept her out of a lot of trouble over the years.

"Were we close?" he asked.

"We slept together, Ryan."

"Yeah, but were we close?"

"For someone like me, that means we were close. We were...friends. We laughed and talked. We'd started reading the same books, just so we could discuss them. I felt like I really knew you."

"I'm sorry, Sarah," he said softly.

She cleared her throat. "How about we stop apologizing to each other and concentrate on getting out of here?"

"Sounds like a plan."

"You know, the chances of this happening are almost as low as you having amnesia. Only about one in eighty-four thousand women are kidnapped in the UK each year, most by people they know. I don't know the numbers for stranger abductions, but I'm going to say those are even rarer. Which means, my chances of finding a pearl in an oyster are eight times higher than the likelihood I'd get abducted."

"And yet here we are." He spread his arms wide.

"Here we are." A shiver went down her spine as she held up her bound hand. "Do you have any idea how to remove this?"

"I can try picking the lock." He tugged his keys out of his pocket and removed the Swiss Army knife attached to them.

"You can pick locks?"

"Don't remember. Here's hoping muscle memory will kick in when I start."

"That's funny. Very funny."

Gently, Ryan reached for her hand and brought it to him. His touch seared her skin, sending flashes of sense memory throughout her body. Leaving a sadness in its wake.

"Don't worry." His smile was playful. "I'm almost certain I've done this before. Your wrist is safe with me. We'll get you out of this cuff and then get both of us out of here."

"I'm scared," she blurted her confession. Scared, confused, bewildered, anxious, stunned, shocked, horrified... Her emotions were on a huge roulette wheel and spinning wildly. Who knew where it'd stop or what she'd feel at any moment? It was out of control. And Sarah *hated* being out of control.

Ryan held her gaze, as though he knew she was dizzy from the spinning and needed an anchor. "I won't let anything happen to you."

"We don't have any control here," she felt the need to point out.

He shrugged. "Then we take it back."

Oh, if only it were that simple. Already, her overactive brain was cataloging all the possible outcomes of their situation, and it wasn't hard to come to the conclusion that most of their options were dire. Even with her limited knowledge, she could tell him that their chances of getting out unharmed were close to zero.

"What if we can't get out?" she said. "There wasn't a way out for those miners trapped in Chile. Or the kids in that cave in Thailand. They all had to be rescued by someone else. At least people knew they were trapped there in the first place. Nobody knows we're here. We don't even know where *here* is. And there's no one looking for us."

"Oh." His smile was blinding. "I wouldn't say that..."

CHAPTER THREE

Benson Security
London Office

"Ryan's missing," Joe Barone said as he barged into Callum McKay's office.

Callum let out an irritated growl, slammed his pen on his desk, and glared at his head of training. "When I was in the service, men knocked before they entered my office."

They'd also cowered outside it until they'd plucked up their courage. Something his team at Benson Security never did—even though *he* was one of the owning partners. Like that impressed any of them. He mentally scoffed at the thought.

To prove his point, Joe ignored his reprimand and threw himself into one of the guest chairs, making Callum wonder if that's where he'd gone wrong—no guest chairs, no guests.

The chairs had to go.

"Did you hear me?" Joe rested his ankle on his other

knee, his foot wiggling in a rare show of anxiety. "Ryan didn't turn up for his firearms proficiency exam, and he isn't answering his phone."

Callum wasn't worried. "He probably found a new cut-price buffet, and his mouth was too full to talk." It'd happened before. More than once.

The tall American shook his head. "It's been hours. Even he can't eat for that long."

"Fine." Callum pinched the bridge of his nose and sighed. "Take a car and go get him. He's probably forgotten."

"He wouldn't. It's all he's been talking about for weeks."

"I give up." Callum threw his hands in the air. "What do you want me to do? Do you want *me* to go find him?"

"No, I want you to mobilize the team. Something's wrong."

Okay, that made Callum sit up and pay attention. "How long has he been missing?"

"Nobody's seen or heard from him since his weekly checkup with the neurologist this morning." A former US Army Ranger, Joe wasn't prone to overreacting. To see him this worried was a serious concern.

"You've talked with his grandparents?"

They'd made the mistake of hiring Ryan's granddad and granduncle to do some carpentry around the place when the London office first opened. The two old men hadn't left yet. They thought it was entertaining to spend their days inventing odd jobs so they could eavesdrop on new cases or "train" with the weapons in the workout room. Right now, they were installing closets in Callum's house, which sat at the back of the Benson Security property.

"I felt them out—didn't want to worry them. They haven't heard from him either." Joe put his foot down, sat forward, and ran a hand through the thick dark hair that was a hallmark of his Italian ancestry. "I've got a bad feeling..."

"You shoulda started with that," Callum said. Because when Joe had a bad feeling, everything usually went to hell. "Get the team together, and I'll meet you in the conference room."

With a chin lift, Joe left. Leaving Callum with a knot in his stomach. It was the same tight sensation he'd endured during the months Ryan had been in a coma. Every day, he'd woken up wondering if it would be the boy's last. *Boy!* Ryan was a thirty-two-year-old man and an ex-soldier with remarkable skills, hardly a boy. But deep inside, far beneath his crusty Scottish exterior, Callum couldn't help thinking of Ryan as another son—although, he'd never admit it, if asked.

"What have you got yourself into this time, lad?" Callum said as he rubbed his hand down his thighs.

Even though his lower leg prosthetics rarely caused pain anymore, he'd found it hard to break the habit. Self-soothing, his physio had called it, before telling him it was common in amputees. Callum had barked at the man, making it clear he didn't need to be comforted, by himself or anyone else. Yet, when times were particularly stressful, his legs—the part that had been torn off by an IED—ached with phantom pains.

And Ryan missing was definitely stressful. The boy often joked that he was the least skilled of the team, but while he'd been asleep, Callum had learned the truth: Ryan was essential to it.

Turned out, he was their heart.

Grabbing his phone, he strode from his office and up the stairs to the conference room on the first floor of the old

Victorian terrace house that was their London base. Although the team had grown in the years since their office had been established, it was only the original members who sat at the table. He scanned the faces that had become family to him—completely against his will.

"Joe, fill them in," Callum ordered as he took his usual position, standing at the head of the table, arms folded over one of his many gray Henleys.

"Don't you dare start without me," a female voice snapped from the doorway.

Callum growled at the sight of Rachel Ford-Talbot, who had once been an owning partner in the business, and a pain in his backside. As usual, she was dressed in some designer suit and a disapproving smirk. She held her iPhone, which would, one day, have to be surgically removed from her hand, and there was a designer handbag slung over the crook of her elbow. The bag probably cost more than Callum's car because Rachel didn't do cheap.

"How did you get here so fast? Joe just told me what's going on." Callum viewed Rachel as the sister everyone hoped wouldn't turn up for Christmas dinner.

"I was already here." Rachel pulled out a seat as her husband, Michael "Harvard" Carter, strolled into the room.

As usual, the former CIA operative was wearing the smug smile he got around his wife. As though he'd hooked a prize-winning fish, when really, he'd caught a piranha.

"Why were you already here?" Callum barked. "You're CEO of a company that's based over two hours away. You do realize you don't work here anymore, right?"

She scoffed. "Like I ever did. I graced this place with my presence and leadership. Something it obviously still needs." Her cool gaze settled on Joe. "You may begin."

"Aye, now that her majesty has given you permission,

you can fill us all in." Callum glared at Rachel, who remained unfazed.

Joe's smile disappeared as he recounted what he'd already told Callum. Expressions around the room sobered, and before Joe had finished talking, Elle Roberts-Knight, their IT expert, had her laptop open with her fingers flying over the keyboard. Her serious demeanor was at odds with her blue hair and pink Minnie Mouse T-shirt. Callum couldn't see her screen, but he'd bet she was hacking Ryan's accounts—if she didn't already have the passwords. Elle had a way of acquiring things she shouldn't have.

"Did you try calling his mum?" Megan Raast, the only other Scot in the room, asked.

The team had become very close to Ryan's family during his months in hospital. Especially to his younger sister, who had Downs Syndrome. Grace had pretty much become the team's mascot during the past year. She was a good kid. One of the few people Callum *didn't* mind having around.

His family had returned to Cornwall after it was clear Ryan would be fine. And, although Cornwall wasn't exactly a day trip from London, they still kept close tabs on Ryan and visited often. Seemed as though none of the people who loved Ryan were quite ready to get over those months he'd been in a coma.

"Yeah," Joe said. "I called her straight after I spoke to his grandparents. I didn't give anything away, just told her I rang to say hi. She hasn't spoken to him since Sunday."

"Girlfriends?" Dimitri, Megan's husband—and keeper —asked.

"He hasn't been seeing anyone since he woke up," Elle said as she typed. "Says he doesn't have time for it. I think he's still a bit freaked that his last Tinder interaction led to our Wi-Fi being hacked and the building getting bombed." She looked up at Callum. "A thing like that can put you off romance."

Honestly, there was nothing to say to that, even if Callum could think of something.

"Friends?" he said instead.

"We're his friends," Elle said.

Her husband stretched his arm across the back of her chair. Unlike his wife, David Knight was the picture of all things ordinary and unassuming. Callum pitied anyone stupid enough to fall for his act. The former CIA agent's skills were deadly. "He hasn't forgotten anything important in months, so chances of today's test slipping his mind are slim."

"Maybe something happened at the doctor this morning that scared him?" Julia Barone was sitting in the corner of the room, partially hidden by a huge office plant that Callum kept having removed, only for it to reappear. "Has anyone spoken with his neurologist?"

Even though Julia now managed to speak without being coerced, Callum still couldn't get her to take a seat at the table. She liked to be able to hide if anyone started shouting. If she hadn't been the best business manager on the planet, he'd have fired her years earlier. Although, her husband, Joe, might have taken issue with that, and he could be a scary son of a bitch when the situation warranted it.

When no one answered her, Julia stood. "I'll take that as a no. I'll call her now." She pulled out her phone as she left the room.

"Has he been feeling sick recently? Any head pain? Migraines?" Megan tossed her long blonde hair over the shoulder of her black leather biker's jacket.

"Not that he's mentioned," Joe said.

Everyone else shook their heads in agreement; he hadn't shared any worries with them either.

"He's remarkably healthy for someone who spent months recovering from a coma," Rachel said dryly.

For once, he had to agree with Cruella. "A wee bit too healthy."

"You think he's hiding something?" Joe asked.

Elle was already shaking her head. "No, he wouldn't. He's been working so hard to get back into shape. All he can talk about is getting to rejoin the team."

"Have to say," Joe leaned back in his seat. "I've spent a lot of time on the firing range with him, and I'm impressed. He can shoot just as well both left-handed and right, and I've never seen any physical issues. Not once."

Callum shared a look with Rachel, who was equally skeptical. They both knew how eager Ryan was to put the head injury behind him. It was a concern that he'd rush things in order to get to his goal as fast as possible. The last thing the boy needed was to relapse, purely because he was pushing himself too hard.

Callum knew exactly how that felt. There'd been a time when he'd been so eager to get back to *normality* that he hadn't properly dealt with losing his legs. He didn't want Ryan to repeat his mistakes.

Julia came back into the room, worry etched on her brow. "The consultant said that Ryan's doing great. The issues that he still has are mild and may never go away, but she's confident he's learned to adjust and deal with them. In fact, she's been talking about dismissing him from her clinic. She doesn't think there's anything else she can do for him that his physio couldn't achieve."

"So, he's as fit and healthy as he tells us all he is?" Callum asked.

"Yes." Julia nodded.

Callum felt his throat tighten as a surge of relief hit him.

"Did you ask about his mood while he was there?" Rachel asked while looking at her phone.

"She said he was happy and excited about retaking his firearms proficiency exam. All he talked about was getting back in the field." Julia nibbled her bottom lip. "Do you think he's been in an accident?"

"I can check the hospitals, just in case," Joe said. "He wouldn't have been driving; he hasn't been cleared for that yet. He's retaking his test next week."

Elle sucked in a breath, drawing everyone's attention. For once, her fingers were still over her keyboard, and her face was paler than usual beneath her blue hair.

David tugged at a luminous lock. "What is it, Blue?"

Her eyes were impossibly wide as she glanced at David before looking up at Callum. "I can't find him."

"Aye," Callum said slowly, wondering if marriage had dimmed her intellect, "that would be because he's missin—"

"No, I mean, I can't find any trace of his cell phone, or..." She shifted nervously in her seat.

"Spit it out." Callum felt a migraine coming on, which happened every time their resident hacker got that guilty look on her face.

Elle batted her lashes at him as she feigned an innocence no one in their right mind would ever believe. "You know how much I worry about all of you, right?"

Joe gave her an indulgent smile. "You're talking about your not-so-secret clandestine hobby of tracking our phones, putting tracers on our cars, and generally snooping on us using GPS?"

"Yeah. Kinda like that, only a bit different..." She glanced at David, who was trying not to grin as he shook his head. "I injected him with a tracking device," she blurted.

"What—" Callum exploded.

"For the love of Prada," Rachel said as she rolled her eyes. "You can't be surprised. I'm more shocked she hasn't tagged the rest of us." She narrowed her eyes at Elle. "Have you?"

"No." There was a very loud and unsaid "not yet" hanging at the end of Elle's reply. She held up her hands to stall any other comments. "To be fair, it was back in the beginning when he couldn't walk down the hospital corridor without getting lost. I was worried he'd wander out of the hospital's front door and we'd never find him again, so I tagged him." She paused. Swallowed. Took a breath. "Twice. Just to be sure."

Callum could feel his blood pressure shoot up into the stratosphere. He pinched the bridge of his nose. "You realize you've broken about a million laws, right?"

"I don't think they count if it's done out of love."

"Elle—" Callum started.

"It doesn't matter anyway because I can't find him." She looked like she was about to burst into tears, so he kept his reprimand for another day.

"What do you mean?" Callum was seriously losing his patience. "The signal is blocked? Or he's out of range?"

"I mean, it doesn't exist." Elle pointed at her screen. "He's only been gone six hours, and after I couldn't find him in London, I increased the search radius to wherever he could travel to within that timeframe. I can't see his signal anywhere."

Callum leaned forward and put his palms on the table. "Explain it to me like I'm an idiot. Is he out of range? Is the system broken? What's going on?"

"I can't explain it." She looked at David for help, and he rubbed her back. "One tracker malfunctioning, I could understand, but two? It's as though they don't exist anymore. They've completely disappeared."

Joe cleared his throat. "Would there still be a signal if something happened to him? Like, if he wasn't breathing?"

"You mean if he was dead?" Elle's voice trembled.

Nobody said anything.

She took a deep breath. "That wouldn't interfere with the signals. No matter what happened to him, I should still be able to find him on here." She pointed at her laptop. "I don't understand."

"Right." Callum's chest was tight, as though a band had wrapped around it. "Joe and David, go to the hospital and see if you can trace his steps from there."

"We might get something off the security footage," Joe said. "But we'll need police help to access it."

"No, we won't. I've got it covered." Their ex-CIA spy casually got to his feet. "We'll get what we need."

If Ryan had been there, he'd have made a joke about David having secret spy ways to do everything. Then Callum would have barked at him to focus, and everyone else would have smiled indulgently.

Callum rubbed at the tight area around his heart. "Dimitri and Megan, call everybody you can think of. Somebody might have seen him or have some idea where he could have gone."

"On it." Megan pushed back her chair, stood, and adjusted the firearm at her hip.

Great. Just what he needed—their most reckless member armed for battle. He glared at her. "You don't need a gun in the office."

Manic blue eyes met his. "I know, but I *want* it in the

office. This place gets attacked and blown up more than the building in *Die Hard*."

"Dimitri?" Callum said with exasperation.

The poor sap just smiled indulgently at his wife. "I'll try to stop her from shooting anyone." He paused. "Including me."

Guess that was the best Callum was going to get. "Elle, you do your stuff online. See if you can figure out when the signal from his tracker, or his phone, stopped transmitting. Dig into his accounts, see if there's been any activity there. Basically whatever you can think of to find even a hint of his whereabouts."

She sniffed. "I can do that."

"Rachel, Harvard, widen the search. Tap into your overseas contacts and see what comes up."

"You know I don't work for you, right?" Rachel stood and smoothed down her pencil skirt.

"You might as well make yourself useful. And, last time I checked, Harvard was still on this team."

She narrowed her eyes. "Only in a part-time capacity."

"At least he has a valid reason for being here," Callum snapped back.

"I have a valid reason." She stuck her nose in the air. When everyone looked at her blankly, she pursed her lips before speaking. "Ryan is one of mine."

"You mean...like a minion?" Megan said.

"Am I one of yours too?" Elle asked. "Are we all? I feel this needs clarifying. Does this mean you like us, Rachel?" She grinned at everyone. "I think she likes us. Possibly even loves us."

Dimitri had the grace to turn his laugh into a cough, but Joe just let it out.

Rachel sighed and turned for the door. "I honestly don't

know why I bother with any of you," she said before she disappeared through it.

"I go where she goes." Harvard saluted them, then followed like a puppy.

With a shake of his head, Callum turned to the rest of his team. "Julia, you liaise with Ryan's family. We can't keep them in the dark. And you have the overview as usual." He glanced around his team. "All information goes through Julia."

She nodded solemnly. "I'll make spreadsheets to ensure we don't go over the same ground. If there's a pattern in anything we uncover, I'll find it."

And that was why she wasn't fired for hiding behind plants. No one was better at sorting detailed data and drawing conclusions from it. Julia could find patterns where other people saw nothing, and more than once, her insight had given Benson Security an advantage they wouldn't have otherwise had.

"What are you going to do?" Joe asked.

"I'll talk to Lake. He needs to know what's happening."

Visibly worried, the team dispersed.

Once they were gone, Callum did what he hoped he'd never have to do. He called the founder of their company and told Lake Benson that one of their own was missing—and they had no idea where he'd gone.

CHAPTER FOUR

As Ryan suspected, it only took a couple of minutes to get the manacle off Sarah's wrist. And no blood was shed in the process, much to her surprise. Which was kinda insulting.

"Thanks." She rubbed her wrist. "That feels better. Now what?"

"We pick a direction and see if it leads us out of here." Ryan held up her handbag. "You mind if I take a look? I want to see what resources we have."

"Be my guest." Sarah climbed down from the platform and stood in the middle of the room, looking a little lost. And cold. There were goosebumps on her exposed skin, and she rubbed her hands up and down her arms.

Ryan grabbed his jacket and tossed it to her. "Put this on."

"What about you?"

"I run hot. I'll be fine."

With a grateful nod, she shrugged into the jacket, pulling it tight around her. Ryan studied her out of the corner of his eye. She was holding it together way better than he would have expected. Most people would have been hysterical by now. Instead, he got the feeling she was analyzing everything, taking her time to come to conclusions. Which was remarkable, considering she was clearly terrified.

"Don't you think it's strange that they kidnapped my handbag too? I would have dumped it."

"Probably didn't want to leave a trail behind," he said as he rummaged through the contents.

There was a small bottle of water, antibacterial wipes, notebook and pen, phone, two protein bars (yes! food!), a travel toothbrush and toothpaste set, an umbrella, tissues, a tiny first aid kit that only really had Band-Aids, antiseptic cream, and aspirin in it, a tiny sewing kit, an iPad, a compact mirror and lipstick, travel hairbrush, and some feminine hygiene products.

Not exactly a goldmine. But then, what was he expecting? A satellite phone and a shovel?

"Why do you carry all this crap around with you?" He tossed the unlit candles in with everything else and added the bottle of water. Then he used the long strap to sling it across his body.

"In case I need it. Why else?"

"I manage to get through the day without needing anything more than my wallet and army knife." He pointed at the bag resting on his hip. "This is just extra weight."

Sarah rolled her eyes and muttered something about men that he didn't catch.

"Here." He handed her the lit candle. "You go first. I can look over your shoulder."

She frowned at him. It was cute. "Are you saying I'm short?"

"If it helps, you're also perfectly formed."

She blushed as she took the candle. The color looked good on her. The small flame barely lit up a foot or two in front of them and flickered wildly when they breathed anywhere near it.

Pausing in the doorway, she glanced at him. "Which direction?"

"Ladies get to pick."

She turned left into the dark tunnel. "It's wider than I thought it'd be." Her voice trembled as she inched her way forward.

"Would have to be wide to allow them to carry us down here. Could use a little more height though." His head skimmed the uneven rock above him, and every now and then, he had to duck to avoid a larger protrusion.

They'd only gone about ten paces when they hit a dead end. Literally. The way was blocked by a cave-in that'd resulted in a floor-to-ceiling mass of tightly packed rocks.

"Guess this is the wrong way." Ryan moved aside to allow Sarah space to shimmy past in order to lead the way back up the tunnel.

But she didn't move past him.

Instead, she stood there, staring at the wall of rocks barring their way. "This is really happening, isn't it?" she said softly.

Gently, Ryan put a hand on her shoulder. "Come on. You need to lead the way."

With a nod, she took the lead again. "How far down do you think we are?"

"No way to tell. Could be twenty feet, could be hundreds."

"The air is so dry and musty. I wonder how far it has to travel to get to us."

"The main thing is that there's more than enough to breathe."

"Yeah, you're right..." She trailed off as she kept stealing glances at the walls on either side of them. "Is this tunnel narrowing, or are the walls closing in on me?"

"It's the lack of light. The shadows play tricks with the mind. Just focus on what you can see, not on what you can't."

She barked out a laugh. "I'll get right on that. How do you stay so calm? I want to run screaming, and it's taking every bit of my self-control not to. My brain keeps telling me I'd feel better if I screamed. It's hard to resist."

"Fight or flight response. It's natural when you're in a dangerous situation. I'm calm because I'm focused on what needs to be done, not on what might happen. Stick to the facts. You're good at that, right? I mean, you were spouting statistics earlier. You must deal in facts all the time."

"I *am* dealing with the facts. We're trapped underground and don't know where we are or how to get out of here. What else is there?" Panic edged into her voice.

It wasn't the sound he wanted to hear. The last thing they needed was for either of them to panic. It was time to get Sarah's mind off the danger and on to something else.

"Well, we could talk about our past," he said. "I've been wondering about some things. We had sex on our first real date, right? It's not fair that I can't remember it, which is driving me crazy. You have to tell me—did I rock your world?"

Sarah tripped over the uneven surface. Ryan's hand shot out to grab his jacket and steady her.

When she turned to glare at him, her cheeks were flushed a pretty shade of rose pink. "I don't think this is an appropriate time to discuss that."

Gently, he turned her back around to face the right way and nudged her forward. "What else are we going to talk about?"

"Oh, I don't know. Maybe how we'll defend ourselves if we run into the people who brought us here. We don't even have any weapons."

"Honey," he drawled. "This body *is* a weapon."

Sarah burst out laughing, as he'd hoped she would, and her shoulders relaxed a little. "Then, I guess we'll be fine."

"Damn right." The darkness loomed in front of them, making it impossible to tell how far the tunnel stretched.

"It's so quiet," Sarah whispered.

Ryan understood. Silence had a strange effect on a person. After a while, you started imagining noises. Once that stage passed, things became really scary. That's when you heard a roaring in your ears as the silence multiplied itself. At that point, you'd do anything to hear a sound you didn't make yourself.

"It'd be a whole lot less quiet if you'd answer my question," Ryan said to distract her. "I think it's only fair you share the details of our night together. After all, you know all about it and I don't."

"I'm not going to discuss my sex life with you." That schoolmarm tone was back, which gave him hope. She might be scared, but she also had a backbone of steel.

"Technically, it's my sex life too," he pointed out.

"Fine, then I'm not going to discuss this with someone who can't even remember seeing me naked."

"I can imagine it—does that help?"

"No. And ew. I'm a stranger to you! The whole thing is too weird."

"Wait. What's too weird? Talking about this, or the sex? And if it was the sex, was it good or bad weird? Are we talking kinky, or did I do something that freaked you out? Because I promise you, whatever it was had to have been a misguided joke. I don't have any strange fetishes."

There was pure mischief in her expression when she glanced back at him. "That you remember."

What?

For a second, Ryan forgot to duck and hit his head on a rock in the ceiling.

"Bandit!" He rubbed the spot.

"Is it bleeding?" Sarah turned to face him.

"Don't think so."

"Let me see."

All he could do was bend for her to examine him. Her fingers in his hair felt strangely intimate, and oddly familiar.

"Only a graze. You really need to be more careful. Did the neurologist say anything about the danger of any further head injuries?"

"Mainly that she didn't recommend having them."

"Let's try to follow her recommendations, then, huh?" A wicked glint flashed in her eyes. "Have any memories suddenly materialized?"

"No..."

"Guess we can rule out hitting you over the head to jog them, then." The way she said it made Ryan think she'd been planning exactly that.

"You can be a little scary, you know that?" And coming from him, that was saying something. His life was filled with scary women. Hell, half of his work team was comprised of trigger-happy, freakishly intelligent, and sneaky women. Sarah would fit right in.

"No, I'm not," she chided. "I'm a very non-threatening person. It's one of my core personality traits."

Oh, not this. "You did one of those personality tests, didn't you?"

"You mean, you haven't? Didn't you have to take one before you were offered your job?"

Now, that made Ryan laugh. Which he did, long and loud. "Uh, no," he said when he'd calmed. "The closest I ever came to a personality test was when Callum asked me if he had to hide the weaponry to ensure I didn't shoot Rachel."

"Rachel? Was she the one who left to run a pharmaceutical company?"

It was very strange talking to someone you thought was a stranger but who knew things about your life. "That's her. She has a mean streak, and without Callum around to act as a buffer, she can get on your nerves. Trust me, it takes a lot to make me mad—unless you're Rachel. She has a gift for it."

"And Callum calms her down?"

That was hilarious. "No. He naturally attracts most of her ire, which spares the rest of us." He started laughing again. *Callum calming? Priceless!*

"What's so funny?"

Ryan wiped his eyes. "The thought of the world's grumpiest Scottish man calming anyone down."

She seemed wistful when she glanced back at him. "You're really close to your team, aren't you?"

"Don't know what I'd do without them." Which was one of the reasons he'd worked hard to get back in shape and was jumping through hoops to take the tests he needed to rejoin the team.

"Must be nice to know you aren't alone." Now, *that* was definitely wistful.

"They're like family to me. You don't have that with your work friends?"

"I work in insurance, Ryan. Most of my colleagues are fifty-year-old men."

"Good point. What about family? Do they have your back?"

She didn't answer immediately. "Sometimes, I forget you can't remember all the things I've told you, then you say something like that." She shook her head. "It's no big deal. My dad drank himself to death, my mum isn't far off doing the same. No brothers, sisters, or other family. Just me, a few friends I see socially, and a whole bunch of middle-aged men in the office."

There was no self-pity in her tone, which somehow made her description of her life that much more brutal.

"It sounds lonely," he said.

"It's no big deal. I'm used to it."

The way she spoke made Ryan think there was a lot in Sarah's life that she dismissed just because she was used to it.

"Well, you aren't alone right now," he said, his voice echoing through the corridor. "We're in this together."

She flashed him a smile. "That's sweet, and trust me when I say, I'm glad I'm not here alone. But you have to remember, I'm not like you, Ryan, and I'm not sure that you're better off having me here. I don't have military training or special security experience. There's a good chance I'll only slow you down."

"Don't say that—"

"But it's the truth. I work in an office and spend my days trying to figure out the odds of random events happening. If someone came to me asking if they'd survive a situation like this, I'd tell them their chances were low and that our company couldn't insure them. The odds are stacked against us, and the chance of us getting out of this alive is slim. The truth is, your odds are significantly better if we take me out of the equation. Of course, if this discussion was taking place in my office, now would be the point where I'd whip out the graphs and talk statistics until your eyes glazed over."

The humor was a chance for him to joke his way out of the conversation. He didn't take it. "You keep talking about the odds of something happening. Only, the truth is, for every situation, there are always people who make it out."

"Yes, and they're so far in the minority you'd need a magnifying glass to spot the number."

"That's not my point. I'm trying to tell you that we're going to be one of the minority. We're the people who make it and screw up the data for folk like you."

"You can't know that." Big eyes caught his as she glanced back at him.

"You can't know it won't happen."

They fell silent as they carefully made their way along the uneven floor of the corridor. There were cracks in the ceiling above them that concerned Ryan. After seeing the cave-in blocking the other end of the tunnel, he had to wonder if the structure of the mine would hold long enough for them to escape.

He wasn't sure what was worse—facing their abductor and whatever he had planned for them, or being crushed to death under a mountain of rubble.

Sarah seemed to be reading his mind. "How much earth is pressing down on us? All it'll take is one crack giving way and we'll be buried alive."

"Not alive," he corrected. "We'd be crushed like a grape under a boot."

There was a second of stunned silence before she burst out laughing. It was slightly hysterical, but he'd take it.

Suddenly, the laughter cut short.

"I see something," Sarah said.

Ryan peered into the darkness. There was definitely something up ahead. "A door, maybe?"

"Oh, I really hope it's the exit," Sarah said.

With each step closer, it became clear that they'd hit a corner. To the right, a new tunnel veered off into the darkness. Straight ahead was a large iron gate.

Slowly, incrementally, the glow from the flame revealed the size of the gate. It filled the tunnel top to bottom, with no space around it or between the bars to squeeze through. It was old, rusted, and obviously made by hand. If Ryan had to guess, he'd say the gate was installed at the same time as the tunnel was built.

As they drew closer, a soft orange lamp clicked on in the area beyond the gate. That was definitely a more recent addition. They froze, waiting to see if the light meant someone was coming. Ryan's ears strained, but all he heard was their breathing. The air didn't stir. There was no movement other than the ones they made. They were alone.

With that realization, he took a steadying breath and became aware of Sarah's whole body shaking.

"Hey, it's okay." He patted her shoulder, a little awkwardly. "Nobody's there."

"The light freaked me out when it suddenly came on," she confessed.

"Motion sensor." He moved closer to get a better look at the gate.

Sarah hurried to his side. "Can we open it?"

"I need more light." A small candle and a dim bulb

weren't going to cut it. He reached into the jeans pocket and pulled out his phone, switching the flashlight on.

Sarah pointed at the rusty lock. "If there's a lock, that means you can pick it, right?"

Unfortunately, he had to shatter her hopes. Angling the light through the bars, he pointed at a brand-new, diagonal length of steel, wedged between the center of the gate and the floor. "See that? It's a security bar. Or, at least a custom-made version of one, and it looks like it's been added pretty recently too. It's fitted into a welded plate on the gate and locked into the floor plate over there. The only way to dismantle it is from the other side. They must leave the gate open when they're on this side of it. Otherwise, they'd be trapped in here with us."

Her hold on the candle tightened until her knuckles were white. "So, we dig under."

"That isn't going to work either. See how the part that opens sits against iron struts? The bits you'd have to step over when going through the gate? Those struts are embedded in the rock, and there's no way to tell how far down they go."

Her shoulders slumped. "There's no getting past this, is there?"

"No." Ryan switched the flashlight off to save the phone's battery.

"Why is this happening to us?" Sarah asked, looking more than a little lost.

"I wish I knew."

"I'm not sure I can handle this, Ryan." Her voice was small. She wasn't seeking pity. She was only stating the facts as she saw them.

Ryan cupped her cheek. "Sure you can. I've only

known you a couple of hours, and even I can tell that you'll be able to handle whatever comes our way."

Her eyelashes dropped. "Yeah. A couple of hours," she said softly before straightening her shoulders and stepping away from his touch. "It seems to me that I have a choice. I can either freak out, have a panic attack, run into a wall, knock myself out, and lie there waiting to die. Or I can pull up my big girl panties, use my brain, work alongside you, and die trying to get out of here."

There was no way not to admire her resolve. Although... "I don't like that both options end in death."

"Might as well be realistic, odds are against us. Roughly twenty percent of all cave rescues end in death for those stuck or lost. Mining accounts for eight percent of the world's death toll. Which is a massive amount when you take into consideration that only one percent of the population work in mining."

Given their situation, it was pretty damn awesome the way she made him want to laugh. "How do you know this stuff?"

"I insured a caving expert once. He wasn't bothered that his hobby had a twenty percent chance of death attached to it. If I'd been him, I'd have found another hobby. Like knitting. If done in moderation, there's only a very small risk of developing RSI. Of course, you couldn't run while holding needles because that'd up your chances of injury."

Yeah, there was no holding it in. Ryan threw back his head and laughed hard.

"What's so funny?" Sarah demanded, looking like she might hit him again.

"Nothing, Stats, nothing."

She feigned a groan. "You can't remember me, but you

can come up with that same stupid nickname all over again. Fabulous."

Suddenly, she stilled, her eyes wide as she stared into the darkness behind him.

"What is it?" Ryan immediately sobered.

"I saw something move," Sarah whispered.

CHAPTER FIVE

In an instant, Ryan morphed from the relaxed guy who was trying to keep her spirits up into a serious, combat-ready warrior. That was when it struck her—he really wasn't afraid. Ryan actually believed there was nothing in the tunnels he couldn't handle. All the stories he'd told her during that month they'd talked almost daily, sometimes for hours at a time, came rushing back. Tales of bravery and hilarity that'd stunned her—as well as entertained her. No, he wasn't someone who'd be scared in the dark.

And she was very glad he was with her.

"Describe it," he ordered, his voice barely a thread between them.

"On the ground. A black shape disappearing into the shadows. Could be a foot?" Was someone standing there, watching them? Listening to them? Waiting to strike.

He leaned in to whisper against her ear. "Take my phone, and as soon as I start running, direct the flashlight at me. Not before, okay?"

Sarah nodded as she took his phone in her shaking hand.

"Right," he said in a normal, relaxed tone. "Guess we should keep on going and find that exit."

He squeezed her arm in reassurance, stepped back, nodded once, and then suddenly turned and sprinted into the darkness. Sarah fumbled with the phone before switching on the flashlight. It felt like an eon had passed, but it had to have been barely a second before the tunnel was bathed in light.

Heart racing so fast it felt like it was trying to escape her body, Sarah focused on Ryan. He toed the bottom of the wall where the small black shadow sat—and something ran out.

"Rat! It's a rat!" He jumped back, banging into the other side of the tunnel as the rat scurried into the darkness. For a second, nobody spoke, then Ryan turned his head to face her. "I really don't like rats," he said with disgust.

No kidding.

She'd just watched the most macho man she knew almost jump out of his pants. "You know," Sarah couldn't resist prodding the bear, "that could have been dinner. Lots of cultures eat rat meat, and I don't see any other options down here."

He paled. "Tell you what, I'll eat it if you catch it and cook it."

And that would happen...never. "Typical. You almost pee yourself at the sight of a rat but have no problems eating one. You really will eat anything, won't you?"

"I'm a growing boy." Already he was back to his confident self. "And it won't be moving if we cook it. Bloody squirmy, scratchy, sneaky, disease-infected wastes of space."

She arched her brows at him. "That was some seriously impressive alliteration. Don't worry, you'll get your dinner. Where there's one rat, there's always another."

Ryan warily examined the space around them. "That's just evil. Come on, Stats, let's see where this tunnel leads."

"You sure you're up for this?" she couldn't resist asking. "I mean, that's the way the rat went."

"You keep on enjoying yourself at my expense," he said. "I'm keeping a tally and there will be payback."

As Sarah passed Ryan, in order to lead the way, she was overwhelmed by the urge to climb him and cling on tight, like one of those clip-on animal toys people brought back from holiday. Although she had no doubt that having her wrapped around him would barely slow him down, she thought it best to resist the urge.

Instead, she forced herself to look down into the darkness of this new tunnel. It was exactly like the last. "It would be so easy to get lost down here."

"For other people maybe, but you have a secret weapon." Ryan nudged her forward.

"You're going to tell me it's you, aren't you?"

"Well, yeah, but it's really only one aspect of me. It's what I did in the army. I was a tracker. We can't get lost. It isn't possible."

"You talk a good game, GI Joe, but what exactly is a tracker?"

"GI Joe was American. I was UK army. Civilians," he muttered before answering her question. "Have you ever seen one of those old cowboy movies where they bring in a specialist to read the markings on the ground so the sheriff can find the bad guys?"

"Of course."

"That's a tracker, only the army version is more so. We're trained to follow trails through all sorts of environments—urban, jungle, and desert. There are only a few soldiers who specialize in tracking these days. We've become too reliant on technology to find things for us. But sometimes technology just won't cut it and you need a real live person. Someone who notices details that software and cameras might think are insignificant and is able to draw conclusions from those clues. It's kinda like being part sniffer dog, part detective, and part mapping system."

It was hard to miss the enthusiasm as he spoke. "You never told me this when I knew you. Mainly, when you talked about your time in the army, you told funny stories."

"I was obviously trying to charm you, Stats—without sounding like a macho arsehole who bores you by boasting about his prowess."

How he managed to make her feel amusement when their circumstances were so dire, she didn't know. "How do these superhuman tracking skills help us then?"

There was a second's hesitation before his reply, which piqued her curiosity. "I have kind of a talent, something that's been supercharged since the coma. I map places in my head. I can tell you exactly how many feet it is from here to the gate, then from the gate to the room where we were held. I can tell you the degree of incline as we walk. And, if pressed, I'm pretty sure that I could take a stab at which direction is north, and I'll probably get it right. With me, you can't get lost."

Sarah's jaw dropped before she spun to face him. "Have you always been like this?"

He shrugged, seemingly nonchalant, when it was clear he felt a bit self-conscious. His ears had turned red, and he didn't look her in the eye. To his credit, he answered anyway. "I've always had a talent for finding things and navigating my way. The army training honed it and gave me extra skills. During the coma, my brain had to rewire itself, and I think some connections were made that weren't there before, ones that make it easier for me to notice things without even trying."

Wow. Just wow. "I've read about this. It's called sudden savant syndrome."

Ryan was already shaking his head. "No, it's not like that. I didn't wake up with the ability to play the piano like a concert pianist, even though I've never touched the instrument. The brain injury just made the skills I'd already been taught a little more...refined."

Sarah didn't understand why he wasn't excited. She was practically buzzing with it. To have something so amazing come out of such a terrible experience? Mind-blowing.

"Do you see maps in your head? Are you counting feet and inches everywhere you walk? Does it work if you're in a car? Have you noticed any other new skills since you woke up? Did you tell your neurologist?"

He held up a hand to stop her. "And this is why I don't tell people. It isn't a big deal, Stats. The talent and skills have always been there; now they're just a little more in my face than they were before."

Something in his tone made her realize there was more going on under the surface of his words. She studied him for a beat before it hit her. "You can't turn it off, can you?"

His jaw clenched and unclenched. "No."

"So everywhere you go, you're measuring distance and drawing maps."

"Yeah. But like I said, it isn't a big deal. I hardly even notice it's happening anymore."

Before she thought twice about it, Sarah reached up to cup his cheek. An electric bolt of awareness shot up her arm, made all the more painful with the knowledge that her touch wouldn't have the same effect on him.

Still, this wasn't about her. She'd deal with the fallout of being around Ryan again once they were out of danger. In the meantime, he had to know how amazing he was. "You've been through so much and you have no idea how remarkable you are, do you?"

To her astonishment, his cheeks turned a deep shade of red. "You had to go make a big deal out of this, didn't you?" he said roughly.

It *was* a big deal. One he obviously wasn't ready to accept—yet. So she shrugged and dropped her hand. "A girl has to amuse herself any way she can. Did you develop any other talents while you were out cold?" Turning, she resumed leading them up the tunnel.

"Not that I know of."

"Then that's what we can do while we're stuck down here. We'll work our way through different things and see if you're any good at them. Sing me a song."

Ryan's laughter was like music in itself. "You're a nut, you know that?"

"Funnily enough, you're the only person who's ever called me that. Most people think I'm sensible, boring, and ordinary."

He snorted. "Bet they don't take the time to see past the buttoned-up clothes to the devil lurking beneath."

And wasn't it interesting that he could?

"If you aren't going to sing, how about whistling?"

"How about we leave the talent hunt until we're out of here?"

"Fine, but only if we get out quickly. If we're in here more than one night, all deals are off. Because by then I'd do anything to distract myself from being stuck underground."

"Anything?" His tone was speculative, and a little hopeful.

"Your mind has wandered into the gutter again, hasn't it?"

"Now, what would make you think that?"

"Experience," she said drolly as the candlelight illuminated dark openings into rooms up ahead. There was one on each side of the tunnel, not exactly facing each other but close.

"There are more rooms." Dread tightened her stomach at the thought of what might be hiding inside of them.

"Could be a dormitory corridor. They used to build them into old mines for workers to live in during the duration of their shift—back when shifts lasted weeks, not hours. The room we were in was probably made for the same purpose. There might even have been more rooms off that tunnel, but the cave-in hid them."

"You seem to know a lot about old mines." Sarah inched closer to Ryan as they neared the gaping maws that passed for doorways. The inky-black openings looked like they could suck you inside if you got too close.

Ryan must have noticed her discomfort because he moved closer to her, the heat of his body offering comfort. "Not the first time I've been in one. Took part in some missions, and rescues, in underground complexes in several countries. After you've been through a few, you start to notice what they have in common, especially older places like this. There's a lot of similarity in how they were built and laid out."

"If they're so alike, is there any chance one of those maps in your head has the exit marked?" It was a poor attempt at a joke.

"Sorry, doesn't work like that. Be great if it did though."

Wouldn't it just? The sooner she put some distance between her and Ryan, the better. Being around him was confusing. Her brain remembered the pain of losing him, but her body only remembered how he'd felt when she was with him. She'd already made one rash decision with Ryan by climbing into bed with him on their first real date. Her heart couldn't cope with two.

"We have to check out the rooms, don't we?" For some reason, staying in the tunnel seemed safer to her. Even though she couldn't see where that led either.

"Afraid so. Don't want to take the chance we miss an exit. How about I go in alone and you stand guard out here?"

"And do what if danger comes? Wave my candle at it?"

His eyes sparkled. "Try spearing it with a witty barb."

"You're not funny."

"I'm adorable. Now, wait here and don't wander off." With a smile he entered the black room, his flashlight app on low to save the battery.

Sarah watched the fluid movement of his muscular frame as he prowled into the room. Every gesture he made betrayed a confidence in his abilities that few people would ever have. He'd been joking when he'd told her his body was a weapon. But watching him now, alert and controlled, she thought it was closer to the truth than he'd meant it to be.

As the glow from Ryan's flashlight moved further away, she shivered. The distance between them made her jittery. Which meant she started calculating odds in her head all over again. What were the chances of the room caving in on him? And what were the odds of her digging him out?

Forcing herself to breathe steadily, she glanced up and down the tunnel. Nothing moved. The only sounds that could be heard were Ryan's soft footfalls. Even then, she suspected he was deliberately making noise to reassure her.

She was pretty sure Ryan could be as silent as a ghost if the need arose.

"Anything?" Sarah had to force herself to speak loudly. For some reason, survival instinct made her want to whisper.

"Nothing yet." Irrational relief slammed into her when he answered. "Gimme a sec. There's a spot in the corner that looks interesting. Might be a passage."

"Okay." Sarah warily glanced at the end of the tunnel, where everything disappeared into darkness. Was there movement? Or was her imagination working overtime?

Something brushed against her ankle.

Her foot shot out.

A rat went flying.

Sarah jerked back, tripped over the uneven floor, and fell into the room behind her. Her backside hit the hard rock. The candle flew from her hand. Its meager light snuffed out instantly. And blackness rushed at her. Even the glow from the room Ryan was in was blocked from her view.

"Okay, you've got this," she muttered. "No big deal. Just stand up and head back into the corridor and over to Ryan. Don't make a fuss. You aren't a child. It's only a dark, sinister cavern filled with...okay, that's not helping. Come on, Sarah. Get your backside up off the floor." She wet her dry lips and fought to breathe evenly.

Her heart was racing so fast she thought she might pass out. Dark places. Her body curled in a ball. Hiding. Scared. Memories from her childhood attacked from every direction.

Completely illogically, she swept the ground for the candle, turning her body until she couldn't remember which way she faced. She wasn't thinking straight, and she was aware enough to know it. Even if she found the candle, how would she light it? She needed her phone. Why was it in the bag with Ryan? Why hadn't she thought she'd need it? She spent her life preparing for every contingency, but *this* she didn't plan.

"Get up now," she snapped at herself as she placed her hand on the ground, ready to push herself up.

Her voice seemed to bounce off the thick, impenetrable darkness as her gaze darted around, trying to find something, anything, to rest on in the blackness. She was becoming disoriented. Even though she could feel the rock beneath her, she was having trouble telling which way was up. Panic messing with her senses.

Her palm slipped forward across the stone, making her lose her balance, falling back on her backside.

Something tangled around her fingers.

Cobweb? Spider?

Awareness seeped into her mind, bringing with it a feeling of absolute horror.

No.

It couldn't be.

Time slammed to a halt as Sarah's universe shrunk to the threads wrapped around her hand. It felt like they were crawling up her wrist, entangling themselves in the silver chains of her bracelet. A scream became trapped inside her head as they held her captive.

"Sarah!" Ryan's voice came from miles away.

And barely registered, because recognition had dawned through her terror. She knew what'd trapped her. Knew it with the same certainty she knew her own name, and the horror of it stole whatever reason she had left.

It wasn't a web her fingers had strayed into.

It was human hair.

CHAPTER SIX

Benson Security
London

It was driving Elle crazy that she couldn't find any sign of Ryan's GPS transmitters. The last time they'd pinged on the grid was right after he'd walked out of hospital that morning. After that, they just disappeared.

"Someone has to have jammed the signal," she muttered to no one in particular. "It's the only explanation."

All she could do now was set up an alarm to alert her when his signal appeared again. In the meantime, she had his online life to dig through. Hopefully, that would shed some light on his current situation.

Swiveling in her expensive, hot-pink gamer's chair, she faced the two screens set up on the right of her massive U-shaped desk. There were six monitors in total, plus her ever-present laptop, an iPad, and several phones—just in case.

One keyboard controlled her empire, and her attention flowed over the screens almost as quickly as her fingers danced over the keys.

Hacking into Ryan's social media accounts would have been child's play—if she'd needed to hack. Which she didn't because she kept a password vault with everyone's passwords in it, whether they'd given them to her or not. Mostly, it was for security, sometimes it was for when someone had forgotten their password and needed help, occasionally it was for something like this.

Elle liked to be prepared.

A Snickers bar appeared on the desk beside her keyboard.

"Thanks, Ryan," she said automatically, then froze.

When she glanced up, it was to find Megan pulling over another chair. "I know he usually keeps you supplied while you work, but seeing as he isn't here..." She settled into the seat.

"Thanks." Elle reached for the candy bar, her throat tight. "Any luck calling Ryan's contacts?"

"Nothing." Megan bit into her own chocolate bar and frowned. "It's times like this that I need some decent Scottish comfort food. A good roll and sausage, or a potato scone roll, or a sausage roll on a bread roll."

"I sense a pattern here," Elle said as she returned to her screens.

"There are only two rules for Scottish cuisine," Megan said. "It has to be deep fried or fit on a bread roll. You'd be amazed what we can fit onto a roll. I've had curry, a full Scotch pie, and Christmas dinner all on a roll. Not the same one, you understand." She heaved a sigh. "Why does thinking about Ryan always lead to thinking about food?"

"Maybe because that's his MO. Sad? Eat. Happy? Eat. Stressed? Eat."

"Awake? Eat."

They shared a bittersweet smile.

Megan brushed her natural blonde hair off her face. "Man, I hope he's okay."

"He has to be," Elle said as she brought up Ryan's old Tinder account. "It wouldn't be fair to go through a near-death experience, months in a coma, then rehab just to end up..." She couldn't say the word. "He'll be fine. We'll find him. Plus, he's capable. If he's in trouble, there's a good chance he'll get himself out of it."

"True." Megan put her feet up on the corner of Elle's desk. As long as her biker boots were nowhere near the machines, Elle didn't care. "I mean, look at the state he was in when he woke up. He could barely stand, his right hand couldn't grip anything, and he couldn't remember half of our names. Now, he's stronger than ever." She stared at the wall for a minute. "I don't want to miss him again. I feel like seven months was enough, you know?"

"Yeah." It had been *more* than enough time without the man she thought of as a brother. She hadn't been able to move on without him in her life. She'd even postponed her wedding so he could take part. Three months earlier, he'd been her proud maid of honor—even borrowing a kilt from Callum because he insisted that a proper maid of honor wore a dress.

Callum had been pissed that Ryan called his kilt a dress, and that's when the fighting started.

Best. Wedding. Ever.

Elle stared at the stream of green-colored code on the black screen to her right and frowned. "That's not right," she muttered.

There was a thump as Megan's boots hit the floor before she wheeled her chair closer. "What?"

"Gimme a sec," Elle said absently as she typed commands into her keyboard. "Oh!"

"What?" Megan demanded. "You can't make noises like that and not tell me what's going on."

There were moments when she wished there was someone else around in the office who spoke code, then she wouldn't have to explain herself to normals all the time.

"Someone hacked Ryan's Tinder account months ago."

Megan was unimpressed. "Aren't those accounts hacked all the time?"

"Not like this." She continued scrolling through the lines of code, already forgetting that there was someone with her.

"I thought Ryan hadn't been on Tinder since he was shot," Megan said, reminding Elle she was in the room.

"He hasn't. This hack is from around the time he went into hospital. Whoever did it was particularly interested in a woman he'd been talking to, somebody called Sarah."

"You mean 'talking,' right?" Megan made air quotes. "I don't think people use Tinder to chat. It's a hookup app."

Elle shook her head. "He was trying something new. We'd had a long talk about how bloody dumb he was with women, and he agreed that he should get to know the next one before they jumped into bed."

"Smart. Less chance they'd steal his car."

"Exactly." Ryan was never going to live down having his new car stolen on the day he'd bought it—by a woman he'd met on Tinder that afternoon.

Megan scooted her seat closer. "Who's this Sarah, then?"

"I've no idea." Elle frowned at the screen. "But there's

like a month's worth of messaging on here." She flicked over to his other message and text apps. "He was talking to her on all of these. It feels wrong to read them."

Megan elbowed her aside. "This is an investigation. We *have* to read these. The fact that it's also a chance to snoop on Ryan's love life is neither here nor there." She paused. "Never understood that saying. Where are they talking about? And why does it matter?"

"Focus." Elle pushed Megan out of the way.

"Look, these messages are obviously important." Megan tried to appear innocent when she was barely containing her glee at poking around in Ryan's private life. "We would be negligent if we didn't find out why."

"I wouldn't like someone reading my messages to David." Elle didn't add that there was a good chance her former spy of a husband would eliminate anyone who dared.

Megan shrugged. "Wouldn't bother me," said the exhibitionist.

"*Quelle surprise,*" Elle drawled.

Everyone in the office knew everything about Megan's love life with Dimitri. It would actually have been a relief if she kept some things a secret. Or at least stopped leaving doors open when she pounced on her husband. There had been times when Elle had wanted to rinse her eyeballs with bleach after passing one of the offices.

"You had no problem snooping with the cameras we'd set up that caught Callum having sex," Megan protested.

"That's different. Callum was suicidal. And..."

"It was hot?"

"I'm not going to answer that on the grounds it may incriminate me."

"Whatever. Have all of his messages been hacked or just Tinder?" Megan asked.

"Good question." Elle did her thing and grimaced. "Everything's been hacked, and all around the same time too. As far as I can see, whoever did this was following every mention of Sarah."

"Maybe this Sarah had people looking out for her?"

"Or a stalker who didn't want her near anyone else."

"We need to find out who she is. Bring up her Tinder profile."

Elle tapped in the command. "It's been deleted."

"Does Ryan mention her full name anywhere?"

"Not that I can see."

"Okay, what about her phone number? Is that there somewhere? We could just call it and ask her who the hell she is and what she's done with Ryan." Megan had that glint in her eye she usually got just before she turned violent. It wasn't a good sign.

"He texted her, so there's a number." Elle rattled it off. "Give it a ring."

Megan already had her phone in her hand. She put it on speaker. "This is Sarah, please leave a message after the tone. If this is a business matter, please call my work number." She proceeded to give it.

As soon as the message was finished, Megan was dialing the work number. "Good afternoon, this is Steele-Shepherd Insurance. How may I direct your call?"

"This is Benson Security. We're hoping to connect with a woman called Sarah. It's a matter of urgency," Megan said. "I'm afraid we don't have a last name. Do you have any Sarahs in the building?"

There was a pause. "Could you tell me what this is about, please?"

Megan shot a questioning look at Elle, who held up her hands to say she didn't know if it was okay to tell her or not.

"One of our colleagues is missing," Megan said. "We found Sarah's number in his phone and we're hoping she has some information that could help us locate our friend."

"Oh dear." The voice sounded suddenly anxious. "Please hold, and I'll get someone to speak with you."

Tinny elevator music filled Elle's office as she frowned at Megan. "I don't like the sound of that."

"Neither do I."

"Are you still there?" a deep male voice said. "This is Officer Mark Jensen with Scotland Yard. I hear you're looking for a woman called Sarah. Would that be Sarah Davidson by any chance?"

What the hell? Megan mouthed at Elle.

This time Elle did the talking. "This is Elle Roberts-Knight. I'm on speaker phone with my colleague, Megan Raast. I'm afraid we don't know her last name, but we're looking for a Sarah. One of our team members went missing this morning, and he had a Sarah in his contacts with this number."

"Benson Security, huh? You guys are famous around the station. Been a lot of trouble since you opened up shop in London."

"You call it trouble, we call it getting the bad guys that the police couldn't catch," Megan drawled.

"Let's just agree to disagree on that." Mark sighed. "Sarah Davidson went missing this morning too."

Elle's mouth was suddenly dry. She wet her lips. "Missing how?"

"You first," he said. "Who's missing and what happened?"

Cops. So trusting. "Ryan Granger, the bodyguard who

was shot last year in the op that exposed the Met's dirty laundry."

"Thought he was in a coma." Suddenly, Mark sounded very attentive.

"Woke up a few months ago. He had an appointment with his neurologist this morning, and no one's seen him since. He's not answering his phone either."

"What makes you think he hasn't just gone for a walk? Or headed to the beach for the day?"

"We, uh, have him tagged with a GPS locator—with his permission," she hastened to add, feeling her cheeks heat at the lie.

Megan rolled her eyes. It took a whole lot more than lying to a cop to make Megan blush.

"Anyway." Elle hurried on. "The signal disappeared this morning."

"What do you mean disappeared?"

"There's no sign of it anywhere. It's like he fell off the face of the earth. What about Sarah, what happened there?"

They heard him take a deep breath. "She went to meet a new client at a local cafe and didn't come back. There's no record of the client other than the note in her calendar, and someone at the cafe saw her get into a black cab with a man she'd just met. Said she was staggering, as though drunk. The guy told them she was ill and he was taking her to hospital. We haven't found a record of her being admitted to any hospitals. What does Ryan look like?"

"You're thinking he was the guy with Sarah, aren't you?"

"I'm not dismissing any possibility, just following the investigation," he said evenly.

It was Elle's turn to take a breath. "He's about six foot tall, broad, muscled, floppy caramel-colored hair, Caucasian with a slight tan. Handsome and approachable, women fall all over him." She looked at Megan for confirmation.

"Green eyes," Megan added. "Small scar on his nose. Clean shaven. Smiles a lot."

"Does it sound like Ryan was the one with Sarah?" Elle said.

"No."

Elle leaned into the phone. "The police don't usually get involved when someone's only been missing a few hours."

"Sarah didn't go willingly. The cafe staff were worried and called us."

"We need to talk in person," Megan said. "Our boss, Callum McKay, will want to share information with you guys. It looks like your missing person and ours are connected. Especially as we've just found out that Ryan's messaging accounts were hacked and someone took the time to read all of his messages to Sarah."

"I'll be straight over," Mark said. "And I'll want to see those messages." He hung up.

"You'd better run downstairs and tell Callum the police are coming," Elle told Megan. "You can update him and Julia while you're there."

"Why does it have to be me?" she whined.

Elle gestured to the monitors. "Still working here."

"Fine." Megan huffed. "But we should really read through all those messages first, so we can censor anything X-rated before the cops get here."

"I'm sure that's your *only* reason for wanting to read Ryan's messages." Elle stretched out her arm and pointed at the door. "Go."

"You used to be way more fun," Megan complained as she left the room.

As soon as she disappeared, Elle brought up the messages and started at the beginning. Not because she wanted to get a kinky kick out of reading Ryan's romantic notes, but because she wanted to know who this Sarah had been to him.

And what she'd done to get them both kidnapped.

CHAPTER SEVEN

Ryan was running as soon as Sarah screamed. The petrified sound ripped straight through him, causing more damage than any bullet ever had. In the few seconds it took to reach the tunnel, the screaming had stopped and a cold, terrifying silence replaced it.

A spike of panic impaled him when he didn't find Sarah where he'd left her. A split second later, the beam from his flashlight swept over her huddled form on the floor in the room opposite. She was facing into the darkness, partially hidden by the wall.

"Sarah!" He fell to his knees beside her, wrapping an arm around her shivering shoulders. "It's okay. I've got you."

There was no response. No recognition at all. She was frozen in place, staring at the floor in the darkness.

"Stats," Ryan cajoled. "Talk to me. You've got to talk to me."

Suddenly, she started to shake violently. A low, desperate moan escaped her that made him break out in a cold sweat.

Grabbing the flashlight, he quickly scanned her, hoping

the problem would be obvious. Hoping she hadn't broken under the stress of their situation and gone catatonic in the darkness. His mind threw random options at him. Were there bugs? Was she injured? Had the bloody rat come back? And then the light hit the floor beside her.

Ryan let out a long breath. "Fuck."

No wonder she lost it.

"Okay, okay." Ryan's training kicked in, and he took charge. With a gentle but firm hold, he grasped her chin and forced her eyes away from her hand. "Look at me. Sarah, do you hear me? I'm right here, and I need you to look into my eyes. That's an order." His tone was steel. It was a command, nothing less, and he expected obedience. "Sarah, look at me. *See* me. I'm right here."

Slowly, she began to focus on him instead of on the horror inside her head. She blinked. Once. Twice. A flicker of recognition ignited the gold in her eyes. Then suddenly, they were liquid.

"Ryan? There's...there's..." It was barely a whisper.

"I know, Stats, I know. I'm going to fix it for you, and I need you to be strong for a couple of minutes more. Can you do that for me?"

Her bottom lip trembled as silent tears escaped to run down her cheeks. "It's around my hand," she whispered.

"I'll get it off," he promised.

Carefully, he moved his hand to cup her cheek, brushing at the tears with his thumb. "I need you to stay very still while I do this. Okay? I want you to keep looking in this direction, and I want you to count to one hundred, out loud, for both of us to hear. Can you do that for me?"

Those cute little frown lines appeared between her brows, and she nodded once.

Still, Ryan wasn't convinced she actually understood

what he was saying. It was obvious she was struggling to focus on him, and he didn't want her to slip back into a dazed state.

"Say it back to me, Stats. You're going to keep looking in this direction and count to one hundred, out loud." Hopefully, concentrating on counting would keep her mind off him freeing her hand.

The tip of her tongue peeked out to moisten her lips as the muscles she'd been holding so tight started to tremble.

"Don't turn around. Keep facing this way. Count to a hundred. That's good, really good. It will help me a lot if you can do that for me. I'll be right here beside you the whole time. Okay?"

The tears were coming faster now.

Slowly, his gaze still on her face, Ryan stood. "Let's hear that counting."

"O-one," she managed. "T-two. Three."

"I'm just going to walk around you." He placed a hand on her shoulder as he did so, grateful she didn't turn her head to follow him.

"Eight. Nine." There was a sob in her voice, but at least she'd stopped stuttering.

Ryan pulled his Swiss Army knife from his pocket and crouched down at her hip. "I'm going to hold your arm to keep it steady. Don't want to accidentally cut you with my teeny-tiny scissors."

"Twenty-five. Twenty-six. Twenty-seven."

"You're doing great." He grasped her forearm, noting that her silken blouse was cool to the touch. Phone light at his side, aimed where he needed it, he started cutting the hair. "This will be over in a few seconds. I promise you."

"Th-thirty," she said through a sob.

Her hand was trembling badly now, making him afraid

he might slip and nip her. Tightening his hold, he quickly, and carefully, cut through the long auburn tresses entangled around her fingers. They were caught in her bracelet and the button at the bottom of her sleeve, clinging to her as though wanting to keep her.

"Forty-four. Forty-five."

Snip. Snip. Snip. "Nearly there."

Ryan kept his attention on his task, refusing to look at the leathery remains of the woman lying against the wall. There would be time enough to examine the body later. When Sarah wasn't there to witness it.

"I'm going to take your bracelet off." The hair was really tangled in it, and it would take a while to get it all out. Something he could do when she wasn't wearing it—or watching.

She whimpered, and he took that as permission. "Sixty-two. S-sixty-two." She hiccupped a sob.

"Sixty-three, Stats. Don't let the side down. I know you're a numbers expert."

"Sixty-three," she repeated. "Sixty-four."

The bracelet snapped free, and the remainder of the hair fell from her hand. Ryan quickly brushed the rest off her, ensuring there wasn't even one stray strand tucked around the button on her blouse. Once he was confident it was all gone, he placed her hand in her lap before sliding his arms under her knees and carrying her out into the corridor.

"Eighty-nine." She sat stiffly in his hold. A brittle energy emanating from her. As though one wrong word would make her shatter. "Ninety."

"Nearly there, Stats. You did great."

Walking a few steps down the corridor, he gently placed her on the ground, propping her against the wall. She drew her knees right up to her chest and held them with one arm. She let the other trail on the ground beside her, as though pretending it wasn't part of her body anymore.

"I'm gonna clean up this hand. While I do that, how about you keep your eyes on my handsome face?" Ryan crouched in front of her and dug around in her handbag for the antibacterial wipes.

"Ninety-three. Ninety-four." Sarah did as he asked, all the while raining silent tears.

Gently, he lifted her hand and started to wipe it. Careful to cover every millimeter of skin. "You're doing great. Let me just get this all cleaned up, and then you can have a sip of water and maybe a bite or two of one of those cereal bars you've got stashed in your bag."

"Ninety-eight." She swallowed hard. "I can still feel it on me."

"That's why I'm decontaminating you." He winked at her. "You're gonna be good as new in a minute. Right now, concentrate on feeling me. That's reality. My skin against yours while I wipe the memory away. Can you feel it disappearing with each sweep of the cloth? I swear I can see it fade as I work. You must be able to feel the sensations disappear, leaving only the warmth of my hand against yours."

"One hundred," she whispered, her eyes still glued to his face.

Once again, he made her focus on reality by speaking it aloud to him. "What does my hand feel like? Describe it to me."

There was a beat of silence, and he hoped she was thinking about her answer instead of what'd upset her.

"Warm," she said at last. "Strong. Big. Rough. There are calluses."

"From lifting weights." He grinned. "Joking. They're

from helping my granddad and granduncle with their carpentry business."

"I remember. You said they looked like gnomes."

"That's them." He tossed the wipe out of sight before rolling her sleeve up twice and entwining his fingers with hers.

"All better. See?" Holding their joined hands up in front of them, he watched as relief made her shoulders slump. But she didn't let go of him. And that was okay with Ryan.

"I didn't mean to freak out," she confessed in a rush. "I didn't think I was the type of person who'd lose it like that. I just, I just wasn't prepared for...for... I know it could have been worse, I was overreacting, I—"

"You," he interrupted, "didn't do anything wrong. Hell, we all freak out at some point. Honestly, I thought you'd have done it a lot sooner. I mean, you've been kidnapped and abandoned underground with a guy you thought was an arsehole—that'd make most people lose the plot."

Her lips twitched slightly at the corners, as though they were trying to smile. "Have you ever done it?"

"Freaked out, you mean?" He sat beside her knees, facing her, still clutching her hand. "Sure." Opening her bag, he took out the water and handed it to her. "You have to let go of me if we're going to open this bottle."

Sarah shook her head, twisting off the cap while he held it, before taking it from him.

Ryan faked a sigh. "I can see I'm going to be down a hand for the rest of this trip." His thumb brushed hers in a caress.

"What made you freak?" She passed the water to him after she'd taken a few small sips.

Ryan was impressed she'd remembered to limit her

intake. He took a swallow before answering, gesturing for her to put the lid back on. "It's sad to say, but there have been many things that've made me freak. The one that sticks out, because of where we are, was the time I had to go underground to find a couple who were missing. I was young, cocky, and full of myself after a run of successful missions."

"This was in the army?" Strength was returning to her voice, along with color to her cheeks.

Ryan nodded and passed her a cereal bar, challenging her to open it without her other hand. Her eyes danced as she ripped it with her teeth. He rolled his eyes.

"The whole mission was a favor for some diplomat who'd heard my unit had a great tracking team, so he sent us in after his daughter and her boyfriend. Of course, knowing my reputation had proceeded me meant I was even more cocky than usual. I practically swaggered into those underground caverns, pretty confident I knew exactly what kind of conditions we would face down there. Only thing was, the locals had neglected to tell me about a colony of bats that called the place home. Since I wasn't expecting them, I did nothing to soften our approach to ensure we wouldn't disturb them. Damn things came at me like a—"

"Bat out of hell?" Sarah's smile was weak, but welcome.

"Smart-arse. But yeah. They bit. They flapped in my face. They crapped all over me while screeching so much I couldn't hear myself think. One of them attached itself to my nose."

"I wondered about that little scar." She passed him the cereal bar.

For once, he didn't wolf the food down; instead, he took a tiny nibble before storing it back in her bag.

Self-control sucked.

"So what happened?" she said, sounding more like herself.

"I lost it. And it wasn't pretty. I turned and ran, waving my arms around my head like an idiot, trying to keep the flying rodents off me while shrieking like a toddler who'd encountered a bee. Ran right past my team and straight into a giant boulder. Knocked myself out and had to be carried out of the cave for medical treatment—mainly bat bites. Had to have a rabies shot." He grimaced. "Couldn't sit down for days after that. On top of everything, we pissed off the VIP who'd roped us in. He was furious we'd lost time getting to the people we were searching for. *And* I lost my rep as a badass." He grimaced. "I hate bats. They're just rats with wings."

Sarah's smile was genuine now, lighting up her eyes. "Did you get the people out of there?"

"Yep. Everyone safe and sound. Except me. I had bat bite marks everywhere. Biggest insult though? Found out months later that they didn't have to give me the shot in the backside; they chose to put it there as payback for me screwing up."

Chuckling, she rested her gaze on their joined hands. After a couple of breaths, she said, "It was a woman, wasn't it? T-the hair. From a w-woman?"

He squeezed her hand. "Yeah."

They sat in silence for a minute or two. Ryan content to stroke the back of her hand as he waited for her to process things. There was no sound in the tunnels to indicate that anyone else was there, which meant they could spare a little time to help her get past this—at least until they were out of the mine.

"We should find out what happened to her," Sarah surprised him by saying.

"You don't need to do that." Although, he was impressed she offered. "You can stay here, and I'll check it on my own. There's really no reason we both have to do it."

Bronze eyes met his through thick, dark lashes. "No, I have to do it too. My imagination will paint a picture of what she was like anyway. It's better if I know the truth. I'll be okay. I'm prepared now. Before…"

"Before—the shock overwhelmed you."

"Yes." She seemed a little lost as she studied their joined hands. "I'm not good with things I haven't prepared to deal with. Usually, I have time to think everything through and work out all the possible things that could happen. This, being here, it's unexpected."

"That's one way to put it," he said through a grin. "Not sure abductions are ever expected, Stats."

A warmth spread through his chest when she smiled. "Are you seriously laughing at me right now?"

"I'm contemplating it. You've no idea how hilarious you are." Ryan got to his feet, tugging her up with him.

"Only to you. And that says a lot."

She probably didn't mean it as a compliment, but that didn't stop him taking it as one. "Let's get this over with so we can find a way out of here."

Sarah squared her shoulders, held onto his hand with a viselike grip, and nodded.

A strange surge of pride overcame him. "So damn courageous," he muttered as he led her back into the chamber that caused her terror.

"Not even close." Sarah squeezed his hand. "Please, don't let go of me."

"No chance of that." Ryan held his phone light in front of them as they stepped through the doorway.

CHAPTER EIGHT

No matter what Ryan thought, Sarah did *not* feel courageous. Mainly, she felt cornered. It was face the fear, or curl into a ball and weep until she faded away. Ryan, on the other hand, was a massive rock—immovable, unbreakable, strong against anything that was thrown at it. Every second they spent together, in their underground prison, made Sarah believe they might actually have a chance of getting out. Purely because Ryan told her so and his confidence was contagious.

"You okay?" he asked, keeping the light away from the corner with the body.

No! "Yes."

"Liar." He grinned at her.

Without asking again if she was ready to continue, he directed the light where it needed to go—at the spot where the hair had ensnared her.

It was possible her heart stopped beating for a split second as she forced herself to look down at the floor. At the spot where the body lay. Adrenaline coursed through her as she realized the remains of the woman were nowhere near as horrific as she'd imagined. The woman looked like a dried-up doll, discarded by a careless child. Instead of horror, all Sarah felt was sadness.

She glanced at Ryan. "Is she...?"

"Mummified? Yeah. That's why we didn't smell any decomp."

The body lay on its side, face pressed to the wall, arms curled up against her chest. Her legs were stretched out into the dark corner. It was impossible to tell what her ethnicity might have been, as her skin had the appearance of tan-colored leather.

Long auburn hair, wild and matted, lay around her shoulders. Chunks were missing where Ryan had cut it, which somehow felt like an added abuse the woman had been made to suffer. Her dress was dirty and torn, when once it had been white with a red flower pattern. Beside her lay a red leather handbag covered in dust.

What a sad and lonely place to die. Sarah's heart ached for her. "She isn't ancient. How can she be mummified?"

Ryan crouched down to get a better look, still keeping hold of Sarah's hand, which she appreciated.

"Under the right circumstances, it can take as little as three weeks to mummify a body. We're surrounded by lime-stone, which absorbs water. The air is dry, the temperature constant. I bet it didn't take long for her to end up like this." When he glanced up to find Sarah gaping at him, he shrugged. "Spent time in Peru chasing a stolen mummy, picked up a thing or two. Do you think you'd be okay if I let go of your hand for a minute? I want to see what's in her bag."

"Can we check the rest of the room first? Make sure there's nothing else lurking in the dark." And yes, she was that wimpy.

"Sure."

Together they walked the room. Thankfully, there were no more bodies. Only an empty water bottle lying on the other side of the room, which Ryan tucked into their bag, and five tiny candles. All used up.

Icy tentacles of unease worked their way up Sarah's spine at the familiar sight of the candles. Then, as the beam of light skimmed over the woman's feet, she gasped. Her hand flying to cover her mouth. There was an iron manacle around one of the woman's ankles, tethering her to the wall with a heavy chain.

He frowned at the manacle. "Now, I'm really glad I remembered how to pick a lock."

Going back to the handbag, Ryan released her hand and crouched down to open it. Sarah stood close, needing to feel his courage and strength to ground her.

"Adrienne Toussaint," he read out loud as he rifled her wallet. "Twenty-six, from Quebec in Canada—that's from her driver's license. Nothing else in here but Canadian-issued bank cards and a photo of, presumably, her and her boyfriend." He held it up for Sarah to see.

"She was so young and pretty." A lump formed in her throat. "No one should die like this. What are her parents thinking? Her boyfriend? How long has she been down here?"

"Don't think too hard about it, Stats, it won't do you any good. Right now, we need to focus on what she can tell us about our situation, and once we're out of here, we can let her family know where she is." He tucked her driver's license into his own wallet before putting it back in his pocket. "There's nothing else in here that would be of any use to us. Mostly makeup and keys."

He put the bag back where he'd found it and leaned over the woman.

"What are you doing?" Sarah hissed.

"Looking for a clue as to how she died. I see something." He angled the light into her chest to illuminate her hands. She was clutching her phone. "I guess she used it for light after the candles went out."

Something glinted, and Sarah pointed at it. "What's that in her hand?"

Ryan peered in closer and cursed softly. "She's wearing an engagement ring."

"How could someone be this cruel?" Sarah asked, not expecting an answer. The world was full of people who took delight in hurting others. None of them made any sense.

Standing, Ryan wiped his hands on his jeans. "I think she died of dehydration."

Like they were supposed to do.

Sarah pressed a hand against her roiling stomach. "This whole situation is beyond anything I've ever encountered. I've never even researched anything like this, and I really don't understand what I'm seeing."

"Neither do I. We can't do anything else here. Let's go."

"I feel like I'm abandoning her, and I hate that we mutilated her by cutting her hair. I wish I hadn't gotten hysterical about it. I wish we'd left her intact."

"All we can do now is make sure her family finds out what happened to her. You aren't to blame for anything she suffered. That's all on the bastard who chained her to the wall."

"Just give me one second." Sarah crouched down beside the body and gently placed her hand on the bony shoulder.

She was cold, and brittle, and everything that made her *her* was long gone. Yet, Sarah still ached for her. It felt like her heart was straining out of her body toward the woman who'd died so brutally. "I'm so sorry about what happened to you, Adrienne. I'm sorry for my part in it too. I know you aren't here, that this is just a shell, and that you're somewhere better now. A place where there's no pain or fear. We'll make sure your family knows about you. You may have died here alone, but we found you and we *see* you. We won't forget."

When she stood, it was to find Ryan staring at her with an unfathomable expression on his face. What she'd just done must have seemed so silly to him, and she felt her cheeks heat.

"There should be some acknowledgment when someone dies," she tried to explain. "Especially when it happens so cruelly."

For a second, he didn't say anything, then he reached out a hand toward her. "We won't let her be forgotten," he said gently. "But we have to go."

She took his hand, feeling his warmth sink into her, replacing the coldness of Adrienne's remains. "I know."

"We need to light another candle," Ryan said. "I don't want to waste the battery on this phone." He rummaged in her handbag and came out with one.

"We don't have anything to light it with—the other candle's flame is long gone."

"Ye of little faith." Ryan shook his head in mock disappointment as he brought out his trusty Swiss Army knife. A tiny cavity in it held two matches. One of which he struck on the limestone wall before lighting the candle. He tucked the barely spent match back into its home. "Might come in handy later."

"You are such a Boy Scout," Sarah told him, making him grin.

They proceeded on up the tunnel, each occupied with their own thoughts. Sarah was grateful the passage was wide enough for them to walk side by side. It seemed safer somehow.

"Looks like there're more rooms," Ryan said grimly.

And sure enough, two more dark holes appeared out of the darkness further up the tunnel.

Dread made her stomach clench. "I'm not sure we should go into them."

"They might hold a way out." He sounded determined, yet unconvinced. "We have to check."

"What if there are more...bodies?" Or worse. People close to death. People they could do nothing for. She couldn't stand the thought of being unable to help someone if they needed it. And she really didn't want to be a witness to someone dying. But she would. If she had to. Nobody should be forced to suffer and die alone down there.

"Still got to check, Stats. This time, you wait in the corridor with the candle, okay?"

It shamed her when all she felt was relief at his offer. "I can't let you go in alone. It isn't fair." Her gaze strayed to the black voids. Who knew what horrible secrets waited beyond them?

"It isn't about fair and unfair." Ryan handed her the candle as they reached the nearest doorway. "It's about skillset. I was trained for this, and if there are more dead bodies in there, it won't affect me the way it will you."

"How can you say that? Of course it will affect you."

"No. It won't. I know you don't understand because your life is far removed from this sort of thing, and that's great, but mine isn't. That wasn't the first dead body I've seen and probably won't be the last. I was trained to deal with violent death." What he left unsaid was that he'd also been trained to dispense it.

"It still must take a toll. You've got a soft heart, Ryan. You can't tell me it doesn't get to you."

"Sure it does, and that's where the training and experience kick in. I compartmentalize. You're strong and have more courage than most, but I'm not sure you're able to put anything you find in a box to examine later. Or to ignore forever. Both work. In fact, I'm a great believer in burying that crap deep and moving on with life. So how about you do you and I'll do me? Let me check out the rooms alone, okay?"

Reluctantly, she nodded.

"Good girl," he said.

To her surprise, Ryan leaned into her and pressed a soft, chaste kiss to her lips. She felt the satin warmth of his touch right to her toes. His kiss was bittersweet, so familiar while reminding her of everything they'd lost. When he straightened, he seemed a little flummoxed by his actions.

"Uh, that was a kiss of encouragement," he said. "It wasn't a come-on because that would be totally inappropriate right now given, well, all of this." He ran a hand through his hair. "I'm usually a whole lot smoother than this."

Sarah couldn't say anything. It took all of her energy not to press the kiss into her lips with her fingertips. As though that might save it forever. And didn't that make her sound like a lovesick teen?

"Right," he said. "Let's get this over with." And then he turned on his phone's light and walked into the first room.

"If we ever get out of here," Sarah muttered, "I'm going to need counseling for sooooo many things." She raised her voice to call after him. "You can't say good girl to a woman. It's patronizing. Plus it sounds like you're talking to a dog."

Laughter echoed out of the empty room.

Dumbass.

Ryan mentally smacked himself upside the head as he entered the room. He had no business kissing Sarah, even in a friendly sort of way. Things were much too confusing between them, and she probably didn't want his lips all over hers again. Especially not minutes after checking out a dead body.

Double dumbass.

It'd just felt natural. Yet it wasn't. The whole situation between them was messing with his head. Part of him felt like he knew her when he had no memory of her at all. There was a comfortable connection between them, an easiness that made him want to relax and just be himself around her. He wasn't sure if it was a consequence of them being thrust together in pretty dire circumstances, or maybe some leftover emotional memory of their time together. Either way, it was weird as hell.

"What's in there?" she called, bringing his attention back to his task.

"Nothing yet." The light swept up the wall and stopped when it hit a candle in a roughly carved nook. The same sort of candle they'd found in their room and the dead woman's room. "Damn," Ryan muttered.

"What was that? Did you say something?"

"Nothing important. I'm still looking." Only, now he stepped carefully, scanning every nook and cranny, expecting to find something that neither of them would like.

When the light swept over another used candle on the platform, a cold acceptance settled within Ryan. There was something bad in the room. The air was heavy with it. Instantly, he was back on high alert, noting every detail as he saw it, weighing its significance and adding it to the already substantial information he'd gleaned from other rooms. At some point, there would have to be an official report about all of this. An investigation.

Justice.

In the meantime, there was only their witness to the atrocities that'd happened far underground.

His feet were on automatic pilot as they zeroed in on the darkest part of the cavern. A second later, the light from his phone revealed his instincts were right. It was two bodies this time, not one. A man and a woman, wrapped around each other in the tight, dark corner behind the platform bed.

The woman was restrained with the same sort of manacle they'd seen before. Broken rocks lay beside the heavy chain, tying her to the wall, making it obvious that they'd tried to free her. Unfortunately, the rocks wouldn't have had any impact on that chain. A dark fury swept through Ryan as he looked at the couple. They'd died in each other's arms. Murdered by some unseen foe who'd played God with their lives.

"What's going on?" There was shuffling at the doorway, telling him Sarah was becoming impatient.

"Don't come in here." His reply was harsher than he'd intended.

Of course, Sarah knew what his tone meant. "You found another body." It wasn't a question.

It was tempting to lie, in a futile attempt to shield her from the horror. But she'd already told him that gathering information helped her to cope. If that's what she needed to get through this, then he was happy to supply it for her. Although, she didn't have to see things to know about them. At least he could protect her from having those images in her mind, haunting her for the rest of her life.

"I found a couple." He heard Sarah gasp. "Mummified like last time. The woman is manacled."

"Don't stay in there, Ryan. Come back out here."

"I'm in no danger, Stats."

"You don't need to dwell on this stuff either."

Ryan didn't know whether to be touched or amused at her worry. Most people took one look at him and assumed he'd cope with whatever was thrown at him.

"I'm coming right out. I need to get their IDs first."

He found both wallets in the handbag beside them. They were German and married to each other. Ryan ran a hand down his face before adding their driver's licenses to his growing collection. German, Canadian, English? What the hell was going on?

As he skimmed the light over the couple again, his hand jerked and he dropped the phone.

"Ryan?" Sarah called.

"I'm coming."

Picking the phone up, he looked at the couple. The man had wrapped himself around the woman, as if to protect her. How completely screwed up was that? To be helpless when his woman was trapped and dying. All he could offer was comfort, right to the end. He'd tried to free her. Had he tried to escape too? Could he have left her behind if he'd found a way out?

"This is a mindfuck," Ryan muttered.

His fist clenched and unclenched with the need to hit something. No, *someone.* He wanted the bastard behind this, and he wanted to hurt him badly. He wanted to make him suffer, the way he'd made his victims suffer. Only, Ryan wasn't sure that was possible. To suffer the way this couple had done, you needed to be able to love.

No one who loved could do something like this.

"Get your backside out here." Sarah was obviously losing patience again.

"Or what? You'll punch me?"

"I apologized for that."

"Yeah, it was sweet. I remember."

He could almost hear her teeth gnashing. "You've got five seconds, and then I'm coming in to drag you out."

He'd almost like to see her try. "I'm coming; hold your horses." With one last glance at the bodies, he strode toward the doorway.

And stopped.

Something glinted at him up near the ceiling.

Something that didn't belong there.

CHAPTER NINE

Sarah watched as Ryan suddenly stopped walking a couple of feet from the tunnel entrance. Honestly, he was deliberately trying to drive her mad. She wanted him out of there. Away from all that death. She wanted him safe. With her. And yes, it didn't make any sense because the bodies couldn't harm him, and Ryan was definitely safer without her than with her. But logic was irrelevant. She'd only believe he was okay if he was by her side.

Still, she was definitely losing her patience. "What's stopping you now?"

"Not sure..." Reaching up, he pried something from the wall and it fell into his hand.

He came over to show it to her.

Sarah poked at the tiny piece of tech with her fingertip. "Is that a camera?"

"Sure looks like one. It's wireless, short range, which means there's a receiver or a relay around here somewhere."

Any impatience she was feeling vanished at this new revelation. "You mean someone is transmitting images from in here? They're watching us?" That was too creepy to comprehend.

"Not sure yet."

She waited, patiently this time, as Ryan meticulously searched the rest of the cavern.

After his news about the bodies, Sarah couldn't bring herself to step inside the room to help. And the candle wasn't bright enough to allow her to search in the corridor. All she could do was wait.

In a matter of minutes, Ryan found two more cameras. "I need to check the tunnels and the other rooms, especially the one they put us in. You stay here; I won't be long."

Oh, that wasn't happening. "I think it's better if we stick together—mainly for my sake."

"You're braver than you think, Stats."

As much as she appreciated the support, it wasn't true. "We're surrounded by people who died horribly. If I'm alone, that's all I'll think about. The only way to keep my mind off them is to stay with you. You keep me focused and help me to bury the thoughts...no pun intended. Everything you do is a distraction. You can't help it."

It was clear he was trying hard not to laugh at her. Again. "That's quite a compliment."

"Don't let it go to your head. As soon as we're out of here, I'm kissing goodbye to any attempts at remaining calm. Trust me, I plan on having an epic meltdown."

He cocked his head. "Can you plan a meltdown?"

"Given enough notice, I could plan anything."

"I bet you could. I still think you'll be safe here for a few minutes and I'll be faster alone."

Sarah glanced around before leaning into him and whispering, "What if they're watching and they want us to split up? What if a huge metal wall suddenly slams down, with you on one side and me on the other?" She made like she was joking, mainly so he wouldn't realize just how much of a wimp she really was. In reality, she wouldn't have been surprised if the whole place had been engineered purely to mess with them.

"You've been watching way too many movies, and that's saying a lot coming from me. Stuff like that doesn't happen in real life."

"Why take the chance? Right? If you're worried about me slowing you down, I can run."

He made a point of staring at her shoes.

They weren't sexy. They were work shoes. And although they had a heel, it was a block, which made it totally possible she'd be able to run in them. No matter what Ryan appeared to think.

"They're perfectly comfortable shoes," she lied. "But if you're worried, we could just walk fast instead of running." If he didn't give in, she planned on rattling off every statistic she knew about heels until she wore him down. There were quite a few.

"That look in your eye is pretty scary." He was smiling while he shook his head at her. "You win; we'll power walk back to where they left us."

That sounded like a terrible idea. Wasn't power walking just running for people who enjoyed wiggling their hips? Sarah swallowed her opinion and straightened her shoulders. "Lead the way."

"You first, shorty, and keep your eyes peeled for more cameras."

"Shorty? I'm five foot four, you overgrown ape."

Of course, he just chuckled.

It didn't take long to find several more cameras, all tucked into hiding spots high on the walls of the tunnel and the chamber they'd been left in. And with each new camera, Sarah's hysteria level inched upward.

"What kind of sicko are we dealing with here?" She wished Ryan would hold her hand again, but his were full of cameras and she was being pathetic. Still, she inched closer to him. Feeling better when he was within touching range. That way, she could reassure herself he was real when logic insisted he wasn't.

"I'd say we're dealing with the kind who has his own killing field." Ryan reached for another camera, just inside the room where they'd started. When he tugged it, a wire appeared attached to it, partially embedded into the rock underneath.

"Killing field?" Oh, that didn't sound good. "You mean, you think there are more dead people down here?"

"I'd be surprised if there weren't. Jackpot," he said as he slowly pulled the wire from the wall and followed it out into the tunnel.

"Why jackpot?" Sarah stuck to his side.

"This one is wired. Which means there has to be a relay close by. You couldn't use Wi-Fi for more than a meter or two, at most, down here before the signal dropped. You'd need another way to get the camera feed out of the tunnels to whoever's watching us. See how this camera unit is bigger than the ones without the wires?" He held out a palm with a few of the cameras they'd collected.

Sarah picked a smaller one and examined it. "These ones are transmitting to the bigger one?"

"Yeah, and the bigger one is connected to a system that has to have been hardwired into the mine."

Her eyes snapped to his. "If we follow the wire, will it take us out of here?"

"Stats." He softened his tone as his expression filled

with sympathy. "This only leads to the relay box, and we already know where the wiring from that leads."

And there it was, confirmation that her IQ was dropping with every minute she remained underground. Suddenly, all those smart women making stupid decisions in every horror movie she'd ever seen made perfect sense. "Straight through the unbreakable gate."

"Yeah. Although, it isn't all bad news. If we can find the relay this is wired into, we might be able to tap into it with our phones, hijack the feed, and get a message out to my team."

"Do you know how to do that? Because I don't."

"Elle's the real expert with this kind of thing. Usually, I keep her supplied with caffeine and Snickers bars, and do what I'm told when she gives me an order." He smiled wryly. "I'm the grunt of the team. All I can do is try my best to make it work."

Oh, she didn't like him referring to himself as only a grunt. Later, when they were out in the fresh air, she planned to set him straight on that issue. "That's good enough for me. Let's look for that relay box." She paused. "Do you think they're still watching us?"

In a flash, the easygoing persona she was used to disappeared, only to be replaced by a man who practically vibrated with cold, contained fury. His eyes darkened, making it clear that he was more than capable of following up on any threats he might make.

"I hope so," he said thinly as he lifted the wired camera until it was eye level. "When we get out of here," he said to whoever was watching, "and we will get out, we're coming for you." It was a promise dripping ice.

As soon as he was done, he bashed the camera against the wall. All they needed was the wire.

Sarah shivered. "You can be really scary, you know that?"

His smile was the one he'd used to get her into bed. "Never to you, Stats. That's all that matters. Now, let's see where this wire goes."

Was it worrying how quickly he could move between anger and amusement? Had he always been like this? Or was this a leftover from his brain injury?

She had to ask. "You were furious a second ago, now you're back to easygoing charmer. It's like you have two personalities. Should I be worried?"

He barked out a laugh. "I love how you just come out and say what you're thinking. And no, you shouldn't be worried. I already told you, I'm good at compartmentalizing. There's no split personality; I just focus on the appropriate emotion for the appropriate situation and bury the rest."

"I'm not sure that's normal, Ryan."

"I'm not sure anybody's normal, Stats."

He had a point.

They continued to follow the wire, which instead of heading toward the gate as she'd expected, disappeared into the rocks blocking the other end of the tunnel.

"Crap." Ryan ran a hand through his hair. "I was worried about this. If there are other rooms beyond that cave-in, then they're all probably wired into the same relay. It'd only take one per tunnel, and I'm guessing the one for this tunnel is on the other side of these rocks."

"We can go back and see if there's another wired camera in the other tunnel." Although, searching the rooms with dead people didn't appeal. It felt like they were desecrating their graves.

"Couldn't see any wiring, and believe me, I looked." He

examined the rocks. "Maybe we could move enough rocks for me to slip through and find the relay."

Sarah didn't want to shatter his hopes, but the rocks were tightly packed into the space. Even if they managed to remove some, the chances of the rest falling on them were high. Instead of being negative, she stepped up beside him and started scanning the wall for a place to start.

"There are some big stones here." She pointed at a space close to the floor. "See how they make a kind of bridge? Maybe we can dig out under it, without bringing the rest of the ceiling down on us."

Ryan crouched down to study the spot. "Might work." He handed her the phone. "Keep it pointed here, and I'll see what I can get out."

"Be careful."

"I'll go slow." He started by moving the smaller rocks under the large stone arch that kept up the rest of the cave-in.

Sarah's knuckles turned white as she clutched the phone and, even though she kept it pointed where Ryan needed it to be, she couldn't help looking up at the cracks above them.

"Death by Jenga," she muttered.

"I heard that," Ryan said. "I happen to be great at Jenga."

"All kids are good at that game."

"Ouch, brutal, Stats, brutal." He removed another rock and bent to peer into the small indent he'd made. "Looks like it's pretty deep. This could take a while."

"Not like we have anything else to do."

"That's the attitude."

One by one, Ryan removed the stones and placed them against the wall of the tunnel. Every now and then, the rockfall would groan and they'd freeze. Fortunately, nothing came down except dust.

Soon there was an indent in the bottom of the wall of rock. Ryan sat back on his heels to look at her. His hands were covered in dust, but there were no cuts that she could see.

"There's a bigger boulder blocking my way." He wiped his brow with the back of his hand, leaving a smudge. "I think I can get it out, but it's gonna go slow. If I knew how deep this went, I'd try to push it through to the other side. Right now, I'm not sure what kind of chain reaction shoving it would cause. Gimme the light."

As soon as it was in his hand, he stuck his head and shoulders into the hole to get a better look. The urge to grab his ankles and drag him away from danger was almost over-whelming. One loose rock, and he'd be crushed. All Sarah could do was stand there, twisting her hands, and praying the rocks stayed in place.

Thankfully, he wasn't in there long. Slowly, he inched to sit beside her. There was dust in his hair, and Sarah itched to brush it out for him. It was hard, remembering that she didn't have the right to touch him any way she liked. Not anymore.

It was for the best though. If there was one lesson she'd learned from their time together, it was that taking risks with a man like Ryan never worked out. Not for someone like her. She was better off with a safe, boring man. One who worked an average nine-to-five job. A man who wouldn't suddenly disappear on her. Or get shot and nearly die.

Or break her heart.

Yep, it was very clear she wasn't cut out to love someone

who put their life on the line every time they walked out the door.

Ryan passed the phone to her. "The slab that's holding everything up is wide and it seems to go over the boulder I need to remove."

"And you'd have to keep your head in there the whole time, right?"

He didn't seem worried about the risk. "I'm sure I can get it."

"I'm sure you can too. I'm also sure that if it all goes wrong, those"—she pointed at the wall of rocks—"will come down and pop your skull like a grape under a boot."

"Using my own imagery back at me. Nice touch." He grinned.

She arched an eyebrow at him. "Accurate though, isn't it? How about we give up and go see what's at the end of the dead body tunnel?"

"That's its official name now, huh?"

"Graveyard seems wrong." She thought about it. "Crypt tunnel? That could work."

"How about this? There's a smaller stone beside the one I'm after. If I pull it out first, it will give me a decent hand-hold on the boulder, and it might give us an idea if it's even worth trying to move the big one."

Okay, she liked this idea better. "Do you have to stick your head in there for the smaller stone?"

"Nope, I can reach it if I stretch. It'll only take one hand to remove."

"Okay then, we can try that."

She got the impression he'd been planning to do exactly this all along, and had only included her in the decision process because he knew she needed to feel in control.

"Crouch down and shine the light into the hole, will

you?" Ryan wriggled onto his belly and stretched his right arm into the space he'd made. His cheek was pressed up against the rocks as he reached for the small stone.

Sarah watched as he slowly, he worked his fingertips into a tiny crack at the right of the stone and began to work it out.

There was an ominous creaking sound from overhead, and they only started breathing again when it faded and everything remained in place.

"I don't like this." Sarah eyed the dust as it fell from the ceiling above onto her head. "Maybe you should leave that little stone alone."

"It doesn't support anything, far as I can see. Removing it shouldn't cause another cave-in. I'm sure we're fine."

She wished she had his confidence.

Carefully, he began to inch the stone out from the crevice it was wedged into. "I feel air behind it." His grin was contagious, and she couldn't help smiling back, although hers was more nervous than excited.

With slow pressure, he pulled the rock toward them until it suddenly popped free. Quickly, Ryan tossed it beside the others while they waited a beat to see if there would be any movement in the blockade.

When nothing happened, Ryan reached for the phone. "Let's see what we're dealing with now."

As he shone the light into the hole, Sarah gasped. Through the tiny space where the stone had been, a rat's head appeared. Its nose twitched. Its black eyes stared straight at them. And then its body contorted, flattening to squeeze through the hole. They stared, in horrified fascination, as it popped out and ran toward them.

Suddenly, Ryan shot to his feet. Sarah, meanwhile, watched another rat's head appear in the same small gap.

Faster than she could suck in a breath, it was through the hole. Followed by another. Then another. And another...

That's when they noticed the noise coming from the other side of the blockade.

Skittering.

Scraping.

Squeaking.

A million tiny claws on stone.

"Run," Ryan barked, grabbing her hand.

Sarah didn't have much choice in the matter because Ryan was already dragging her up the tunnel. Behind them, the squeaking and scratching grew louder as more and more rats poured through the dam that'd kept them at bay.

As they reached the curve where the gate sat, Sarah glanced behind them. In the split second before the tunnel fell into darkness, she could just make out the floor.

It was a carpet of rats.

CHAPTER TEN

Benson Security Office
London

When Joe and David returned from the hospital with the security footage from that morning, they headed straight to Callum's office. Only to be stopped by Julia.

"The police are in with him." Her complexion was even paler than usual, and Joe didn't like it one bit. "A woman Ryan knew went missing this morning too. Elle's busy digging up everything she can on her and will fill us in once she's done."

"Was she abducted?" David asked.

Joe's wife zeroed straight in on the implication behind the former spy's question. "Yes, the police think Ryan might be behind it. He wasn't, was he? He was abducted too." She covered her mouth with her hand.

Joe stepped up beside her, slung an arm around her

shoulders, and tucked her into his side. "Yeah, baby, somebody took him."

Anxious eyes looked up at him as she took a deep breath. "The police will want to know what you've found. Let me get my iPad, and we'll interrupt the meeting. Do we need to do this in the conference room?"

David shook his head. "No, but we'll need Elle. Meet you back here in a few." He jogged up the main stairs as Joe followed Julia into her office.

As usual, it was meticulously organized, with everything arranged in sets of three or seven. The three brightly colored notebooks he'd given her the day before sat on her desk in pride of place. They were precisely spaced, as though she'd measured the gaps between them. Joe knew she hadn't. Julia didn't need to.

She rounded her desk to pick up her iPad from its designated spot. She kept a running list of each completed task on it, as well as a spreadsheet with every piece of information that came across her desk for each job. The one she'd started on Ryan would already be stuffed with detail. Nothing got past Julia. She saw patterns in data that other people could never spot, and she was careful to assess every single piece of information to ensure they didn't miss anything of importance.

She was a genius. And Joe would never figure out why she'd fallen in love with someone as ordinary as him. All he knew was that he was damned glad it'd happened.

"You okay?" He came up behind her as she gave into the urge to adjust some Post-it notes on one of her many whiteboards.

He swept her shoulder-length hair aside and placed a kiss in the crook of her neck, breathing her in deeply. Home. That's what Julia was to him.

She melted into him, giving him her trust in a way that humbled him. For someone who found it so difficult to negotiate the world, having her at ease around him was a gift.

Julia turned in his caress and threaded her arms around his waist. "I can't bear the thought of anything happening to Ryan. He's only now coming right from the coma and was so upbeat about getting his life back. I want him home. Where he belongs."

"We all do." He held her close, and she pressed her ear to the spot above his heart. Softly counting the beats to soothe herself. "You don't need to stay in the office. You can compile notes from home. No one would think anything of it."

"Yes, they would." She rubbed her cheek against his shirt. "They'd think I don't care, and I do."

"Not if we told them about the baby." He knew his voice was softer when he mentioned their pregnancy, and he didn't care one bit.

She leaned back in his arms to look up at him. "I'm not ready. Soon, I promise. I've barely passed the twelve-week mark, and I'm still worried that..."

He hated the pain in her eyes. "That we'll lose this one too?"

Julia focused on a spot in the middle of his wide chest. "Once Ryan is safe, then we'll tell everyone."

"Whatever you need, Jules. You know that."

"Thanks," she whispered.

Gently, he angled her chin up and covered her lips with his. She tasted like saltwater taffy, straight from his home-town's boardwalk. Maybe, once Ryan was safe and sound, they could take a trip back to Atlantic City, just to rest up and enjoy the sea air. It would do them both good.

Reluctantly, Joe eased his lips from hers as he heard David and Elle coming back down the stairs. "Time to deal with Callum," he said.

She nodded, clasped her iPad to her chest like a shield, and followed him out of the room.

Harvard had tagged along with David, and Joe lifted his chin in hello.

"Thought he might see something we didn't," David said.

"More eyes, the better," Joe agreed as he knocked on Callum's door.

"What?" came the charming response.

Joe shared a grin with the other two men as he opened the door. "We've got something you should see," he said as he entered the room.

Callum had obviously been pacing again because he wasn't behind his desk; instead he was over by the window. He inclined his head to the police officer taking up one of his guest chairs. "Officer Mark Jensen, Scotland Yard. Joe Barone, head of training."

Joe shook hands with the cop, whose eyebrows rose as the rest of the team filed into the room.

"We need more chairs," Elle said to David, who turned around and went to fetch some.

"No, we don't," Callum shouted after him. "I've already got too many bloody chairs."

"Bad day, boss?" Elle asked as she plonked her laptop down on his desk and made herself comfortable in his seat.

Joe, meanwhile, made sure Julia took the other guest chair and didn't decide to hide in a corner instead. She gave the police officer a shy smile before focusing on her iPad.

David came back with a couple of folding chairs, and

when Joe shook his head, Harvard took one and David set the other beside Elle before sitting in it.

"We all comfy now?" Callum glared at them.

The cop seemed bemused as everyone else grinned and Elle gave Callum a thumbs-up.

"The chairs have to go," Callum muttered. "No more chairs. I don't care if the Queen comes to visit; she can bloody well stand."

"If you're done having a meltdown about the seating arrangement," Joe said, "we've got the security footage from the hospital to look at."

The cop's radar pinged, and his attention zeroed in on Joe. "They just handed it over to you?" He cocked an eyebrow. "Without a lawyer or a warrant?"

"David has superpowers." Joe grinned at the man. "He asked nicely, and the security team handed it over. I think it's a Jedi Mind Trick, but he isn't sharing."

"Just play the bloody footage," Callum barked.

"All righty," Elle said as she tapped her laptop and the footage from the flash drive David had given her appeared on the huge monitor facing the window.

"The blinds?" Julia said to Joe.

With a smile for his wife, Joe edged Callum out of the way and closed the blinds so they could see the screen better.

The footage was in black and white and had come from a camera over the front entrance of the hospital. There was a time stamp in the bottom right-hand corner of the screen. As one, the team leaned forward, each intensely focused on the video as, at just past ten, Ryan strolled through the front doors. As they watched, he smiled at an elderly woman before lifting his hand to call one of the idling black hackney cabs over to him.

When the taxi pulled up in front of Ryan, he opened the rear door and leaned in to say something to the driver. Just then, a tall man with broad shoulders bumped into Ryan's free side. Next thing they knew, Ryan was being helped into the cab and the man followed in behind him. The door closed and the cab drove off. No one near Ryan seemed to notice that he'd just been kidnapped.

"Oh," Julia muttered. "That isn't good."

"Does the abductor have something in his hand?" Harvard rumbled, staring at the screen. "Can we replay the bit where he helps Ryan into the cab?"

Elle typed in some commands, and the video jumped back to the spot Harvard wanted.

"Can you zoom?" Harvard asked.

The image became bigger, but not clearer.

"I can't increase the pixels, which means this is as sharp as it'll get," Elle told them.

"There's definitely something in his hand." Harvard pointed at the screen. "By Ryan's throat. See?"

David nodded. "Looks like a syringe. Classic drug and drop. It's a technique we learned in the agency, for use if we needed to quietly extract someone for questioning."

"You can say torture," Elle said. "We're all friends here."

David tugged a lock of his wife's hair before he addressed his fellow spy. "Harvard, you recognize that guy?"

"I don't think there's anything to recognize," Julia said. "All we have is his rear view."

"And that's all we need." Harvard smiled at her before turning to Elle." Can you play it again? Slower, this time."

They watched the whole thing in slow motion.

"You thinking what I'm thinking?" Harvard asked David.

David nodded. "Yeah, he never did learn to change his gait or body language. I'd bet my life we're looking at Stephan Prentice, American. Special forces washout and current mercenary. Our paths crossed on a couple of jobs." He cocked an eyebrow at Harvard.

"I met him in a hot zone. Guy nearly got us all killed. I'd know that walk anywhere. Plus, he's got the build and the moves."

Callum placed his hands flat on his desk. "You're thinking someone hired him to take Ryan?"

"It's the only possible explanation," Harvard said. "Prentice doesn't have personal vendettas. If there's no payday, he ain't interested."

"Then we find out who's paying him." Callum glanced at Joe.

"Or," the cop said, standing and tucking his hat under his arm, "you hand this over to the police and let us do our job."

Joe caught David's eye, and the spy gave a slight nod, letting Joe know that Elle had already made copies of the video.

"Wouldn't do anything else, officer," Joe said with an alligator's smile.

The cop wasn't fooled, but he didn't push the issue. He held out a palm for the flash drive.

"No' so fast." Callum pointed at the screen. "Does that guy match the description you got for the woman's abductor?"

Officer Jensen gave a terse nod. "Going off the time stamp, it looks like the woman was taken first." He let out a sigh. "The brass will want to take over when they see this."

"Aye, I bet they will." Callum folded his arms and

stared the man down. "Just you make sure they keep us in the loop when they do."

"I'll try." Again the cop held out his hand for the drive.

"Try hard," Callum ordered as Elle handed it over.

Once he had the footage, the officer headed to the door and opened it. "I'm going to assume this is the only copy, apart from the one at the hospital," he said. "And I'm going to give you some advice. Let the police do their jobs, and don't go running off like a bunch of cowboys looking for wild west justice. We've dealt with situations like this before. Stand down and let the experts handle it."

When there was no reply, he shook his head and closed the door behind him.

As soon as it clicked shut, Callum turned to David and Harvard. "Do you two know how to get to this Prentice guy?"

They shared a look, then nodded.

"Leave it with us," David said.

CHAPTER ELEVEN

There was no way in hell Ryan was going to survive being shot in the head just to end his days as a Happy Meal for rats.

"Faster," he ordered as he pulled on Sarah's hand and she stumbled over the uneven surface.

Her shoes were totally fine for running—yeah, right...

He broke out in a cold sweat as they ran. Rats. It had to be rats. Not just one, no. A whole bloody army of the disease-carrying vermin. Anything else and he'd have been fine. But a swarm of rats? Pack of rats? Plague of rats? Did it really matter what they were called? All that mattered was that they were right behind them. With their dead black eyes that reminded him of sharks, and their weird pink paws that looked like tiny baby hands but thinner. And the tails? Those thick, nasty, naked tails...

Just thinking about the tails made him want to vomit.

The tails were the worst part of a rat. Not the ever-growing teeth that gnawed through concrete, or the disease they spread, or the way they could contort to get into the tiniest space. No. It was the tails. The tails were just wrong.

Like someone stuck a worm or a baby snake onto the backside of a rodent and called it good.

And why did they need to be so long? And squirm? It was like a rat's tail had a life of its own.

"Ryan, we can't outrun them. We need to stop and think."

"Hell, no."

They could totally outrun them. Okay, maybe Sarah couldn't, but he definitely could. Of course, he couldn't leave her behind to get gnawed to death. Which meant they couldn't outrun them after all, not like this.

He knew just what they needed to do. "Kick off your shoes—they're slowing us down."

"I'm not taking off my shoes." She sounded breathless.

Ryan should have quizzed her on her fitness level before this whole thing started. At least then he'd have been prepared when she couldn't keep up.

"Ryan, rats can run faster than humans. We can't outrun them. We need another plan."

They what?

They needed a new plan.

"Climb on my back," he ordered. "I can carry you while I run." He'd carried heavier packs in the army, he was sure of it. "No bloody rat is going to outrun me."

"Uh, unless you won an Olympic medal for the hundred meters, the rat is going to win."

"Now isn't the time for rat facts. We're being hunted."

"No, we're not. Will you please stop and listen to me for one second?"

He didn't even grace that lunacy with an answer.

Behind them, a million tiny nails scraped against rock. It was a sound that would give him nightmares for years to come. No way in hell was he looking back to see all their beady little eyes on him, or their whiskers twitch as they scented their next meal—him! Oh, man, what he'd give for a gun. No—a flamethrower! Then he could toast their little arses.

"We need to stop." Sarah yanked at his hand.

"Are you hurt?" *Are you mad?*

"The rats are more afraid of us than we are of them," she said, answering the question of whether or not she was mad.

"Not when they outnumber us, they're not."

"Ryan." She jerked his arm back toward her. It was like being manhandled by a kitten. "We need to stop, right now. I know how to get them off our trail, and I need your help."

"Yeah, I don't think so." He kept running.

"Stop being a big sissy and listen to me," she shouted.

Okay, that brought him up short.

The pause was clearly all she'd needed. Sarah snatched her hand from his and quickly took off his jacket.

"Take off your shirt," she demanded.

"What?" Movement caught his eyes further down the tunnel. "Run, Sarah, run!" He reached for her, but she deftly stepped aside.

Suddenly Sarah's hands were on either side of his face, forcing him to look down at her. "Take off your shirt. Now. Everything will be fine if you do what I tell you."

She wasn't making any sense. "This isn't the time to get me naked, Stats."

She kicked him in the shin. Hard. "Take off your damn shirt and copy me. Right now! And stop making me hit you. I hate how it makes me feel."

She hated how it made *her* feel?

Ryan resisted the urge to rub his sore shin. It was clear she wasn't going to take another step unless he did as she asked. He couldn't leave her alone with the rats, which meant he had to help her. Damn it, being an honorable guy could really suck sometimes.

Dumping the bag on the floor beside them, he pulled his T-shirt over his head. "This had better work, Stats, because if I get bitten and turn rabid, I'm coming for you first."

She sighed. "I know you're scared. I'm scared too. That doesn't mean we can't think logically about this."

"I'm not scared," he protested. "I'm...disgusted. Rats carry disease." Yeah, that sounded much better. Or at least, a whole lot less pansy-arsed.

"Whatever you say." He couldn't see her face because she was rummaging around in her bag, but he was pretty sure she was rolling her eyes. When she stood up, she had her phone in her hand. "Aim the light at the rats—"

"Are you nuts?" He didn't want to see their black stares of death.

She glared at him. "No. But I'm losing my patience. Aim the bloody light, wave your bloody shirt, and make a lot of bloody noise. Okay? I can get us out of this. All I need is for you to follow orders, soldier!"

As she barked at him, she started waving his jacket around while yelling at the rats. Her enthusiasm was impressive, although Ryan took issue with *what* she was yelling.

"Back! Get back now! Get back before Ryan faints and squishes you with his oversized body!" Her flashlight hit the edge of the rat wave, and to his surprise, it slowed.

"What the hell?" he muttered.

"Ryan, I swear, if you don't help me, I will feed you to them myself," Sarah said between yelling.

Hastily, he brandished his shirt while stomping and

shouting at the rodents. Unlike Sarah, he mainly used curse words. It took a helluva lot of self-control to aim his light at them, but he did it. And what he saw nearly made him pass out with relief.

The rats were scurrying away from them.

The wave split, like the Red Sea, and flowed into the two rooms holding the dead bodies. And that's when he realized Sarah had intended for that to happen all along.

So freaking smart.

He could have kissed her. If she wasn't so bad-tempered.

As soon as the last rat disappeared, Sarah turned off her light and held out her hand to him. "Now, we run."

He didn't need to be asked twice. Holding his shirt, he slung the bag over his body and took her offered hand.

"How did you know they'd do that?" he managed to get out as they raced along the tunnel.

"They're scavengers. Cowards. They want an easy meal." She paused. "I gave them one." Her voice sounded strangled, and Ryan knew it'd cost her to send them after the dead bodies.

"It was them or us, Stats. At least the bodies won't suffer."

"It's still wrong."

Yeah, they'd argue about that later. In the meantime, he focused on putting distance between them and the rabid pack behind them while he tried to get his heart rate back under control. It felt like Dave Grohl was inside his chest, knocking out a fast-paced blast beat on his drums.

Every few steps, Ryan had to glance over his shoulder to ensure they still weren't being followed. So far, so good, but who knew how long that'd last?

About ten minutes after the rats had dispersed, they came to a fork in the tunnel.

"Which way?" Sarah asked him.

"Now, you want my opinion?" He cocked an eyebrow at her.

She made a big deal out of looking back up the tunnel. "Nope. Don't see any rats. Wonder why that is?" She folded her arms and glared at him. "I'd have asked your opinion if you'd shown any indication that you had a plan. As far as I could tell, you intended to run until we both collapsed and died. And the rats ate us anyway."

Okay, he'd give her that. Letting the subject drop, he took a few steps up the tunnel on the right. The air was foul.

"The other one," he told Sarah. "This way smells wrong." It smelled like decomp, which he didn't think she needed to know.

On the plus side, if any rats did follow them, the stink in that tunnel would appeal far more than Sarah's floral perfume.

"Are we finished arguing about the rats?" She clearly wasn't going to move until they'd settled things.

"Yeah." He sighed. "You were right. I was...hysterical and I should have listened to you. I really don't like rats."

"No?" She gasped, placing a palm over her heart. "I didn't know that. If I'd known that, I wouldn't have bullied you into avoiding them. My bad."

"You're not funny." Although, she really was and he couldn't help grinning.

"You're impossible," she told him again.

"That's probably true." He hesitated. "Thanks for dealing with the rats. Perhaps we could keep this part of the story to ourselves once we're out of here. Deal?" His team would rib him over this forever if they knew.

"I'll think about it." She stuck her nose in the air as she entered the tunnel he'd indicated. "It will cost you though."

"I like a woman who doesn't shy away from blackmail," he teased.

Sarah grinned at him before eyeing the tunnel. "This one is single file only. Do you want to go first?" She batted her lashes at him. "That way you'll have something between you and the rats."

"Not funny." Although, he'd never admit it was also tempting. "On you go."

They walked single file, Ryan behind Sarah, who carried the light. The candle they'd been using was long gone, snuffed out in the run from the rodent horde. They didn't stop to light another, aware that the rats could reappear at any second. Instead, they used the phone, keeping it on the lowest setting possible to save the battery.

"I'm sorry for kicking you," she said as they walked.

Ryan shrugged. "I would have slapped me."

"I'll try very hard not to hit you again," Sarah said solemnly. "Unless, you know, something else scares you into a catatonic state."

"Are you ever going to let this go?" He groaned. "You're as bad as my team, and that's saying something."

"It's hard to let go of. I mean, you're this big tough guy who is totally unfazed by everything—except an itty-bitty rodent." She was grinning again; he could hear it in her voice.

He had to fight not to smile back. She didn't need the encouragement. "Millions of rodents. Get your facts straight."

"Millions of fluffy, cute, itty-bitty rodents." Now, she was just amusing herself.

"You're one of those people who had pet rats, aren't you?" He shuddered at the thought.

Sarah barked out a laugh. "Where I grew up, rats were considered wildlife, not pets. Taking out the rubbish was something you did in pairs, with one of you brandishing a big stick, just in case you got jumped by a dumpster-diving rat."

Huh. He'd had her pegged as strictly middle-class, never having seen the seedier side of life at all. "Then where the hell does all this rodent love come from?"

"Research. I once had a client who bred rats. He wanted to insure his business, so I did some research." She glanced back at him again. "They're really smart and make a laughing sound when you tickle their bellies. They can jump two feet in the air and scale pretty much any surface."

"Now, you're being evil. Don't let me stop you, but keep in mind, there will be payback."

"Payback?" She sounded a little worried.

"You might want to keep in mind that I've had years of army and security team experience with this kind of razzing. I know how to bide my time before giving as good as I get."

Her eyes were wide when she looked back at him. "Rats are bad. Evil. Terrible. No sane person wouldn't be scared of them."

"Damn straight."

He couldn't help wondering if it had been like this between them before. It felt easy, fun, intimate—even though he barely knew her. He could become addicted to this feeling.

Their new tunnel led upward, which Ryan took as a good sign. What he didn't like was that the ceiling became lower with each passing step, until he was painfully hunched in order to avoid another head injury.

Sarah wasn't happy either. "I feel like Alice in Wonderland. You know, during that part where she's big and walking toward the tiny door."

"If a rabbit in a hat appears, we can follow it out of here."

"So rabbits are okay, but rats..." she muttered.

Ryan decided to act like he hadn't heard her.

"Maybe we should go back?" Sarah said. "The roof is getting lower with every step we take. At this rate, we'll be crawling."

Back meant rats. Ryan was okay with crawling. "Let's see how far we can get before we give up."

He was beginning to wonder if he'd have to crouch in order to continue down the tunnel, when the ceiling suddenly disappeared above them.

"Whoa." Sarah angled the flashlight upward. "I was *not* expecting that."

The light dropped off, making it impossible to see how high the area went. "Might be an old mine shaft." Ryan glanced around, hoping there was a ladder or something they could climb to get out. No such luck.

"Uh, Ryan, we have another problem here." Sarah shone the light on the opposite side of the tunnel where there was nothing but wall.

They'd hit a dead end.

"Well, that's disappointing." And nauseating, because it meant heading back to the rats.

As the light swept around the narrow chamber, it reflected off a section of floor to the right of them. Ryan eyed it curiously, wondering what had caused the reflection.

CHAPTER TWELVE

There was a pool in the corner of the mine shaft.

Crouching down, Ryan gestured to Sarah to bring the light closer so he could get a better look at the water. There was a roughly hewn trench, filled with milky white water and smelling like chalk. It was about four feet wide and who knew how deep because you couldn't see the bottom. But the most interesting thing about it was that it ran under the wall.

"I know what you're thinking." The light shook in Sarah's hand. "You're thinking we swim through that to the other side. I vote for checking out the other tunnel first."

There was no avoiding it. He had to tell her why the other tunnel wasn't an option. "There was a strong smell of decomp in the tunnel, Stats. I don't think anything good will come from going that way."

"More bodies?" Her face had paled again.

"I'd say so." And by the odor, he'd say these ones weren't mummified. He pointed at the pool. "This isn't so bad. I mean, I'm already topless. Might as well see where this goes."

Her eyes strayed to his chest, and her cheeks flushed. "You could get stuck down there. I don't want you to drown."

"I don't want to drown either, but this could be our way out."

Standing, he kicked off his shoes as Sarah slipped his jacket back on. She wrapped it tight around herself, as though seeking comfort rather than warmth.

Ryan handed her the bag and shirt. "I won't go far. I'll only take a peek."

She chewed her bottom lip for a second before answering. "The water is too cloudy to see anything."

"You can make out about a foot in front of you before visibility drops off. Think of it like fog; as I go through it, I'll see my way. Can you get your phone out of your bag for you to use and hand me mine?"

Clearly hesitant, Sarah handed over his phone. "We don't know what's making the water that color. It could damage your eyes."

"I'll be fine."

"If you're taking this route because you're worried about the rats following us, you should know that the water won't stop them. They can swim for days. And hold their breath for three minutes at a time."

He shuddered. "Thanks for that imagery."

"Sorry. I just...it's just..." She glanced about the place, looking a little lost. "You could die."

And there was the heart of the problem. "Come on, Stats, get that big brain of yours in gear. What are the chances I'd die in there?"

"I can't think. I need a minute."

Suddenly, she turned and placed her forehead on the wall beside her. She closed her eyes and seemed to concentrate on taking slow, even breaths while little shivers ran through her body.

Ryan didn't know what to do to help her. He wished the strange boundaries of their relationship were clearer, so he'd know whether or not she'd welcome his comfort. Because he desperately wanted to comfort her.

Eventually, she placed her palm on the cool rock and pushed back from the wall.

"Sarah?" Ryan tentatively touched her shoulder.

"I'm okay." She stepped out from under his touch, putting a distance between them that he *really* didn't like. "There's a lot to think about, and it's all coming at me so fast. I'm used to having time to gather information and think things through before I make decisions. This is a little over-whelming. But, I'm fine. What about trying to get to the relay station on the other side of the cave-in? Now that the rats are occupied, we could try again."

"We'd still need to spend time trying to make a passageway in the wall of rocks—without bringing it down on our heads."

Wide eyes blinked at him as her mind raced. Ryan gave her the time she needed to come to the conclusion he'd already reached.

"Then I guess we need to investigate the pool," she said at last.

"If it looks even the slightest bit risky, I'll come straight out and we'll find another way, okay?"

She nodded but was less than convinced.

Unable to do anything else to reassure her, Ryan sat on the edge of the pool and lowered his legs into the water. "Hm, it's not that cold."

"Limestone reacts with the hydrogen in water which causes a release of heat that will have kept the temperature from dropping lower than the cave air. It's probably also the reason the water is cloudy." She took a breath. "It won't hurt your eyes; in case you were worried."

Man, she was cute. "Thanks for letting me know." Keeping his phone out of the water, he eased the rest of his body into it. To his relief, his feet hit the bottom by the time the water was mid-chest. "Not so deep. Guess we're about to find out if this phone is as waterproof as they tell us it is."

Sarah came over to the side of the pool, clutching her phone in her hand. She tucked the stray curl that'd escaped from her bun behind her ear and took a deep breath. "What can I do to help?"

So. Damn. Brave.

And so damn irresistible too.

He flashed a cheeky smile. "How about a kiss for good luck?"

Her gaze dropped to his lips as she sucked in a breath. "I don't think kissing you is a good idea, Ryan."

"Do it anyway," he tempted.

"Bloody catnip," she muttered as she knelt at the side of the pond. "You aren't good for me."

"Oh, I don't know about that." He closed the distance between them and waggled his brows. "Stop stalling. You're kissing me, remember?" He held onto the edge of the pond, pressing his hands into the stone to stop from taking over.

"I'm not the one with memory problems," she said haughtily. "I just need a minute to think."

"That's the problem. Too much thinking, not enough kissing."

She let out a strangled growl of frustration, leaned forward, cupped his face in both her hands, and pressed her lips to his. As kisses went, it was pretty tame. Yet, he felt it right to his toes. Full satin lips teased him with gentle touches. While her hands trembled slightly against the rough texture of his jaw.

Her tentative touch felt deeply familiar. As though his lips remembered hers, while his mind had lost the memory. It felt—right. As though they were both where they were meant to be.

And then she sat back, taking her touch with her, and the strange sense memory floated away.

Her cheeks were flushed, and there was a shyness about her that hadn't been there before. "There," she said. "You have your luck."

"I'm thinking that for this trip, I might need a double helping," he teased.

"Then come back in one piece and we'll renegotiate," she said with a smile that was pure temptation.

"I can do that. Right, I'm going in." Ryan turned back to the water. "Keep an eye on the time; I'll be back before ten minutes are up."

"You better be."

He flashed her a grin before lowering into the water.

"Don't you die, Ryan Granger," she ordered. "And don't get another concussion either. Remember, you're just peeking at the other side then coming straight back, so don't dally." Worry laced each word.

"Yes, ma'am," Ryan said. "No dallying, concussions, or death."

And then his head slipped under the surface.

Sarah watched Ryan disappear below the surface of the milky water and fought the instinct to jump in after him and pull him out. It was something she was doing a lot lately. Fighting her nature when he did something danger-ous. Everything they faced, every choice they made, it all flew in the face of common sense. Part of her still believed they should wait for help. The rest of her knew that if they waited, they'd share the fate of poor Adrienne and the couple Ryan found.

Keeping her eyes on the surface, her breath hitched at the exact moment when Ryan disappeared from view. He was gone. She was alone. A massive wave of anxiety hit her as she willed Ryan to be safe. Willed him to return.

Trembling fingers pressed against her lips as she ques-tioned the sanity of kissing him. No good would come of any physical contact with the man. She hadn't been joking when she'd said he was her catnip. He was addictive. A temptation she couldn't afford.

But his kiss? That was her Kryptonite.

Her palms were clammy, and she wiped them on her skirt. The whole situation was completely out of her control, and she didn't have the information she needed to change that. Where were they? Who was doing this to them? How would they get out? How were they supposed to know if the decisions they were making were the right ones?

When her stomach clenched, she rolled into herself to try and ease it. She hadn't felt this helpless since she was a child, forgotten by parents who only cared about their next drink. Sarah had been making her own decisions for as long as she could remember. And she'd learned the hard way that you needed to do careful research before committing. Otherwise, you'd choose wrongly and things would get worse.

She *never* did anything without looking at all of her

options. Without knowing all the possible outcomes. Without weighing the odds. Until now…

Well, unless you counted her brief relationship with Ryan.

There had been *no* way to prepare for him.

A tiny, somewhat hysterical laugh erupted from her. It bounced off the hard cold walls, making the emptiness seem even more stark, the silence more oppressive. She wet her dry lips and, keeping her eyes on the water, spoke out loud to stop the emptiness from eating her whole.

"How do you prepare for a whirlwind to blow through your life?"

An ache settled in her chest. She should never have signed up for Tinder. It'd been such a dumb idea. A temptation she'd been unable to resist, so she'd justified the risk. She'd just been so desperately lonely, and the only men she knew were middle-aged and married.

Barely days after she'd committed to the app, Ryan sauntered into her life, with his spontaneous decision-making and ability to find the fun in every situation. His teasing sensuality had called to the recklessness she kept locked up deep inside of her. He was a temptation she couldn't resist.

Their conversations quickly became the highlight of her day, and she'd begun to wonder if meeting him in person would be a disappointment.

She'd been wrong.

Everything about their night together was a fairytale. They'd shared a wonderful meal, strolled through London, danced in an open-air roller disco, and gone home to her staid and boring house, where they'd made love until the early hours.

It had been magical.

For one glorious night, Ryan had made her feel secure enough to release the reins on her reckless tendencies. It'd been as though there was a safety net beneath her, ready to catch her if she fell. She'd stepped out of her comfort zone, believing he'd be there for her, letting a part of her personality that was usually locked away tight have a taste of freedom. Not since she'd been a child, and brutally disappointed, had she trusted anyone with all of her.

And she was the only one who knew about it because Prince Charming didn't remember her at all.

"And doesn't that sum up your life perfectly?" she asked the walls. "One day, this will be amusing...maybe..."

The cool air was sharp in her lungs, slicing at her with every breath she took. Her skin vibrated with awareness, automatically cataloging her environment, never letting her forget that she was alone and helpless. A glance at her phone told her Ryan had been gone almost seven minutes.

Shouldn't there be some sign of him by now? Or was he resting on the other side before he made the swim back? Was there even another side to get to?

Unasked-for facts flooded her mind. Tidbits she'd picked up over her years accumulating data. No matter what she learned, she had no problems retaining it, which meant that any time she was stressed it all came rushing back.

That's how she knew that the average person could hold their breath for between thirty seconds to two minutes. Whereas Navy SEALS were trained to hold it for three to five minutes. Free divers could go much longer than that, ten minutes or more. For most people, the urge to take a breath kicked in after a couple of minutes, and panic made them give in to it.

She couldn't even imagine Ryan panicking, so she could rule that out.

How long could he hold his breath? And why hadn't she asked that before he went underwater? He'd been trained, of course. Army, he said, not Navy. Did that make a difference?

Seven minutes twenty-two seconds.

Was he stuck?

Should she go in after him? Would she be any use if she did?

Surely, he was fine. Tom Cruise held his breath for six minutes in a *Mission Impossible* movie. Ryan could definitely beat that. Right? Ten minutes, he'd said. She shouldn't worry before then.

"How exactly are you going to stop yourself?" she asked the silence.

There was no response.

Sarah glanced at the clock again. Seven minutes and thirty-one seconds.

"He's capable, and calm, and absolutely confident that he can do this. There's no reason to freak out."

If they ever got a minute when they weren't trying to escape danger, she was going to give him a questionnaire on his skills and abilities. That way, she'd know exactly what he could do under any given circumstance. Knowledge meant control. Control meant safety. Safety made her feel secure.

She let out a long breath, feeling better now she had a plan.

Seven minutes and forty-three seconds...

Sarah caught herself rocking back and forth, a leftover behavior from the anxiety of her childhood, and forced herself to stop. Rubbing her arms, she scanned the darkness around her. Staring into the blackness made it feel endless. Like the flat black color that sculptor Anish Kapoor used to make his audience feel like they were falling into his work.

There was no way to get her bearings in the old mine. Every wall looked the same. The color never changed from beige. Even the air had the same musty smell in every room and tunnel. They could have been going around in circles since she'd first opened her eyes, and she would never know.

"Ryan would know, wouldn't he?" Her heartbeat slowed at the thought.

Swallowing hard, she checked the phone again.

Eight minutes and five seconds.

A noise startled her, and she spun to face the wall behind her, straining for the slightest sound, peering into nothing. When there was no movement, or noise, she turned back to the pool. Her heart raced, her hands shook, her stomach was one huge knot.

Instantly, she was transported back to her childhood. Jumping at every sound in the dark. Waiting in the bottom of her wardrobe for her parents to come home. Even drunk and useless, they were still more comforting than being alone in their run-down council flat.

She hated the dark. It brought back the fear she'd felt when her parents had been unable to pay their electricity bill. The stark terror of nights spent alone and forgotten, while they were off drinking. The memory of being hungry and afraid was far too close for comfort. And the box inside her mind, where she stored everything she was helpless to change, cracked open.

She saw herself as a child. Small, scrawny, with dirty brown hair and eyes that were far too big for her face. Curled in a ball in the corner of the old wooden wardrobe. A thin blanket covering her and a death grip on Fuzzy, her ratty stuffed bear. She'd taken a knife from the kitchen to protect herself and clutched it tight as she startled at every creak and groan the old building made. She still remembered the smell—stale sweat, damp, and a mustiness that could have come from the mine she sat in now.

"That isn't now," she muttered. "It isn't here. I'm not that person. I'm stronger. I can pay my bills. My home is warm. My fridge is full. The past is gone."

There was no doubt a therapist would rub their hands together in glee at the thought of dealing with Sarah's head. Unfortunately, she was too cheap to pay for one. Plus, what could they tell her that a Cosmo quiz couldn't? She'd endured a crappy childhood. So what? Millions of people went through the same or worse. No, she wasn't one of those folk who had to dig up their inner child and give it love and attention, or a stern talking-to, or whatever you were supposed to do with it. Her childhood was what it was. Her adult life was pretty darn awesome.

Usually.

When she wasn't stuck in a cave with an ex who couldn't remember her. Not to mention the dead bodies and the rats.

She looked at the water.

She didn't even want to think about going in there.

Eight minutes and forty-six seconds.

The surface of the pool remained calm.

There was no sign of Ryan.

CHAPTER THIRTEEN

Surely ten minutes didn't actually last this long? Maybe there was something wrong with her phone and the clock wasn't working?

Around four hundred people drowned in the UK every year, most of them men. She cocked her head. Why more men than women? She shrugged. Probably because women were more sensible. Drownings were less common in pits or wells, which was as close as she'd ever seen to a statistic for a mine. So, if she followed the facts, the chances of Ryan drowning in the rocky pool were very low compared to other places he could drown.

Then again, she didn't know the overall number of people who went into rocky pools and didn't drown. It could be two out of ten, which would make Ryan's chances of drowning as high as eighty percent.

"Helpful, Sarah, really helpful..."

Nine minutes and thirteen seconds.

What was she supposed to do when the time ran out? Go in there and find him? How would she do that when visibility was so low? Chances were high, she'd drown too.

Her stomach clenched and unclenched in a nauseating cycle set on repeat.

Even if she could find him in there, how would she get him out? He was huge, and muscled, and heavy, and she... wasn't.

"Please be okay, please be okay, please be okay." The whisper bounced around the chamber, and she imagined the words floating up the shaft above her.

Would shouting his name help? Or would it just attract the rats?

"Please be okay, please..."

Her palms were so damp that the phone almost slipped from her hands. She grasped at it, a little light-headed at the thought of losing it in the water.

Nine minutes and twenty-two seconds.

"Ryan," she begged. "Please. Please don't leave me alone here. Please don't die."

Sarah instinctively knew that if Ryan was gone, she would be too. It would only be a matter of time. She didn't have the skill or confidence needed to get out of there on her own. This kind of adventure was Ryan's wheelhouse, not hers.

A faint ripple on the water's surface caught her eye, and she held her breath, refusing to blink in case she missed something.

Air rushed out of her as the light from a phone appeared followed by the dark shadow of Ryan's body. The top of his head broke the surface. He wiped his hands down his face as he strode through the water toward her.

"Hey, Stats," he said with a grin. "Miss me?"

As he reached the edge beside her, Sarah launched forward and wrapped her arms around his neck. Solid. He was solid and real. Not a hallucination brought on by being alone in the dark.

"Shush," he said softly as his arms came around her. Even though he didn't know her at all, he didn't hesitate to hold her. "It's okay. I'm here, back in under ten minutes. It's okay."

Sarah knew she was holding him too tight. Too long. Clinging like a desperate woman. And yet, she didn't let go. She couldn't. Not yet. Not until her heartbeat was steady and her runaway imagination believed he was real.

"I found a passageway that looks promising." His voice rumbled through his chest, vibrating against her cheek. Strong hands stroked her back. "It looks good, Stats. I think it might get us out of here. There was graffiti, which means at least one person has been in there. If they got in, we can get out. So, don't worry, we're going to be fine."

She swallowed hard, trying to get a grip on herself. It took longer than she would have liked. Slowly, she separated from him and sat back on her heels. Threading her hands together to stop them shaking.

"You didn't think something would happen to me, did you?" He ran his hands through his sodden hair to sweep it back from his face.

Suddenly, she became all too aware of the cut wet chest in front of her. So much broader than she remembered. Her eyes strayed to two round white scars—one low on the right side of his chest, the other beneath it.

Bullet wounds.

"Your job is very dangerous," she whispered.

"Not all the time." He gently tipped her chin up until she looked him in the eye. "I told you I'd be back so you wouldn't worry."

"You know worry doesn't work like that, right?"

His eyes sparkled at her. "You mean, you don't just take my word as gospel? Huh. I thought you were back here having a nice, relaxed nap. Secure in the knowledge that I'd be fine."

Sarah feigned a frustrated sigh. "Tell me what we're dealing with." She needed to prepare, mentally at least.

"Yes, ma'am." He cocked his head and smiled. "Can I get out of the water first?"

All she could do was roll her eyes at him, then watch in silent appreciation as he flexed his muscles and climbed out of the pool with no effort at all.

Sarah wanted to fan herself at the sight. The man was cut. Lean, muscled torso tapering down into a narrow waist before those V muscles disappeared into tight, wet jeans. And his thighs! His thighs alone made her mouth water. Thick, strong. She was going to swoon. It was like watching a real-life version of one of those Levi commercials from the '90s. The ones she'd, ahem, *researched* many times on YouTube. For work, of course...

"Like what you see?" the devil drawled.

"Yes." Sarah sighed, her eyes still on his pecs. "Sweet heavens, yes."

A deep, wicked chuckle snapped her out of her lust-induced daze, and she smacked a hand over her own mouth and prayed that wasn't drool she felt at the corner of her lips.

***

Ryan wanted to kiss Sarah all over again, and this time do it thoroughly. But she was skittish and they had a hurdle ahead of them. No matter; unlike the woman in front of him, *he* had patience.

"Now that I have your attention on *other things*"—he grinned at her—"we need to talk about the pool. First, it isn't a channel someone dug out, although they did refine this edge some. It's a natural underground pond. Which means, no straight lines down there."

It was clear she was paying close attention to every word he said. No doubt recalculating odds with every new piece of information he gave her.

"The other thing you need to know." He pointed at the wall above the water. "That isn't a wall. It's a huge mass of rock that goes back several feet. Right under the middle of the rock, the pool splits off into about half a dozen passage-ways. I found one that looked good on my third try."

She nodded slowly. "But?"

Damn, this was hard. Ryan knew what he was asking of her, and it wouldn't be easy. "It's about a two-and-a-half-minute swim to the other side."

She tucked her hair back with a shaking hand. "Under-water all the way?"

"Yeah."

There was a long, heavy pause before she replied. "I can't hold my breath that long, Ryan."

He'd already figured as much. "Which is why we'll practice before we go for it. I'm going to give you a crash course in military techniques for underwater missions." Well, the part that would help her to get into the right head-space anyway.

Her hand fluttered to her throat, and she forced a smile. "Do you remember the techniques well enough to pass them on?"

The woman had a reservoir of strength if she was able to make jokes of this. "Cheeky arse. I'll have you swimming like a seal in no time."

"Do they hold their breaths when they go underwater?"

Huh. "I actually don't know. They're mammals, so they'd have to. And you don't hear of many drowned seals, which means they have to be pretty good at it." He grinned, pleased with his reasoning. "I'm gonna go with yes. You're cleared to swim like a seal."

"I'm so reassured."

She was also a smart-arse. "Let's eat the rest of the cereal bars and drink some water. The bars' packaging won't survive being underwater anyway. Then I can take you through some breathing exercises up here before we get in the water to practice. Sound good?"

"No, Ryan. The whole thing sounds very far from good. But what doesn't kill you makes you stronger, right?"

"Or leaves you in a coma," he felt the need to add.

"That too." She got up, grabbed the bag, and came to sit beside him, handing him the untouched cereal bar while taking the partially eaten one for herself. "You're bigger than I am and need more energy," she explained.

"We can split them evenly. I might be bigger, but I'm also trained to go long periods without food and still function." Of course, his belly decided that was the perfect moment to remind both of them that it was sorely neglected. The rumble echoed off the stone wall and made it sound like there was a bear in the dark along with them. "Just ignore it," he said wryly. "I am."

"Eat the bar; I'm good with this piece. My stomach is a little upset right now. Plus, I'm used to going long periods of time without food and I honestly won't notice whether I ate or not."

"To hell with that." Ryan snapped his bar in two and handed half to her. "We'll both survive a little hunger and can afford to share the nutrition we have. And what do you mean you go hours without food? Please don't tell me you're doing some weird starvation diet because those things are bad for you. It isn't natural to not eat. And you don't need to lose any weight either. Trust me on that."

Her cheeks turned that pinky peach color that made her hair glow and her eyes look molten. "I'm not on any sort of diet. It's just that up until after university, when I got a steady job, food was unreliable. Some days I had it, some days I didn't. It was better once I was able to fend for myself though."

Oh, he didn't like the sound of that at all. "What do you mean it got better when you started fending for yourself? You mean once you had a degree and a job?"

"Yes, then too, but before that as well," she said between nibbles of the bar. "I told you about my parents' drinking? Well, sometimes they'd forget to buy food. Or forget they had a child who needed to eat. There wasn't a lot of money kicking around anyway; Dad couldn't hold down a job and Mum was too wasted to try. Food was a low priority for them. When I turned sixteen, I left home, and things got a bit better then."

The way she spoke, so matter-of-factly, made his hackles rise. She might not feel fury at her parents' neglect, but he sure as hell did. "I'm sorry you had to live like that."

She shrugged. "It was a long time ago. No big deal."

"It's no big deal?" He would have let the comment drop if it'd been thrown out flippantly to end the conversation. Instead, it looked like she really meant it. And that made Ryan mad all over again. "You obviously don't know me, or you would never tell me food isn't a big deal. It's one of the reasons we live. And I don't mean eat to live, I mean live to eat. Food—good. The more, the merrier. And not just nutritious crap. I'm talking about the good stuff—cake, and pie, and cheese, and pizza. Everybody should have as much food as they want. All the time." He frowned at her, offended by the stupidity of her comment. "Especially kids."

Sarah burst out laughing. "Thanks for sharing your manifesto with me."

"I'm serious," he said.

"I know you are, and it's sweet. You also need to remember that you're reacting to something you just heard. Whereas I dealt with my parents' neglect a long time ago. I know what it's like to be hungry, cold, alone in the dark, and scared. And I'm sure that sounds awful, but those are also good lessons to learn, aren't they?"

"Stats." He slapped a hand over his heart. "You're killing me here. Those aren't things a kid needs to learn."

"How else am I supposed to look at it, Ryan? Should I bemoan how tough I had it? Constantly live in the past? Hold a grudge against the people who should have cared for me instead of abandoning me? What's the point in that? The only person it makes suffer is me. So, I take the good and I move on. Look at it this way. Assuming I live until I'm eighty, less than twenty percent of my life will have been crappy because other people were in control of it." She beamed at him. "Plus, it wasn't all bad. School was good."

Damn it. He really wanted to kiss her again. "I'm really regretting that I can't remember you, Stats," he told her instead.

He'd expected her to blush and lower her eyes. As usual, Sarah didn't do the expected. "If you're very good and we live through our swim, I might find the time to remind you of all the things we did together that you've forgotten." She blinked, and her eyes widened as though surprised at herself. "I mean, verbally. I'll tell you about them. Most of them. Not all of them. Crap."

Ryan couldn't help laughing at the hole she'd dug for herself. "Sorry, Stats. I heard you the first time. There was no mention of a nice little chat. So, I'm just gonna let my imagination fill in the details on what that memory jog will look like."

"Pervert," she muttered as a blush crept up her throat. She took a deep breath. "Ryan, I really can't hold my breath that long. I don't see how I can get through to the other side of the pool. I think it's probably best if we split up. You can go ahead and bring back help to get me out of here."

What? Hell no!

All humor fled. "That's not happening, so get it right out of your head."

"It's logical. If I go in there with you, I'll panic and we could both drown. I'll be perfectly safe here until you come back with help."

He was already shaking his head. "We don't know how long it will take for me to get out of here. It could take days, weeks even. Who knows? We've got no idea where we are or even how far underground we're sitting. You could starve to death before I make it back. Or run out of water."

Sarah gestured to the pool. "I have water."

"Stats, drinking that will make you sick. It isn't just the limestone that's making it cloudy; there's a whole load of crap in there." Including one bloated rat carcass that he really didn't want to dwell on. "It's nowhere near clean, and we've no way of filtering it or boiling it to make it even remotely drinkable."

"It makes sense, Ryan, you ha—"

He reached out and cupped the back of her neck, bringing her face closer. "I'm not leaving you here alone. It isn't happening, so stop telling me to do it. If we can't swim out, we'll find another way. Together. Got it?"

Sarah nodded and wet her lips before replying. "What do I need to do?"

Damn, she slayed him with her courage. Reluctantly, he released her. "First, we practice staying calm."

"Well, that should be easy," she muttered.

CHAPTER FOURTEEN

For more than two hours, Sarah practiced different types of breathing. Ryan made her lie on the stone floor and place a hand on her abdomen while he taught her how to breathe properly.

"Deep breaths make the belly move. Shallow moves the shoulders," he explained. "We want to use all of our lung capacity for this. Okay?"

When that was over, they moved on to a technique called box breathing that Ryan had learned in the military to keep calm while under fire or in enemy territory. Inhale for four seconds, hold for four seconds, breathe out for four seconds, hold for four seconds, and then repeat.

"This will help you to relax before we go under the water. The more relaxed you are, the less oxygen you use," he said. "You want to move as little as possible too. That's why all you're going to do is float while I swim us both to the other side."

And bang went the relaxed breathing. "What about you? Won't you use a whole lot more oxygen if you're dragging me along with you?"

"Stats," he said, "I can hold my breath for five minutes while swimming full out, and for a whole lot longer if I'm just lying there."

"Show-off," she grumbled.

He tucked her straying hair behind her ears. "You need to concentrate on not breathing. That's your only job. I'll do the rest."

Her heart raced at his touch, undoing all the hard work she'd just put in to slow it. "You know those team-building challenges where you're supposed to fall back and let other people catch you?"

He nodded.

"I've never once managed to do one of those. I tried, but I just couldn't trust anyone enough to catch me. If I can't do that, there's no way I can do this. You have to knock me out and drag me through."

"First, I can't. You won't be able to hold your breath if you're unconscious. Second, I'm not some random work-mate who doesn't have the upper body strength to catch you if you fall. You said you know me. If you really do, you know that if anyone can get you through those tunnels, it's me."

Sarah glanced down at her hands, which were clenched into fists on her lap. "Have you ever been so terrified that you can't do something?"

"Like confront a tunnel full of rats?"

She narrowed her eyes at him. "I *made* you do that."

"I can make you do this, but you won't be calm while it's happening and we want calm."

"Maybe I could just read a book for half an hour. That helps me relax. I have my iPad; there are books on there." And maybe, after some time, he'll have given up on his crazy plan to drag her through the water while she suffocated from lack of air.

Of course, he was on to her. "And what book would you read to avoid doing this?"

"Pride and Prejudice, probably," she grumbled. "Although, Darcy is nearly as annoying as you're being right now."

Ryan's head fell back as he laughed. "Jane Austen is on my list, but I haven't reached her yet. For some reason, since the coma, I've been reading like a nutter. I was working my way through one of those lists, you know, one hundred classics you should read before you die. But I got side-tracked by the thriller genre. Those books are like Pringles—you can't stop at one."

"Maybe we could read a thriller together?" Sarah asked hopefully. "It will give us time to think about this plan. And, you know, calm us both down."

"Good try, Stats, but it's not happening. You can do this. You might not have faith in me, but I have faith in you. You're one of the bravest people I've ever met."

"That would mean a lot more if I didn't know you couldn't remember everyone you've met."

"I'm serious, you've got this. You just need to stop stalling."

Sarah held up her hands so he could see them shake. "I'm not brave, I'm just good at hiding how scared I am."

He enfolded her hands in his. "That's the definition of bravery, babe. Feeling the fear and doing it anyway."

Sarah closed her eyes and let her head drop forward. This whole thing was impossible; why couldn't he see it? He was asking her to go into a dark, enclosed space where she would be submerged in water and unable to breathe. Every nightmare scenario from her childhood was lurking in that water. Just one of those memories could trigger a panic attack that would take them both down.

"Stats," he said, understanding and compassion in his voice. "I really believe you can do this. Besides, it's drown with me or get eaten alive by rats alone."

Her head shot up as she glared at him. "That's not helpful."

"Oh, I don't know." He smiled. "The water's looking pretty good right now, isn't it?"

"I think we should time me holding my breath again." She really didn't like the determined expression on his face. It didn't bode well for her. "Only I want to know how long I can do it for this time."

"Nope. No more practice runs. And definitely no numbers in your head. If you have a target in mind, that's as far as your subconscious will let you go. Much better if you put that brain of yours to use by concentrating on resisting the urge to take in air, instead of on how much time has passed."

It was no use. She wasn't ready. There hadn't been enough time to prepare—physically or mentally. There might *never* be enough time for her to get ready for something like this.

"Maybe we should sleep on things before we try swimming out of here. It's late. We're both exhausted. It's been a long traumatic day. What do you think?"

"I think you're still stalling." Ryan took her hand and firmly led her to the water's edge. "Time to go. The longer we wait, the more you'll think about it. The more you think, the more you'll freak. Sometimes, you just have to jump in and hope for the best." His eyes sparkled. "Pun intended."

The water glimmered in the dim light from Sarah's phone. It didn't appear threatening; in fact, it seemed almost peaceful. Any other time, in any other place, she'd have found it soothing. But not here. Not like this.

Shivering, she cast a longing glance at Ryan's jacket, which lay discarded against the wall. It was too thick to take with them. It'd weigh them down and take forever to dry out, so it'd been sacrificed. Beside it sat a pile of things from her handbag that were also useless if they got wet. Their bag was lighter now. The stash of items that might help them survive was already dwindling.

Just another sign that they had no control of the situation at all.

Ryan slung her handbag over her body before crouching down at her feet. "Gonna have to tear this skirt. It's a damn shame because it's sexy as hell, but I'd rather you had full maneuverability in the water, just in case you need it."

As he spoke, he matched action to words and ripped a split right up the side of her skirt from the tiny tear that had already been there.

"That's better," Ryan said, his voice rough and his attention firmly caught on the bare expanse of thigh in front of him. He cleared his throat before climbing into the pool. "Let's get this show on the road," he said as he placed his hands on her waist and lifted her into the water.

Sarah's palms slapped his bare shoulders. "I'm not ready."

"You're never gonna be ready. That's why you need me. Without me gently nudging you along, you'd still be back in the cavern weighing up your options."

The water slid up her legs, over her hips, and to her shoulders as she clung to Ryan. "You call this gently nudging? It's like being hit by a sledgehammer."

She was aware that her fingernails were digging into his shoulders, yet she couldn't seem to uncurl them. Milky water lapped at her chin, slid under her clothes, and wrapped around her body. There was no way to process this reality. She was standing up to her chin in water, in her office clothes, with a man she thought she'd never see again. It was a lot to deal with. And that was without getting into the whole dead people and kidnapping part of her day.

"I want to scream at the top of my lungs that we're going to die," she confessed.

"I don't appreciate the death part because I'm sure we'll be fine. Other than that, if you think it will make you feel better, go for it."

"Well, I don't want to do it now that I have permission," she grumbled.

The darkness was closing in on her again. Their only light was from her phone sitting on the edge of the pool. Ryan's phone, which had less charge than hers now, was in her oversized handbag, along with her shoes and his shirt. Ryan had tied his shoes together and secured them to the outside of the bag.

Her teeth started to chatter, even though the water wasn't that cold, and she found her gaze straying to the black silky depths that disappeared under a massive expanse of rock.

They were going in there.

Where there was no light.

No air.

Nothing.

Her heart was hammering so hard inside her that it was almost painful. All the breathing exercises she'd done to help lower her heart rate and keep her calm were rendered pointless. There was only blind panic and absolute terror.

"Lie back and float while we do some box breathing," Ryan said.

As soon as he started speaking, she was shaking her

head. "This isn't going to work. I can't. I just can't. I'm sorry. I really am, but you have to do this without me."

She tried to push away from him, to clamber back out of the water, but his hands held her in place.

"It's going to be fine. You just need to get control of your thoughts," he said evenly.

"No." She twisted in his hold, not making it very far. "No. I can't go in there."

"Sarah," he said firmly. "Think of something else. Something soothing."

Was he crazy? "Let me out of here."

Why wasn't he letting her go? Couldn't he see that she wasn't equipped to do this? She'd kill them both.

"Sarah Jean Davidson," he snapped, making her look up at him.

His tone left her expecting anger and disappointment; instead she found understanding and empathy on his face. The sight made her want to weep.

"The strongest muscle you have is your mind," he said. "You need to break the cycle of fear that has you caught up in it."

"How?" Her voice, like the rest of her, was trembling.

"We give you something good to think about." His smile was rueful. "I'm going to kiss it all better. Okay?"

Although she nodded, she wasn't entirely sure she understood him because her fears were still too loud in her head.

Ryan's hands shifted as Sarah clung to his shoulders. One cupped the back of her head; the other pressed her close to him at the small of her back. His mouth moved in to hers and pressed a gentle kiss to her lips. Their eyes were open, staring into one another's. Sarah barely felt it. All she did was remain frozen in his arms.

"You're brave," he said before kissing her again. "You're smart." Another gentle kiss. "You're funny." One more, and this time the sensation began to register. She felt her lips relax against his. "You're sweet, and I'm not talking sugar here, although I taste plenty of that when I kiss you, I'm talking about the way you think of others." Another kiss, this time the tip of his tongue caressed the seam of her mouth. "You're sexy as hell." His eyes grew darker as he gently sucked on her bottom lip. "You're sensual but shy with it." He rubbed his lips back and forth over hers. "You're so damn beautiful, it hurts to look at you." He nibbled at her lips. "But it's that courage of yours that slays me. Every." Kiss. "Single." Kiss. "Time." Kiss.

Sarah felt herself melting into him as her eyelids drifted closed.

"And, kissing you is like getting a hint of a scent that brings back a flash of a memory. One you can't quite put your finger on."

His lips lingered this time, teasing and tasting.

"But you know it was a good memory," he whispered, "because you can still feel the emotion that came with it."

"Ryan?" she breathed.

But her brain wasn't functioning any longer; her body was in control, and it wanted more.

As though knowing exactly what she desired, Ryan angled his mouth over hers and invaded. As little moans of pleasure supplied the music for their tongues to dance, Sarah felt the world fade away. There was only Ryan. Only his touch. His taste. His scent. Only the dark, delicious sensations he made her feel as he led her through a kiss that swept away all reason.

They fed from each other until they were breathless

and desperate for more. Slowly, Ryan pressed gentle kisses to her swollen lips as he led her up out of her daze.

"I've got you," he whispered. "I promise."

And in that moment, she could do nothing but believe him.

Feeling almost euphoric and a little light-headed, she let Ryan ease her back until she was floating on the surface of the water. With one hand under her to support her, he caressed her cheek with the other.

"Box breathing," he said softly before counting her through the breaths.

She didn't take her eyes from his. She felt like she was floating—in her mind, as well as in reality.

"You are amazing," he told her, and even though it was hard to believe, she found herself clinging to the words.

"Three deep breaths and then hold, okay?"

She didn't reply because she didn't want to break the spell he'd cast over her.

"One." He breathed with her, his hand moving from her face to her abdomen to check she was filling her lungs.

"Two." Again, they breathed in unison. "You're doing great," he said with a smile that was blinding.

"Last one and then under. Close your eyes, focus on that kiss, count if you have to, and let me do the work." He didn't give her time to think. "Three," he said.

When her lungs were full, he sank into the pool, taking Sarah with him.

Water rushed over her face.

Sarah grabbed hold of her mind with a steely grip. Forcing it to concentrate on the heat from Ryan's arm as it wrapped under her shoulders and across her chest. He held her firmly. His strength and confidence in his touch.

In turn, Sarah placed her hands on his forearm and fought to remain relaxed.

She didn't dare open her eyes, knowing that anything she saw would pull her straight out of the calm she felt and right into a panic attack.

A panic attack under water.

Her heart picked up speed. Her stomach lurched.

No!

She forced herself to visualize Ryan. Tall, strong, casually confident. She felt safe with him.

Water rushed past. Her leg dragged along the rough stone wall. Her chest felt tight. Strained and stretched with air that had nowhere to go.

Breathe!

Just breathe!

The air was desperate to get out. It pushed at her throat, demanding release. But Sarah knew if she let it out, she'd want to take in another breath. And there was no air to breathe.

Ryan's kiss!

His lips. His taste. The gentle yet firm caress that left her weak and desperate for more. She played it over and over in her mind, forcing herself to ignore the burning in her lungs.

Something banged into her shoulder. Ryan's grip tightened. Her chest hurt. Her diaphragm was painfully tight. It was the engine that made her breathe, Ryan told her. Try to relax your diaphragm and fool it into thinking you're fine.

If she could have laughed, she would have.

There were pins and needles in her fingers now. Her face felt tingly, and her limbs felt like they were drifting away.

How long had it been?

Don't think about time.

She dug her fingers into Ryan's arm as she felt his body move beside her. Strong. Sure. Confident in the water as he pulled her along with him.

Were they close to the other side? How long had passed? Her chest felt like it would burst and panic edged at her thoughts. There was no way she could hold it any longer. She had to breathe. And even though her mind knew there was no air to take in, her body didn't believe her. She needed to let out the air. It was causing her pain. She had to get rid of it.

Stubbornness fought with terror. Logic with pure emotion. Her body at war with her mind in a way that it'd never been before.

Breathe!

NO!

Cold, slimy water, thicker than usual, caught in her clothes like long fingers pulling her down. Seeking to keep her forever.

Her lungs were on fire. The pressure unbearable. Her teeth ached from clenching her jaw shut against the urge to breathe. It was too much. She couldn't take any more. She had to breathe.

SHE HAD TO BREATHE.

She was going to do it.

There was no stopping it.

Her chest was in agony, her throat on fire. Spasms wracked her diaphragm and her brain screamed and screamed and screamed and—

Suddenly calm enveloped her.

The enticing edge of sleep beckoned her over.

A peace like she'd never known stole through her body,

making every muscle relax to the point of feeling nothing at all.

She was floating away.

And it was beautiful.

The taut tension that was her mind's constant companion fled. There was no need to think, or worry, or plan. All she had to do was feel.

For the first time in her life, she experienced true freedom.

And it was glorious.

The water that'd felt so menacing became a soft cocoon.

A cradle.

A haven.

A place of safety, where she could rest and just be.

So, Sarah smiled, this is death...

CHAPTER FIFTEEN

Benson Security
London

Megan was feeling antsy. She didn't want to be in another meeting. She wanted to be out there, pummeling bad guys for information. The problem was, they didn't have any bad guys to pummel—at least not until David and Harvard tracked their one down and brought him back to base. She hated waiting. She wished the boys had let her tag along with them while they hunted down a lead in East London, but they said she'd attract too much male attention.

Megan knew they were more worried she'd shoot the idiot before they had a chance to question him.

Sometimes, this security specialist gig wasn't all it was cracked up to be. It was still better than hairdressing though, and she did get to work with her sexy husband. There just really needed to be a little less talking and a whole lot more action.

Dimitri elbowed her and leaned in to whisper. "Pay attention. There's probably going to be a quiz after."

If only that was funny.

"We boring you two?" Callum snapped at them.

Dimitri clamped a hand over her mouth before she could tell her boss the truth. Traitor.

"We're good," Dimitri said. "We're all about the focus, aren't we, Buffy?" He grinned at her.

Megan bit his hand, making him wince.

While Callum glared at them, Elle tapped her laptop and a picture of a woman appeared on the conference room screen. She was pretty, a bit uptight looking but pleasantly plump—as her mother would say. She looked...ordinary.

"Sarah Jean Davidson," Elle said. "Twenty-seven. An actuary with Steele-Shepherd insurance. In the month before he was shot, Ryan sent her hundreds of messages and called her several times. As far as I can tell, they only met in person once—the weekend before Joe blew up the office."

"Hey," Joe drawled. "The explosives were Callum's idea. And it was your brother's fault we had to trigger them."

Megan grinned. The explosives were great. They should blow things up more often.

"I don't understand." Julia looked confused. "Were Ryan and Sarah pen pals?"

Oh boy. Megan loved Julia, but she lived in a different world from, well, everyone else. There was naive, then there was Julia. It was good she had Joe to stand in front of her, otherwise the world would have chewed her up years ago.

"Kinda," Elle said, flashing Julia a sweet smile. "They met on Tinder and were getting to know each other before they—"

"Got to know each other." Megan finished by wiggling her eyebrows.

"Oh. Of course." Julia started blushing, and Megan sighed.

Next girls' night, they'd have to explain modern dating to Julia—again. At least there would be wine.

"That doesn't sound like Ryan." Dimitri took a Danish pastry from the huge platter in the middle of the table. The sight made Megan sad. If Ryan had been there, that platter would have been empty by now. "Since when did he want to talk to a woman before getting her into bed?"

"He was trying something new," Elle replied primly. "He was fed up being conned, robbed, and generally misused, and it was pointed out to him that possibly he was the problem and his attitude to dating might need some tweaking."

Megan couldn't help grinning at Elle. She could just imagine how that was pointed out to Ryan and wished she'd been a fly on the wall.

"Anyway," Elle said, "someone hacked all of their conversations, and as far as I can see, there wasn't any reason to read them. Sure, they're flirty, but mainly it's two people talking about everything and getting to know each other. She sounds smart and funny, and he was really opening up to her. Did you know he reads? Like a lot?"

"You mean books?" Megan was confused. "I know he reads comics."

"Yeah, books. There's a whole conversation about Moby Dick in their messages."

"Are you sure he read it and didn't just think it was a porn movie?"

"No." Elle shook her head at Megan. "He read the book."

"Apart from his reading taste," Callum growled, "did you find anything that might give us a clue as to what's going on here?"

"No, there's nothing." Elle looked deflated.

"But you dug into her background too, right?" Callum frowned.

Elle shrugged. "There wasn't much to find. She's the only child of two alcoholic parents. Her dad drank himself to death years ago, and it looks like her mother could join him any day now. She hasn't had any contact with either of them since she turned sixteen. The place she grew up...let's just say it makes a war zone look good. There are school records mentioning that she often came to school in little more than rags and was malnourished. Sarah definitely didn't have an easy childhood."

Julia looked like she might burst into tears. "That's so sad."

"Yeah," Elle agreed. "But she got out of there by working hard, being smart, and never setting a foot out of line. Seriously, this woman has only one reprimand noted in all of the records I combed through. Just one. There were no work problems, no speeding tickets, nothing."

Megan tossed her long blonde hair over her shoulder. "I have to know what the one reprimand was."

"When she was thirteen, and top of her year academically, two boys got grabby during swim class and she decked them. Broke one of their noses." Elle's grin oozed appreciation. Then she scowled. "The boys got away with it, and Sarah was suspended for three days as punishment."

Okay, now Megan was beginning to like this girl. "Typical. A woman gets assaulted, defends herself, and the guys get off scot-free."

"I wouldn't say scot-free," Dimitri had the nerve to say.

He held up his hands in surrender when he saw her face. "I mean, they were in the wrong and deserved to get punched, and the school should totally have backed up Ryan's woman. But at least they got hit, right?"

"You narrowly talked yourself out of that hole, buster," she told him.

"Can we please bloody focus on the job?" Callum barked. "Ryan is missing, unless you've forgotten."

"Anyway," Elle said hurriedly, no doubt to deliberately stop Megan from snapping right back at their grumpy-arsed boss. "As far as I can tell, Sarah Davidson has a few casual friends that she hangs out with now and then. She doesn't have any debt, she works hard, gives to charity, and leads a pretty regimented life. She only joined Tinder a few days before she met Ryan. He was her first date, and her last. She deleted her account a few weeks later."

"Any trouble at work?" Joe folded his arms, making his shoulder muscles bulge and Julia's mouth water.

"Nope." Elle shrugged. "She's squeaky clean—no upset clients, no disgruntled colleagues, nothing. Trust me, I did a deep dive on this woman and there isn't anything that raised alarms."

"Past boyfriends?" Rachel asked, her eyes on her phone.

One day, Megan was going to get that phone off Rachel, just so she could find out what she did on it that took so much attention.

"There were only a couple. One is married, the other transferred to Germany for work."

"Hobbies? Weird reading or TV habits? Did she write to death row inmates? Or have a long-lost cousin in the mob?" Dimitri asked.

"Not everybody is lucky enough to have mob connections." Elle stuck her nose in the air. "She reads—a lot. Which is hardly a crime."

"And also explains why Ryan was suddenly literary," Megan said. "That boy will do anything to get laid."

There were groans all round.

"What?" Megan said. "You know it's the truth."

"Anyway," Elle said. "Sarah collects handbags, although never to the point where it threatens her savings or paying her bills. She picks up shopping for her elderly neighbors, writes to her MP about stuff she disagrees with, and follows too many Instagram accounts dedicated to Chris Hemsworth. Apart from that, there's nothing in her life that'd attract the attention of a mercenary for hire. The most dangerous and exciting thing Sarah Davidson has done in the past five years is meet Ryan on Tinder."

Sitting still for so long was making Megan itch. She stretched her arms onto the table. "She sounds dull as dishwater. What the heck did Ryan see in her?"

"I don't think she sounds dull," Julia blurted, taking on Megan—something she never would have done when the London office had first opened.

You go girl! Megan beamed at her.

Julia swallowed but carried on. "I think she sounds like a really nice person."

"Exactly." Megan pointed at Julia.

Confused, Julia looked to her husband for clarification. And instantly got it.

"You're talking to the wrong person, Jules," Joe said. "Megan lives on the edge. According to her, if you aren't constantly in danger or causing trouble, then you don't know how to live."

"Amen, brother." Megan grinned, making her husband groan.

"I found a video that might answer your question." Elle pressed a button, and Ryan appeared on the screen next to a pretty brunette woman.

They were part of a crowd, walking along the Embankment beside the Thames late in the evening. Ryan was chatting away, definitely in entertainment mode. Sarah looked like she wasn't sure how to relax and enjoy herself, which made Megan wonder what he was doing with her. Not only that, her hair was in a tight bun at the nape of her neck—for a date! And she wasn't even showing any skin. Her lilac blouse was high-necked, her cardigan matched it, and she'd color coordinated with white pants and lilac sandals. Which, no surprise, had a sensible heel.

"She is so not Ryan's type," Megan said with a shake of her head.

"That's the whole point," Elle said. "Ryan's type kept treating him badly."

"Ryan's type thought Spandex was outerwear," Rachel said in disgust.

Dimitri nodded. "The more flash and sparkle, the better. If they had supermodel in their resume, then they were a shoo-in."

"That's not true," Elle said. "He had a thing for that woman in South America, and she wasn't like that."

"She did rip him off though," Dimitri pointed out. "Which fits his type to a T."

"You're all wrong," Julia said quietly. "Ryan has always wanted someone who needed him. Everything else was just window dressing. He's a white knight."

Megan thought back to the way Ryan had cared for Dimitri's sister after she'd been rescued from being sex trafficked. For a second there, she'd thought they might end up as a couple one day. Once Katrina was healed enough to cope with him.

"You know," she said to Julia. "I think you might be right."

Callum slammed his palms on the table. "Are we done discussing Ryan's taste in women? Or should we send out for ice cream and nail polish and do this properly?"

"Sexist," Elle said through a cough.

She also unpaused the video, and their attention turned back to it once again. On-screen, Ryan and Sarah were passing the roller park that was nestled under the concrete monstrosity that was the South Bank Center. Sarah's eyes strayed to the pop-up roller disco that'd taken over the area for the night, and a look of longing passed over her face before she turned back to Ryan.

Of course, he didn't miss the look, and taking Sarah's hand, he led her to the park—even though she was shaking her head to tell him it was a bad idea.

Elle cleared her throat. "This was taken by a blogger who'd been asked to cover the pop-up disco and promote it. When he saw Ryan and Sarah show an interest, he kept the camera on them."

It took quite a bit of gentle, good-natured cajoling on Ryan's part to get Sarah to agree to go roller skating, but she eventually gave in. It was kinda sweet, in a PG sort of way, to watch her face light up as she put on the skates. It was clear she'd never have joined in if Ryan hadn't been with her, even though she wanted to skate.

Their first turn around the rink didn't involve any dancing. Ryan held her hand, and Sarah seemed to blossom as they skated. After two rounds, she threw back her head and laughed at something he said before stripping off her cardigan and tossing it over the rail. Her blouse was sleeveless, and even Megan had to admit it looked sexy with the white pants. Ryan leaned in to say something in her ear, and she unclasped her hair, letting bronze curls fall to her shoulders. Unlike Megan's waves, Sarah had naturally curly hair that cork-screwed around her jaw. Suddenly, she wasn't so much the Plain Jane Megan had thought her to be.

Beaming at each other, Ryan and Sarah stopped going in circles and started to dance. With each passing second, Sarah loosened up further, her moves naturally sensual and uninhibited. She practically glowed as she waved her hands in the air, skating to the beat around Ryan.

And Ryan, he couldn't take his eyes off her. Every move he made was to protect her from the people crowded around them, all the while gently coaxing and teasing her out of her shell.

"I didn't know he could skate," Megan said, feeling awestruck. "Let alone dance."

Even Rachel had put down her phone to watch the couple enjoy themselves. It was mesmerizing. As they skated close to the camera, Sarah looped her arms around Ryan's neck and they spun slowly, staring into each other's eyes. It was the perfect romantic movie ending.

The video froze on that shot, and for a moment there was silence.

"Do you see it?" Elle said quietly.

A little breathless, Julia said, "He's the rain for her desert."

Rachel made gagging sounds, and Megan elbowed her hard. "Have some respect, Cruella. Unlike you, some people have feelings."

Rachel's icy glare promised payback. Megan grinned, *bring it on.*

Joe ignored both of them and spoke to his wife. "We see

it, Jules, they were falling in love. Might even have already been there."

"I really am going to vomit," Rachel muttered.

Why a sexy, easy-going man like Harvard had married Rachel was anyone's guess. Personally, Megan thought his kink was pain.

Elle sniffed. "I can't believe none of us knew about her. What must she have thought when Ryan suddenly disappeared? I should have looked through his email and messages at the time, but I was too upset and figured we'd contacted everyone who was important to him."

"Stick to what we're dealing with now," Callum said gruffly. "We cannae change the past."

"No, we can't." Elle switched off her laptop and the screen went blank. "I honestly don't think Sarah, or anything in her life, had anything to do with the disappearances, Callum. If there was something hinky, I would have found it."

"Then we start a deep delve into Ryan. It's clear from this that we didnae know as much about him as we'd thought." Callum started to pace. A man of action, he didn't like being holed up in the office on the best of days. Megan could relate. "For some reason, somebody investigated their relationship over a year ago and waited until now to pick them up." He folded his arms and frowned at his team. "What are we missing?"

For once, Megan couldn't think of a smart-arse reply.

CHAPTER SIXTEEN

Ryan knew the instant Sarah lost consciousness.

Her fingers uncurled from his forearm as all tension slid from her body in one silent wave. Limp and heavy, she began to sink toward the floor of the pool, dragging him along with her. Ryan tightened his grip on her, kicking with all his might to keep their forward momentum. She was a dead weight under his arm, slipping from his grasp with ease.

And he would not lose her.

Curling a fist into the material of her blouse, he twisted in the water to put himself under her. If he could support her body with his while powering through the pool, they'd make it. But he had to get them there in under three minutes.

Any longer, and it'd be too late to save her.

If this had been a normal, water in the lungs drowning, he'd have had more time. Five or six minutes before her oxygen levels were too low to bring her back. But this was a silent drowning. Shallow water blackout, the professionals called it. Meaning the oxygen in her brain had gotten perilously low and she'd blacked out. Like fainting under-water. And now, without her consciously fighting to hold her breath, her body automatically took in air—when there was no air to breathe.

He'd thought this might happen. Sarah had been so dead set that she'd panic and take them both down, yet he'd only seen stubborn determination from the woman since the moment she'd opened her eyes. A person like that didn't give up easily. A person like that held her breath long past the point where her body could handle it.

So, he'd planned every detail of what he'd do to get them to safety, going over and over it in his head until it felt like second nature.

Fool.

He'd forgotten to factor in his feelings.

Forgotten how paralyzing they could be.

Fear, insidious and malicious, grew inside him. Like vines around a tree, it choked his confidence. Strangled his reason. Made him want to kick, and fight, and struggle to get free from it. When he should have been clearheaded and focused. Sarah needed him.

Get a grip! Callum's voice barked in his head. *Use your training, Soldier, and get the two of you out of there!*

Swimming on his side, one arm around Sarah, the other holding the phone out in front of them, Ryan did as he was told. The water was cloudier now. Made thick by the slurry they'd kicked up as they swam. He could barely see a few inches in front of him, but his innate sense of direction was functioning fine.

Powering through the water, as fast as he dared in such a dangerous, closed-in space, Ryan brought them into the central pond area. Their tunnel was second on the left. It was narrow, lined with jagged rock, and it would be a squeeze. Not impossible with Sarah as a dead weight in his arms, but definitely harder. Part of him couldn't help but wonder if all the months of training were for this moment. He'd never been stronger. And he'd never needed it more.

Watch out for that sharp rock! Callum's voice bellowed.

Ryan dodged to the side, taking Sarah with him. They skimmed along the rough surface of the wall, barely managing to avoid the piece of stone that would rip through flesh. Eyes stinging from the thick white water, he maneuvered them deeper into the narrow channel.

That same dead, bloated rat carcass floated in front of his face, and Ryan pushed at the water to get it out of his way. He glanced back to check on Sarah. Her hair had come loose and billowed around her face, while her arms and legs floated out from her body. They were going to get hurt. Maybe even broken. He couldn't take her through the tunnel like this. And he couldn't afford the time to stop either. But a broken bone. Or torn and bleeding flesh...he couldn't risk it.

Keeping her wedged between him and the wall, he deftly brought her hands in front of her and buttoned both sleeves together, effectively cuffing her in place. Her legs were trickier. All he could do was tie both sides of her ripped skirt to constrict their movement.

His heart seized at the sight of her.

Bound and unconscious.

Drowning before his eyes.

Dying...

Less than two minutes left, Callum snapped. *Get in that tunnel, Soldier!*

Kicking against the water, he launched them into the tunnel. Visibility was even worse now. He was essentially swimming blind. Hugging Sarah to him, he shielded her body as best he could while negotiating bumps and turns.

His lungs were burning. His eyes stinging. His heart wildly out of control.

He ignored it all.

Laser focused on his goal, he swam toward the end of the tunnel.

A minute left, Callum said. *Put on some speed.*

Ryan did as he was told, well aware that one day soon, he'd be talking to his neurologist about his boss living in his head. Although, right then, he'd never been more grateful for the grumpy Scot.

Pushing the water behind them with the hand that held Sarah's phone, he kicked down. Aiming them through the part of the channel that became tight and low. Rocks skimmed their bodies as they passed, and he hoped none had injured Sarah. There was no way to tell if they had.

Not that any scrapes would matter if he couldn't get her out of the water in time.

Kicking through the narrow part of the tunnel, he dragged Sarah with him. With one strong arm, he propelled them forward to where the tunnel widened again before opening up into the cavern above. Nearly there. A few more strokes, and he could help Sarah.

Ignoring the agony in his lungs, he pressed onward.

Only to be jerked back.

Spinning around, he waved the light behind him. Only to find that the strap of the bag had caught on something. And there was no way to unhook it because Sarah's body was in the way. And the tunnel was far too tight to maneuver her out of it.

He needed to break the strap.

Pulling at it didn't work, so he placed his feet on the

ground to get some momentum. The damn strap still held. Letting go of Sarah, Ryan ducked and contorted himself in an effort to get the bag over his head. It was impossible. There wasn't enough space.

Sarah was dropping rapidly, and afraid he would lose her in the murky water, he grabbed hold of her. And dropped Sarah's phone. It floated down into the mud and rock-covered bottom of the pool. The light slowly fading as it went.

Now, there was only blackness.

The bag was wedged against his back and immovable because of the stuck strap. There was no way to retrieve his phone from it. Which meant they were stuck in the darkness.

Get out of there now! Callum bellowed.

Using every ounce of strength he'd built since waking from his coma, Ryan held Sarah tight and pushed off from the rocks with his feet. The leather strap dug into his shoulder until he thought the bone would give before the bag. A bubble of air escaped him, making his diaphragm flex. Time was running out. For both of them.

Move it! Callum shouted. *Break that bloody strap.*

Ryan pushed with all his might, propelling them forward. And, just as he was about to give up and try something else, there was a pop as the strap snapped and the bag slid into the darkness below.

Exertion made his lungs burn with a ferocity that was almost unbearable. He'd used too much oxygen. Exerted himself far too much. If he didn't breathe now, they'd both be in trouble.

Propelled by fury and desperation, Ryan swam forward as best he could. Navigating the way by feel, which slowed them down.

You need to get out now, Callum ordered.

I'm growing weak, Ryan replied, *and we can't speed up, or I'll swim us straight into the wall.*

Aye, and the last thing you need is another head injury, Callum said. *You can do this. You were trained to do this. You're a warrior. A soldier. Don't let me down. If you do, I'll kick your backside from here to Scotland.*

With Callum's prosthetics, that would be like getting beaten with a steel pipe.

Nearly there, Ryan told him.

But he knew they weren't going to make it. His hands were tingling, and there were strange lights flashing before his eyes.

Don't you dare pass out on me! Callum shouted. *You get your arse out of there now and save that girl.*

Woman...she doesn't like being called a girl. He was finding it hard to think now.

His limbs felt heavy and dull. Each movement was like swimming through treacle.

Callum? he called as he felt around in front of them.

There was no reply.

Callum?

Mustering what strength he had left, Ryan kicked off the bottom in order to feel what was above them.

And his hand hit air.

Not rock.

Air.

Propelling them upward, he dragged Sarah onto the rocky bank, going by feel and memory. He sucked in the musty air like it was pure filtered oxygen. Weak, tired, his limbs heavy, all he wanted to do was rest. Sleep. Perhaps forever.

But he couldn't.

He wouldn't.

Kneeling beside Sarah, he felt for a pulse. Nothing. Closing his eyes because he couldn't see a damn thing anyway, Ryan started CPR. Thankfully, his training kicked in, helping him function on autopilot as his foggy mind fought to stay conscious.

"For drownings, you start with breathing, not compressions," he muttered.

Five breaths to get started. That's what they were taught. The air all the more important because Sarah had been without it for too long. He tilted her head, using his fingers to check her mouth was clear of anything she might have taken in while they were underwater. Satisfied her airway was clear, he pinched her nose, and taking a deep breath, he pushed air into her lungs. Five times, deep breaths. Each one making him dizzy.

There was no response.

But he'd pushed some water out of her lungs. He'd felt it dribble down her chin. That was something.

"You're not going to die here," he vowed as he felt his way down her sternum to the spot he needed for compressions.

One hundred and twenty to start. One minute's worth of compressions. His limbs felt heavy, and his coordination was off. He shook his head, hoping to clear it, but the movement only made things worse.

"Get with it!" he snapped at himself.

Straightening his arms, he knelt up over her and, hands together, started a series of rapid pushes against her chest. Too much pressure and he'd crack her ribs, or worse, break one and puncture a lung. Too little pressure and it wouldn't get her heart started.

Drips from his forehead landed on his hands. "Come

on, come on," he muttered as he fought to save her. "You're young, you're healthy, your bones shouldn't break..." But all he could think of was her fragile ribs under his meaty hands.

He moved to her mouth, pushing air deep into her lungs. Now it was two breaths and thirty compressions per cycle.

"Focus, Ryan," he said before sucking in a deep breath.

Fitting his mouth over hers while he held her nose closed, he pushed air into her. And then he repeated the process before quickly returning to chest compressions.

"Sarah," he barked at her in a good impression of Callum, "don't you fucking die on me."

His head was pounding, and his limbs were heavy and awkward. Only adrenaline kept him going. Without it, he'd have been out cold beside her.

As he pushed at her heart, he strained for any sign she was breathing on her own.

There was nothing.

Yet.

He shifted back up to her face to breathe for her. Two more deep breaths pushed into her lungs. His life inside of her. No response. He returned to her chest and started compressions all over again.

"Please, Stats, you gotta breathe. I need you with me." He pushed as hard as he dared, knowing that keeping her heart going was more important than giving her air.

Each tiny movement he made brought a round of protest from his muscles. Ryan knew he was fast approaching his limit, but he couldn't give up. Not until the decision was taken from him and his body collapsed beside her.

All his training. All his experience. It was all for this

one moment. For this one task—saving this woman. *His* woman. He felt it. Deep inside, where his emotions remembered even though his brain couldn't. He felt for *her*.

"Please, baby, please," he begged as he returned to her mouth. "Please breathe. Please come back to me."

Yet again, he filled his lungs to bursting before pouring as much of it as he was able into Sarah. One breath. He took another deep breath, only to let it out in a rush of air when she made a gurgling sound. He felt her body move and almost passed out with relief.

But they weren't out of the woods yet.

"You've got this, baby. You can do this."

Quickly, Ryan rolled her to her side, holding her steady as she coughed up murky water from the pool. It was the most amazing sound he'd ever heard.

"It's okay, Stats," he whispered to her. "Everything is going to be okay."

Her weak body spasmed violently as she convulsed with each brutal cough. It wasn't long before the coughing turned into vomiting. And all Ryan could do was hold her, stroking her hair away from her face, as she retched and writhed in pain.

An eternity passed before she stopped, slumping into his arms. He heard her swallow and try to clear her throat. She needed a drink, but all of their clean water was in the bag at the bottom of the pool.

"I'll get it for you as soon as I can," he promised. He'd have gone back in right then, if he hadn't been aware that his body was slowly shutting down on him.

Sarah sniffed and burrowed into him. Her movements dull and weak. She groaned softly, and he stroked her back.

"I've got you. You're okay now." He rolled the two of them away from whatever mess she'd made.

Lying on the cold, hard stone, he tucked her tight into his side, her head on his chest, her arm over his stomach. It still didn't feel close enough. One hand on her back, he measured her breathing, reassuring himself that it was steady. Keeping track of any breaks in the rhythm.

His other hand caressed her throat until he found the spot where her pulse beat strongly against his fingertips. She cleared her throat again as she lay limp against him.

"Good, this is good. You're doing great, Stats. I'm so proud of you," he cooed to her.

There was no indication she'd even heard him. The stress and exhaustion of her experience had won, and she was out cold. Good. She needed to rest.

Slowly, Ryan's own heartbeat began to slow. They were soaked, chilled from the water and the cool air, but he could hold her close, and together they'd stay warm.

"You scared me," he whispered into the black, impenetrable darkness.

He couldn't remember the last time he'd felt that scared. Maybe never.

"Who are you to me?" he whispered. "You feel...important."

Once he was sure that her breathing and heart rate were normal, Ryan allowed himself to relax. As sleep swept him under, he thought he heard Callum's voice.

You did well, son, he said.

CHAPTER SEVENTEEN

Sarah opened her eyes to find only black. She blinked several times, but all she saw was endless darkness. For a brief second, she was right back in the closet she'd hidden in as a child. Afraid that the monsters would get her in the dark or that her parents would forget her entirely and never come home.

She curled her fingers into the bed beneath her—only to find it wasn't a bed. It was warm, solid flesh.

"Ryan," she whispered as everything came rushing back.

They'd been in the water. She'd held her breath, then...nothing.

"Ryan?" Her throat ached when she spoke, and her voice sounded hoarse.

Gently, she shook Ryan, feeling naked abs beneath her hand.

He shifted, and an arm tightened around her waist. "Hey, Stats, you're awake." There was a smile in his voice.

"What happened to the light?" There wasn't a smile in her voice. Nope, there was borderline panic.

He rubbed her back. "Lost it in the pool. Gimme a minute to get my head on straight, and I'll go get it. Or at least get the bag. That should be easier to find."

"We lost the bag?" And all of their meager resources? "What happened down there? I was holding my breath, and I thought I was going to die. But there's nothing between that and waking up."

"Welcome to my world," he drawled.

Carefully, he moved, taking her with him until they were both sitting on the stone floor.

"Are we on the other side or back in the shaft?" Sarah gripped his arm. Afraid she'd lose him in the dark if she took her hands off him.

He shuffled around some. "We're on the other side of the pool, where we wanted to be."

"But?" There was definitely a but in there, something he was reluctant to tell her.

His hand brushed her arm until it found her fingers. Threading them together, Ryan answered. "You lost consciousness halfway through our swim."

Sarah swallowed hard, feeling a raw ache in her throat. Slowly, she realized that wasn't the only ache she felt. Her chest hurt too, as though she'd pulled something while trying to hold her breath.

"You swam me out of there?" She blinked at nothing as the cold implications of his words sank in. "Did I drown?" Her free hand moved to her chest, testing the pain she felt when she touched it. "Did you have to revive me?"

"All that matters is you're fine now," Ryan said firmly. "But the bag got caught on the way through the tunnel and we lost it. I'd planned on getting it before you woke, but I guess we both crashed."

Sarah barely registered what he was saying. She had a

vague recollection of vomiting, which would explain the nasty taste in her mouth.

"Did I die?" she said.

"No!" He gripped her hand tightly. "You just had a minute where your heart didn't beat and you weren't breathing."

She felt light-headed. "Which is literally the definition of dead."

"No, there was still brain activity, which meant your system had just stalled. It was nothing more than a hiccup."

"A hiccup where I stopped breathing and my heart didn't beat?"

"Yeah."

Her mind was blank. How did you process information like this? Was she supposed to rush up and contemplate the meaning of life? Was she supposed to cry? Mainly, she felt stunned. And sore.

"I don't know what to think," she confessed.

"Don't think anything. It's over and we move on to the next thing now."

"Uh..." Nope. There wasn't a thought in her head. She had no idea how to react or what to say. She swallowed again, her lips feeling dry, her mouth disgusting, and her throat sore. "I guess I'll put this in a box to deal with later."

"Or never. Never is good too."

"Thank you," she said, aware that the words weren't anywhere near enough to cover everything he'd done. "Thank you for saving my life."

His fingertips found her face and stroked her cheek. "I'd say anytime, Stats, but I never want to repeat that. For a second there..." His hand dropped away.

"You thought I was gone," she said before trying to clear

her throat. It was like swallowing sandpaper. "I think I might have been sick too."

"Oh, there was definite vomit. Don't move around; it's still out there, somewhere in the dark."

"Delightful. Well, that explains the taste in my mouth." Her cheeks suddenly heated. "My breath—I'm sorry, it must smell awful."

"Hadn't noticed."

She was pretty sure he was lying. "What do we do now? Can you remember which way to go? Can we feel our way out of here?"

"You're only saying that because you don't want me to go back in the water, but it'll be fine. The bag isn't far up the tunnel and the water is pretty still. It should be around the spot where the strap broke, which isn't far from here. It won't take me long to get it."

"You're right, I don't want you to go back in the water." Especially after everything that'd happened last time.

"I'll be fine. Anyway, we need that bag. It has the tooth-paste in it."

She smacked his bare chest. "Not funny. I'm not sure there's any point retrieving it," she said. "The electronics will be waterlogged by now and completely useless."

"I don't know how long we were out; it might only have been a few minutes. And they have some protection from your bag."

"Now you're just being optimistic."

"It's how I roll," he said with laughter in his voice.

She inched away from him, still holding his hand. Careful not to go too far in case she landed in vomit, or worse, fell back in the water. "Go then, so we can get out of here." The pool was giving her the creeps.

"Yes, ma'am." He moved around some, letting go of her hand and patting her shoulder. "I'd kiss you for luck, but…"

Oh, that was just evil. "If I could see the water, I'd shove you in it," she told him.

He squeezed her shoulder. "Don't go anywhere. I'll be back in a couple of minutes."

There was a gentle splash followed by the sound of water lapping at him, and then silence. Sarah twisted her hands in her lap as she closed her eyes in an attempt to block out the nothingness of her surroundings. Then she repeated the trick Ryan had taught her and started counting aloud.

"One, two, three, you'd better get back here in one piece, Ryan Granger, four, five…"

She was almost at three hundred when she heard the water splash and Ryan gasp.

"Are you okay?" she rushed to ask.

"All good. Got the bag. Keep talking so I climb out in the right spot."

"What should I say? That for a second date this experience really sucks?" It was a poor attempt at a joke, but Ryan laughed anyway.

"When we get out of here, I'll take you on a real second date." He paused. "Or in my case, a first date."

"I wasn't fishing for a date. I was being funny. Or trying to." She sighed. "Plus, honestly, I don't think that's a good idea."

"Are you kidding? I kiss like a god. That's totally second date motivation right there."

He brushed against her before sitting close. Unlike Sarah's clothes, which were just damp now, Ryan's jeans were dripping again.

"It's not about your kissing," she said, carrying on the

world's most ludicrous conversation. "It's about your life. You can do the whole life-on-the-line thing without even missing a beat, but I'd drive myself to an early grave worrying about you. I'm pathetic like that."

"Is this about the coma thing? Because I hear the chances of that happening twice are pretty low."

"Oh, how you amuse yourself at my expense. No, it isn't about the coma. You have bullet wounds on your chest, a scar on your shoulder, another on your back. Who knows what else I haven't noticed? You live life on the edge. I worry if it's too dangerous to take up knitting."

Suddenly, light flooded the cavern, making her blink fast as her eyes adjusted and the room came into focus. Then, there he was, sitting facing her, looking like a hunky Poseidon who'd just emerged from the deep after frolicking with mermaids. She glanced down at herself. It was as she'd suspected. She looked like a damp pile of seaweed.

"iPad still works, then," Ryan said cheerily. "Haven't tried my phone yet, but if we use it on the lowest light setting it should still have some life left in it. Here, drink this and then you can brush your teeth." He handed her the smaller bottle of water, along with the travel toothbrush and toothpaste set.

There were scratches on his arms, probably from swimming against the rocks. But other than that, he looked good. A little too good. A little too hard to resist—if she let her guard down, which she couldn't. Not without risking the security she'd worked hard to acquire.

Taking the items he handed to her, she looked around the cavern and stopped at the sight of a gaudily painted tag on the wall near the mouth of a tunnel. Wide-eyed, she turned back to Ryan.

"We really might be able to get out of here," she said, feeling a little shocked.

"Ye of little faith," he muttered.

It didn't take long for them to freshen up. Ryan was back to wearing his shirt, which was soaked, but he insisted it would dry faster on his body than off. Sarah wasn't particularly worried about how wet the shirt was; she was more upset that his abs were under it.

Perv.

His phone was still working, so they were using up its battery before they switched to the iPad. Mainly because the phone was easier to carry. The clip Sarah used to tie her hair in a bun was long gone, so she brushed it out and hoped it wouldn't look like a bird's nest when it dried. And yes, it was stupid and shallow to worry about the state of her hair considering all the other things they had to worry about. Still, Ryan was a freaking cover model, even after everything they'd been through. The least she could hope was that she didn't resemble a haystack.

"I think I should take my shoes off until they dry," she told him as they walked down yet another tunnel. If she never saw a tunnel in her life again, it would be too soon. "They're soaked and rubbing against my toes."

"You'll regret it if you do," he said from behind her. "One sharp rock underfoot, and you'll have to limp out of here."

Sarah sighed, wishing every little thing wasn't so blooming hard. Each step she took jolted her chest, pulling at abused muscles and sending spikes of pain throughout her body. Her throat felt slightly better now that she'd had something to drink, and she was very grateful that her teeth were clean and minty fresh. But overall, she was desperate for a shower. The slimy water from the pond had coated her skin, and she couldn't even bear thinking about what might have been in it. If she had a fear of bacteria, she would have lost it right about now.

Thankfully, Sarah wasn't a delicate flower. Heck, she'd grown up in one of the UK's toughest areas and could negotiate her way through any slum. She still wanted to be clean though. No, what she *really* wanted was to get out of there, but she would settle for clean if she could get it—for now, anyway.

On top of everything else she had to contend with, they now had a musical accompaniment to their trek through the mine—Ryan's stomach had become very vocal about being neglected. With each step he took, it rumbled. Each one louder than the last. It would have been funny, if she'd had the energy to laugh.

"Ryan?" she asked, mainly to break the monotony of miles of beige stone walls. "What happens if you don't get fed regularly? I mean, apart from the sound effects, do you turn rabid? Should I fear for life and limb? Will my leg start to look tasty at some point soon?"

"Hilarious. Nothing happens. Although, the longest I've gone is two days, and by the end of it I was ready to gnaw on my shirt. Not sure what would have happened if it'd stretched out beyond that. Don't think you can die from eating a cotton shirt, can you?"

It was slightly worrying that he sounded like he might be seriously considering it as a future option.

"I don't think you should eat anything you can't digest," she felt the need to say.

"Some women eat coal when they're pregnant, and they don't suffer."

"If we find some coal, you have my permission to nibble it. What's the weirdest thing you've eaten, just because you were hungry?"

"Elle's cooking? She went through an experimental phase. Thankfully it didn't last long."

"I'm serious, I want a serious answer."

"Okay, there was snake meat and guinea pig in South America. Deep fried tarantula in Cambodia. Rocky Mountain oysters—"

"That doesn't sound weird," she interrupted.

"It's what people in Denver call fried bull testicles."

Ew, no! "The Scottish are right—you really can deep fry anything. That's even worse than the spider."

"Then there's frogs' legs, chicken feet, huhu grubs, and pan-fried crickets," Ryan continued. "I once ate an out-of-date—by about six years—jar of mustard while I was laying low in an abandoned house. It was the only thing in the cupboard." His stomach rumbled ferociously. "It knows we're talking about food," he said. He patted his belly lovingly.

Sarah shook her head at him. "You do know it doesn't think for itself, right?"

"How little she knows," he reassured his stomach. "So, what's the weirdest thing you've eaten?"

"Haggis." Sarah was totally out of her league when it came to Ryan and food. "And German blood sausage. I guess I'm not as adventurous as you."

"Or you're smarter," Ryan said as he tugged at a lock of her hair. "This is really curly. Is that why you keep it tied back?"

Sarah sighed. "It's neater, and people don't touch it so

much when it's in a bun. Plus, nobody takes me seriously with this hair. They think I'm a grown-up version of Shirley Temple." Which was also why her hair straighteners were her most prized possession.

"Shirley Temple was awesome." Ryan sounded enthusiastic. "People only remember the child movie star, but she was an Ambassador for the US government, and a United Nations delegate, and an environmental activist. She even had a cocktail named after her."

"A nice, safe, boring cocktail," Sarah huffed.

"She had an IQ of one hundred fifty-five—that's Mensa level."

"And she sang *On the Good Ship Lollipop*," Sarah reminded him bitterly.

Ryan burst out laughing in that deep, rumbling belly laugh of his. "Is it the good girl image that bothers you or just the curls?"

"Both. Probably. I think..."

He tugged another curl. "We can totally sort the good girl image. Say the word, and I'm happy to lead you over to the bad side."

He'd already tempted her with that once; she wasn't sure she'd cope a second time. "I'll pass."

"For now," the devil said.

As they rounded yet another bend in the tunnel, they suddenly stepped into a large cavern. It was long and narrow, and the ceiling was low overhead. There were rows of built-up dirt mounds running the length of the room, and it looked like there were—

"Mushrooms!" Ryan ran past her, heading straight for the fungi.

He crouched beside a dirt mound. "There's a lot of mold in here, but I think we might still find some edible ones." He poked around before lifting a white button mush-room as though it were an Oscar statue. "Look, Stats, food."

Honestly, she wasn't sure she'd ever seen him happier.

Cautiously, Sarah walked further into the room. "I've heard about this. People using old caverns and mines to grow mushrooms."

Ryan nodded, already moving down the row to see how many more he could find. "There was a woman in Inver-tary, the town in Scotland where Benson Security was founded, who ran a mushroom farm in an old mine." He glanced around. "Looks like this one was abandoned a while ago."

"But—" Exhilaration rushed through Sarah. "They had to have a way to get the mushrooms out of here, right?"

Ryan was much too focused on the mushrooms to care about an exit. "Let's eat first, then we'll search for the exit."

"Ryan, if we find the way out first, we can have a proper meal aboveground."

"Oh. Okay." With his harvest tucked into a pouch he'd made with the front of his shirt, he stepped over the mounds to join her. "Guess we just follow the walls until we find it." His eyes were on the mushrooms, rather than the walls. And there was a tiny bit of drool in the corner of his mouth.

"Don't you dare eat those without cleaning them," Sarah told him. "If there are mushrooms down here, then there has to be a water source that they used to grow them. Clean first, eat later."

"I don't think a little dirt is going to upset my stomach," he said as they slowly made their way along the first wall.

"Do you really want to risk food poisoning when we're this close to getting out of here?"

"I can wait," he said. But he didn't sound happy about it.

CHAPTER EIGHTEEN

David managed to track Prentice, the mercenary hired to abduct Ryan, to a ratty old bar in London's East End. He'd been in worse places, as had Harvard. Although, from the look on Harvard's face, you wouldn't think so.

"Is being married to a millionaire ruining your appreciation for the grubbier side of life?" David asked as he sipped his warm ale.

They sat in the far corner of the small bar area. David was grateful the crowd wasn't just made up of locals because they would have stuck out like two sore thumbs.

Harvard flashed a smile while keeping his eyes on their prey. "Do I detect a note of jealousy in your tone?"

It was famously difficult to rile Michael "Harvard" Carter. The man was born cool—in all senses of the word.

"Elle could be rich if she wanted," David pointed out, but

then conceded with a shrug. "Wouldn't be legal though, and would, most likely, end with me breaking her out of some high-security prison because she'd hacked the wrong people. Probably safer if we earn our money the good old-fashioned way."

"Hard work, low pay." Harvard toasted him before giving a chin lift. "Looks like our boy might be ready to call it a night."

"About time. If you grimace at the carpet one more time, I might lose it."

"There's a carpet. In. A. Bar." Harvard's lip curled. "No way they can get that clean."

"Rachel's silver spoon is spoiling you, man." David took another sip of beer, watching Prentice in the mirrored signs hanging beside the bar—next to several Toby Jugs that could use a good clean. "You met the Queen yet?"

"They're not that close family members; they only get together at big events. It's not like they're having tea every Sunday."

David bit back the urge to roar with laughter, it would attract too much attention. "Listen to yourself. You didn't even bat an eye at the idea of meeting the Queen."

"I'm married to the aristocracy. I've met more lords and ladies than you can count. Hell, half the House of Lords was at our wedding."

"Not to mention William and Kate. Wait, do you call them by their first names, or is it Your Royal Highness?"

"It's good you're enjoying yourself. One of us should be."

David placed his pint glass on the old mahogany bar. The wood was varnished to the point where it looked like it'd been shrink-wrapped, and the scrollwork around the edges had years' worth of dirt enhancing the design.

"Another, luv?" the barmaid asked.

The woman was pushing seventy, had bleached blonde hair, a heavy hand with blue eye shadow, and those little spider web lines around her lips that only smokers developed.

David's smile was designed to make her feel like the Mona Lisa incarnate. "I'm good, thanks."

She batted her false lashes before sauntering on to the next customer.

"I'm telling Elle you were flirting," Harvard said as a group entered the bar, taking the small room to bursting capacity. "Heads up, we have movement." He touched his earpiece to activate comms. "Joe, Dimitri, we've got Prentice and two friends heading out of the door nearest Brick Lane. Follow, don't engage."

"Copy that," Joe said.

David threw some bills onto the bar as they pushed up out of their stools. Slowly, they made their way through the packed pub. Someone had cranked up the music, and Rick Astley was playing. David suspected that in this bar every night was eighties night.

Pushing through the heavy wooden door, they ducked to avoid the hanging flower baskets that adorned the front of the pub. Each strategically placed to cover areas of flaking plaster on the exterior wall.

A yellow light illuminated the bar name, Cock & Bull. Right beside it, some helpful vandal had drawn a huge dick in black marker pen. David wondered how long it'd been there because he couldn't see the owners making the effort to paint over it in a hurry.

"They're heading to a curry house in Brick Lane," Dimitri said through the comms unit. "Are we picking him up before he loads up on curry? Because I don't fancy an interrogation after he's eaten."

David and Harvard casually strode along the narrow, one-way road that led to Brick Lane at the end. Brick Lane had once been famous for its exotic markets and for being the stomping ground of Jack The Ripper. Now, it was known as Banglatown because of its large Bangladeshi community and many curry restaurants. But it wasn't all curries and spicy food; there were weird little shops selling everything from cheap Chinese knock-offs to handmade ceramic toilet seats.

As they turned into Brick Lane, the street became busier. Some people were still shopping, while others were out for an evening meal. Orange street lights illuminated the vast range of graffiti that seemed to cover every building. There was everything from unreadable tags scrawled with hasty black ink, right through to gallery-level murals that covered whole walls.

Dodging around trash bags that had accumulated on a corner, they continued up the narrow brick-lined street to the area housing most of the Bangladeshi restaurants.

"They're heading for Curry King," Joe said with disgust.

"No taste," Dimitri added. "All these fantastic restaurants, and they choose a chain."

"The beer doesn't care if it gets a gourmet," David pointed out. "The beer just wants to be fed."

"And this is why you shouldn't drink warm beer on an empty stomach," Harvard said.

"Or at all," Joe amended. "The English need to catch up with the rest of the world and refrigerate."

He was preaching to the choir. All four of their current team hailed from the States.

"We need to get him away from his boys," Joe said. "Don't want a showdown in the middle of the street."

"How do you want to play this?" Dimitri said.

Harvard glanced at David. "They're the decoy?"

David nodded. They were closing in on the three men; only a few feet separated them.

"There's a good chance Prentice might recognize one of us, so you two hustle his boys into the restaurant while we pick up the package."

"Copy that," Joe said.

As Dimitri and Joe approached the Curry King, they became rowdy and loud, laughing at each other as they played their parts as hungry drunks. To the annoyance of the three men, Dimitri and Joe elbowed their way in front of Prentice, crowding him out as they followed the other two into the restaurant.

It was all the gap David needed.

As Harvard came up on one side of the mercenary, David took the other.

"Hey there, Prentice," David said as he jammed a gun into the mercenary's ribs.

"What the fuck?" Prentice executed a move to free himself, but Harvard grabbed him and held on tight.

David rammed the gun further into Prentice's side, making the man grunt. "Don't think I won't shoot you."

Prentice growled at David. "The fuck you will. We're in the middle of the fucking street."

"Language," Harvard reprimanded, drawing his attention.

Prentice's head spun around to face the former spy, and he visibly paled. "Fuck."

"Been a while." Harvard kept a friendly smile on his face as they frog-marched Prentice past the restaurant doors. "I see you haven't learned any new words. How have you been, Prentice?"

"What the hell do you want?" He craned his neck, looking for his friends, who'd been waylaid by Joe and Dimitri and wouldn't get to him in time.

Angling Prentice toward the next corner, they made their way up Hanbury Street where one of their SUVs was parked. All the while, Harvard continued to smile and chat in that easygoing tone of his. "We want to talk. A nice, easy conversation between professionals. That's okay with you, isn't it?"

"I don't have anything to say to you," Prentice snapped. "So you might as well shoot me now."

"I'd like that," David said. "Been a while since I shot a man."

Prentice frowned at him as recognition slowly dawned in his eyes. "Fuck, you're David Knight."

"You're right," David said to Harvard. "His language skills need work."

"You really should make the effort," Harvard said as they reached the SUV. "You'll attract a higher class of criminal employer if you do."

Harvard unlocked the car with his fob and swung the back door open for Prentice. They'd been expecting him to make a break for it at this point, and sadly, he didn't disappoint.

Pushing back against the car, he swung at Harvard—making the mistake of assuming the bigger man meant the bigger threat.

David slammed a hand over the man's mouth to muffle any shouting as he angled the gun and shot Prentice in the leg. Shoving him head-first into the car, David leaned in over him and secured his hands and feet with zip ties.

Leaving him face-down and bleeding on the leather of the back seat, secured with seat belts that were threaded through his arms and legs to keep him firmly in place, David let himself into the front of the vehicle.

Harvard was already behind the wheel. "You just had to show off, didn't you?" he said as he put the car in gear and pulled out into the narrow road.

"You've never seen me show off," David drawled.

"I'm fucking bleeding back here," Prentice shouted from behind them. "I need a hospital, assholes."

David twisted in his seat and aimed his gun at the man. "From now on, every word you utter earns another bullet. Let's see how many we can put in you before you bleed out."

Prentice clenched his jaw tight as his eyes blazed fury.

Satisfied that the mercenary understood him, David settled back in his seat as Harvard negotiated the maze of roads that made up East London.

"We're in the car," Joe said over their earpieces. "Heading to the office."

"David shot Prentice," Harvard tattled.

"It was the fastest way to handle things. He isn't dying, and he's able to talk," David defended his decision.

"Joe," Dimitri said. "You owe me ten bucks."

CHAPTER NINETEEN

The entrance to the mushroom farm had been bricked up.

Sarah stood in front of the brick wall, staring at it, wishing there was some way to get past it. Some way to knock it down. To get through and out of the damn mine.

"How easy do you think it is to knock down a brick wall?" she asked Ryan, who'd gone back to foraging for mushrooms that weren't covered in mold.

"If you have the right equipment, I'd say pretty easy." He looked over at her from where he was crouched beside a mushroom bed. "We don't have any equipment, let alone the right stuff."

"Couldn't you just, I don't know, run at it?" He was big and strong, so surely it would give.

"Absolutely, if you want me to get another head injury."

"What if we pick at the mortar around one brick, poke that out, and make the wall weaker? Could you kick it down then?"

"Pick at the mortar with what? Our fingernails?"

"No! I have a nail file."

"Great. Wake me up in about two years when you've loosened the brick."

"Ryan." She pointed at the offending wall. "This is the way out."

"Stats, it really isn't. You're assuming it's one brick deep, but it could be way more solid than that. There's no way of knowing. Go clean up, and once we've eaten, we'll look for another option."

With a frustrated huff, Sarah went back to the tap they'd found near the blocked exit. At least they had water now, which meant they'd both drank their fill. And that brought other problems. The far corner, in the darkest part of the cavern, was now the designated bathroom.

Ryan was right—she needed to clean up. She felt feral. If only there was soap. If—when—she got out of here, she was going to hoard soap like it was going out of fashion. All kinds and colors. Every scent under the sun. Her house would be filled with it.

Right now, all she could do was use an antibacterial wipe as a cloth and clean up as best she could.

"Don't peek," she ordered Ryan as she undid the zipper in her skirt and pulled it down over her hips.

"I let you peek when I cleaned up." He grinned at her. "Actually, I'm pretty sure it was more staring than peeking."

Her cheeks flushed at the memory. "You stripped without any warning. What was I supposed to do?"

"Turn away?"

"You caught me by surprise, and I slipped into a shocked state."

"Stunned is more like it. I saw you drooling."

Oh, she'd totally been drooling. It was like watching a Michelangelo sculpture come to life. And then, there was water sliding over his biceps and pecs, over his shorts to his glorious thighs. Yeah. There'd been drooling. She'd only caught herself when he'd hooked his thumbs into his boxer shorts and cocked an eyebrow at her. Then she'd turned away.

Why had she turned away?

It wasn't like she hadn't seen it all before.

"Because you aren't going there with Ryan, remember?" she muttered to herself.

"You say something?" Ryan called.

"Talking to myself, don't worry about it." Trying to talk some sense into herself, more like. A few kisses shared during a stressful situation didn't make for a relationship. Not that she wanted a relationship. The thought of sitting at home waiting to find out if Ryan had made it back from a mission in one piece was stomach churning. She knew herself, and there was no way she could cope with that.

Yes, a relationship was definitely out. Even if he wanted one, which he'd made no indication that he did. But surely there was nothing wrong in getting a little solace? Some hot, sweaty, mind-blowing solace?

She rolled her eyes at herself. No matter how politely she put it, she was just looking for an excuse to jump the man. Any excuse. Hell, at this point, "I tripped and fell onto your penis" would work fine.

"Nearly ready for round two," Ryan called, making her jump.

"Round two?" Was that a squeak in her voice?

"Mushrooms." He held up her handbag, which he'd been using to collect his latest harvest. "We can eat again whenever you're ready."

"Yes, of course, mushrooms." Which was not where her dirty mind had gone. "I'll just be a couple of minutes."

It didn't worry her that he'd starve while he waited. Not

only had they already munched their way through his first collection, but he'd been snacking while he picked the new ones—even though she'd warned him to wash them first.

She sighed. If he could eat a fried spider, he'd survive a grubby mushroom.

Slipping her underwear off without removing her blouse or skirt, a trick all women learned early, Sarah washed out her bra and panties, wrung them tight, and hooked them on a nearby rock to dry.

"I'm getting washed now. Don't turn round," she told him.

"That hardly seems fair," he protested. But he was in the far corner of the room, and if she could barely see him, he could barely see her.

They'd left the phone balanced on some dirt halfway between them, and the glow was just enough to enable her to see what she was doing. Sarah stripped off the rest of her clothes and made fast work of washing her body as thoroughly as she was able. When she was done, she struggled into the damp underwear and then rinsed her blouse and skirt. Or what was left of them. Basically they were rags now.

She hesitated, considering putting her clothes back on, but Ryan was only in his boxers, and her underwear covered more than most bikinis. Plus, it wasn't like she was shy. People just assumed that her reserved nature equated with shyness. But deep inside, where no one could see, Sarah had a wild side. One that was whispering to her to remove her underwear, saunter over to Ryan, and see what happened.

She kept it on.

Her wild side had gotten her into trouble before, and Sarah was wise to it.

"Hey," Ryan called. "Look what I found."

She glanced across the room, but all she saw was him holding up something large for her to see.

"What is it?"

"Hessian sacks. A pile of them. I think they used them to pack the mushrooms. We can make a pallet with them, which means we won't have to sleep on the stone."

He was so pleased with himself that it made her smile. "That's great."

Obviously feeling like the great provider, Ryan sauntered over to her and stopped dead when he saw what she was wearing.

"Whoa, that's the ugliest underwear I've ever seen. And that's saying something because my friend Julia once wore granny knickers with the days of the week printed on her backside."

Where to start? "First, my underwear isn't ugly. It's plain. Which is fine for work. You know, the place where I was before someone abducted me." She looked down at the beige cotton bra and panties set. There was nothing wrong with it. "Second, why were you looking at your friend's knickers?"

And why did she feel a flush of jealousy about it too?

"It's a whole story, involving a stolen mummy and a very high fence. I'll fill you in later." His eyes slid down her body and lingered at her little pooch of a belly. "Is that a tattoo? You rebel. What is it?"

She was about to remind him that he already knew, when she remembered he didn't. "None of your business," she said instead.

"Oh, I think it is." He grinned as he kept coming toward her. "It's got to be something really meaningful. Is it some weird statistic?"

She slapped a hand over the tattoo—another consequence of letting her wild inner child free.

"Come on, Stats, let me see." He pouted. "I'll beg if you like."

Oh, he was the devil. It was on the tip of her tongue to offer a quid pro quo situation. She'd show him her tattoos—because yes, she had more than one—if he took off his boxers. Not so she could perv at him, you understand, but so things would be fair. She was *all* about the fairness.

"It's a quote, isn't it?" he said, taking a step toward her. "I bet it's some cr—"

Suddenly, he fell to his knees. His hands clasped his head, and the bag with the mushrooms spilled onto the floor, its contents rolling across the rock.

"Ryan!" Sarah crouched down beside him. Hesitant about whether she should touch him or not. "Are you okay? What's happening?"

He groaned, a horrible pain-filled whine.

"Ryan, speak to me. I don't know what's happening. Please, you're scaring me." She gently put her hands on his shoulders.

"Migraine," he gritted out.

Sarah had seen migraines before, she'd even experienced one herself, but they'd looked nothing like this. He was in agony, doubled over and groaning as he held his head. Did migraines come on that suddenly?

"What do you need? Wait, I have some aspirin."

He didn't reply. All he did was rock back and forth. She'd seen Ryan hurt, and he'd just shrugged it off, too tough to let a small thing like an injury stop him. Yet there he was, huddled on the floor, unable to answer because of the pain in his head.

Sarah rushed over to the spot where they'd stored the

contents of her bag. Grabbing the aspirin and one of the water bottles, she hurried back to Ryan.

"Take this. It'll help." It had to. It was all there was to give him.

She held out the aspirin, but he didn't take it. His eyes were closed, and he didn't seem to hear her.

"These are painkillers," she said gently as she placed the pills against his lips. "Open your mouth, Ryan." Once he'd taken them, she held the water to his mouth and gently encouraged him to swallow.

Helpless to do anything else, she could only watch as he slumped to his side and curled into a ball on the ground. His hands never left his head, and every now and then, he let out a low, pain-filled moan.

Sarah was scared. Had he hit his head when he was under the water and not told her? What if he'd suffered another concussion? His neurologist was worried about that happening again, although Ryan didn't seem that bothered. Or maybe, he just didn't *want* to be that bothered about it.

Hurrying across the room, Sarah retrieved some of the hessian sacks he'd found earlier. Quickly, she made a pallet to lie on to keep the cold stone from seeping into them. It took a few trips to retrieve the sacks, and a hefty amount of effort to maneuver Ryan onto them, but she managed it.

Once he was settled, she wet her blouse and placed it on his forehead. Then taking the phone, she sat down beside him. Gently, she raised his head to rest it on her thigh.

She stroked his shoulder, more to reassure herself than him, as he clearly wasn't aware of anything now. He was locked inside his head, consumed with pain.

"It's going to be okay," Sarah said. "You'll get through

this, I promise. You aren't alone, I'm here and I'll take care of you."

Knowing from experience that light aggravated a migraine, Sarah turned off the phone. Immediately, they were plunged into absolute darkness. But this time, she was more afraid *for* Ryan than she was of anything she couldn't see.

As the silence settled in around them, she stroked his hair, adjusting the damp blouse to keep his forehead cool. There was nothing else she could do, except wait.

Ryan woke up thirsty. There was a dull throbbing pain in his head, along with an awareness that time had passed. How much time, he didn't know. Smooth, warm skin was a pillow beneath his cheek, and he let out a breath knowing Sarah was there. He vaguely remembered her resting his head on her thigh. Now it seemed that, sometime during the night, she'd shuffled down to lie flat, and his head was now on her belly.

Her fingers threaded through his hair, as though she'd been stroking it in an attempt to soothe his bruised brain. It was sweet, but pointless. When the pain hit him, there was nothing anyone could do to help—short of knocking him unconscious.

"Ryan," she said, her voice husky from sleep. "You're awake. How do you feel?"

"Better. I could use a drink."

"I've got some water here." She shifted, and he felt a bottle being pressed into his hand. "Can you cope with the light on?"

"Not yet," he said honestly.

As he drank, he took stock of how he felt. His head was throbbing, his eyeballs felt firm and swollen, his right arm felt weak, and his thinking seemed sluggish. There were still some sparkling lights going off randomly in the corner of his vision. Lights that were purely in his head. Thankfully, he didn't feel nauseous. Probably because the only thing in his stomach was raw mushroom.

"Have you always had migraines?" Sarah said as she gently brushed at his hair with her fingers.

Ryan lay his head back on her soft belly. "They started after the coma."

The ache in his head seemed to ease as Sarah carefully massaged his scalp. "Do they happen often?"

"Depends on how you define often." He deflected the question.

Obviously not enough. "How do *you* define often?"

He curled his hand around her thigh. She was warm, and smooth, and felt like heaven. "Couple of times a month."

He felt her stiffen in reaction but then quickly relax again. "Does something trigger them?"

"Like all the bright lights we've not been experiencing?" He traced the curve of her inner thigh with his fingertips.

Her breath quickened. "No. Would hitting your head again set them off?"

"I haven't hit my head recently." His fingers smoothed down to her knee and back up her thigh. "It's no big deal, Stats. It's just another weird side effect of being shot in the head."

"Like the spasms in your hand that you think I don't notice?"

Oh, she was tricky. If his dull, thudding brain wasn't so preoccupied by the curve of her leg, he'd probably put more effort into being a whole lot more careful around her.

"The headaches are getting better," he said as he slid his hand, very slowly, up the inside of her thigh. "I don't have as many episodes as I did when I first woke up."

She sucked in a breath as his knuckles brushed the V between her legs, skimming over the cotton of her underpants. He stilled, his heart loud in his ears, waiting for her to object to his touch. She didn't, and with a smile, he teased her by sliding his hand back down her thigh.

"Does the neurologist think these episodes will disappear entirely?" She sounded a little breathless. It suited her.

"She says there's no way to know for sure. They could vanish one day, or the time between them could increase until they just don't happen anymore, or this could be as good as it gets."

"Do they always come on that fast and so brutally?"

"Yeah."

But he didn't want to think about how a headache could render him paralyzed and helpless. He'd buried that crap months ago, swearing he'd only dig it out when forced. Because the implications of what the headaches and the spasms might mean were too stark to consider.

Instead, he'd concentrated on things he could control— like getting fitter, re-sitting his certifications, and resuming his place with his team. Everything else would sort itself out once life was back to normal.

And he definitely, absolutely, did *not* want to think about what his neurologist had told him. That if the headaches continued, one day they could trigger a stroke that would render his right arm useless.

No, he had much better things to think about. Like the soft, squirming woman beneath him. Ignoring the brutal hardness of his cock, which demanded immediate attention, Ryan stroked back up Sarah's inner thigh. Her fingers tightened in his hair as his knuckles brushed her warm sex through her panties.

"Ryan, I don't think this is a good idea," she said hoarsely.

"I promise you won't regret it," he teased, using the universal argument of most teenage boys.

She barked out a laugh before moaning when he pressed a little firmer against her ugly cotton underwear. "Oh, I know," she said. "I'm talking about your sore head. I don't think you're in any condition—"

"This is exactly what I need," he said. "Is it what you need, Sarah?"

"Oh sweet heavens, yes." She widened her legs, making him grin with delight. "But I want to be on top this time."

"I've got something else in mind first." With a deep chuckle, Ryan hooked his finger inside the leg of her panties.

CHAPTER TWENTY

"What?" Sarah gasped the word as his fingers lazily toyed with the hair covering her mound. "What's your idea?"

"You never told me about the first time we had sex." A finger dipped lower, skimming her clit, making her moan. "I wouldn't want to repeat myself and bore you, so I think you should describe it to me. In detail."

"Wait, you want me to what?" Her hand tightened in his hair before she remembered his lingering headache and gently soothed any sting she'd caused.

"It's simple." The devil traced the lips of her sex in a soft, barely-there caress. "You talk, I touch. You stop talking, I stop touching."

"This is evil." Or genius. She wasn't sure which.

She was swollen and wet, and definitely wanted more than just the hope of release. But this? Could she do it?

"Are you shy?" He teased those wicked fingers of his, unrelenting in their slow caress of everything except where she needed it most.

"It's..." Damn it, he was making it too hard to think straight. "It's private. Talking about it feels too intimate."

"Baby, my hand is in your underwear. You don't get much more intimate than that." He was grinning, she could hear it.

The devil was having fun at her expense.

"Plus," he said. "It isn't like I wasn't there experiencing it with you. Isn't that right, Stats?" One finger trailed between the lips of her sex, making her arch up into his touch.

"More," she gasped, clutching the bare muscle of his shoulder.

"You want more, you know what to do." He traced the crease at the top of her thigh.

"Fine." *Demon man!* "We were in my bed—"

"Nope." He smacked her sex, a small teasing pain that sent sparkles rushing through her brain. "Start from the beginning. I want to hear the buildup. I want to hear about how crazy and desperate you were to get me inside you."

Sweet heavens, she was going to come just from listening to him talk.

"There were small touches all evening," she said, her mind playing the video of their one night together as Ryan caressed closer to the hard little nub that needed him so. "Hot glances across the dinner table, brushing into each other as we walked beside the Thames."

"You're doing great," he purred as a finger dipped into her wetness. "And you smell like a bakery, early in the morning, when the heat wafts out into the cold, dark air."

A giggle escaped. Of course, she smelled like food to him.

"Hey." He tugged at the hair over her mound. "No laughter. I'm being poetic here."

"You're being hungry there," she corrected.

"Now we're talking. Once you're done telling me all

about that night, I'll have to get myself a snack. I bet you're delicious. My mouth is watering just breathing you in." He paused with his gentle teasing. "I don't hear you talking."

Head spinning, Sarah tried to concentrate on what she was telling him. "You held my hand as we walked along the South Bank. And then you spotted a roller disco and talked me into it. We skated and danced in the darkness. The music so loud we could barely hear ourselves think. That's when the touching became more sensual. We held each other as we danced, caressed as we moved. It felt like the beginnings of making love."

"Did I kiss you?" A fingertip started a gentle massage of her painfully aroused clit.

Heaven.

She was drifting on a cloud of pure, delicious sensation.

"Yes." She was breathless from need. "Soft, teasing kisses."

"Did my hands wander?" His rhythmic touch was driving her wild.

"Not to anywhere X-rated. You touched everywhere else though, leaving sparks behind."

"I bet I was so hard, I ached. Did you notice?"

"Yes," she gasped. "I wanted to rub myself against you right there at the rink."

"What happened next?" His finger kept up the painfully slow circles on her clit. Just enough of a touch to drive her out of her mind, but not enough to send her over into oblivion.

"We made it back to my place, with a lot of touching and kissing along the way."

"Did I jump you as soon as we were inside your house?"

"No, I jumped you." She let out a long sigh as she wriggled against him. "More, Ryan, please," she begged.

"Shh, we're just getting to the good part. Be patient, baby, you'll get there. How did you jump me?"

"I didn't even pretend to be sociable or polite. I just took your hand and dragged you straight upstairs to the bedroom, where I pressed you up against the wall and slid my hands under your shirt and over your abs. I kissed and licked and sucked every exposed piece of skin that I could reach while I pushed your shirt over your head."

"Fuck, I like that." His touch lost its rhythm for a second, but when it started again, the pressure increased.

It was glorious.

Sarah was lost between worlds now. Caught in the sensations he made her body feel, there in the darkness of the cavern, while her mind replayed every single touch from their night together.

"Our mouths met. Hot, heavy kisses that were almost violently desperate. I was losing myself, but you could still think and you took over."

"What did I do?" He sounded almost as breathless as she felt.

Her fingers curled into his shoulder, absorbing his strength, wanting to rub against it and roll in it until she was high from the feel of him.

His hand suddenly withdrew from her panties.

"No," she wailed.

"No talking, no touching." He sounded like the declaration caused him pain.

His breath was warm against her stomach, his facial hair a new sensation against her skin.

"You lifted me." She fought to get her thoughts under control, to relay them to Ryan. "You just picked me up like I weighed nothing."

"That's the reason I work out," he said as his hand

slipped back into her underwear and his fingers unerringly found her little pleasure spot. "Ladies like the muscle."

She playfully slapped his shoulder, and he flexed to prove his point. Oh, yeah, she loved his muscles.

"I wrapped my arms and legs around you and held on tight," she said as he continued to touch her.

Her breath was coming in pants now, and it was so hard to think straight. There were stars in her head. Whole galaxies begging her to come explore. But she forced herself to stay tethered to planet Earth so she could keep telling Ryan what he wanted to hear.

"You pressed me up against the wall and kissed me until I was delirious. Clothes came off—I'm not exactly sure how. I remember your hands on my breasts, massaging, teasing, tugging at my nipples until I thought I'd go insane from wanting you."

He dipped a finger deep into her wet heat, making her body arch. "Did you beg?"

"Yes," she gasped as he slowly moved his finger in and out, mimicking what she'd wanted so badly, what she'd been dreaming about for over a year. Ryan. Inside her. Filling her up.

"And then what?" He slid back to her clit.

The stars were rushing at her now. Swirling planets in her mind. "I felt the soft comforter on my bed at my back. It was cool compared to your hard, hot chest. Your mouth was at my throat, my fingers in your hair. I love your hair. It was so thick, but short and hard to grab, which somehow added to the excitement."

His finger circled her quicker. She wanted more. She wanted all of him.

"Your mouth was on my breast, kissing, teasing, suckling, while your hand wandered lower, like now." She sucked in a breath, feeling light-headed. "Please, Ryan, please take me over."

"Not yet," he said. "What happened then? I want to hear it all."

"You said you couldn't wait, that you'd go slower next time. That you'd taste me and make me beg. But right then, you were going to go crazy if you weren't inside of me."

"I feel the same way now, baby," he said, his voice strained with need.

"The look in your eyes," she said, remembering, seeing it all over again in her mind. "So, dark and intense, but soft and...mine. Your arms strained as you balanced above me. I couldn't stop myself from touching you. I was drunk from it. Your arms, your chest. I raised my head and bit your pec before soothing it with my tongue."

"Did I spread your legs wide?"

"So wide." The room was spinning. The stars were flying around her. She lost track of what she was saying. "I felt you. Wide, hard yet soft, pressing into me, and I wanted you there. I wanted all of you."

His finger pressed on her clit, making her moan echo through the room.

"You took forever to seat yourself inside me."

"How did it feel?" His voice was a croak.

"So, so good. Endless. You filled me up. I could feel every inch of you. And my muscles tightened, holding you inside me. Keeping you there. I didn't want it to end. I didn't want you to leave me. I felt connected. To you."

"Like I belonged there?"

"Yes," she moaned, her fingers digging into his flesh as his touch drove her higher.

"You moved," she gasped. "Rocking into me. Explosions

in my head. So many explosions. I could taste you. Feel you. Surrounded by you. Only you."

"Fuck," Ryan said. "I can't take anymore. I need to be inside you, but first, you need to fly for me, Stats. You hear me? It's time to fly."

He pressed her clit, rubbing deftly, and the universe inside her head exploded. Planets were formed. New stars in a dark night. Just for them.

Panting for air, Sarah slowly floated back down to earth and gradually became aware that Ryan had shifted position. He was no longer lying beside her; now he knelt at her feet as he slid her underpants down her legs.

She heard his rapid breathing, felt his shaking hands, and knew his desperation.

Through the lifting fog of her mind, she heard him mutter.

Only, it wasn't coming from Ryan, but from further away.

She stilled, adrenaline making her senses acute. There it was again. A voice. A voice that wasn't Ryan's.

She jerked, sitting up and grabbing his hand to still him. "Did you hear that?"

"I heard and loved all of it." Ryan leaned in, nuzzling her cheek and neck.

"No, not that. The voice." Sarah grabbed two handfuls of his hair and raised his head. "I hear voices."

"Stats, I'm in the middle of something here. Let go of the hair."

"I'm serious. Listen."

"Baby, if you've changed your mind, that's fine, just tell me. I mean, I'll be in agony, but I can wait."

"Will you shut up and listen? I hear people talking."

"Other people?" He asked, proving once and for all that men really did switch off their brains during sex. "Not us?"

"No! Listen."

Their sense of hearing more acute in the darkness, they listened.

And heard murmuring.

Ryan stiffened and Sarah released his hair. They froze, listening.

There it was again.

"Talk about crappy timing." Ryan was on his feet in an instant. Light from his phone came on straight after but quickly dimmed as the battery died. "Where's the iPad?" he said, before finding it and switching it on.

Sarah blinked against the sudden brighter light, noticing that Ryan had already pulled on his jeans and was working on his shoes.

"Get dressed, Stats, but keep it quiet. I need to find where the noise is coming from."

She grabbed her bra and did that fasten at the front then swivel it to the back routine to get it on. Meanwhile, Ryan took the iPad and went searching for the source of the voices.

Sarah kept her eyes on him as he headed straight for the far wall.

"Hello?" Ryan called. "We need help."

Dressed, Sarah tossed their belongings into her handbag before hurrying over to his side.

The voices were louder now but still too far away to make out words.

"Hello," Ryan shouted. "We're trapped and need help."

There was a moment of silence before someone shouted back. "Hello?"

Sarah's knees went weak, and she slid to a crouch beside Ryan.

"There!" He pointed to a hole, high up in the corner of the room. "It's coming from there."

"We're stuck in an old mushroom farm," Ryan called to the stranger. "Is there a way out from your end?"

"But of course." A very dim light appeared through the hole, probably from their flashlight. "You must come through this tunnel. Can you see it?"

"Yes. Please, stay there. We need help finding our way out of here," Ryan said.

"We will stay," the voice replied. It sounded male, young, and very formal.

"Where are we?" Ryan called again. "We woke up in here."

There was a murmur of conversation before the voice replied. "My English is not so good. I am unsure we understand you. These are the catacombs."

"Catacombs?" Sarah said, staring at Ryan.

He lifted his voice again. "What catacombs?" he shouted. "And which city?"

CHAPTER TWENTY-ONE

Benson Security Basement
London

Rachel was in testosterone hell.

"Bloody Americans and their bloody guns," Callum exploded when he saw the state Prentice was in. "Couldn't you have knocked him out?" He pointed through the two-way mirror to the man in Benson Security's interrogation room. "I just had that floor redone, and he's dripping blood all over the new carpet."

Rachel'd had enough. "Boys, focus. Ryan first, carpet second. For the love of Prada, go in there and beat some information out of that man before I die of boredom."

"Aye." Callum scowled at her. "Because stopping you from being bored is my first priority."

Her husband smothered a grin while the other three men resumed their stupid argument. Obviously, it was up to the women to take control and sort things out. As usual.

With a look of disdain towards the Neanderthals, Rachel walked out of the viewing room and into the interrogation room. Flicking the lock behind her so the boys wouldn't follow and continue to annoy her.

The plain white box of a room contained only a table and two chairs, one of which was bolted to the floor, and a two-way mirror—mirror side showing. Rachel eyed the new blue carpet. It was ugly. Callum should have saved his money and left the old blood-stained one alone.

"Good morning," she said to the glowering man who was cuffed, hands and feet, to the bolted chair. "My name is Rachel Ford-Talbot, and I'll be your interrogator today."

She dusted off the chair on the opposite side of the table from Prentice before sitting. After placing her Chanel handbag on the floor beside her, she crossed her legs and assessed the mercenary. He was made up of muscle and scars, with a touch of intelligence thrown into the mix. Thug for hire. How cliché.

"Rachel," Callum's voice came over the intercom. "Get your backside out of there!"

"Please forgive my associate," Rachel said. "He obviously hasn't had his medication today. Now, tell me who paid you to kidnap Ryan Granger and where did you take him?"

She glanced at her phone; there was an urgent email from her brother, who was head of research and development at their pharmaceutical company. She held up a finger. "Hold that thought. I have to deal with this email first."

As she typed, Prentice looked around the room. "Is this a fucking joke?" he snarled. "Candid fucking camera? Am I on some stupid-ass TV show?"

"Not with that language, you aren't," Rachel said

absently as she focused on the email. "Please be quiet, this is important."

The door rattled and someone thumped it. "Rachel, open the door," her husband called, sounding far more reasonable than he probably felt. Harvard was very good at sounding reasonable. He seemed to do it quite a bit around her.

"Done." Rachel rested her phone on her knee as she turned her attention to their prisoner. "You were saying?"

"Fuck all," he spat. "That's what I was saying."

Rachel picked a piece of lint off the skirt of her black Prada suit as her husband thumped the door again.

"This isnae funny, Rachel," Callum said, obviously through a clenched jaw. "You're slowing us down."

"Honestly." She rolled her eyes. "He's so dramatic. Of course, he has reason to be concerned. After all, I'm only a part-time interrogator." She didn't hide her disdain as she looked at the man. "Normally, I run a pharmaceutical company."

"Bitch, I don't give a fuck," Prentice growled.

"You should, you know. Because, as CEO of the company, I have access to a lot of interesting drugs. Ones that couldn't be traced back to me, if I happened to use them."

His eyes shifted left then right, a hint that she was making him nervous. "What the hell do I care what drugs you take?"

"Oh, they wouldn't be for me. They would be for you. In fact, that email I just sent." She waggled her phone, with its black case that looked so good against her dark red nails. "It was to order some drugs for you. My assistant is organizing them for me now."

"You're full of shit. There're no drugs, and you ain't

gonna use them on me. People like you follow the rules." He snorted. "Send in the men. You're wasting my time, bitch."

"You really do have a potty mouth, don't you? And a disdain for showering."

"Fuck off."

"I will, once we're done. Tell me, Mr. Prentice, have you heard of something called chemical castration?"

For the first time since she'd entered the room, he looked genuinely wary. "What the fuck are you talking about?"

Rachel curled her lip at his language. Honestly, if this was what an American education got you these days, then it was no wonder the country was going downhill.

"It's really quite fascinating as a medical procedure," Rachel said, appearing bored. "Some people advocate the long-term approach, where an inmate—because we're talking sexual offenders here—is forced to take pills or is given regular injections to achieve castration. I favor the speedier approach. One injection, straight to the testicles."

He turned gray. "You're a fucking psycho, bitch."

"True." She inclined her head. "Do you know what chemical castration does? It eliminates any sexual desire you might have for whatever hairy creature of the night you mate with. It also vastly reduces the testosterone zipping through your veins, which will turn you into a frightened little kitten who cries when people threaten him." She looked thoughtful. "I don't imagine that would be helpful in your line of work."

"You wouldn't," he sneered. "You think I'm gonna fall for this shit, you're mistaken."

"Look around you," Rachel said. "Nobody knows you're here. I can do whatever I want, secure in the knowledge that you'd never go to the police, would you, Mr. Prentice?"

"I'd fucking kill you, bitch."

"Not if you were crying like a baby and too scared to leave your house. I bet the other mercenaries wouldn't even play with you anymore. You'd be the laughing stock of your community and hardly a threat to anyone. Let alone a woman who's surrounded with the best security money can buy. I'm afraid your threats are as lame as your sexual prowess would be. Shame."

Rachel wasn't impressed by the stunned look of horror on his face. He wasn't nearly as scared as he should be. Because she wasn't bluffing. She'd use any drug her company produced on the man to make him talk—even if it landed her in jail. Not that it would, of course. She had money and upper-class connections that wouldn't allow such a thing to happen.

"But I'm forgetting the best part," Rachel told the worm staring at her as she leaned forward, closing the distance between them as if imparting a secret. "The part I personally enjoy the most is that the injection causes testicular atrophy." She held up a hand to forestall any questions, not that he seemed eager to talk. "I realize you probably don't know what that word means, so I'll explain. Your testicles, or balls if you prefer, will shrivel and die on your body. They'll become a black mass of dead, rotting flesh under your flaccid, useless penis." She sat back in her seat and folded her arms as she smiled. "Isn't modern medicine wonderful?"

He gaped at her as sweat broke out on his brow. Strangely, he seemed to have run out of things to say.

Thankfully, there wouldn't be an awkward silence because Rachel wasn't finished. "Of course, you won't have the courage to seek medical help for the issue, but it wouldn't do you any good anyway. The process is irreversible." Her phone chimed, and she beamed as she checked the screen. "Excellent, the drugs are on their way."

She picked up her bag and stood, smoothing her skirt as she faced him. "I won't be here for this part. I don't have any desire to see your sexual organ. The men will hold you down and perform the injection. I hear it's painful but, in my opinion, worth it. Now, I really must go. I have a facial at ten."

As she strode toward the door, Prentice shouted. "Fuck it, I'll talk."

Rachel smiled over her shoulder. It was her shark smile. The one that told people she was just about to eat them. "Oh, I'm sorry. I no longer care if you'll cooperate. You're a vile, uncouth bull of a man who confuses muscle for intelligence. And, you aren't the only person who can tell us where Ryan is. You wasted your opportunity to talk. Now, I only want to see you suffer."

With that, she unlocked the door and stepped outside, closing it quietly behind her.

Five horrified men stood in front of her, staring at her with a mixture of fear and revulsion. Beside them was a bouncing Elle and a grinning Megan.

"That was awesome," Elle said. "Do it again!"

"I would have just used an elastic band," Megan said. "No circulation. No penis."

"Aye," Callum said with a grimace, "we remember."

"Is that true?" Dimitri looked shaken. "About the one injection to ruin a man's life?"

"Don't be an idiot," Rachel said and watched as the men's shoulders slumped in relief. "It takes a *few* injections to cause atrophy. Although, I'm sure you could up the dose to achieve the same result faster."

"I'm going to be sick," Dimitri muttered.

"Then my work here is done," Rachel said. "I have some phone calls to make. Callum, I'm using your office." She slung her bag over the crook of her elbow. "Let me know what he tells you."

"I don't think I can go in there," Joe said. "I might vomit."

"I'll do it." Megan narrowed her eyes at the door.

"No," all the men shouted together.

"I'll go," David said. As he passed Rachel, he inclined his head in a show of respect. "You ever want to change careers, let me know. There are governments who would kill to have you."

"I know." Rachel sailed past the team and headed for the stairs out of the basement. "Harvard?"

"Yeah, Princess?" he said, a smile on his face.

"Don't get blood on that suit," she told him. "I'd hate to have to throw it out."

"Yes, ma'am," he said.

Callum's office was on the ground floor, and Rachel nodded at his wife, Isobel, as she passed. Isobel, as usual, was royally screwing up her job as receptionist. This time by tormenting a courier with her complete lack of organization.

With a sigh, Rachel let herself into Callum's office and brought out her phone. If David didn't get the information they needed, she fully intended to inject Prentice's tiny little balls all by herself. Harvard would hold him down for her. He understood her need to make predators suffer.

She was on her third call when the door opened and Harvard strode in.

"We know where he is," he said. "You need to pack a bag, and the team need to borrow the plane."

Rachel switched off her phone. "If they blow this one up, I will make them pay." In more ways than one.

"I already told them." He held the door open for her.

As she passed her husband, she stood on tiptoe to press a kiss to his lush mouth. "And that's why you're the only person on this planet that I can tolerate for more than five minutes at a time," she said before sailing through the door.

"You're such a liar," he drawled.

"You wish." She glanced at him over her shoulder. "Where exactly are we going?"

CHAPTER TWENTY-TWO

"Which city are we under?" Ryan asked again when there was just confused silence from the other side of the tunnel.

"We are under Paris, of course," the voice replied. "Are you ill? Injured? Have too much wine?"

There was laughter from the strangers, making Sarah wonder exactly how old they were.

"We're in Paris," she said to Ryan, as her brain worked a mile a minute trying to make sense of it all. "How did we even get here without passports?"

"Yeah, let's worry about that part later," Ryan said to her, before calling through the hole again. "We're coming through."

"We will be here," was the reply.

"Come on, Stats, we're getting out of here. I'll lift you up, then climb in behind you. We're crawling out."

Oh, she didn't like the sound of that at all. But as with everything else that'd happened since they'd entered the vast network of caves and tunnels under Paris, it seemed she didn't have a choice.

"I'll take the bag," she said. "The straps are long

enough to hook over my shoulder. And it would be best if you kept your hands free in case there's trouble on the other side."

"That's my girl." He stroked her cheek and looked like he wanted to kiss her all over again.

"We need to hurry," she said. "In case our guides change their minds."

"Yeah. Worst timing in the world." Ryan clasped his hands to make a foothold for her. "Leave the bag. I'll hand it up to you. Get yourself in there first."

Grasping his shoulders, she stepped into his hands and boosted herself up and into the hole in the wall. At least, she got most of her upper body into the small tunnel, but that was as far as she could pull herself.

"This is no use," she said. "I don't have any upper body strength, and I can't see anything to grab so I can pull myself in."

"Don't worry, I've got this." Large hands grasped her backside and shoved. There may have been some massaging in there too.

"There are other places you could have held," Sarah complained.

"Yeah, but if I'd touched *that* area, we'd be right back on the mat."

"Pervert," she muttered and heard him chuckle.

On hands and knees, her bum sticking out of the tunnel, Sarah waited for Ryan to hand her the bag and iPad.

"I'm liking this view, Stats." He slid her bag between her knees.

"Could you please get your mind off sex for five minutes?"

"I'll try, but I make no promises."

Sarah wriggled to get the bag over her shoulder. The

sharp edges of the rock above scraped her head, and there was barely any space on either side of her.

It was too narrow. Too low. Too confining. Every instinct she possessed was screaming at her to get out of the tunnel. It was only the desperation to escape the mine altogether that kept her in place. That, and the small voice in the back of her mind that kept repeating: *you aren't stuck, you have a light source, you can get out if needed, you aren't alone, you'll be fine...*

She had to be. This was their only way out.

"Hand me the tablet," she said as she reached back for it. Ryan placed it into her hand.

She wasn't sure if having a light made her feel better or worse, because now she could see how far the tunnel stretched in front of her, how low the roof was in places, and how thick the debris was that covered the floor.

"I'm not sure you'll fit in here," she told Ryan.

"I'll fit." Confidence poured from him.

It was clear that carrying the iPad would make it harder to crawl, which meant she had to find a way to keep her hands free. There was only one other option. She slid it into the front of her blouse, used her bra to keep it in place, and hoped it didn't fall out.

"The tunnel seems to go up," she said to Ryan as she crawled forward to make space for him. "It's going to be a tight squeeze though."

It helped that there was light coming from the distance, where the strangers waited for them. Sure, it was only a small glowing dot of light, but it was something.

There wasn't enough room for her to look over her shoulder to see how Ryan was doing getting into the passage. All she could do was listen to him scuff and grunt behind her, while she tried very hard not to think about the fact his face was practically plastered to her backside. It wasn't like he hadn't seen it before. But, of course, he couldn't remember the view.

"This is mortifying," she muttered.

"We'll be fine as long as you don't fart."

"Ryan!" Her cheeks were burning. "I can't believe you said that."

"What? It's funny. Now get going. Or do I need to headbutt you to get you to move?" He paused. "Head. Butt. Literally!" He dissolved into laughter.

"Boys." Sarah rolled her eyes as she started to crawl forward. "So easily amused."

The narrow passage was littered with stones and rocks, making each inch forward an exercise in pain. She took her time, brushing debris aside so she could place her hands and knees with the minimum of discomfort. But one glance ahead, and she knew that tactic wouldn't be possible for long.

"There's a lot of rubble further up the passage," she told Ryan. "Can you see anything? Are you getting any light back there?"

"A little. Don't worry about me though. There's no chance of me getting lost, seeing as there's only one way to go."

The tunnel became even tighter, and Sarah had to angle her body to get it through the narrow space. Thankfully, it widened up again on the other side.

"Be careful here, it's very narrow," she said. "There's a rock sticking out on our left that you need to shimmy past."

"Got it, thanks."

How he managed to get through that space, she couldn't guess. It'd been a squeeze for her.

The rubble was really piling up now. From the look of

the ceiling, parts of it had come down at some point, shedding small stones that were sharp if you happened to press on them. There were larger rocks too. Some strangely smooth and round. She picked up one to move it out of her way.

Instead of being heavy, as she'd expected, it was lightweight in her hand. Frowning, Sarah set it beside the wall and watched as it rolled toward her. That's when she realized it wasn't rock.

It was part of a skull.

"Hey," Ryan said as he bumped up against her. "Don't stop now."

Sarah couldn't speak. She dug the iPad out of her shirt and shone the light up ahead, sucking in a horrified breath at what she saw. It wasn't rocky debris that covered the passageway floor. It was bones. The rest of the tunnel was littered with them. Skulls. Femurs. Ribs. Tiny bones from a hand or foot. A broken pelvis wedged against the wall. Some were in pieces, most were intact.

All of them were human.

They were crawling through a grave.

"Stats," Ryan said. "What's the holdup?"

There was ringing in Sarah's ears. Her eyes remained glued to the sight in front of her as her brain tried, and failed, to make sense of it. The bones came in all sizes, from child to adult. All of them scattered. Discarded. Filling the space. There was no way around them. No way not to touch them. Their only option was to go over them.

To crawl, hand and foot, over human bones.

No.

Nonononononononononoo...

"Sarah, talk to me," Ryan ordered.

"Are you people coming?" a voice called from the other end of the tunnel.

"Yeah," Ryan answered. "We're in the tunnel. We're going as fast as we can." He lowered his voice, speaking only to her. "Why have you stopped? Tell me what's going on."

Sarah wet her lips. Knowing, somewhere in the back reaches of her mind, that she had to tell him what she was looking at. The words seemed stuck in her throat.

"Sarah?" he demanded.

"Bones," was all she managed to get out.

"Bones? What are we talking about, Stats? Describe what you're seeing."

She cleared her throat as her palms became clammy. "The tunnel. The whole tunnel. It's filled with bones. S-skulls. I-I touched a s-skull. There are other ones too. L-leg. Hand. There's h-hundreds. Thousands. There's no way past them."

She heard Ryan curse and knew what he was going to say. She was already shaking her head, even though he hadn't uttered a word yet.

"We have to go over them, Stats," he said gently but firmly.

"I can't do that."

It wasn't possible. These were human remains. She couldn't crawl over them. It was wrong. Sick. The stuff of nightmares. And she already had enough material stored for a lifetime of nightmares. She didn't need more.

"We don't have a choice, baby. It's the only way out of here." He sounded so reasonable, but he couldn't see what she was seeing.

So.

Many.

Bones.

She didn't move, and she didn't know what to say. All she could do was stare at the skulls peeking out from various places throughout the tunnel. Their hollow eyes staring at her in judgement.

"Are they old or new?" Ryan asked, but his words barely registered with her.

One skull was smaller than the rest...

No, she couldn't even think what that might mean.

Several were broken. Did that mean they were brittle? Would they crumble if she touched them?

She couldn't.

She wouldn't.

Just no.

Ryan's hand wrapped around her ankle. "Sarah, are the bones old?"

She blinked several times. "How do you tell?"

"I don't know. Do they look dusty, or broken, or do they look fresh?"

She shuddered. Fresh was not a word she wanted to use in their current situation. All it did was bring back memories of the bodies they'd found. And the horrible way she'd mistreated them by sending the rats in their direction.

No, she couldn't think of that. Not now.

"Sarah," Ryan pressed. "Are they dusty and old looking?"

"Does it matter? They were people. I can't crawl over them." She wanted out. She couldn't go forward, which meant she had to go back, but Ryan was blocking the way. "Let me out. I need to get out of here."

"No." His hand tightened on her leg. "We're in catacombs, remember? The Paris catacombs are full of old skeletons. Come on, Stats, surely you know the numbers."

There'd never been any reason to research the catacombs. She only knew about them from a passage in a novel she'd read once years earlier. That story hadn't mentioned the bones.

"Six million," Ryan said when she didn't answer him. "In the seventeen hundreds, they dug them up from overflowing graveyards and moved them down into the abandoned mines under the city. These are really old bones, Stats. They've been dead a very long time, and they've already been moved from their graves."

She wasn't sure how knowing that was supposed to help. "I can't. I just can't."

Crawl over bones? Hands touching them? Hearing them crunch and crumble beneath her? What if a sharp piece pierced her skin? Cut by a human bone. No. No, she wasn't doing this.

"I can't," she repeated. "I'm sorry. I can't." She started to back up, but Ryan wouldn't budge.

"Wait." Ryan stopped her. "Hold on a second." He raised his voice and called to the people waiting for them. "Is there another way out of the mushroom farm?"

"Non, Monsieur," came the reply.

"Baby, listen to me, okay?" Ryan soothed. "I can't carry you through this tunnel. There isn't the space. I can't do anything to take your mind off what we have to do. I'm helpless here, and I really wish I wasn't. I'd do anything to take this from you so you wouldn't have to do it, but I can't. This is the only way out. You have to keep going. Please, baby, you can do it. I know you can."

"I can go back and wait. You'll find another way to rescue me." She had complete faith that he would. Unlike her, Ryan could do anything.

"There isn't another way. This is it. It's just a few moments, and then it'll be over. You can do it."

It wouldn't be a few moments. It would be forever. She'd close her eyes and see this tunnel forever. She felt tears slide down her face and splash to the stone beneath her.

"One hand at a time," Ryan coaxed. "You don't have to hurry."

She sobbed. She couldn't stop herself.

"Please," she begged.

"Wait," Ryan said. "I have an idea. Stay here. Don't move an inch."

She heard him shuffle behind her, doing something, she didn't know what. For a second, she thought he'd backed up and left her alone in the tunnel.

"Ryan?" she called.

"I'm here," he said. "I went to get these."

He had left the tunnel and she'd missed her chance to return to the mushroom farm. That's why he hadn't told her what he was doing. Somehow, it felt like a betrayal.

"Reach back, Stats. I have something that will help." He pushed something up the tunnel toward her. "I picked up a couple of hessian sacks. You can put one down, crawl on it, then put the next one down to crawl on that. I'll hand them to you when you move off them. This way, you won't have to touch the bones."

She took the rough sack from him. "I'll still hear them crumble. Feel them give way under the sack."

"You aren't going to hear them because I'm going to be making noise. And you won't know what you're feeling through the sacks. It could be stones or rubble. You won't know for certain that it's bones."

She stared at the tunnel and saw only bones. But maybe, just maybe, she could convince herself that there were rocks and stones in there too.

"Okay." She sniffed as she spread the sack in front of her. "We'll try."

"You are amazing," he told her. Then the fool kissed her backside. "That was for encouragement."

She hiccupped a brittle half laugh. "Only you would think so."

To her surprise, having the sack cover the floor from wall to wall actually helped. Now, she just had to hope none of the sharper pieces would stab her through the hessian.

"I'm ready," she lied. "But if this doesn't work, you have to back up and let me out of this tunnel. Promise me."

"It'll work."

"Ryan," she pressed.

"I promise," he conceded. "I'm going to start making some noise now. Once you're on the sack, just pause and I'll hand the next one to you. You ready?"

"That depends. What kind of noise are we talking about here?" she asked worriedly.

At that, he started singing *Ninety-Nine Bottles of Beer on the Wall*. And singing was *not* his gift.

Laughing through tears, Sarah gingerly crawled onto the first sack. She felt the packed surface beneath it move with her weight, but all she could hear was Ryan's awful singing.

Okay. Okay, she could do this.

"One done," she yelled to be heard over his caterwauling.

"Good girl," he purred as he handed her the other sack.

Sarah decided they'd deal with him calling her that later. Right now, it took all her concentration to focus on placing the sack in front of her while blocking out Ryan's tuneless wail.

Slowly, she made her way onto the second sack, and keeping her eyes from what lay ahead, she waited for Ryan to pass her the other sack.

"You're doing great," he said. "If it'll make you feel better, you can sing with me."

With a hysterical laugh, Sarah crawled onward.

CHAPTER TWENTY-THREE

It turned out their rescuers were two teenage boys. One of whom couldn't keep his eyes off Sarah's breasts. Ryan wondered if the kid would still be able to ogle her with two black eyes.

"How far are we from an exit?" Ryan stepped in front of Sarah, blocking the little pervert's view.

"It is about a day from here," the boy Ryan *didn't* want to punch answered.

This boy was taller than his friend, with a scraggly, stretched look to him that either came from growing too fast, eating too little, or doing drugs. He'd given his name as Le Chat, the cat, which apparently was his graffiti tag. The smaller, pervier one was called La Fosse, the pit. It suited him.

When Ryan had followed Sarah out of the passageway and into the much wider and taller tunnel they now stood in, he'd found the boys writing their names in spray paint across the stone wall. Of course, they'd packed up pretty damn quick when they'd spotted Sarah.

He would have been worried about the looks she was

getting, but seeing as both kids barely came to his shoulder, and he could easily grab one in each hand and knock them together without even breaking a sweat, he figured she was safe.

"A day?" Sarah asked as she tried to step out from behind him.

He moved with her to keep her out of The Pit's sight.

"Oui, Madame," Le Chat said. "We are very far into the catacombs." He cast a furtive glance at his friend. "This is as deep as we go in this tunnel. You are lucky we came here today."

Oh, yeah, these two couldn't be trusted. Ryan wasn't sure if it was because they were both about sixteen years old or that they looked like they practically lived in the caves, with their ratty jeans and dirty faces, or the way one of them had eyes that kept straying to his woman. It could also be that sexual frustration was coloring his view of the world. But hey, they were to blame for that too.

"How long have you been down here?" Sarah asked the teens.

Le Chat glanced at his friend before answering. "A couple of days. We have a, how do you say it, burrow? A few hours from here."

"A hidden place we protect for ourselves," La Fosse added.

"A den." Sarah smiled at them, like they were children.

Oh, how naive she was. When Ryan was sixteen, he'd been far from a child. Mainly, he'd been an overgrown walking hormone with only two things on his mind—sex and food.

Actually, not much had changed.

His belly rumbled in agreement.

"Oui, a den. We can rest there." The Pit was looking at her chest again.

Ryan was done. "La Fosse. Your eyes stray to my woman's breasts one more time, and I'll remove them from your head."

"Ryan!" Sarah's jaw dropped.

The Pit looked like he might crap himself but nodded furiously. Good. They understood each other.

"What he means," Sarah said completely unnecessarily because Ryan had been pretty damn clear, "is that we're very grateful you waited for us and will show us the way out of here. Aren't we?" She elbowed his side.

"Sure." Ryan flashed a smile that was all teeth.

"So, which way now?" Sarah asked, stepping closer to him as she did so.

It was obvious that she was putting on a brave face for the teens. Ryan was glad she didn't try to fool him, too, because they were past stuff like that. Instead, she leaned her shaking body into him and let him support her.

The last tunnel had been tough on her. Hell, all of the tunnels had been. And as soon as they were out of there, he was booking them into the best hotel in Paris, running her a bubble bath—while he showered for about a week—and then he'd make love to his woman.

Possibly after a hearty meal. They needed their energy after all.

Le Chat, the least offensive of the boys, pointed behind him. "We go up," he said with a smile.

"Lead the way." Ryan jerked his chin to the tunnel. "Let's get out of here."

He made sure both boys were in front of them where he could keep an eye on them while still protecting Sarah. "Gimme the bag and iPad," he told her.

She didn't protest, just handed them over.

Ryan took her hand in his as they followed the teens. Sarah was moving slower than usual, so he matched his pace to hers and made sure the boys never got too far out of sight.

This tunnel was different from the ones they'd been in. The walls were made of old worn bricks, which were covered in colorful graffiti. There were the usual tags, but now and then they passed a genuine work of art. Although, he had to look twice at some of the subject matter: Satanic symbols and sex acts seemed to be popular, although so was Mickey Mouse.

Every now and then, they passed some discarded bones —all human—just lying against the walls. They were old, mostly broken, and had been left as litter in the passageways.

The Pit looked back over his shoulder and saw Sarah staring at a skull someone had tagged with their name using black marker pen.

"Macabre, non?" the teen said.

"I thought the bones were kept in the ossuary, but they seem to be everywhere," she said, meaning the place where bones had been arranged into sculptural shapes in order to make them neater and therefore more attractive to the tourists. They loved to walk under the sign welcoming them to the city of the dead before taking selfies with pillars made out of skulls or walls built from thousands of femurs. Sometimes Ryan didn't understand people.

"The bones are spread over all of the catacombs." La Fosse grinned, showing a missing tooth. "Most of the ones in the passage you came through were once in these tunnels. The artists moved them over the years to make space for their work." He waved a hand at a wall painted with the image of a horned man with a goat's legs.

"Is that what you're doing down here?" Sarah asked as she tiptoed past some smashed and broken ribs.

"Oui," Le Chat answered. "We have the desire to be famous. Like Banksy." He beamed back at them as La Fosse frowned.

"Not Banksy, he is a sellout." He spat on the floor in disgust. "We will be true graffiti artists. We have no need for galleries. The world is where we show our art."

"Do you want to see one of our works?" Le Chat asked eagerly.

Of course, Sarah was much too polite to say no. "I'd love to."

Ryan bugged his eyes out at her, but she didn't pay any attention.

"Here," Le Chat said, waving his arm toward a painting on the right. "We have done this."

Sarah turned pink when she saw it was a naked woman with massive breasts, surrounded by black cats. At least, Ryan thought they were cats. It was hard to tell. The only thing that was really clear was the breasts. And there was no need to guess who'd painted those.

"Oh, that's..." Sarah seemed a little lost for words. She cleared her throat. "You have a lot of skill. I'm sure you'll be very famous."

The pair elbowed each other, grinning widely.

"We paint witches," Le Chat said. "Because we are la féministe."

"Witches have the women power," La Fosse added, as though that cleared everything up.

"She's a witch?" Sarah sounded a little strangled.

"See?" Le Chat pointed at a mark on the woman's belly. "She has the pentagram. And of course, the cats."

"I see," Sarah muttered. Although, how she saw anything beyond breasts the size of beach balls, Ryan didn't know. "Thank you for showing me your art. Should we carry on now?"

The teens didn't move. "You want a photo with our painting and the artists?"

"I, uh, wish we could..." She turned to him, apparently out of reasons why they couldn't.

"Don't have enough battery, kids." He held up the iPad. "Once this runs out, we're in the dark."

"A pity." Le Chat gave a very Gallic shrug, making Ryan wonder if the French had the move wired into their genetics.

They didn't say much after that, just concentrated on walking through the tunnel, which seemed to gather filth as they went. There was a used condom beside some pieces of bone, beer bottles, cigarette ends, and junk food wrappers. Ryan had to wonder why, if the artists had managed to clear out the bones, they couldn't pick up after themselves too.

When the tunnel was wide enough, he wrapped an arm around Sarah and let her lean on him. It was clear she was exhausted and running on fumes. They'd been underground for days, with only two cereal bars and some raw mushrooms to keep them going.

"Do you have anything to eat?" Ryan asked the boys.

"Oui." Le Chat dug into his backpack and produced a paper bag with the word pâtisserie stamped on it. "Please, eat." He handed it to Ryan.

Peeking inside, Ryan found two bashed, but edible, pains au chocolat. Instantly, he was drooling.

"How much can we have?" he had to ask.

Le Chat shrugged. "All of it."

"Thanks," Ryan said, meaning it.

Taking out the larger of the two chocolate-filled pastries, he handed it to Sarah. "Time to top up your energy, Stats."

She smiled weakly before nibbling on the pastry. Ryan didn't like the limp she'd developed since they got out of the bone-filled passage. Her leather shoes had become stiff after being in the water and were obviously rubbing against her feet. The Band-Aids she'd kept in her bag were long gone, the adhesive ruined by the same water that'd turned her shoes into torture devices. But she couldn't walk like this. More to the point, he wouldn't let her.

"Wait a minute," he said to the boys before turning to Sarah. "Let's have a look at your feet."

She held up a hand in protest. "They're fine."

"Then you won't mind showing them to me."

With a sigh, Sarah steadied herself by putting a hand on the wall beside her and stepped out of her shoes—with a wince. There was a burst and bloody blister on one heel, and red raw toes on both feet.

"You're wearing my shoes." Ryan kicked his off before delving into their bag for the precious antibacterial wipes. "We'll get you cleaned up first."

"I can't wear your shoes. They're far too big for me, and besides, what will you wear? I'll be fine in my own shoes. Some padding or something to stop them rubbing would be good though."

"We're way past that, Stats. I didn't realize your shoes were this solid and had dried in some weird shapes. You might as well be wearing those wooden shoes they have in Holland."

"Clogs," Le Chat said helpfully.

"Yeah, those." Gently, he took each of her feet in turn and wiped them clean.

"I can't wear your shoes," Sarah protested. "You can't go barefoot."

"Of course, I can. My feet aren't all ripped up, so they'll cope a helluva lot better than yours will." He looked up at the boys. "You two got an extra pair of socks?"

Again, it was Le Chat who came to their rescue, while The Pit concentrated on keeping his eyes off Sarah.

"They are clean." He passed them to Ryan.

"Thank you," Sarah said, making the boy blush.

Ryan ripped a strip from the bottom of his T-shirt and gently wrapped Sarah's heel before helping her into the socks. He then used his own socks to stuff the toes of his trainers, so Sarah could wear them without them slipping. It looked like she was wearing clown shoes.

"Try not to trip," Ryan told her, taking her hand.

"Thanks. That feels so much better." She tugged him down until he bent over far enough for her to press the sweetest kiss to his lips.

Unfortunately, the moment was ruined by twittering teens. Ryan scowled at them before gesturing toward the tunnel.

"Let's get going," he ordered.

They made slow progress through the dark, dirty tunnels. Apart from the endless graffiti, there was nothing to differentiate one section of dusty old brick from another.

"Our place is near," Le Chat told them after they'd been walking for hours.

"You must speak of it to no one," La Fosse added.

"Don't worry, kid. Our lips are sealed," Ryan said.

In a shallow alcove off the tunnel sat a large chair-sized

rock that'd been tagged one too many times by talentless artists. The teens stopped in front of it.

"This is it," Le Chat said as he checked the tunnel for anyone watching.

If he means the rock is his den... Ryan was going to kill someone. Probably the little pervert.

Le Chat angled in behind the rock and dropped to his knees. Then disappeared.

"We crawl through," La Fosse said. "You go first because I must seal the door behind us."

"Sarah, you're up." There was no way, he was letting the creepy teen crawl behind her.

Without protest, she shuffled into the narrow space behind the rock, then slowly lowered to her knees before crawling into a dark hole that'd been hidden from view. La Fosse made a big show out of looking everywhere but her backside, which was fine by Ryan. The kid needed to learn some respect.

It was a tight squeeze for Ryan. The space wasn't designed for adult male shoulders, but he forced his way through, hiding his relief when he made it to the other side. La Fosse was fast on his heels, pulling a painted board behind him to hide the hole. Ryan had to admit, unless you knew where to look, you'd never guess there was an entryway hidden behind the rock.

The room that made up their den wasn't large. Fortunately, it was tall enough to stand in, which helped stave off any claustrophobia he might have felt. The teens had obviously been bringing stuff in, a bit at a time, to pad their nest, and it was surprisingly clean.

There were two ratty rolled sleeping bags, a plastic cooler that functioned as food storage and table or seat, a lantern and a few candles, lots of spray cans, and a bong. All the comforts of home, along with the smell that accompanied teenage boys. Thankfully, the bong hadn't been used recently and the smell of weed wasn't strong. He couldn't say the same for the boys' body odor.

Le Chat pushed the cooler against the wall and motioned to Sarah. "Seat," he said.

She sank on top of it with a grateful sigh. It worried Ryan that she seemed so deflated, rather than her usual bright, confrontative self. There were dark circles under her eyes, marring the ivory perfection of her skin. Her clothes were stained, torn, and wrinkled. And there were small scrapes, scratches, and bruises on almost every area of visible skin, making him wonder how many more there were under her clothes. Damn, but he wished he could fix it all for her.

Ryan crouched in front of her, brushing the wild curls that he loved from her face. "Do you need to go somewhere to clean up?"

It'd been hours since they'd used the toilet corner in the mushroom farm, and Ryan was a bit annoyed with himself that he hadn't thought to mention this before they'd crawled into the teens' den.

"I'm fine, for now. Tired." Her small, intimate smile was pure sunshine in the dimly lit cavern. "Nap, then decisions, okay?"

"Sounds good to me." He dug into the bag and handed her a bottle of water to drink, while he spoke to the teens. "How much longer until we hit the exit?"

La Fosse had unrolled his sleeping bag and was sitting tailor-style in the middle of it, staring at the bong with greedy eyes. "Do you mind?" he asked as he pointed to it.

"Yeah." There was no way in hell he was going to spend

the night in a tiny room while the guy smoked dope. "So give me an hour estimate," he asked Le Chat.

"Six or seven," he said as he fixed his own bed. "We sleep, then we walk. Tomorrow you will be free." He lay down on top of the sleeping bag, facing out toward Ryan and Sarah. "How long have you been lost here?"

"Years," Sarah muttered.

"A few days," Ryan said, settling in beside Sarah. Sitting against the wall between her and the boys.

Instantly, she angled herself to rest her head on his shoulder, and he slung an arm over her knees to keep her close. There was no way in hell either boy would get past him to Sarah. And yeah, he was aware of how paranoid he sounded. But as Callum often told him, *paranoia keeps us alive.*

"Sleep, Stats. We'll be out of here soon." He hated that she was shivering and all he could do was keep her close in the hope he shared his heat.

"Ryan," she whispered, her eyes already closed. "Don't worry, it's going to be okay."

Damn, she slayed him. Over and over again.

"I still don't understand how you got down here," La Fosse said, lowering his voice for Sarah's sake.

"Neither do we." Ryan didn't trust the kid enough to share details with him. That information was being hoarded for his team and the cops. Plus, they were still kids, and there was stuff they didn't need to know.

He flicked off their iPad, leaving them with only the light from the battery-operated lantern that the boys had stored in the room. It wasn't bright, but it gave them enough of a glow to see each other.

"How do we get out?" Ryan asked, keeping his voice low. "I mean, if we split up, somehow."

"You follow the red graffiti," Le Chat replied before his friend started shouting at him in rapid French.

"Hey," Ryan snapped. "Sarah's sleeping." And hadn't even stirred at the noise. "What's the problem?"

"I told you a secret," Le Chat said as Pit boy glared at him. "We cataphiles do not share our ways of the tunnels. It is enough that we tell you about our space. The ways in and out of the catacombs are protected. We each have our own path, and we do not share."

Honestly, Ryan couldn't see what the big deal was. Guess he wasn't the only one suffering a little paranoia.

"Don't worry. We won't tell a soul about your den or the way out of here. And seeing as we're never coming down here again, I'd say your secrets are safe."

La Fosse continued to glare, splitting his venom between his friend and Ryan. Yeah, that guy was a teenage delight.

"We better get some sleep," Ryan told them. "We've got another long walk tomorrow."

He squeezed Sarah's knee and hoped she was up to it. No matter, he'd get her out of there even if he had to carry her the rest of the way.

As Ryan closed his eyes, he heard the boys settle. Holding Sarah tight, he let himself drift off into a light sleep. Confident that should either boy come near them, he'd wake instantly and deal with them. In a way they probably wouldn't like.

CHAPTER TWENTY-FOUR

Benson Security Team
Paris, France

As soon as he pulled up in front of their Paris hotel, Callum knew Rachel had interfered with their reservations. He knew this for two reasons: first, Julia would never book somewhere this costly, and second, the place had a bloody spa. Since when did security operations need spa facilities? He'd never needed a spa when he'd been in the special forces.

The façade of the hotel was festooned with red sunshades and color-coordinated flower boxes on every window. There were ironwork Juliet balconies, carved stone pillars, and Art Nouveau glasswork everywhere he looked. The hotel screamed money. What it didn't do was whisper covert operation.

The valet took the keys for his hire car, and while the

doorman held the door for him, Callum scowled at Rachel—who'd arrived by limo. Of course.

"This is your doing, isn't it? Do I need to remind you, again, that you're no longer a partner in Benson Security? Which means you don't get to intimidate my office manager into booking five-star hotels."

"Your lips are moving, but all I hear is Cheap Scot." Rachel passed him, her nose in the air. "I'm paying for this, not the company."

"Nobody asked you to," he pointed out, feeling like a complete moron in his work jeans and T-shirt as he walked through a lobby filled with celebrities and what looked like half the Saudi royal family.

She rolled her eyes at him. In that patronizing yet long-suffering way only Rachel could pull off. "Did you honestly expect me to slum it in a backpackers or whichever chain hotel you thought would be suitable?"

"No," he gritted out. "I didnae expect you to come at all." It was like talking to a can of paint.

Harvard slapped him on the shoulder as he passed, grinning like a lunatic as usual, as though Rachel was the funniest woman on the planet. "Just go with the flow," he said. "She can afford it, and it makes her happy to do this for her friends."

"No, it does not!" Rachel snapped.

"Can't you no' do something about her?" Callum appealed to the American.

Harvard cocked an eyebrow. "Manage to fire your wife yet?"

Callum felt his ears burn. Isobel was, without a doubt, the worst receptionist he'd ever come across. She was a hazard to their business. And yet, she was still behind the front desk at Benson Security.

"I'm waiting for the right time?" he said.

"Yeah, so you are." Harvard sauntered away, amused again.

"Yes!" Elle literally jumped for joy when she came through the main doors. Her head angled every which way to take in the splendor. "Rachel totally came through for us, didn't she, boss?" She beamed at Callum, who didn't beam back.

"Come on," David told him. "We're all here to get Ryan back. And if that means sacrificing budget accommodation for a luxury hotel, then that's what we have to do."

"This isnae funny," Callum grumbled as they headed to the lifts.

"Little bit," David said.

Of course, Rachel had booked the Royal Suite. It had six bedrooms, six bathrooms, two living rooms, a dining room, an office, and a kitchen. And a view of the Eiffel Tower. It was also full of delicate antique furniture and soft silk furnishings that'd stain easily.

"The office isn't big enough for all of us, so I'm setting up in the dining room," Elle announced as she passed. "I've been going through Ryan's history with a fine-tooth comb, and we need to talk about it."

"Did you find something?" Callum followed her into the dining room and winced when she plonked her laptop down on the polished wood of the antique table.

"No, I found *every*thing. The list of people Ryan has offended is as long as my arm and getting longer every minute I investigate. It's like looking for a dickhead in a country only populated by dickheads."

"Colorful," Callum said drolly.

Julia slipped into the room and sat in the chair nearest the exit before consulting her iPad. "We could start cross-referencing your findings with the information Mr. Prentice gave us. It might help narrow things down."

"I don't know." Elle tightened the blue ponytail she had right on top of her head. It looked like a whale spout. "He didn't give us much."

"We have the name of the man he dealt with, his bank account information, and the fact that we're in Paris. The location has to be relevant, doesn't it?" Julia checked with Callum.

"Aye." Callum scratched his stubble-covered chin. "What do we have on the man Prentice handed Ryan and Sarah over to?"

Her computer already open and running, Elle tapped in a command. "Leo Fournier. They call him The Baker."

"Because he cooks the books?" Megan asked as she strolled into the room carrying a bag full of weapons.

"No," Elle said. "Because Fournier translates to baker."

"Well, that's boring." Megan held up the bag. "Joe told me to clean the guns. Can he do that?"

"Aye." And knowing Joe, he'd done it to keep Megan out of trouble. Smart man.

"Bummer." Megan tipped them out onto the other end of the table.

"Put a bloody cloth down first," Callum snapped. "What are we? Barbarians?"

"I knew you should never have let him see the bill for the new carpet," Elle told Julia. "I warned you he'd go mental over every penny we cost him from there on in."

"If you took care of the things around you, we wouldnae have to spend so much to replace them." Callum pinched the bridge of his nose. It was worse than talking to his kids.

"You should have left the bloodstained carpet alone,"

Rachel said, taking a seat at the head of the table. "More intimidating when you're questioning someone."

"Aye, but the cops tend to get suspicious when they find a room covered in blood."

"That guy had a nosebleed," Megan protested. "It wasn't my fault."

"You punched him in the face, which started the bloody nosebleed." Callum stared at the ceiling, as though he might find patience in amongst the rococo cornices.

"And here I was worried I'd missed the briefing," an English voice drawled from the doorway.

"Lake!" Elle bounced out of her seat and hugged the founder of the company.

Lake Benson seemed a little bemused by the show of affection, but his eyes crinkled in what passed for a smile.

"What are you doing here?" Rachel asked.

Lake cocked an eyebrow at her. "Ditto."

She sighed. "Just what we need, another taciturn macho man."

"Well, we already have our quota of bitches." Megan smiled sweetly at Rachel.

Callum ignored them and clasped his business partner's hand. "I wasnae expecting you."

"One of our own is missing," Lake said, as though that explained everything.

"Elle was just telling us about the French connection," Callum said. "Elle? You want to carry on?"

"Sorry, yes. It's just, is that the universal badass pose?" she pointed to the men dotted around the room.

All but Harvard were standing feet apart, arms folded, with frowns on their faces.

"Do you get this kind of respect in the Scottish office?" Callum asked Lake.

"I get respect wherever I go," Lake drawled before giving Elle a chin lift.

"So, about my report," Elle said, suddenly all business. "Leo Fournier, The Baker, runs his business out of Paris and subcontracts with guys around the planet, depending on what the job needs. He's known for getting you whatever you want, for a price. No job is too dirty. He's been in business a while, probably because he knows how to keep his mouth shut. And he looks a little like Christie's Poirot—David Suchet version. No kids, no girlfriend, nobody you could use to get to him. As far as I can see, he runs a tight crew. His people are loyal or they're dead. There's nothing in between."

"This is the go-between who hired Prentice to kidnap Ryan and Sarah?" Lake asked.

Elle nodded, making the blue spout dance. "He hangs out in a bar in Pigalle. Not the tourist area around Moulin Rouge—we're talking a seedy back-alley type bar with topless waitresses, illegal strippers, and a brothel upstairs. He's classy like that."

"Then that's where we start." Callum glanced at Joe. "Take a couple of people and scout the place out. We need to know what we're walking into and how best to approach this. We're also going to need somewhere quiet where we can talk to this guy once we pick him up."

"You can bring him here." Rachel waved a hand to indicate the most expensive hotel suite in Paris. "Trust me, no one will bat an eye at a little violence and torture. I've heard what rock stars do in these rooms."

Yet again, Callum had to be the voice of reason. "We're no' interrogating a criminal here."

Rachel sniffed, as though *he* was being difficult. "Well, I'm sure they could give us another room, if we needed it."

"Yeah," Megan said. "Why don't I call down to the concierge and ask if their torture dungeon is free?"

Rachel was unfazed. "This is Paris; I honestly wouldn't be surprised if they had one. Be sure to mention my name. It comes with VIP benefits."

Before Callum could explode, David piped up. "I know a place," he said, surprising no one.

"Secure?" Callum asked.

David just stared at him.

"Stupid question," Callum muttered. "Joe, you ready?"

"On it." Joe indicated for David and Harvard to follow before leaving the room.

Callum turned his attention back to Elle. "Can you hack this Baker guy?"

She cracked her knuckles. "Is the Force with Leia? Seriously though, we need to expand the tech team. Recruitment has been leaning too much toward brawn rather than brains these past few years. I could use some help." She pulled on a pair of over-ear headphones, started humming the Star Wars theme tune, and instantly tuned out the world as she stared at her screen.

"This is going too bloody slow for my liking," Callum complained to Lake. "Ryan's been out there for far too long."

"He's skilled. He'll be fine." Lake was confident, even though his presence made it clear he was just as worried. "Once we find out who hired Fournier, it'll go fast."

"And if he doesn't talk?"

"He'll talk." There was no give in Lake's tone.

And that was why people paid the big bucks to deal with him. Lake was a scary guy. In his forties, his blond hair turning gray, Lake should have lost his edge. But the man was even more intimidating than he'd been back in their

Special Forces days. With his connections, his willingness to do whatever it took to get the job done, and his vast array of skills, Lake Benson wasn't a man you crossed.

"Holy hotcakes, Batman!" Ripping off her headphones, Elle suddenly pushed back from the table. "The alarm went off. The alarm I set up for Ryan's tracking devices, that alarm. His phone is back on the grid, and it's here in Paris."

CHAPTER TWENTY-FIVE

Sarah woke to the sound of Ryan's steady breathing and the dim flicker of candlelight. Angling her head, she studied his profile. Sweet heaven, he was beautiful—inside and out. Well, except for the obsessive eating, and an inability to carry a tune, and a gung-ho attitude that led him into trouble.

If only she was courageous enough to keep him.

But Sarah knew herself well enough to admit it wasn't possible. It would kill her to have to wait for him to come home after every mission. She wasn't strong enough to deal with the terror that he might never return—or might come home changed. He deserved a woman who could support him in his career, without damaging herself doing it. Because if there was something she'd learned from this awful underground experience, it was that Ryan was very, very good at what he did, and nothing should get in the way of him doing it.

She traced her fingertips along the edge of his jaw, feeling the thick stubble that any male sex symbol would kill to sport. Even barefoot and with a chunk ripped off the bottom of his shirt, he could have sauntered into a Michelin-starred restaurant and been given a table without objection. Whereas, if she'd turned up with him, they would call the police to deal with a vagrant.

Long dark lashes fluttered on his cheeks before his eyes opened and searched for her. They lit up, turning warm when he found her, and Sarah tucked that memory into a safe box for the days when he was no longer in her life.

His wide hand flexed on the outside of her thigh. "Hey." His voice was rough morning perfection. "You feeling better?"

"Mm." With a smile, she nuzzled against him. "Much better."

"Your feet?"

"A dull throb. I can walk." Heck, she would hop, skip, and jump through agonizing pain if it meant getting out of there.

His eyes darkened. "Good girl," he teased.

"Seriously, *not* a girl," she chastised because he expected her to.

"Oh, I know."

She blushed at the intimacy of his tone.

"Okay," Ryan said loudly as he got to his feet. "Let's get —" He broke into a stream of creative cursing before looking back at her. "The little shits have gone."

He stepped to the side so she could see past him, and sure enough, the sleeping bags, paint, bong, and boys were nowhere to be seen.

Sarah was genuinely shocked. "How could they?"

Didn't the boys see the state they were in? Didn't they realize how much Ryan and Sarah were relying on them to get out of the catacombs?

"Easily." Ryan kicked the wall. "I'm more pissed that they managed to get out of here without waking me up." He rubbed the back of his neck. "Must have been the lingering headache. It probably made me slip into a deeper sleep than I intended. At least I was smart enough to ask them how to get out of here before I fell asleep. I'm going to break their scrawny necks when I catch them though."

From the fury emanating from him, Sarah had no doubt he meant every word he said. Unfortunately, he was about to get even madder.

"Ryan?" She hesitated as she dug through her handbag. "The iPad is missing. And your phone. Oh!" She looked up at him. "Our wallets are gone too."

Ryan didn't speak or even move a muscle. He didn't need to; his whole body practically pulsed with rage.

"We still have our water," she hurried on in an attempt to calm him. "And they left us the candles." Three stubby candles, to be precise. But their ID, credit cards, and most importantly, their light source were gone.

Ryan growled, deep in his chest. It was a menacing sound that made it clear he saw no silver lining in their situation.

And he was right.

Her shoulders slumped as she considered the few items they had left to get out of there. "I have to be the world's worst judge of character because I thought the boys were nice—well, apart from the whole boob obsession thing."

Suddenly, Ryan crouched in front of her, cupping her cheek. "I *will* get you out of here," he vowed.

"And *I'll* get you out too."

They were a partnership. Sure, most of the skills were in his half of it, but that didn't mean she couldn't do her bit to make sure he was safe.

His lips curled in a sweet, gentle smile. "I'm counting on it, Stats."

"Now, can we forget about the klepto teens and move on? I don't have time for anger right now. I just want to be aboveground, where there's fresh air and toilets you can sit on."

His lips twitched as his good humor returned. "I still get to kill them later though, right?"

She inclined her head as though in thought. "You don't want to kill kids, Ryan. But I'm sure we can come up with an equally satisfying way to make them suffer."

With a chuckle, he placed a kiss on the end of her nose. "Ready to go?"

There was nothing to get ready, so Sarah just nodded. "Better grab the candles; we're going to need them. Wait! We can do that thing they did on Indiana Jones. You know, where he wrapped some cloth around the end of a bone before setting it on fire and using it as a torch." She shuddered. "Bad joke. I couldn't use a bone like that."

Ryan's smile lit up his face as he stood. "Just when I think you can't get any better, you bring in Indy."

"I'll even sing the theme tune if you're good. Now, let me get what we need out of this bag. There's no point carrying it. You can just shove things in your pockets, and I'll carry the water bottle."

Sarah stood, and using the cooler as a table, she went through the contents of her bag. The only useful things it held were her travel toothbrush set and a few remaining antibacterial wipes.

A hand snaked around her stomach as Ryan pressed up behind her. His lips found the crook of her neck, where he placed a lingering kiss. Instantly turning her knees to noodles.

"I can be good," he rumbled against her skin, sending shivers, of the best kind, through her. "I can be really, really good." He nipped at the sensitive spot between shoulder and neck.

"Stop it," she protested weakly. "I have no willpower when it comes to you. One more bite, and I *will* jump you again."

His chuckle was dark and delicious. "If only you knew how tempted I am right now." With a sigh, he released her. "But we have to get out of here. I am going to keep that little revelation in mind for later though."

Well, hell.

"Well, hell," Ryan said as he held the candle up to the wall filled with graffiti. "How are we supposed to tell which red the little shits meant?"

Visions of hanging the teens, by their ankles, over a pit of squirming rats filled Ryan's mind. Maybe he'd even go all blockbuster villain on them and light a candle under the rope that held them in place. Naw, that was too clichéd. He'd tie them by their ankles under one of the Paris bridges and swing them like a pendulum, watching as they narrowly missed the boats and sobbed for their lives. Yeah, better.

"I think that's orange." Sarah leaned past him to point at a tag scrawled across the brick. "And that one looks more magenta than red. I'm going to go with this one. I think that's definitely red."

"You sound very convinced," he drawled. "Also, I think you're putting too much faith in those idiots. I'm not sure they knew the difference between magenta and red."

"They were artists, of course they did."

Oh, sweet, naive child. "Stats, you saw their artwork. It didn't instill confidence."

She slapped a hand in the middle of a huge, unreadable tag. "This one is red."

"It's as good a choice as any, I suppose."

"That's the spirit." She glared at him.

It was cute. Kinda like an irritated puppy—a poodle puppy! The hair was totally in poodle territory, although he'd never mention that to Sarah. Somehow, he didn't think she'd take it as a compliment. One day, though, he was buying them a poodle.

"Stop grinning at me," Sarah snapped as they headed down the corridor that'd been tagged with the chosen red paint.

"Somebody woke up on the wrong side of the bed this morning." He wrapped an arm around her shoulders and hugged her to his side.

"I wish there had been a bed," she said woefully before looking up at him with those big bronze eyes of hers. "Ignore me. I'm just tired and cranky."

"At least you aren't terrified or unconscious," he joked, "so we're on the up."

Sarah stared at him for a second before grinning. "True." She leaned away from him and held up their water bottle. "Do you need another drink?" It was barely a quarter full.

"I'm good, thanks."

"We need to find some water soon, or we'll be in trouble." She took a couple of sips before holding his hand, making him grateful that there was enough space in the tunnel for them to walk side by side.

"Really hoping we'll be out of here before the need for water becomes an issue." Ryan squeezed her hand. "The idiots said it was about a six-hour walk to topside."

"We can do six hours," she said firmly.

"Yeah, we can." He smiled over at her, but her focus was on the tunnel ahead of them.

The brick part of the catacombs seemed to have been built a whole lot more recently than the space they'd first started in, and the wider tunnels gave him hope that they were nearing an exit.

They walked in silence for a while. Sarah was still limping, and his huge shoes couldn't have been comfortable, but she didn't complain. He'd noticed that she rarely complained about anything, preferring to accept her situation and try to make the best of it. It was pretty amazing to watch, especially as she had to have been beyond exhausted and completely strung out from the emotional toll of their abduction. Really, it was a miracle she was still standing.

Ryan eyed the ceiling. There seemed to be more cracks than usual, and it was raining dust down on them. Not that you'd notice the extra dirt amongst the crud they were already sporting. They were a pair: torn up, battered, hungry, and exhausted with no clue as to whether they were heading in the right direction or not. On top of all that, the pains in his stomach were a constant companion now. His poor neglected belly had even given up on rumbling. It was as though it'd lost all hope of ever seeing food again.

"Careful." He tugged Sarah aside as a few small chips fell from above.

"Is it just me," she said, "or is this tunnel looking a little abandoned?"

"Nope, it isn't just you." The graffiti was sparse, and

there was more rubble and dust than before—most of it undisturbed. If this led to an exit, then it was one that hadn't been used for some time. "Looks like we picked the wrong shade of red."

"I was sure it was the right red," she huffed as they turned back to try again.

"Told you, Stats, you might know your colors, but those little shits sure as hell didn't."

"Stop calling them that. They were probably desperate and had no choice but to steal our stuff."

Yep, she needed a keeper. With a soft heart like that, the world would walk right over her. "You've been desperate— did you steal somebody's iPad to get you out of it?"

"No. But I stole toilet paper from the public bathrooms because I couldn't afford to buy it. And I'd go to church on Sundays, purely because they had a shared meal after the service. You were supposed to bring something for it, but I never could. I'd offer to help clean up because when no one was looking, I could clear leftovers into my bag to eat at home later. If I'd had the courage, I might have stolen from people. You never know..."

No, he knew. She'd never have gone that far. Ryan's chest tightened at the thought of her sneaking food and feeling shame because of it. It was all kinds of wrong.

"Stats..." Stopping right there, he pulled her into a hug. And he didn't even pretend she was the one who needed the comfort.

"It was a long time ago," she said. "I'm fine now."

As he held her close, feeling her soft body against his, he pressed a kiss to the top of her head. "I'm fighting the urge to go on a toilet paper spending spree as soon as we're out of here. I suddenly have the need to fill your house with it, so you'll never have to worry about it again."

"I think that's probably the nicest thing anybody ever said to me." She looked up at him and smiled. "Please don't do it, though."

Ryan was laughing when his hand spasmed and he dropped the candle. "Damn it," he spat as it fell to the floor and the flame snuffed out, plunging them into darkness. "Sarah, I'm sorry. Gimme a sec, and I'll light another one."

"It's okay, I—"

Whatever she was about to say ended when the ceiling started to crumble. A piece of brick skimmed the side of his head, hitting his shoulder.

"Ryan!" Sarah screamed at the same time, he yelled, "Run."

But she didn't run.

He felt her palms hit the middle of his chest and she pushed hard. Catching him off guard, she sent him sprawling back down the tunnel, away from the falling bricks.

"No!" Ryan shouted, scrambling to his feet.

A loud rumble shook the tunnel, and the roof over their heads collapsed.

"Sarah!" he bellowed before dust and grit made him gag and cough.

He pulled his T-shirt up over his nose and mouth as he tried to make sense of what'd just happened. Light. He needed light. Fumbling in his pocket, he pulled out a candle. Going by feel, he retrieved the unused match from the sealed space in his Swiss Army knife. It took a couple of tries to strike it before he quickly lit the candle.

After what felt like hours, Ryan faced the damage. Blinking back the dust cloud that still lingered around him. Feeling the grit scrape his eyes. The same way it'd scratched at his lungs. Fighting panic, he managed to see through the dust.

Only to find that the spot where they'd stood was filled with rubble.

And there was no sign of Sarah.

CHAPTER TWENTY-SIX

Ryan paced the old brick tunnel. He felt caged. Trapped. Helpless. A tiger behind bars, measuring his prison with each prowling step.

And *he* wasn't the one with a wall of rubble between him and freedom.

He stared at the mess. Hating it. Wanting to pummel it into submission. Knowing it wouldn't help.

There was no way to get past the cave-in. Not without bringing the rest of the ceiling down on himself. There was also no way of knowing how far it extended into the tunnel. Or if it was even possible to dig his way through.

Or dig Sarah out.

Fuck!

Ryan doubled over as his vision blurred. This wasn't happening. It couldn't be. She wasn't buried under the rock.

What if she was buried alive?

What if she was under there? Bruised. Broken. Whispering his name.

He stood, curling both hands into his hair as he stalked back and forth in front of the candle at his feet.

Think.

He needed to think.

There had to be another way around the collapse. They'd passed other passageways, maybe one of those merged with this tunnel, on Sarah's side of the cave-in. The problem was, there was no logic to the way the catacombs were laid out. Even with his sense of direction, there was no guarantee he'd choose the right tunnel—even if there was one.

No, it was too risky. The odds that he'd just waste time instead of finding her were too high to take. He had to find another way.

Stalking back to the rubble, careful of where he stepped because standing on a sharp rock wouldn't help his situation in the slightest, he examined the cave-in again.

Bricks, rubble, dirt, and dust. A wall of tightly-packed stone. And it was still coming down. Trickling through the gaps above. The whole thing was far too unstable to touch, let alone dig through.

"Sarah!" he bellowed for the millionth time. "Sarah!"

Think. You need to think.

He crouched down at the base of the rubble. Okay, what did he have that he could use to dig her out? Anything? There were sacks back in the mushroom cavern. A cooler chest in the teens' den. Some bones scattered around the place. Empty spray paint cans... And that was it.

There were literally no resources that could help him now.

He hung his head, clasping his hands on the back of it. He'd never felt so helpless in his life. Was she hurt? Unconscious? Dead?

Hell no!

He had two choices—find a way to her, or try to find the

way out to get help. How was he supposed to decide? Especially knowing the wrong choice would cost her life.

They were no better off than the couple whose bodies he'd found in the mine. His woman was trapped, and he had to decide whether to escape for help, or stay and work to free her. Was this what that couple went through? Is this how the man had felt when he couldn't save the woman he loved?

All this effort. All this time, struggling to get out of the catacombs and they'd ended up right back where they'd started—Sarah was trapped and he was useless.

And wallowing in self-pity wasn't going to help anyone.

He shot to his feet. "Sarah!"

The only reply he got was the sound of shifting rock.

He'd told her he'd protect her. That he'd get her out of here. That he wouldn't let anything happen to her. When, in reality, this was all his fault. If he hadn't dropped the candle. If he hadn't left them in darkness when the tunnel started to fall. Maybe then, they'd have had enough warning to run together.

This was on him.

By denying he was still dealing with fallout from the coma. By believing everything would be okay and he could function the way he'd always done. By ignoring reality, he'd risked the woman who'd filled a hole inside of him that had been empty since she'd been wiped from his mind.

This was all his fault.

"Sarah!" he hollered. "Sarah!"

It was a six-hour walk to the exit. That's what the teens had told him. They'd wasted an hour following the wrong graffiti. Which meant it was now a seven-hour walk to get help.

Seven hours was a lifetime.

And that wasn't even counting the time they'd waste getting back to this spot. Realistically, they were looking at fourteen hours before he was back with help—at least. That was a helluva long time to leave her in the dark, afraid and alone, wondering if he'd forgotten her.

Damn it.

He wasn't thinking straight. He didn't have to walk—he could run. Crap, not with a candle for light, he couldn't. The flame would go out seconds into his sprint. Those bastard boys. They had no idea what they'd done to Ryan and Sarah.

But, walking fast. He could do that. Maybe even a gentle jog. As long as the candle stayed lit, that was the main thing. At least he could cut a couple of hours off the walk out of the tunnels. And he could run back, if he managed to get a flashlight. So that would take it down to six, seven hours total—if he didn't hit an obstacle that slowed him down.

If the teen hadn't lied about how to get out.

He wished Sarah was there. She'd have calculated the odds of each choice and told him the best option. But then, if she'd been there, he wouldn't need the information to begin with.

Pacing back to the rubble, he listened for any sign of her.

Nothing.

"Sarah!" His voice echoed off the brick walls. It was the only sound that came back to him.

This had to be the worst decision he'd ever faced. Leave her? Try to find her? Stay put in the hope he'd be able to dig through the rubble, once the cave-in settled? He wanted to rage. To lash out. He wanted something solid to deal with, a clear-cut challenge he could face head-on.

Instead, he had risk percentages running through his mind, and a gnawing, clawing, screaming fear in the pit of his stomach.

He didn't have time for indecision.

And neither did Sarah.

Where the hell was Callum's voice when he needed it?

"Fuck!" he roared.

Okay, okay, he could do this. He *had* to do this.

"Sarah," he called loudly. "I hope you can hear me. I'm going to get help. I'm not abandoning you. I'll be back. I'll get you out. Stay where you are. Don't move, okay?"

Waiting for a reply, he heard only silence.

Ryan wiped his face and blinked to clear his eyes. Dust must have gotten to him because they were leaking.

With one last look at the rubble, he sheltered the lit candle in his hands and started to jog up the tunnel. Each step he took away from Sarah was like a nail being hammered into his chest.

This was worse than losing her in the water. This felt like he was abandoning her. Like he was letting her down, even though he knew he wasn't. It was torture.

Yet, he kept putting one foot in front of the other.

For Sarah.

CHAPTER TWENTY-SEVEN

Callum focused on Elle—the pixie-faced genius. "You've found his phone, but no' the GPS implants?"

She shook her head. "Just the phone. But it's here, in Paris, and it's on the move. Someone has it. Someone else, not Ryan, because there are no other signals setting off alarms."

"And it's definitely Ryan's?" Lake asked.

"Definitely."

"Dimitri, Megan, Lake, you're with me." Callum grabbed his weapon and shoulder holster from his duffle. "Where we heading?" he asked Elle.

"Corner of Rue Daguerre and Rue de Grancey. About fifteen minutes from here."

"Keep me up to date on the phone's movement." Callum strode to the door. "Julia, call down and tell them I need my car brought round." He glanced at Lake as they rushed for the elevator. "You got a gun?"

Lake pushed back his beige denim jacket to reveal the holster on his hip.

It took a millennium to get out of the hotel, into the car, and drive to Montparnasse. Callum abandoned their vehicle near the Metro entrance at the end of Rue Daguerre, and they walked up the long, narrow street.

A café on the corner had tables spilling out into the road. Not that it mattered since there wasn't any traffic, only pedestrians shopping at the market stalls lining each side of the street.

"I know he isn't here, that it's just his phone, but this is exactly the kind of place he'd gravitate to." Megan pointed at the Fromagerie, with its bright red stall covered in hundreds of different types of cheese. "There's a patisserie up there, a crêperie, cured meats... This is Ryan's Nirvana."

She wasn't wrong. Callum took out his phone and called Elle, his eyes scanning the crowd, looking for anything that might lead him to Ryan.

"Where is it?" he asked when she answered.

"It's stopped moving. Gimme a sec."

They passed a fish shop, its stall loaded with mussels. Then a fruit stand, piled high with all colors and kinds of fruit. The smell of fresh strawberries merged with warm baked croissants as they hit the patisserie.

"If he's here, just eating his way along the street, I'm gonna kill him," Dimitri muttered.

"Okay," Elle said in Callum's ear. "You'll never believe this—the phone is in a McDonalds. No way this is Ryan. He wouldn't walk past French food to get a cheap mass-produced hamburger."

"Where's the bloody burger place, Elle?" Callum was seriously losing his patience.

"Sorry, on the right. Just past the florist. It's bright red; can't you see it?"

"It's no' red. They tried to make it blend."

This McDonalds was beige and gold. And it still looked out of place. Especially seeing as it took up the ground floor of a classic French apartment building, complete with iron-work balconies and wooden shutters.

They made their way past the many buckets of brightly colored flowers covering the pavements. "I'll text when I need you to call Ryan's phone," he told Elle.

"I'll be ready." She hung up.

"You can't call yourself?" Lake asked as they pushed through the doors into the long, narrow fast-food restaurant.

"No, we need the ringtone Ryan gave Elle."

Callum glanced at Dimitri, who nodded and led Megan through to the back of the restaurant. Together, they'd block any chance of escape from that direction. Lake lazily leaned against the wall beside the door, pretending to check his phone. No one could leave without having to get past him.

That left Callum to find their prey.

The room wasn't packed, but it was busy. Mainly with teenagers and American tourists. None of them looked like they had any reason to have Ryan's phone. Flicking a text to Elle, Callum scanned the diners and waited.

When the *Star Wars* theme tune started playing, Callum zeroed in on it. There were two boys sitting at a table near the window. They were mid-teens and scruffy. One of them switched off the phone and slipped it into his backpack, while the other carried on wolfing down his burger.

Callum nodded at Dimitri, and together they closed in on the boys.

"You have my friend's phone," Callum said in fluent French. "Get up and follow me out the front door, right now. I have questions for you."

The boys shared a look before laughing. "I don't think so, old man. You're crazy. We don't have anybody's phone. Now piss off."

Callum leaned over the table, a smile on his face for anyone watching. "In about two seconds, I'm going to pick your scrawny arse up and carry you out of here. Unless my colleague shoots you first." Dimitri brushed back his jacket to flash his gun. The boys went pale. "We only need one of you. I'm happy to let him shoot the other. You can choose. Which one gets the bullet, and which one answers my questions?"

"The cops—" The skinnier one had gone ashen.

"Will arrive long after you're dead." Callum stood back. "Your choice. Make it now. I'm done talking."

The teens scrambled, grabbing their backpacks as they stood. "We'll follow you," the taller one said.

"Good decision." Callum led the way to the exit as Megan and Dimitri closed in on either side of them.

As they reached the front entrance, Lake flashed a cold smile at the teens as he opened the door for them.

"The courtyard." Callum pointed to the archway that went through the building facing them, leading to a communal garden behind it.

Flanking the boys, the team casually walked across the street and through to the courtyard garden. As soon as they were on the other side of the building, out of view of the street, Lake indicated he was going to check the area out. It didn't take long.

"Older couple feeding birds in the back right corner," he said when he was done.

Backing the teens up against the wall, Dimitri and Megan played sentry as Lake and Callum faced the boys.

"Hand over the phone." Callum held out his palm.

The shorter of the two dug around in his backpack, removed the phone, and tossed it at Callum. He thumbed the screen, and instantly a photo of Ryan and his sister Grace appeared. A cold fury settled in his stomach.

"Where'd you get it?" he barked at the boys.

"We found it," the short one said, looking every bit the liar he was.

"Now, we both know that isnae true." Callum pointed a finger at him. "Shoot this one—we don't need him."

Dimitri took out his gun. And the teen lost control of his bladder.

"We got it in the catacombs," he blurted, his face red and his eyes wide as he tried to cover his accident with his backpack. "There was this couple. They said they were lost, and we helped show them the way out. They gave it to us as thanks."

Callum frowned at the latest line of bullshit. Meanwhile, Dimitri cocked his gun.

"We stole it!" the other teen blurted, his eyes on the gun. "We stole the phone."

"What else did you steal?" Callum asked calmly.

"There was an iPad," he said. "But we don't have it anymore—we sold it."

Callum waited.

"We took their wallets too. We gave them to a guy we owed money."

Callum's jaw clenched. "Did you help the couple to get out of the catacombs, or did you just leave them there?"

Their shared look of guilt was all the answer he needed. And for the first time in his life, he wanted to hit a kid. But he didn't. There were other ways they'd answer for their crimes.

"You're going to take us to the place where you left our

friends," he said through gritted teeth. "And you'd better hope they're alive and well, because if they're no', they won't be the only ones who don't come out of the catacombs. Do you understand me?"

It was the other boy's turn to pee himself.

CHAPTER TWENTY-EIGHT

The teenagers called themselves Le Chat and La Fosse because they were sixteen and thought they were cool. Dimitri thought they were headed to prison, probably sooner than they expected.

The boys led them to a hospital, not far from the street market where they'd found them. The complex was a mixture of old and new buildings, with the newer ones in worse condition than the older.

"Where's the entrance?" Callum asked from the driver's seat.

The teens were wedged between Dimitri and Megan in the back seat. Dimitri would have rather they'd ridden in the boot, but he'd been outvoted. The back seat was cramped, and it smelled. But not as badly as it could have done. The boys each had spare pants in their backpacks, and Dimitri had ensured they changed before getting in the car.

"It is in the bottom of the old car park," Le Chat, the slightly more cooperative of the pair, said. "Behind the eye hospital."

"Is it a public parking garage?" Callum asked as he stopped at the entry barrier for a ticket.

"Oui, I think so. We usually do not have a car."

Callum drove them into the right building, then spiraled downward into the basement parking level. The space was everything you'd expect from an old car park: bad lighting, cramped, and dirty.

"Where?" Callum barked again.

"You see the garbage containers? Over there." The boy pointed to the huge wheelie bins, several of which were lined up in a row on the far wall.

"It's always rubbish," Megan complained. "This is a hospital. Couldn't the entrance have been through a nice sterile room?" She stroked her favorite leather biker jacket. "Now it's going to smell like medical waste."

His wife had her own priorities. "You could leave it in the car," he pointed out.

Her smile was blinding. "You're a genius."

As she shrugged out of her jacket, La Fosse leered at her cleavage, angling himself ready to grope when the car slid to a halt. His moves weren't even covert. He was too busy drooling to put the effort in.

Dimitri knew there was no need to deal with the boy. Megan could look after herself. And she did. With one quick move, and two fingers, she poked La Fosse's eyes in the best Stooges impersonation Dimitri had seen in a while. The kid howled as tears streamed down his cheeks.

"You ogle me, touch me, or generally pant after me one more time," Megan said sweetly, "and I start tearing off body parts. Got me?"

There was much nodding and apologizing through the sobs.

Man, he loved his wife.

"You two are a delight," Megan said with disgust. "You perv on women, steal stuff, lie, and abandon people who're lost and alone. People who might die without help. I'm wondering if it's worth leaving you alive at the end of this. Seems to me you don't have anything of worth to add to society."

The boys started to protest, but she held up a hand. "One more word, and my gun comes out. I'm so pissed with both of you that I can hardly keep my hands off it."

There was silence. During which Lake turned to the back seat and smiled at Megan. Not a lip twitch, a full-out smile. Dimitri's chest puffed with pride.

After they'd piled out of the car, Le Chat told them to move one of the bins. When they did, it revealed an old manhole cover.

"We go down there," he pointed.

"Of course, we do." Megan glared at him, making him squirm.

As the teens removed the cover, Callum nodded to his team. "I'll stay up here and coordinate."

"You won't slow us down," Dimitri said, "if that's what you're thinking."

"I wasnae. But the prosthetics will make it hard going and we need someone to run things up here."

There'd been a time when Callum didn't even mention his prosthetics, let alone the impact they had on him and the team. If Ryan had been there, he would have faked tears, patted Callum on the back, and told him he was proud that his boss had finally grown up. Man, he missed Ryan.

"What's the plan?" Lake asked as he watched the teens.

"It's basic as hell." Callum ran a hand through his already messy hair. "You go in, mark your path, and send someone back if you need help. We don't have much in the way of useful equipment, but we have the basics."

"Maybe we should wait to go down until we have more resources," Dimitri said. "We don't know what condition they're in or what kind of help they'll need."

Callum eyed the boys. "What state were they in when you saw them last?"

Le Chat hurried to answer. "Dirty, hungry, thirsty, and the woman had injured feet, so the man gave her his shoes."

"He doesn't have any shoes?" Megan narrowed her eyes. "No shoes, no light, no food, and nobody to guide them out. I'm feeling murderous again."

"You can play with them after we get Ryan and Sarah out of there," Lake decreed, making the teens back away from Megan.

Meanwhile, Callum bent over and unlaced his Nikes. He handed them to Lake. "I sure as hell don't need them."

Le Chat went white when he saw Callum's state-of-the-art metallic feet. "Le Terminateur," he whispered.

Callum opened the boot of his rental and unzipped the duffle he'd brought with them. "Flashlights, water bottles, protein bars." He handed them to his team. "Everything else in here is useless."

"Got a marker pen or paint?" Dimitri said.

"I bet they do," Megan pointed at the reprobates.

Without being asked, Le Chat delved into his backpack and handed Dimitri a can of black spray paint.

"I'll mark our route with LTW," Dimitri decided.

"LTW?" Megan asked as Lake and Callum groaned.

Dimitri grinned. "It's the Army Rangers motto— Rangers Lead The Way."

"It should be WDW. There are two SAS officers here," Lake said.

Megan reached over and took the can out of Dimitri's hand. "We're using MR for Megan rules." She arched an eyebrow at the men, and there were no objections.

"Time to go," Callum said. "Those two idiots say it's a six-hour walk to where they left Ryan and Sarah. If you run, it should cut that time in half. I'll give you seven hours, just to be safe, before I call in the cavalry."

"Who's the cavalry?" Megan asked as she lowered herself into the hole, grabbing the rungs as she did so.

"Everybody I can think of," Callum growled.

Lake caught his eye. "Start with L'Inspection Générale des Carrières. Ask for a guy called Paul la Tour. He's an engineer with subterranean rescue experience."

Callum nodded as Megan's voice came out of the hole. "Is there anywhere on the planet where you *don't* have contacts?"

And miracle of miracles, Lake smiled again.

Ryan's foot was bleeding, and he was on his second candle. There was only one left. Without a phone, there was no way to tell how long he'd been jogging through the tunnels, but the pedometer in his screwed-up brain told him he'd covered about fifteen miles. Which meant, at an average jogging speed of about five miles per hour, he'd been away from Sarah for roughly three hours. Although it was probably more because there'd been areas where he'd had to slow down because it was too dangerous to jog.

By his calculation, he was about an hour away from an exit—assuming he could find it. And assuming he'd followed the right shade of red this time. It was all taking far too long.

Was Sarah awake and wondering where he was? Was she worried he'd left her? Was she suffering alone?

Stupid, useless questions.

They only made his heart beat faster and his stomach clench. Man, he was thirsty. Sarah had been holding their only bottle of water when the tunnel collapsed, and Ryan hadn't spotted any other source during his jog. Still, if he'd had to choose, he'd have left the water with her anyway.

There was more graffiti on the walls now, along with evidence that people had been cleaning up after themselves. An old ceramic tile embedded in the tunnel told him that he was beneath Rue du Faubourg Saint-Jacques. It meant nothing to him except that civilization was closer than it'd been three hours earlier.

Ducking under a low-ceilinged archway, Ryan paused. There were voices. Murmurs in the distance. And, if he wasn't mistaken, the sound of running feet.

The echo made it hard to tell which direction the sound came from, or even which passageway. All he could do was look for the red mark he'd been following and carry on, hoping it'd take him to someone who could help.

He jogged on for a few minutes more, feeling hopeful as the voices got louder. And, if he wasn't mistaken, they were speaking English. Relief surged through him, knowing that he wouldn't have to try to explain what he needed in French.

The passage widened into a chamber with several offshoots. One wall had been painstakingly carved into a 3D relief, depicting ocean waves. The graffiti artists had treated the carving with respect, and there were no tags to mar it. In the top right-hand corner of the carved mural were the words, life is a wave, surf the wave.

Or get drowned...

He was so busy staring at the mural that he wasn't paying attention to the candle. Until it flickered and died. Ryan didn't move as the reality of his situation sank in. He had one candle left. And now, he had no way to light it.

Bloody, stupid, idiot...

The running feet were closer now.

"Help," Ryan shouted. "I'm in the mural room, and my light has gone out. Are you there? Can you help?"

There was a pause before a very familiar voice called, "Ryan?"

Lake Benson?

Damn.

He was hallucinating.

Too long underground, without food or proper rest. Too much stress and disorientation. Of course, he was hallucinating. He should have expected this and prepared himself.

"Ryan?" the voice he'd imagined called again. It sounded so like Lake that it could only have come from his head.

Because why would Lake be in the Paris catacombs? Even if his team did know where he'd been taken, the chances of them finding him were about a billion to one. There were over two hundred miles of tunnels under Paris. Probably more. Most of them hadn't even been mapped. So the odds of Lake picking the one Ryan was in were pretty damn low.

Sarah...

She was relying on him, and he'd screwed up. How could he follow the red graffiti when he couldn't see a thing? He was stuck. In the dark. Directionless and helpless. And he was imagining a savior in the form of the company founder. All the while, the reality was that Sarah was back with the cave-in and suffering without him.

Unless…he'd imagined everything.

Suddenly, he wasn't sure what was real and what wasn't.

Sinking to his knees, Ryan gasped for air, even though there was plenty around him. Was this *all* a hallucination? Had he made everything up? Was he still drugged and trapped in the room where they'd left him?

Sarah had to be real, right?

She felt real.

She felt like she was…his.

A light hit his face, blinding him, and he held up a hand to shade his eyes.

"Ryan!" He felt arms around him and found himself looking into Megan's grinning face. "Are you okay?"

His heart sank.

He was definitely hallucinating because Megan didn't do affection.

"Ryan, are you okay?" That was Dimitri's voice.

Ryan looked up to find Lake and Dimitri looking down at him.

There was no getting past it, he had to ask. "Are you guys real?"

"How about I punch you and you can see how real it feels?" Megan asked with a smile.

That was more like her.

Lake crouched down in front of him. "Are you hurt?"

Ryan's brain was still trying to fathom whether this was all a mirage or not. "How did you know where to find me?"

There was shuffling in the darkness as the baby arse-holes who'd stolen from him came into view. "Never mind. I can see how you found me. Pretend you never heard me asking if you were real. I was having an existential moment."

Dimitri's hand clamped on his shoulder. "Did you hit your head again because that's an awful big word you just used."

"Are you injured?" Lake asked again, holding out a bottle of water, which Ryan gratefully took.

"Scrapes. Bruises." He took a long drink, reveling in the feeling of the icy cold water as it slid down his throat. "We need to get back to Sarah. There was a cave-in and she's trapped."

"Is she injured?" Lake asked, his intense gaze demanding clarity.

It was the anchor Ryan needed, and he answered as he would an army superior. "I don't know. We were separated when the ceiling came down, and she didn't reply when I called."

"How far from here are we talking?"

"About three hours at a jog. It's just a guess though. I didn't have any way to tell the time after those bastards stole my phone. With your flashlights, though, we can make it in less time." A thought occurred to him. "Elle tracked my phone, didn't she?" He looked at the teens. "Guess you weren't fast enough getting rid of it."

"If it's any consolation"—Megan patted his arm—"they peed themselves when we politely asked for it back."

"It's a small consolation, but I'll take it." He looked back at Lake. "There's a lot of rubble between us and Sarah. The ceiling is still unstable, and there was debris coming down when I left. I'd have tried to dig her out, but I knew it'd make things worse. I considered trying to find another tunnel that joined with the one she's in, but I didn't want to get lost down here. All that would have achieved was both of us dead. The only option was to try and find help." He swallowed hard, then cleared his throat. "I had to leave her there."

"You did the right thing." Lake handed him a protein bar.

As hungry as he was, Ryan wasn't sure he could eat. "It doesn't feel like it."

"Then trust me. You did the right thing." Lake stood, glancing at the boys before talking to Ryan. "Describe where Sarah is to these two. If they know of another way to get to her, I want to hear about it."

When Ryan described the graffiti they'd been following, the boys shared a worried look.

"You followed the wrong color," Le Chat said. "I told you to follow red."

"Well, it's hard to tell colors apart in candlelight."

Le Chat winced. "We don't use the tunnel you mention. It is unstable."

"No shit, Sherlock," Megan drawled.

"There were warning signs." Le Chat looked at The Pit for confirmation, and he nodded.

"Again. Hard to see much with just one small candle," Ryan gritted out.

Lake handed him another protein bar, probably to get his focus off killing the teens.

"Is there another way to get to Sarah?" Lake asked them.

The two boys had a spitfire conversation in their native language that Ryan couldn't follow, making him wish the coma had given him a gift for languages. But nope, he got the ability to measure distance without a ruler and the urge to read thrillers. He was beginning to think that nothing good came out of being shot in the head.

"It's worth a try," Lake said to the teens, because of

course, he spoke fluent French. "Apparently, there's another passage above us. One that crosses over the tunnel where Sarah is trapped. There are access points between the two. One may lead to Sarah."

Ryan's hands began to shake with relief that they had a plan. A chance to get to her.

"Megan," Lake said, "run back and fill Callum in. Tell him to call emergency rescue, just in case we need them. Once they arrive, take them to the point where the tunnel collapsed. They can work the rescue from that side while we try to find Sarah from above."

Megan nodded as she got to her feet. "How will we lead the rescue team to the cave-in? I've tagged this far, but I don't know where to go from here."

Lake considered the teens before speaking to Le Chat in French. When he was done, the boy was shaking and nodding furiously.

"He'll wait here for you and show you where to go," Lake told Megan.

It spoke volumes that no one questioned whether the boy would actually do what Lake told him to do. Nobody doubted he would. It'd take someone a whole lot more dangerous than Le Chat to cross Lake.

"I'll be back," Megan said in a bad Arnie accent before running off into the tunnel.

"Lake," Ryan said. "There were bodies. Other people who'd been abducted, like Sarah and me."

Le Chat sucked in a breath and looked like he might run. La Fosse muttered some curses. While Lake and Dimitri went still.

"You can find them again?" Lake asked.

Ryan nodded.

"Then we'll deal with that later. Sarah first."

"Yeah," Ryan agreed. "Sarah first."

He pulled on the shoes they'd given him. Obviously, the teens had updated his team on his bare feet situation.

As he laced them, he realized they were familiar. "Are these Callum's?"

"Gotta love a boss who'll give you the shoes off his own feet," Dimitri said with a grin. "He's running around on cyber feet topside. Just for you."

"I'd be touched, only his cyber feet are a size smaller than my flesh and bone feet."

"Don't understand that," Dimitri said. "If you could choose whatever size your feet were, wouldn't you go bigger?"

Seeing as Megan wasn't around, Ryan assumed Dimitri was talking to himself.

Once on his feet, and feeling stronger than he had in days, Ryan faced La Fosse. "Lead the way, and make it quick. I'm holding you responsible for whatever state we find Sarah in. You hear?"

The teen didn't look him in the eye; he just nodded and turned in the opposite direction of the mural.

"We go this way," he said.

As one, the men started to run, dragging the teen along with them, while Le Chat waited for Megan to return.

CHAPTER TWENTY-NINE

Sarah didn't want to open her eyes. Because she knew what she'd find—the nothingness of endless darkness. Fighting to keep the silence from derailing her thoughts, she cataloged her injuries. There were going to be bruises, a lot of bruises, but as far as she could tell, nothing was broken. She hadn't been hit by the bulk of the collapse, only by some of the smaller rocks at the edge.

It had been pure instinct to push Ryan out of the way while jumping back herself. Now, she wished instinct had made her throw herself into the same part of the tunnel as Ryan. Because instinct had left her alone. In the dark. With no clue how to get out.

Brushing the debris off herself, Sarah sat up and leaned back against the wall. The same wall she'd rammed her head into in an attempt to avoid the falling ceiling. There was a lump on the back of her head, but no blood, which was something. Of course, there was also no way of telling how long she'd been unconscious. Minutes? Hours? Her internal clock was silent.

"Ryan?" she called, but her voice was hoarse and useless.

She felt around for the water bottle, grateful when her fingertips bumped into it straight away. The water was tepid and stale. And she was thankful she had it. After a few sips, she tried calling again.

"Ryan?"

There was no reply. No sound at all. It was eerie. Even in her childhood home, when she'd hid in the dark, there had been the creaks of the old building and the distant voices of neighbors to keep her company. Here, all she had was the sound of her own heart thumping, fast and furiously, in her chest.

"Ryan," she shouted again.

All she heard was ringing in her ears.

Pulling her knees up to her chest, Sarah went over the facts as she knew them.

One: She'd shoved Ryan out of the way, so he had to be fine. Unless the rest of the tunnel came down after she'd been knocked out...

No.

It wasn't likely. She'd spotted the crack above them a split second before the candle went out. The crack had run horizontally across the tunnel, not down it. In fact, there were no cracks in the section just before the one that collapsed. She'd noticed because the tunnel seemed to be full of them. When the one overhead had groaned and started to crumble and the sprinkling of dust became a torrent, she'd known there were only seconds to spare until it all came down. The area they stood in would be buried—and them along with it. Her only thought was to get Ryan out of the way before it collapsed.

And she was *sure* she'd shoved him hard enough.

Which meant the odds were good that he'd been safe on the other side.

She nodded. Okay. That made sense. She took a deep breath and carried on.

Two: If Ryan was okay, that meant he was looking for her or had gone to get help.

Or, he left you...and forgot about you...again...

"Get out of my head!" she snapped at the voice from her childhood. "I don't have time for abandonment issues."

The chances of Ryan forgetting her were slim, unless he'd been hit on the head again. Which was unlikely, seeing as she'd shoved him hard so that wouldn't happen again. Anyway, he'd never leave her there alone. *Never.* Every fiber of his being was designed to be the hero. His honor wouldn't let him leave her. She knew that now. Only something completely out of his control would keep Ryan from returning to get her—like a coma.

Which led her to three: She had to stay where she was so he knew where to find her.

She blinked against the black void. Where was she going to go anyway? For all she knew, there could be a pit five steps from her, waiting for her to walk into it, and she would never know because she couldn't see a thing.

Yes. Staying put was a *very* good plan.

Four: She didn't have much water left, so she had to conserve it until she was rescued.

Five: She should also conserve her energy, which was fine considering she wasn't going anywhere anyway.

All she could do was wait.

And seeing as she wasn't the hero of the piece, that was fine by her.

Her hands shook as she grasped the water bottle, reminding her that she was barely keeping it together. Her mind kept straying into areas it shouldn't go, and she fought to bring it back. To keep herself focused on the facts—and not on the bodies that'd dehydrated and died alone, lost in the tunnels.

Absently, she felt a tingling on her neck and brushed at her hair. A bug crawled over her hand. Gasping, Sarah shook it off. It felt big. Lots of legs. Spider? She felt movement on her other shoulder. Then her knee.

Jumping to her feet, she dropped the water bottle and swept her body and hair with her hands. Brushing away everything and anything that might be there. She was panting now. Imagining all kinds of unseen things crawling over her.

Any second, and her hyperventilating would result in a full-blown panic attack, which would send her into an oblivion where bugs crawled over her unconscious body.

Oh! No!

Had they been doing that while she'd been out cold?

She flapped her shirt to get anything stuck in there out. Followed up with running her hands up and down her legs, under her skirt, checking every inch of herself. Lastly, she doubled over and combed out her hair with her fingers.

That was the best she could do.

"Calm down," she told herself. "You need to stay calm."

There were bugs on the floor—she was sure of it. She might be unable to see them, but she sure as hell could imagine them. Great big spiders coming for her. She could see them in her mind as they crawled over Ryan's huge shoes and up her—

Ryan's shoes. They were like anvils. Sarah stomped in place, imagining squished bug bodies and spiders running for their lives. As she stamped, she waved her arms, making sure to dust her hair every now and then, just to get anything that might have dropped from the ceiling.

Okay, you can do this.

So much for conserving energy, but at least things weren't crawling over her skin. She repeated the facts in an attempt to ease her heart rate.

"One: Ryan's fine. Two: He'll rescue you. Three: Stay put. Four: Water." She'd forgotten the water! Bending over, she felt for the bottle, hoping she didn't find bugs instead. When she found it, she carefully wiped it down and sighed with relief when the lid was screwed on tight. "Five: Conserve energy. Yeah, that's pretty pointless."

She struck five off her list and added a sixth item. If Ryan was looking for her, he needed a clue as to which direction to head in. Which meant, six: Make lots of noise.

Plan sorted, Sarah took a deep breath and started to sing.

"Ninety-nine bottles of beer on the wall..." All the while stomping in place to keep the bugs away.

The passageway La Fosse led them down seemed to be an old utility tunnel. Ryan spotted evidence of dated wiring and broken fuse boxes. Overhead, the Metro rumbled periodically, sending vibrations through the earth and shaking dust down onto them.

"Why would anybody come down here willingly?" Dimitri complained from behind Ryan.

"La liberté," La Fosse said, sounding very out of breath.

"Freedom, huh?" Dimitri said. "Like the freedom to rob people who're in need? That kind of freedom? I'm thinking you should exercise your freedom to only talk when absolutely necessary, kid."

Ryan glanced at his phone. Now that it'd been returned to him, and helpfully charged, he could keep track of the time again. Two hours, with brief rests for the kid, that's how long they'd been going. All that time spent on a steady but shallow decline into the catacombs.

"Wait," La Fosse said.

Lake, Dimitri, and Ryan came to a halt beside him, as La Fosse pulled a worn and well-used piece of paper from the side pocket on his backpack. He studied it intently, with all three men doing nothing to hide that they were examining it too.

The paper appeared to be a crudely drawn map, with notes scrawled all over it.

"We must be careful now," La Fosse said. "From here forward, this tunnel is very close to the older one. There have been many holes that have opened up between them."

"Can we get around these holes if we have to?" Ryan asked.

The kid nodded, still panting for air. It was pathetic. Lake was at least thirty years older than junior and he hadn't even broken out in a sweat.

The passage was wide enough for them to walk two abreast. Ryan and The Pit went first, eyes on the ground, looking for hazards.

"There weren't any holes in the section of tunnel Sarah and I went through," Ryan said.

Hopefully that meant any gaps between passages that they found were on the side of the tunnel that held Sarah.

"Kid," Dimitri said. "Where are we on your map?"

"We are over the part that intersects with the tunnel below. Like a diagonal." He used his arms to illustrate that their tunnel crossed over the other tunnel in a long slant, not in a perpendicular way.

"So there's a decent length where these two tunnels overlap," Dimitri said. "That's good. Ups our chances of finding her."

"If we're over the right tunnel." Ryan glared at The Pit, who hurriedly averted his eyes.

A few minutes later, they came across the first hole. It wasn't big enough for anyone but La Fosse to get through, which meant it wouldn't work. Although, Ryan was tempted to dangle him down there by his ankles as a crude sort of recon.

The next three holes weren't even big enough to fit The Pit's skinny frame.

"Do people actually use this tunnel to get down to the one below?" Ryan asked, just to be sure.

"Oui," La Fosse said.

There was nothing for the next few minutes, until their flashlights skimmed a wooden segment of the tunnel floor.

"An entrance." La Fosse pointed to the boards that were placed side by side, covering the stone floor. "We look under here."

Together, Ryan and the kid moved the planks, leaning them against the tunnel wall. Beneath them was a dark gaping hole about four feet wide and at least twelve deep. Someone had fitted a couple of Glue-in U-bolts to the soft rock between the levels, and a climber's rope was dangling from them by a carabiner. The rope had been knotted at points to make it easier to use as a ladder. From the looks of it, the same people had embedded some randomly placed rungs for climbers to hold on to, if needed.

"We have a winner," Dimitri said. "Rock paper scissors to see who goes first?"

Ryan was already lowering himself to his belly, feet dangling into the hole.

"Guess Ryan wins," Dimitri said.

Holding the rough rope, he lowered himself down into the tunnel beneath them. Flashing his light in both directions, he checked for signs of Sarah or the cave-in. There was nothing, so he anchored the rope for the others to climb down.

Once they were all at the bottom, Lake turned to La Fosse. "Which way?"

Pit boy wiped his nose with the back of his hand. "Uh…"

"Get the map out," Dimitri ordered.

"There is nothing on the map for directions in this tunnel. I am not lying," The Pit whined.

"Let me see." Lake held out his hand, and La Fosse quickly passed it over. "This map is a mess. It's a miracle we even made it here in the first place. We'll just have to choose a direction and see where it leads."

"Wait. Gimme a second here." Ryan held up his hands for silence as he closed his eyes and concentrated.

"Uh, Ryan," Dimitri said. "Is this really the time to pray?"

"Shh," Ryan hissed as he tried to tap into his freaky gift.

A map of the tunnels he'd been through appeared in his mind, like a 3D model he could spin to look at from every angle. It showed the different levels and entrances to passageways he hadn't taken, as well as faint outlines of things he knew were there but hadn't actually seen—like the Metro. He waited, getting a feel for the map in relation to where they were standing.

Opening his eyes, Ryan pointed down the tunnel. "It's that way."

"You sure?"

Ryan couldn't blame Dimitri for being skeptical. "Yeah, I'm sure. Tracker training."

"This seems a little extra for standard army training," Dimitri said.

"Yeah, it's a coma thing." Ryan shrugged, deciding there was no point in hiding the crazy. "I see maps in my head now."

They started jogging down the tunnel in the direction he'd indicated. Dimitri kept shooting him curious looks, while Lake seemed to take the situation in his stride.

"Is this like a Rain Man thing?" Dimitri said.

Ryan rolled his eyes at him. "Megan is really rubbing off on you, you know that?"

"Ray-man! That's what I'm calling you now. We gotta think of a way to monetize this new skill of yours. Maybe we could blindfold you and spin you like a bottle, then take bets on whether you know which way you're facing at the end of it."

Ryan let him know what he thought of that idea using sign language.

Dimitri was unfazed. "Does your woo-woo mapping system tell you how far it is to Sarah?"

"No, it doesn't." *Soon. They had to find her soon. Right?*

Dimitri clasped his shoulder. "It's cool, Ryan, we'll get her."

All he could do was nod as his stomach churned and exhaustion nipped at the edges of his consciousness.

The tunnel didn't go in a straight line. It was as though the people who'd made it were either drunk or confused. Either way, there seemed no rhyme or reason to the layout.

"Halt," Lake snapped, receiving instant obedience.

He held up a fist for silence.

"You hear that?" Lake asked quietly.

A voice.

A female voice.

Sarah.

They picked up speed, and the voice became louder.

"Is she...singing?" Dimitri asked. "And keeping a weird beat?"

Ryan grinned as the lyrics to *Ninety-Nine Bottles of Beer on the Wall* drifted toward them.

"Head injury?" Dimitri asked Lake.

"She's letting me know where to find her." Ryan ran around the corner, and his flashlight landed on Sarah.

He didn't know whether to laugh or cry. And he sure as hell didn't know what she was doing. As well as singing at the top of her lungs, she was stamping randomly while swinging her arms wildly.

When the light hit her face, she covered her eyes. "Ryan?" she said, sounding shaky. "That'd better be you. I'm sick of singing this song, and there are spiders trying to eat me."

He rushed to her, scooping her up into his arms and clamping his mouth over hers. Their kiss was long and hard and kind of frenetic.

They broke apart and Ryan ran his hands over her, checking for injuries. "I thought...I was worried you were..."

"I'm fine. I knew you would come back." She stroked his cheeks, and he felt like he was drowning in her eyes.

Alive.

Safe.

Well.

At last, it felt like he could breathe again.

Someone cleared his throat, and Sarah's head shot around, her mouth dropping open. "Uh, Ryan?"

"You want to introduce us?" Dimitri was grinning like a demented chimpanzee.

"Sarah, this is Dimitri, my teammate, and Lake Benson, he owns the company. You know the teenage arsehole already."

She pushed at his shoulders to get him to put her down. Yeah, that wasn't happening. Not yet. Not until he could handle having space between them. Maybe in a year or two.

"Uh, hi." Sarah ducked her head shyly.

"Nice to meet you, Sarah," Lake said, his lips twitching.

CHAPTER THIRTY

They climbed out of the catacombs under the hospital just as the rescue services were ready to go in. To Sarah's uneducated eye, the scene seemed chaotic and far too bright after being underground for days. There were police, ambulance crews, official-looking men in hard hats, a woman shouting instructions—and even a camera crew from the local news.

One group of people, relief on their faces, beelined straight for them.

"Ryan!" A tiny blue-haired woman bounced on the spot before rushing him.

"Ellie Blue," he called back, letting her know this was his best friend.

Elle ran at Ryan, jumping up to throw her arms and legs around him, laughing loudly when he caught her. Her eyes shone with pure joy.

Ryan said something to Elle, and her gaze shot to Sarah. Next thing she knew, Sarah was being hugged by a woman she'd never met.

"You're Ryan's Sarah," she exclaimed. "I'm so happy to meet you." Then she turned somber, holding both Sarah's hands in hers as she looked up at her earnestly. "If I'd known about you, I would have told you he was in a coma. I'm so sorry that I didn't think to check his online profiles to find you. I can only imagine what you must have thought, and it's all my fault."

"No—" Sarah started to say.

"Yes." Elle nodded. "This is on me. Which means you get favors for life. Just ask and it's yours. You want someone on the no-fly list? I can do that. You want to hack some top-secret facility? I'm your woman."

She was so earnest that all Sarah could say was, "Thanks?"

Ryan's laugh caught both of their attentions, and they turned to see him pull a pristinely dressed woman into a hug.

"That's Rachel," Elle said. "She doesn't hug."

"This is how normal people show affection," Ryan told Rachel, laughing as he did so.

"This is how a perfectly good Prada suit ends up in the rubbish bin." Rachel curled her lip. "Stop touching me and take a shower."

"She's an acquired taste," Elle said with affection.

A scary blonde woman, who turned out to be Dimitri's wife, Megan, sidled up to Sarah.

"I'm glad you're alive and safe," Megan said. "But if you ever hurt Ryan, I'll use you for target practice." Then she was gone.

"Is that normal?" Sarah asked Elle.

"It's how Scottish people tell you they care." Elle nudged her. "Speaking of scary Scottish people, don't let this one freak you out. Really, he's a teddy bear."

A sandy-haired man strode toward her on mechanical

feet, holding out his hand as he scowled. When Sarah hesitantly took it, he clasped her hand between both of his.

"This is our boss, Callum," Elle said.

Intense green eyes met hers. "You shouldnae be standing," he said gruffly. "You look like you've been through hell. Let's get you some help." Then he turned and bellowed at a paramedic to get his arse over there and do his job.

Sarah honestly wasn't sure what she was supposed to do. Was she supposed to head over to the terrified paramedic or stay with the scary Scottish guy?

"Let go of Sarah," an American man said. "You're freaking her out."

"I am not," Callum barked before looking down at her.

"Maybe a little," she admitted.

With a grump, he dropped her hand and headed over to harass the poor paramedic.

"I'm Joe," the American said. "This is Julia." He held hands with the woman at his side.

Everything about Julia called to Sarah. She had kind eyes and a soft smile that instantly put her at ease.

"The first time Callum barked at me," Julia said, "I fainted."

"You did?" Sarah could totally understand that.

"Yeah." Joe grinned at Julia. "And then spent almost a year hiding under her desk or behind office plants so she wouldn't have to deal with him."

"Or you." Julia batted her lashes at him before giving Sarah a wry look. "Or any of the men. They can be a little...intimidating."

"No kidding." Sarah agreed. "Elle says he's a teddy bear."

"Elle grew up in the mob. It's all relative," Joe drawled.

"Sarah," Callum shouted. "Get over here. The para-medic is ready to do his bloody job now."

Joe laughed while Julia looked sympathetic. "I can come with you, if you like," she said.

"It's okay. Looks like someone already intercepted him."

Callum had been waylaid by two more ferocious-looking men, and Sarah hurried over while he was still occupied. When his conversation finished, he nodded at Sarah, growled at the paramedic, and headed over to talk to Lake Benson.

Meanwhile, the two men who'd been talking with Callum came to see her.

"I'm Harvard, Rachel's better half," said yet another American. "Welcome to Paris." There was a twinkle in his eye that made Sarah like him instantly.

A smaller, nondescript man stood beside him. "David, the blue-haired wonder belongs to me. I'm glad you made it, Sarah. I just wanted you to know that we're following leads on who's behind your abduction, and I can promise you we'll get answers soon. In the meantime, if you need anything, call out. We're all here for you." He smiled before heading over to his wife.

"He's kinda scary," Sarah found herself saying to Harvard.

"Most people don't pick up on that," he told her. "Don't worry. He's on our side." He shook his head at the sight of Ryan annoying his wife. "I have to go rescue Ryan before Rachel runs out of patience with him."

Sarah thought it was interesting that he didn't feel the need to rescue his wife. As they passed each other, Ryan and Harvard slapped hands, as though they were tag teaming Rachel. It struck Sarah then that this team was closer than family. They were bound together by a trust that ran deeper than most relatives ever had. It was amazing, and a little intimidating, to witness.

"How you doing, Stats?" Ryan said as he sat close beside her on the ambulance tailgate.

"Bit overwhelmed," she said honestly. "And hungry. And tired. And desperately in need of a bath."

"Let's get you checked out properly first, then we'll deal with the rest of it." He tapped the paramedic on the shoulder. "I had to perform CPR on her after she almost drowned. Can we get an X-ray to check her ribs? And I think some of her scrapes might be infected; it wasn't clean down there. Oh, and maybe a saline drip. She hasn't had much to drink for days, and I'm pretty sure she's a little dehydrated."

"Ryan!" Sarah felt her cheeks heat. "Don't tell the man how to do his job."

He shrugged and spoke to the paramedic. "There's a bump on her head, so we should check for a concussion. And her feet were pretty torn up too."

The paramedic grinned. "Best we go to the ER and do this properly," he said.

"Good man," Ryan agreed.

"Welcome to Benson Security," Elle called to Sarah, flashing a cheeky grin. "The men were born arrogant."

"And sexy," Ryan replied.

"True," Elle said. "That *is* a plus."

"Climb inside, both of you," the paramedic said. "It's easier to drive you over to the ER building than wheel you there."

"Come on, Stats." Ryan took her hand and pulled her into the ambulance. "There's bound to be a snack machine in the hospital."

With perfect timing, his belly rumbled as the driver closed the door.

Sarah was absolutely mortified to find that she had to walk through the lobby of one of Paris's most prestigious hotels while she looked like a disaster victim.

"Somebody could have brought us clean clothes," she whispered to Ryan, who seemed not to notice all the staring eyes.

"Julia offered, but I didn't see the point. We need a shower first."

"She offered and you said no?" And yes, her voice had gone back up into dog whistle territory again.

"The lift is right there, Stats. Just smile at the curious people and get in it. They'll have forgotten us by the time we make it to Rachel's suite." He grinned wickedly. "Wave if you want to. It'll give them a thrill."

She groaned and moved closer to him, using his over-sized body as a shield from prying eyes. He wrapped an arm around her, but she could feel his chest move and knew he was silently chuckling.

It had taken a couple of hours to get out of the hospital. Sarah had been declared concussion-free, and there were no cracked ribs from Ryan's CPR—something he'd been worried about. There was no denying they were in poor shape though. Both of them were covered in cuts and bruises, and Sarah felt like every step she took pulled at overused muscles.

Joe, who'd picked them up, jogged from the front desk where he'd been talking to someone and met them in the elevator.

Sarah winced. "I'm sorry about the smell," she told him. "I'm sure it's even worse in such a small space."

"Don't smell a thing," he managed to say with a straight face.

Sarah didn't know if that was the truth or not. It was hard to tell, from her perspective, just how ripe they both were. They'd both cleaned up a little in the hospital, but she felt gross. All she could think about was a shower and a soft, clean bed.

"Please tell me somebody ordered food," Ryan said, proving his priorities were different.

Joe was clearly entertained. "Julia stocked up as soon as we got word you were coming home. Temporary as this home might be."

"I love Julia," Ryan said on a sigh.

"I'm going to let that pass," Julia's husband said. "On account of you being starving and in no condition for me to punch."

The elevator opened into a foyer area with one set of double doors. There was no hotel corridor, no multiple numbered rooms, just one set of ornate doors and a discrete brass plaque declaring it "The Royal Suite."

Ryan opened the door and gestured for her to enter. "This is Rachel's idea of mission accommodation. She only does five stars."

The vast living area was elegance itself. Furnished with baroque antique furniture, purple silken cushions, and heavy matching drapes, it screamed wealth. And it made Sarah feel far too dirty to touch anything.

Ryan didn't have the same problem. There was a coffee table laden with sandwiches and pastries, and he headed straight for it, dragging her along with him.

He loaded up a plate for each of them before plopping back into one of the expensive sofas.

"We can't sit there," Sarah told him. "We're too dirty."

As she stared at Ryan, who was too busy eating to answer her, Rachel swept into the room, followed by pretty much everyone else.

"The hotel will clean it," Rachel said. "That's why we pay them. Sit."

Sarah sat, feeling a little like a well-trained dog. But she couldn't relax, so she perched on the very edge, hoping she didn't leave a mark. Ryan, on the other hand, had no problem spreading out on the sofa.

"Elle," he called. "What we got to drink?"

"What do you want?" Elle asked from the other end of the room.

"Milk," Ryan said, making everyone laugh. "What do you want?" he asked Sarah.

"I'd love a cup of tea," she said. "But I can make it."

"Don't be daft. I'm on this," Elle said as she left the room.

"I'd better help." Julia stood. "Elle's tea isn't very good."

"I heard that," Elle called from the other room.

As Sarah nibbled at a sandwich, Ryan went back for seconds, piling his plate high again.

"Do you two have the energy for a debrief?" Lake asked.

Ryan studied her for a beat. "If it's short. Sarah's wiped. And we need to get cleaned up."

"Summary now," Callum said, standing beside Lake. "Details tomorrow."

"We've set up a room for you," Joe added. "Julia put some clothes in the drawers for both of you, and there's food and drink in there too. If you tell Julia your sizes—especially shoes, Sarah—we'll get items that fit and have them delivered for when you wake."

"That's very kind," Sarah told him. "I'm afraid I don't have any money on me right now. Our wallets went missing."

Ryan's hand covered hers where it sat on her knee. "They didn't go missing. The little assholes stole them. But you don't need money, we've got it covered. Right?"

"Absolutely," Joe said firmly, shutting any further discussion down.

Soft conversation broke out around the room as everyone settled into the many sofas and chairs. Well, all except Callum and Lake, who preferred to stand. Julia brought a cup of tea in for Sarah, placing it on a delicate table at her side. She added two bottles—one of orange juice, the other water.

"I didn't know what else you might want, so I brought a couple of options. If you'd like more tea, or something else, just signal me. It's no trouble at all." She smiled shyly and whispered, "I enjoy looking after people."

"Me too," Sarah whispered back.

With a smile, Julia took the seat nearest Sarah.

"Okay," Callum barked. "Let's get this done before these two fall asleep. Elle, fill them in."

Elle was sitting tailor-style on a large ottoman, her laptop open beside her. "Okay, peeps, here's the summary. You were both lifted off the street by a mercenary called Prentice. After Rachel scared the ever-loving out of him, he told us he'd been hired by a fixer called Leo Fournier, here in Paris."

"The Baker," Ryan said around a mouthful of almond tart. "I've heard of him. He'll do anything if the price is right. Who was he working for?"

"That we don't know," Elle said. "Yet. We have a lead on where he's hanging out, and the boys plan to pick him up tonight." She glanced at David, who took up where she left off.

"We have a room set up to talk to him." David's eyes were cold, and Sarah knew there would be a whole lot more than talking going on in that room. "You want in?" he asked Ryan.

To her surprise, Ryan glanced at her, then shook his head. "Not tonight. I want to make sure Sarah gets settled. You can fill me in once you're done."

David nodded.

"Apart from that," Elle said, "we know that someone was investigating both of you during the time you were dating. Why they waited until now to pick you up, we don't know."

"They investigated us?" Ryan reached for more pastries.

"Read every piece of correspondence between the two of you. They seemed very interested in your relationship."

Sarah suddenly lost what little appetite she had. Handing her plate to Ryan, who'd vacuum up what was left, she picked up her tea. The warm liquid was nectar from the gods.

"Did you find out who hacked us?" Ryan said.

"A hacker for hire called Bubba—would you believe it? I got in touch with him, but he said everything happened through a broker and he had no idea who wanted the information." Her eyes narrowed. "Bubba had some unfortunate luck after our talk. He's now being questioned by the FBI in some unrelated matters."

Ryan grinned. "Only the FBI?"

"Possibly the NSA too. I'm biding my time." Elle had a look on her face that Sarah had only seen on Bond villains.

"Do you have any idea why you were lifted?" Callum asked.

"Nope." Ryan looked at her, and she shook her head.

"I don't understand any of this," Sarah said honestly.

"I can tell you this though." Ryan moved on to the plate of cookies. "We were held in somebody's killing field. Sarah was manacled to the wall while I was free to roam. When we broke her out, we found two other women who'd died manacled to the walls in different rooms. One of the women was part of a couple. Her husband died with her. It looked like they'd tried to escape. The couple was German, and the woman was French Canadian. I took their driver's licenses for ID, but they were in the wallet that the kids stole."

Sarah swallowed hard before addressing the room. "The Canadian woman was Adrienne Toussaint, twenty-six, from Quebec City. She was engaged. The couple was Stefan and Iris Muller, from Leipzig. They were twenty-nine and twenty-four, respectively." She looked at Ryan. "I read the licenses."

He took her hand in his as his eyes softened. "It's good you did."

"German, Canadian, English?" Joe said. "It's all over the place."

"I think there were more bodies too," Ryan said. "One of the tunnels that we didn't take was stinking of decomp. And there were more rooms sealed up behind a cave-in. The place was wired for video, and someone had installed motion sensor lighting in the part of the tunnel that was sealed off to us. There was some brand new welding on an old gate to keep the victims from opening it."

"Cameras?" Elle leaned forward.

"They were using a Wi-Fi system that fed into a wired-in relay. I couldn't get to that though, or I'd have tried to hack it."

"But if we get back down there, I could use the system to trace who was running it." Elle looked thoughtful as Sarah shuddered at the mere mention of going anywhere near those tunnels ever again.

"Can you find your way back to the area with the bodies?" Lake asked.

"Yeah." Putting his empty plate on the table, Ryan sat back in the sofa. "But we'd have to go the long way—which means crawling through tiny tunnels and swimming under rock. I couldn't get past that gate, so I don't know how to access it from the other side. If we take the right tools with us, we can dismantle it and see where it leads, which will make things easier when we bring the authorities in. Otherwise, they'd have to swim through the tunnels too."

Sarah shuddered at the memory of being in the water, making Ryan zero in on her.

"We're done here," he told his team. "We'll talk tomorrow. Which room is ours?"

As Julia told him where to go, Sarah felt herself shutting down. There was no more energy left. Not for talking, or being polite, or even eating. She wasn't even sure she'd be able to shower before she fell asleep. All she wanted to do was crawl into a proper bed and sleep forever.

CHAPTER THIRTY-ONE

Their room was beautiful. Light, airy, and clean. It also wasn't a room—it was an apartment. There was a sitting area, complete with sofa, chairs, and footstools. A coffee table held platters of snacks and drinks in buckets full of ice. The bed was vast, with a canopy you could draw around it to make your own little world. And the windows had a view out over the Seine and the Eiffel Tower.

"Not sure you're up to a bath tonight." Ryan led her into a bathroom that was as big as the ground floor of her house. "You'll only fall asleep, and I don't think I have the energy to carry you to bed."

Although she gazed longingly at the massive tub, she had to agree. "Shower it is."

After Ryan turned on the shower heads—yes, there were more than one—he gazed around the room. "It looks like Louis the Sixteenth puked up in here. Is there ever a reason for decorative columns?"

There was no stopping the giggles that erupted, even though they sounded a little on the delirious side.

"Oh, you're beyond exhausted." He stalked toward her and started unbuttoning the rag that used to be a blouse.

"Um, what are you doing?" Sarah watched his fingers deftly deal with the buttons.

"Helping. The faster we shower, the quicker we get to bed."

She held the sides of her blouse together. "We're not showering together."

How he managed to look both sexy and cute at the same time, she didn't know. "Stats, this isn't the time to be shy. You can barely stand on your own, and I'm genuinely worried you'll fall asleep as soon as the warm water hits you. This is purely about showering. We'll save the good stuff for when we're both awake enough to appreciate it."

She still didn't let go of her shirt. "I can shower on my own." *Maybe...*

"You can't be self-conscious," said the man who looked like he'd stepped off the cover of a fitness magazine. "I've been all over your body."

"Yes, in pitch darkness." Where he couldn't see her little pouch of a stomach, or the stretchmarks on her boobs, or the cellulite on her thighs.

"I would offer to turn the light out, but I think we've both had enough of the dark. How about I close my eyes instead?"

"Promise?"

"No, Stats, I can't promise." He seemed amused.

"Then what's the point of offering?"

"What was it you called me? Oh yeah, stop being a big sissy and get in the shower." He pulled his ripped shirt over his head and tossed it in the corner of the floor.

There were scratches and bruises marring his perfect torso. It was as though someone had vandalized a

Michelangelo, and it physically hurt her to see them there.

"You're right. I'm being a big sissy. Worse, I'm being irrational." She gathered her courage and tossed the blouse on top of his T-shirt.

"I wasn't going to say..." Ryan smiled cheekily.

He toed off his borrowed shoes before slipping his jeans and boxers down his legs.

Sweet heavens, she was going to faint!

"You seem to be a bit stalled there, babe. Let me help. Otherwise, we're never getting to bed." He stepped in front of her, all muscle and man.

"You are so beautiful," she sighed, her hand going to his chest. It was warm, and solid, and oh so tempting under her touch.

Crouching, Ryan carefully removed the shoes he'd given her. "Please, don't ever say that in front of the guys. Men aren't beautiful, they're handsome or rugged. Yeah, I like rugged. Use that."

Sarah stroked her fingers through his hair as he undid her skirt, letting the abomination fall to the floor.

He sucked in a breath as his hands rested on her well-padded hips. "Now, *you* we can call beautiful. Or voluptuous." He hooked his fingers into her underpants and dragged them down thighs that hadn't seen a gap since she was a toddler. "Lush is another good word for you. And Rubenesque." He grinned at her as he stood. "Bet you didn't think I knew that one."

Oh, what the hell, she was going to give him the benefit of the doubt and believe he genuinely thought her rounded body was perfect.

While he got rid of her bra, she stroked his cheek. "I think you know all the right words," she said.

"Until you're naked." His hands cupped her breasts, making her sigh into his touch. "Then I forget how to speak."

"You're doing okay right now," she pointed out.

"Only because you're too tired to do anything else, and I'm being chivalrous. I can totally get why chivalry died out." His thumbs brushed her nipples, sending tingles straight south. "Shower. Bed. Everything else later."

Seeing as she could hardly keep her eyes open, Sarah was in no position to object.

The shower was big enough for several people, with two wide rain-making heads above them and two smaller detachable showerheads at right angles to them. It was like stepping into a tropical storm. The water pressure was so strong, it felt like it was massaging her aching muscles. Unable to stop herself, Sarah's eyes closed as she drifted to the beat of the water.

Hands found her hair, and gentle fingers massaged exotically scented shampoo into her scalp. Sarah leaned back against Ryan, reveling in the feel of his bare skin against hers.

"I could get used to this," she moaned as he rinsed her hair before carefully adding conditioner.

"So could I," he said.

He reached past her for the shower gel and Sarah complained, although not very enthusiastically, she'd admit.

"I can wash myself," she said.

"Let me." It was a purring temptation she was helpless to resist.

All she could do was stand there, halfway between reality and heaven, as Ryan softly soaped and rinsed her body. There was a reverence in his touch that brought tears to her eyes. Sarah honestly didn't think she'd ever felt so cared for.

"I should have taken better care of you," he said as he traced a bruise on her shoulder.

"You took the best care of me, considering it wasn't your job anyway. We're both banged up, which means I didn't take the best of care of you either."

"Hey, don't ruin my macho fantasies. It's my job to do the caring." His eyes were twinkling as he turned the water off, making Sarah wish they could have stayed under it. But seeing as she was already falling asleep, that wasn't a good idea.

Grabbing an oversized white towel, Ryan wrapped her in it. It was so thick and fluffy it felt like being enfolded in a hug. Would it be terrible of her to steal the towel? Probably best if she found out if the gift shop stored them first.

Even though she insisted she didn't care about going to bed with damp hair, Ryan dried it for her. In a way that only people without naturally curly hair would do it. Come morning, she'd look like she was wearing a clown wig. Still, he was sweet to do it.

Julia had set out night clothes for them, but they were too tired to bother. Instead, Ryan lifted her into bed and brought the comforter over her. Bliss. Pure bliss. She was floating on a cloud of Egyptian cotton, and she never wanted to come back to earth.

When Ryan climbed into the other side of the wide bed, he reached for the lamp to switch it off.

Sarah rushed to stop him. "No, please, leave it on."

Thankfully, he didn't object. All he did was roll into her, snuggling her close. And, secure in Ryan's arms, with the lamplight glowing and the duvet warming her, Sarah fell asleep.

Ryan woke to screaming, and it took a second to realize where he was. Beside him, Sarah thrashed in her sleep. Her hands pushing at an unseen foe.

"No," she begged. "Don't take me. Please don't take me."

She was having a nightmare.

"Hey, hey, wake up," Ryan said softly, trying to wake her without freaking her more.

It was pointless. Because while he soothed, half his team burst into their room, armed to the teeth.

The noise woke Sarah, who shot upright, the duvet falling around her waist. She spotted the team. Screamed at the top of her lungs and dove under the covers.

Ryan patted her through the bedding. "Nightmare, guys. You can stand down."

The men holstered their weapons and retreated, but not before Dimitri gave him a wide grin and a thumbs-up. The door closed loudly behind him, and Ryan glanced at the clock: two a.m. The team was obviously heading out to pick up Leo Fournier.

Ryan paused, waiting for the urge to join them to kick in. When it didn't come, he shrugged. He had better things to do.

"Are they gone?" Sarah's muffled voice came from under the bedding.

"Yeah, you can come out now."

The wildest hair he'd ever seen appeared from under the duvet, followed by wide molten bronze eyes.

"I flashed your team," Sarah said woefully.

"They've got a tough night ahead of them. They deserved a treat."

She groaned loudly and retreated back under the covers. Ryan decided to join her. In their little cocoon, breathing each other's air, he stroked her cheek.

"You okay?" Damn, she was beautiful.

"Bad dream," she whispered.

"Want to tell me about it?" His caress moved to her throat, reveling at the silky sensation of her skin beneath his fingertips.

She nibbled at her full bottom lip. "We were back in the water. The bodies were there, of the people we found. They were holding me. Pulling me down."

"Oh, baby, they can't get you here. Nothing can. You're safe."

"I know." She shuddered. "It's only a stupid dream, but it felt real."

"It isn't stupid. That was a helluva thing we went through. We'll both be having nightmares for a long time. It's normal and healthy. Just not so much with the fun." He traced over her shoulder and down her arm, hating the sight of the bruises and scratches that marked her skin. Hating that she'd been hurt. That she was still in pain.

"You have nightmares?" She sounded skeptical.

"Sure. Everybody does." His fingers moved to the curve of her hip. Shakespeare could have written sonnets about the way her waist dipped in before her hip flared out in a perfect curve.

"You don't seem the type," she said.

"Too manly, I know. It's a curse." There was a shallow indent between her thigh and hip that fascinated him. "I had nightmares while I was in a coma."

"I didn't know that was possible."

"Nightmare, vision, delusion, whatever it was, the same thing repeated in my head for months. I was lost. The map didn't make any sense, and no one could give me directions. I remember feeling confused, and scared, and helpless, desperate to wake up from the dream. But I never did. At least not for seven months."

"That sounds awful."

His compassionate woman. He wondered if she was even slightly aware that her feelings were written over her face for everyone to see. She probably thought she was keeping everything hidden, so she wouldn't get hurt. But she was failing miserably because he could read the truth in her eyes. His woman was hopelessly in love with him, and getting in deeper every minute.

He drew an invisible line from her hip to her cute little belly button. Her belly was soft and round, not the muscled plane of a fellow warrior, nor the skin and bones of some of the models he'd dated. He loved it.

"Do me a favor," he said as he made circles around her belly button.

"What?"

He looked into those bronze eyes of hers. "Never do any sit-ups or anything else to make this flat and muscled." He spread his palm over her belly. "If I wanted to feel something hard, I'd touch myself." He stilled. "That didn't come out right."

Sarah's whole body shook as she laughed at him.

Yeah, he probably deserved that.

"Ouch," she groaned, clasping the area where he'd pressed to revive her. "Still a bit sore. I shouldn't laugh so hard."

He frowned at the spot below her breasts. "Here, I can help." He rolled her onto her back.

"How?" Her hand caressed his shoulder.

"I'm going to kiss it better."

"Is this like a military medical thing?" she teased as he shuffled down the bed.

"Absolutely. I kissed all of the men's boo-boos if they were injured in the field."

Her laughter turned to a gentle gasp as he kissed the spot he'd had to hurt in order to save her. Her fingers softly combed through his hair, and he knew that even if the scar disappeared entirely, he'd always keep it longer for her.

"You know," he said against her skin, "I ought to be thorough. There is more than one area on your body that needs my medical attention."

"Far be it from me to get in the way of the medical profession."

"That's what I like to hear. Lie still. This won't hurt a bit."

She giggled again as he kissed the scrape on her hip before moving down to a series of bruises that ran down her thigh. He knew she'd gotten some of them when he'd been dragging her through the water. Others must have occurred during the cave-in. She'd been hit by far more rocks than she'd let on.

He nipped her outer thigh with his teeth, making her yelp.

"What's that for?"

"Shoving me out from under the tunnel collapse, only to get injured yourself."

"Other people would thank me for saving their life."

"Other people are dumb." He kissed his way down her leg to her poor, abused feet. "Are they sore?"

"Not right now," she said.

He lifted a foot and pressed a kiss to the instep, making her gasp.

"Problem?" he asked, feigning innocence.

"That shouldn't feel that good," she said, disarming him with her openness.

"Oh, I think we can make you feel a whole lot better than that." He kissed and stroked his way up the inside of her leg, taking his time with the sensitive area at the back of her knee.

As he moved back up the bed, he widened her legs to make space for himself. Her scent drew him, like a bee to nectar. He trailed kisses up her inner thigh, homing in on his destination with a gentle kiss to her bronze curls.

Hands tightened in his hair. "Hey," she said breathlessly, "I don't think I'm injured there."

"Better safe than sorry," he said huskily. "You never know when an injury may occur."

The air was warm in the duvet fort they'd made to keep out the world. And the intimacy of hiding together made everything else seem all the more intense. Including the sweet and salty taste of her desire.

"So, this is preventive?" she grated out as he stroked her with his tongue.

"Yes," he said solemnly.

"Sexual healing?"

She giggled and gasped at the same time, resulting in a weird kind of strangled noise that she so deserved to make after that cheesy dig.

"Could you please take this seriously?" Ryan demanded. "I'm administering first aid here."

"Could you administer it faster? I feel an injury coming on."

"Really?" He lifted his head to look at her. "We can't have that. Tell me where it hurts?"

"You are sick, and twisted, and evil for torturing me like this—"

Her tirade ended on a moan as Ryan got back to kissing everything better.

CHAPTER THIRTY-TWO

Sarah was floating four feet above their bed, gasping for air, as Ryan coaxed her back down. She'd been in the stratosphere. He'd taken her so high, so fast, she wasn't sure what exactly had happened. She only knew she wanted to do it again.

And again.

As soon as she could catch her breath.

"Wanna touch," she managed to get out before speech became impossible.

"You can touch," the devil drawled. "As soon as you're able. I'm not stopping you, but you're looking a little mellow there. You'd better not go to sleep on me, we're nowhere near finished."

"Good," she rasped.

His sinful, sinful mouth found her breast and sucked her nipple deep into his hot, wet mouth. Sarah came off the bed again. Every nerve ending in her body electric with sensation after he'd made her explode.

"Please," she begged.

"I thought I *was* pleasing you." He sucked her again as his hand massaged her other breast.

His body was heavy against hers. Her legs wide on either side of his hips. She could feel his hard, hot length against her thigh—which was totally the wrong place for it to be.

He was driving her crazy on purpose. Enjoying himself at her expense. Or she was enjoying herself at his... Either way, there was too much enjoying going on and not enough joining!

There was no way she could wrestle Ryan to get him where he needed to be. He'd win every time when it came to body strength.

Sweet heavens, she so loved his body. And his strength.

Logic. That's what she needed. If she could just think of some. Right then, all she wanted to do was sink her teeth into his bicep. Just a little. Actually, there were quite a few places she wanted to touch, and taste, and nibble.

"My turn," she complained.

"Yes, it is." He did something with his tongue and her nipple that made her claw at his back in desperation for more.

What had she been thinking?

His rough stubble hadn't quite turned into a full-blown beard yet, and she loved the feeling of it rasping against her skin. Had it left burn marks? Would she look down later and see red patches on her inner thighs?

Oh, boy, she hoped so.

He nibbled and kissed the crook of her neck, biting down on the muscle of her shoulder before swirling his tongue to soothe the sting. That same tongue then teased the shell of her ear, driving her crazy when the sound of his heavy breathing became all she could hear. She arched up against him, rubbing herself along his hard length.

He moaned in her ear, and it was like rockets went off inside her, propelling her forward. With more force than finesse, she toppled him onto his back and climbed on top of him.

Damn.

He was a work of art.

Hers.

She scraped her teeth over his small nipples, feeling his hands curl tight in her hair.

"What do you want, baby?" he rumbled, sending vibrations straight from his chest right through her body.

Sarah was past words. Instead of answering, she trailed her tongue over the contour of his abs while her hands strayed. He tasted salty and was hot to the touch. His thick hard cock rubbed against her sensitive wetness, making her moan and writhe. She was losing her place again. She couldn't lose her place. She needed to stay on task. She needed...

She just *needed.*

Slipping a hand between their sweat-drenched bodies, she grasped him. Reveling in the feel of all that soft satiny skin encasing hard, throbbing flesh. He moaned, pressing up into her hold, and she bit his nipple. Delirious with wanting him, she positioned him at her entrance and sank down on top of him.

Her head fell back as she sat up straight, letting her weight take him deep. Feeling every thick inch of him as he impaled her. The world was spinning. Her body felt like it was made of bubbles and she could float away. Or pop, one at a time in a cascade of tingles.

Hands grasped her hips. Muscles beneath her tensed.

Ryan pushed up into her, and those special nerves that only he could reach were plucked like harp strings, sending musical vibrations throughout her body.

"Sarah," he moaned, his voice tight. Her name stretched between them.

She rotated her hips and fireworks went off inside her eyelids. Lifting her hands, lost in the feelings, she raised them above her head. Reaching to touch the stars only she could see.

His hands moved to her breasts, kneading, massaging, caressing.

She was on fire.

Flames dancing over her skin.

Ryan flexed and his hips thrust up, pushing deeper into her. She was going to faint. Pass out. Right there on top of him. And it would be amazing.

"Kiss me," he growled.

And, with effort, Sarah opened her heavy eyelids to look at him. His eyes were ablaze. His cheeks flushed. His lips swollen. And the muscles in his neck and shoulders were stretched tight.

Hers.

She collapsed onto him, finding his mouth with hers. Clasping his face in her hands as she devoured him. Ryan held her hips. His kisses just as desperate as hers as he pistoned up into her. They moaned and gasped. Clinging, feasting, moving in a desperate rhythm that drove them both higher and higher until there was nothing but Sarah and Ryan.

Her legs began to tingle. Her kisses lost their focus. Her mind was soaring.

"Now," she moaned.

"Now," Ryan agreed as he thrust upward.

Together, they exploded. Coming apart in a cascade of colors and sparkles that showered the earth.

Sarah's muscles lost all tension, and limp, she fell to Ryan's chest. Where she lay, listening to his rushed breathing and racing heart. There was nothing else that mattered.

***

Ryan gently massaged Sarah's backside as she slept on top of him. They were messy, sticky, but he didn't care. A vague thought swam in his mind, telling him he should care. That sticky meant no condom, and he didn't know if Sarah was on anything that would protect them. There could be consequences. But even that passing thought didn't cause him worry. Because, it was Sarah.

He was floating on a cloud of pure contentment. He didn't want to move, he wanted to bask. She'd stolen his breath, and his heart. Had it been like that before? Had she been wild in bed and blown his mind? Had he wanted to keep her as much then as he did now?

Already he wanted her again, even though they were both too exhausted to go for round two. Sleep, then sex. Lots of sex. Although, he wasn't sure he could sleep. He felt wired, his mind racing, his body flush with endorphins and adrenaline. Yet, he was at peace. Because this was where he belonged.

There was a soft knock at their door, and Ryan pulled up the duvet ensuring Sarah was covered.

"Yeah," he called softly, but Sarah didn't even stir.

Dimitri's head peeked around the door, and he grinned when he saw Sarah on top of Ryan. "We picked up the Baker guy. You want in?"

It was the perfect use for all the extra energy he suddenly had, at least until Sarah was rested.

"Gimme fifteen," he said, and Dimitri closed the door quietly.

Gently, he moved Sarah onto the bed beside him before going to get a warm cloth to clean her up. She slept through everything. Ryan jumped in the shower quickly and dressed even faster. Pausing to write a note before letting himself out of the room.

Dimitri and Callum were waiting for him in the sitting room.

"Who's staying to watch the women?" he asked.

It was the first time he'd asked that question of the team when he'd been the one who had a woman who needed protecting. It made him want to strut. Yep, Elle was right—he was basically a teenager.

"Joe and Megan are staying here," Dimitri said.

Ryan's eyebrows shot up. "Does Megan know she's on watchdog duty?" Because the suite was pretty silent if she did. Usually there was a whole lot more shouting.

"She's asleep. I tried waking her up, but she just complained." Dimitri shrugged, grinning as he did so. "You snooze, you lose."

"Your relationship is a mysterious thing." And one that might end suddenly once Megan woke up.

"Are we done yakking?" Callum said. "Can we go hit someone now?"

Sharing a grin with Dimitri, Ryan followed his irritated boss down to the car. Twenty minutes later, they pulled up to an ugly concrete office building. The kind that was built the world over when budget was more important than aesthetics.

They were in a business park in the middle of the night,

which meant the place was dark and deserted. Just the way they liked it. As they approached a nondescript side door, it swung open and Harvard appeared.

"What is this place?" Ryan asked.

"CIA safe house. You haven't been here. You've never heard of it. It doesn't exist."

"Gotcha."

They followed him into the building and down into the basement, where he swung a metal cabinet filled with cleaning supplies out of the way before they entered the door behind it.

"We have control of the cameras," Harvard said as he led them down a long gray corridor. "And there's no one in the building. Even if we aren't done by office hours, it's safe to leave him here. But it shouldn't take that long." He eyed Ryan. "You up to date on the game plan?"

"Got the rundown in the car. Did you have any problem picking the guy up?"

Harvard grinned. "Funny thing. We had it all planned out—how we'd distract his muscle and separate him from the rest of his people. But when we got there, Lake said to give him a sec. He sauntered in through the front doors of the strip bar and came out a couple of minutes later with Fournier on his heels. No bodyguards. No guns. Nothing. Lake just opened the back door of the car and Fournier climbed in."

Ryan burst out laughing. "Does anybody know what he said to Fournier?"

"Nope." Harvard shook his head. "But I'd like to. Because—damn."

"And that's why *we* work for *him*," Ryan said.

"No kidding," Harvard muttered.

Through another metal door. Down another set of

concrete stairs. They entered a plain, empty room. There was one chair, bolted to the floor, and a man was cuffed to it.

Lake, Callum, Dimitri, Ryan, and Harvard spread out around their prey and watched as he nervously licked his lips. A lizard with a shoestring mustache and oiled hair.

"All this for me? I'm flattered," he said in English.

When his gaze skimmed over Ryan, he seemed to falter for a second. A sign that he recognized the man he'd abducted and thought dead. Fournier shifted in his seat but remained calm. He was, after all, a negotiator. And it was clear he felt he could bargain his way out of his predicament.

"I don't talk," he said to Lake. "You must know this. My clients pay for my silence. But perhaps we could come to another arrangement that is satisfactory for all of us."

Ryan and his team just stared at the man, as the menace in the air became thick enough to taste.

With another furtive glance at Ryan, Fournier changed tactics. "It's about this one, isn't it?" He pointed at Ryan but continued to talk to Lake. Who, so far, hadn't moved a muscle in reply.

"I was paid to deliver him," Fournier said. "What happens then is not my concern." He shrugged. "We are men of the world, Monsieur Benson. You know how these games are played. It is nothing personal."

It'd felt pretty damn personal to Ryan. Even more so because they hadn't just picked him, they'd picked Sarah too.

Callum took a step toward Fournier, and the rest of the team followed. Still no one spoke. There were dots of perspiration on Fournier's brow now. But he appeared calm and unconcerned.

"I made my peace with this life many years ago," he

said. "I knew one day someone would come and ask questions I could not answer. C'est la vie. But you must know, there are people who will not be happy if The Baker is gone."

"Like Abramovich," Lake spoke for the first time. "We dealt with him after he trafficked one of our team's sister."

Dimitri didn't even bat an eyelash at the mention of Katrina's ordeal.

"Or Carlos Esteban," Callum said. "But then, he died after involving one of my staff in his crimes."

"Maybe you mean the Martinez brothers," Harvard said. "But I do believe we put that cartel out of business after they messed with a friend of mine."

"Must be the James Gang." Dimitri's voice was ice. "But they didn't survive a run-in with us either when they went after one of ours."

"Looks like you're losing friends faster than making them," Ryan drawled. "Kinda makes you wonder who'd come looking for you if you disappeared."

Fournier paled, his tongue darting out to lick his lips again. "Is this supposed to make me nervous? I have many more friends."

Harvard's phone buzzed, and he looked down at it. A slow smile, much like that of a shark, spread across his face.

"Is one of those friends Uri Petrov?"

Fournier was quick to cover the flicker of shock that crossed his face.

"Because that dude is going down." Harvard held up his phone. "Seems all the records you had on him are now in the hands of Russian authorities." He glanced at the phone. "Oh, and the CIA. That's cool. One for the home team."

"C'est impossible," Fournier said tightly. "My records cannot be accessed."

"Whatever you say." Harvard shrugged as Dimitri's phone pinged.

"Well now, this is interesting. Seems you're close to a guy called Albescu who runs women out of Romania. Not the nicest guy. You really should be choosier when picking friends, Fournier. Anyway, looks like his info is winging its way to Interpol as we speak." He looked at Callum. "Aren't they coordinating an international investigation into human trafficking?"

"Aye," Callum said. "I believe they are."

"Non!" Fournier snapped. "This is but a ruse. It is not possible for you to have my files."

Lake walked the few steps to stand directly in front of the Frenchman. He folded his arms and looked down at the man. There was no expression on his face. "Here's the thing —Albescu? Petrov? They don't know that. As far as they and the authorities are concerned, the information came from you."

Fournier was sweating profusely now.

"Says so right here." Harvard held up his phone again.

"They will know this is not true." Fournier looked at each of them. "You cannot know what jobs I have fulfilled for them."

"Aye, we can." Callum stepped up beside Lake. "See, we have a hacker and a CIA agent who've been digging into your business. Those two have a lot of connections between them, and they might not know the details of your operations, but they know enough to point people in the right direction. You tell us you won't talk, but there are people out there who are happy to tell David Knight anything he wants to know."

"Le Chevalier?" Fournier blustered. "He is but a myth."

"He's a myth who's dusting your ass right now," Harvard said.

"As things stand," Lake said, "you only have to watch your back for Petrov and Albescu. We can keep going. The list will grow. It's going to be hard for you to hide from that many of your ex-customers. And sure, you can try to convince them we're behind the leaks. You might even manage with one or two. But not with ten. Or twenty. Or thirty. Because we will keep going until we pull on every string that even hints at having you at its source. We'll expose it all, Fournier."

It was the most Lake had said in years, and Ryan was kind of awestruck by it.

"And, meanwhile," Callum said, "our hacker will find your files. It's just a matter of time."

"Especially seeing as the guy who wrote the security program the UK government uses was a silent partner in Benson Security." Harvard was smiling again. "I'm sure he'd be happy to help his friends destroy your ass."

"I-I can't talk." Fournier was pleading now. "If it gets out, I will be killed."

"Baker man," Dimitri said. "Your days are numbered anyway. Now, you gotta choose whether you want two bad guys on your tail or twenty. I know what I'd pick."

Ryan crouched, bringing himself eye level with the Frenchman. "We only want to know one thing—who hired you to abduct me and Sarah Davidson. That's it. Nothing more. You give us a name, and we walk away."

Fournier's shoulders slumped, then he cursed them out in his native language.

Looking into Ryan's eyes, he said, "Professor Garnier."

CHAPTER THIRTY-THREE

They were back at the hospital where they'd surfaced from the catacombs. Sarah's anxiety grew with every step they took toward their destination. Although, she wasn't afraid. That would have been impossible when she was surrounded by members of the most exclusive private security team in the world. The only two missing were Rachel and Julia.

"You doing okay, Stats?" Ryan asked as he squeezed her hand.

"No," she said honestly, earning grins from everyone who heard.

"Me neither." His smile settled something within her.

As they entered one of the older buildings at the back of the complex, a security guard approached them. Dimitri and Megan broke off from the group to deal with him, while the rest of the team never even paused as they walked down the corridor in search of Professor Garnier.

There was a secretary in the outer office. She took one look at the group and reached for the phone. Joe gently removed it from her hand, smiled, and took care of the situation. Meanwhile, Harvard positioned himself in front of the outer door as a sentry.

Lake opened the door to the inner office, and everyone else streamed in.

"Who are you? What do you want?" Sarah heard a voice say in French and English.

Sarah's hands began to shake, and she fought the urge to run as Ryan sent her a reassuring glance.

"Professor Garnier?" Callum rumbled.

"Oui," came the terse reply. "Please leave and make an appointment. I'm very busy."

"This won't take long," Callum said.

The group parted, spreading around the large room and allowing Sarah her first look at the person who'd orchestrated her abduction.

Behind the wide mahogany desk sat an elegant woman, who looked to be in her late fifties, possibly older. Her hair was in a classic twist at the back of her head. She wore a tastefully patterned silk scarf, knotted at her throat, over a cream blouse. There were understated diamond earrings in her ears, although her manicured hands were without adornment. She was thin, to the point of being pinched, with a sharp intelligence in her brown eyes that never stopped assessing as she looked at them.

"I don't know you," Sarah said, feeling strangely disconnected from the whole experience.

Those sharp eyes focused on Sarah. They skimmed down to where she still held hands with Ryan, then up to Ryan's face.

Recognition flickered. "Ah, now, I see."

It vaguely registered that her accent wasn't French—it was North American. USA or Canada. Sarah had never been good at telling them apart.

Garnier pushed away from the desk, and Sarah noticed something she hadn't before—the woman was in a wheelchair. She rolled around her desk and came to a halt in front of them. There was an iPad in her lap, and she took the pen from it, opened a document, and faced them with a look of cold assessment.

"I wondered if you'd made it out of the catacombs," she said with an eagerness in her voice that made Sarah's stomach turn. "I need to know how you did it. Forgive me." She waved a hand. "I have a lot of questions. You're the first of my subjects that I've had the opportunity to meet in person."

"Subjects?" Sarah whispered. Nothing the woman said made any sense.

"You're part of a very important study. Please, take a seat. We have a lot of ground to cover." Garnier motioned to a corner of the office that had a leather sofa in it. She seemed to have tuned out the other people in the room, now that she had her attention on them.

"I don't understand," Sarah said to Ryan.

"I think I do." Ryan practically vibrated with rage.

Around them, Lake and Callum were rifling through cabinets and drawers, while Elle and David concentrated on the bank of computer monitors against the far wall.

Voices came through the door, angry and commanding. But Joe and Harvard were on sentry duty and no one got past them. Sarah heard someone mention the police before Joe calmly replied they'd already been called. Dimitri and Megan were waiting for their contacts downstairs.

"Callum," Elle said, her voice tight. "I have the video feed. There are stored video files of past victims. They're couples. All couples. There are several here, going back years."

Professor Garnier seemed to take issue with Elle's terminology. "Not victims—participants. Carefully chosen to enhance this study. And don't touch that; I can't have you corrupting years of data. In fact, it's time that everyone left this office." She looked at Ryan and Sarah. "Except you two."

"You were studying us?" Sarah said, frowning in confusion.

"Yes, of course," Garnier said. "Please sit. I'm getting a pain in my neck from looking up at both of you."

"Lady," Ryan said. "I might just fix that for you. Permanently."

Garnier cocked her head at him. "Aggression. Interesting." She made a note.

"The effects of the male self-preservative instinct on romantic love," Lake read from a file he'd gotten from her desk. "Utilizing a controlled environment, subjects are confronted by an unwinnable scenario. The female partner is secured to the location and unable to escape. While the male partner is free to roam. The author hypothesizes that romantic love would have little to no impact on the male's overwhelming instinct for survival. When given the choice of dying with his loved one or having a chance at survival alone, the author proposes that the male will always choose the latter." He tossed the file onto the desk.

"You left us to die, for a study?" Sarah had to sit down, but the last thing she wanted was to do it in that office.

"No, I gave you options." Garnier's smile was cold. "I made a mistake leaving you with your belongings; I see that now. I didn't realize how resourceful you could be. Of course, that means you didn't actually confront the issues raised by the test, as you simply bypassed the challenge by releasing your partner. You're an anomaly that fooled the test criteria, but there is still important data that can be gleaned from your experience. It's obvious that the test conditions need some tweaking in order to ensure compliance going forward. It's very important for me to know how you got out of the catacombs."

"She thinks you're Kirk," Elle said in disgust. "And this is the Kobayashi Maru. She wanted you in a no-win situation and you won. Guess you're not such a big brain after all, huh, Professor?"

"Please don't speak to me," Garnier said. "You're irrelevant." She sighed as she looked up at Ryan and Sarah, disappointment on her face. "And it would seem that you are too. If you aren't willing to share information, then you must excuse me. I have work to do." She turned her chair and addressed the rest of the team. "Get out of my office, or I'll call security."

Ryan dropped Sarah's hand and spun the wheelchair back around to face them.

"Who put you in the wheelchair?" he said.

"That isn't relevant," she snapped.

"It was a lover, wasn't it?" Ryan looked around, taking in the few personal images in the room before drawing his own quick conclusions. "Did it happen during rock climbing or caving? Because the catacombs weren't just a convenient location. You aren't from Paris, are you, professor? You're Canadian, and I'm betting you moved here to be near the catacombs."

"This is none of your business," Garnier said. "Charlotte," she called. "Get security."

Ryan ignored her. "He left you when you were injured, didn't he? Left you to die instead of dying alongside you like a crazy, in-love man should have done. I mean, where was the practical evidence of all those declarations of everlasting love? When he'd whispered that he'd die for you, had it only been metaphorical?"

"Shut up," Garnier snapped as she tried to wheel her chair out of Ryan's grasp.

"When he was confronted with the choice to make the ultimate sacrifice for the woman he loved, he chose himself, didn't he? He left you to die. Only you survived, and you've been trying to prove that he couldn't help it ever since. It's the male instinct, right? It wasn't because he was a selfish coward, or maybe you weren't worth saving. It was biology. Or environmental conditioning. Or anything other than the truth." Ryan bent over the woman, staring her in the eye. "Am I close?"

Garnier struck out, slapping Ryan across the cheek.

Without thinking, Sarah reacted and slapped the woman hard in return.

Hand burning, she blinked at Ryan in shock.

"It's only *me* who makes you violent, huh?" With a shake of his head, he stood and took her stinging hand in his before looking at Callum. "I'm taking Sarah back to the hotel."

Callum nodded. "Cops can talk to you just as easily there as here."

Ryan strode from the room, taking Sarah with him, as Garnier started to rant about how she was suing for assault.

The rest of the day was a blur of official activity. Sarah had to tell her story to several different police officers as the investigation covered multiple jurisdictions, some international. By the time evening came around, she was tired of repeating herself. More than that, she was tired of hearing herself talk about an ordeal she'd rather forget.

The Parisian police contingent, headed by an associate of Lake's, gratefully accepted Benson Security's offer to help with their investigation. Which meant Elle and David were holed up at cop central, digging through all of the digital records taken from Garnier's office. So far, they'd found evidence of eight couples who'd lost their lives after being randomly chosen by a madwoman to take part in her sick experiment. They suspected there would be more names added to their list in the coming days.

It turned out that the couples were chosen from a blog called Love in the City. Normally, the blogger was based in Paris. But sometimes, he took jobs in other cities. He'd taken one in London to help promote a pop-up roller disco that Ryan and Sarah had spontaneously attended. The video he shot of them caught the eye of their abductor. It was only because Ryan had been shot that they hadn't ended up in the catacombs a year earlier. Instead, she'd bided her time and picked them up when it suited her.

Why the woman hadn't just forgotten about them, only she knew. And unless she started talking, it would stay that way. As soon as the professor had stopped worrying about her data, she'd asked for a lawyer and hadn't said anything else since.

Sarah wasn't sure what was worse—being the random victim of senseless violence, or having come to an evil person's attention because she'd fallen in love. And, she had fallen in love. Possibly that very first night she'd met Ryan in person. Or even weeks earlier, during their first silly, intimate, wonderful conversation.

The sad thing was, even though he'd unintentionally

hurt her when he disappeared, and even though she definitely knew better, she was still in love with him.

She just couldn't have him.

"Hey, you okay?" The object of her musings plopped down beside her on the sitting room sofa. A bag of chips in his hand. "Hungry?" He angled the bag toward her.

"No, thanks." She rested her hand on his knee, allowing herself this time with him before it all ended. Storing each memory for the day when she'd feel strong enough to take them out and revel in having known him.

He covered her hand with his. "The police didn't upset you, did they?"

She shook her head. "I'm exhausted. How are things going with you?"

"Good. We've got oxygen tanks coming in for the pool we swam through. Better safe than sorry. Either way, we have to go back through the water to get to the original cavern. Once there, we'll dismantle the gate and see where that tunnel leads, but it should be an easier route out, don't you think?"

Honestly, Sarah didn't want to think about it at all. "Yes, I think you're right."

Memories of sending the rats in after the bodies flashed through her mind, and she cringed. If she had to choose all over again, would she still have done that? Sadly, she would. Especially if it meant saving Ryan—even if it was from a few rats.

"You realize I'm only showing these guys the way, right? Once they're in there, it's all on them."

"I know." But she also knew that he was too good at his job, loved it too much, to resist the temptation of staying underground to help with the investigation.

"Ryan," Callum snapped from the dining room. "Get your arse in here. We're no' finished yet."

"Gotta go." He pressed a quick kiss to her lips before hurrying from the room.

Once he was out of sight, she made her way through the crowded suite to Rachel's room.

"Come in," Rachel called after Sarah had knocked.

The room was much like the one she'd been sharing with Ryan, only with a tad more gilt. Rachel sat at a delicate desk in front of the windows, looking out over the Eiffel Tower. A laptop was open in front of her, and her phone was in her hand. Harvard sat on the sofa, drinking coffee while reading a report Elle had sent him. Sarah knew it was a report on the bodies because the photos were hard to miss, even from a few feet away.

Harvard's smile was welcoming, while Rachel looked slightly bored.

"I'm sorry to bother you," Sarah said to the woman who scared her a little. "I want to go home and wondered if you could arrange that for me. I don't have a passport or any access to my money, but I can sort that out when I'm home. It's just getting there...you seem like the kind of person who'd know how to do that and could make it happen. Will you help me?"

Honestly, she expected Rachel to tell her to get lost. From what she'd seen of the woman, she didn't exactly play well with others.

The brunette swept her long silken hair over her shoulder as she considered Rachel. She arched a perfectly plucked brow. "Ryan?"

"It's finished," Sarah said, although it hadn't really started, had it? A few stolen days, under extreme circumstances, did not a relationship make. "I need to go home."

The woman considered her for what felt like endless seconds before she stood. "We'll leave now."

Sarah wanted to weep with gratitude.

Harvard wasn't so thrilled. "You can't just walk out on Ryan, honey," he said gently. "And the cops might have a few more questions. Don't you think it would be better to hang around for a few days?"

Before she could reply, Rachel spoke, "She said no, Michael. We respect the no."

Harvard stood, clasped the back of Rachel's neck, and pressed a sweet kiss to her lips. "Yeah, we do," he rumbled. "What will I tell the crew?"

"Tell them the truth." Rachel slung her handbag over the crook of her arm. "I'm smuggling Sarah back into the UK, and I'll send the plane for them later."

"Got it." He nodded, and then to Sarah's surprise, enfolded her in a careful hug. "You're in good hands, honey. Rachel will get you home safe, and if you need anything, just call us, okay?"

"When I get another phone," she said, feeling suddenly weepy.

"Oh, for the love of Prada, you don't have a phone? How have you been managing?" Rachel waved her iPhone to emphasize her point. "We'll pick up one on the way."

And then she strode out of the door, expecting Sarah to follow. Before she did exactly that, she reached into the pocket of her jeans and took out the letter she'd written for Ryan.

"Will you make sure he gets this?" she asked.

"Absolutely." Harvard took it from her.

And then Sarah hurried after his wife.

CHAPTER THIRTY-FOUR

Three weeks later
Benson Security Office
London

Ryan had been running on fury, frustration, and fear for the past three weeks. And all of it was because of Sarah. She'd left him in Paris without saying goodbye, instead writing him a crappy Dear John letter that reeked of martyrdom. *She couldn't ask him to choose between her and his job...bullshit!*

Like he hadn't known from the minute he'd met her— the second time—that she wasn't cut out to be an army, or police, or even private security "widow." Some women could take having their men walk out of the door and straight into trouble. Sarah couldn't. And there was nothing wrong with that.

Except in her head.

He huffed in exasperation. What was it with intelligent

women and their need to overthink everything? Sometimes you just had to go with your gut. Or in this case, your heart.

Yeah, he was seriously pissed.

But first, he had a team meeting to deal with.

Rachel smacked her handbag onto the boardroom table and glared at Ryan. "I hope you didn't drag me all the way over here for a briefing on the psycho killer."

"Qu'est-ce que c'est," Elle said grinning.

Ryan couldn't help laughing, while Rachel scowled.

"At least she didn't sing it," he said.

"Why are you calling meetings anyway?" Rachel pulled out a chair and graced it with the presence of her backside. "Are the people at the bottom of the totem allowed to call meetings?"

"Give it a rest, Rachel," Callum barked from his usual spot at the front of the room. "The boy has something to say."

"The boy is the same age as I am," Rachel pointed out.

"Yet, you're CEO of Drugs, Inc. and I'm bottom of the totem pole. Life is cruel." Ryan grinned at her.

Callum ran a hand through his hair, making it stand up on end. Not that it ever looked combed, but he'd managed to make it worse than usual. "No' as cruel as it's going tae be if you two don't stop bickering and we get to the reason we're here. I haven't been home in three weeks, and I have a family I'd like to see."

"I've seen you," his wife, Isobel, said from the doorway. "And I'm good for at least a couple of hours." She batted her eyelashes at him, making his face turn beetroot.

"Did you use his office?" Megan stretched her arms out onto the table as she spoke to Isobel. "Because if you want to change it up, the workout room has awesome acoustics."

That little revelation earned loud groans and

complaints from everyone. Except Julia, who whispered something in Joe's ear, then turned luminous when he answered her.

"I bet she asked if they were singing," Elle said to Ryan under her breath.

Man, he loved his team. His friends. His family. Looking around, he knew he'd made the right decision. They were tight, and they'd have his back. Even Rachel. Sure, she might put a knife in it while she was there, but she wouldn't let anyone else do it to him.

"Get back to the reception desk," Callum told his wife, who cheekily saluted him before closing the door behind her.

"So, she's still employed, then?" Harvard drawled, making everyone cover their laughter.

"Hey," Elle said. "I've just realized something. Did anybody else notice the parallels between Rachel and the creepy professor? They're both independently wealthy, they both dress like Prada Barbie, and they both think other people are only there for them to play with." She beamed at Rachel. "You could have been a serial killer."

Rachel rolled her eyes. "No. I couldn't. I prefer the people I experiment on to live."

Harvard's laugh was deep and contagious. As everyone else joined in, Ryan decided it was time to get things back on track.

"Okay, let's get to the reason for this meeting," Ryan said, tapping out a drum roll on the tabletop. "I'm handing in my resignation, effective immediately." *Ta-da!*

There was a moment's silence before all hell broke loose.

Elle demanded he "take that back," or she'd give him a noogie. Julia asked if he was healthy and looked worried while doing it. Rachel told him he wasn't coming to work for her. Dimitri and Megan wanted to know what else he could do because, according to Megan, his skills were only suitable for Benson Security and he'd die without them. Joe, David, and Harvard just sat back, looking amused at everyone else.

Then Callum bellowed, "Shut up!"

And, funnily enough, people did. Once there was silence, under the eye of death from Callum, Ryan got the nod to continue.

"It's like this," he said. "I've been lying to all of you. And to myself. The truth is, no matter how hard I work at it, I'm not fit for the field." He held up his right hand, which wasn't shaking even though he'd expected this part of his explanation to make him nervous. "I get muscle spasms and can't grip whatever I'm holding. Then there are the migraines—although they could be seizures. We're not really sure. All I know is they come out of nowhere and are totally debilitating."

"But that doesn't mean you can't be part of the team," Elle said. "You can still work with us while you heal."

He patted her fuzzy blue hair. "I'm not going to heal, sis. It is what it is."

"You can't know that." She looked at David. "Can he?"

"I'm gonna guess and say his neurologist has been over it with him, Blue." David tugged her closer to him.

"I didn't want to face it." Ryan looked around the room at the people he loved. "But a hand spasm almost got Sarah killed in the tunnels. And things down there could have been a whole lot worse if I'd had a sudden onset migraine in the middle of them." He thought of the swim through darkened water. "It was pure luck that I didn't. I'm a liability, guys. And that was before the international press attention."

The group groaned, and Rachel rolled her eyes so hard, he thought her head might follow.

Being involved with a female serial killer had meant that all of them had been hounded by the press. But they *loved* Ryan. Not only was he photogenic, he was one of only two survivors left behind by the Valentine Killer, as they'd named her. Several times, Ryan had called out journalists for their lack of originality in naming the professor, but none of them listened.

"Anyway," he said. "My face is everywhere. Kinda makes covert ops a problem. Hell, even straight bodyguard work would be impossible if I was getting more attention than the guy who hired me."

"But it will pass," Dimitri said. "There'll be another news story to replace it soon enough."

"I don't know." Ryan sighed. "I've been offered book deals and asked to sell the movie rights. The BBC wants to do a documentary. There are podcasts dedicated to the professor's screwed research. This isn't going to go away any time soon. And whether I like it or not, I'm the face of the story while we keep Sarah's name out of things, and while Garnier refuses to talk. Where I go, the press goes. Which means you guys are on the news too. We can't function as a security company with that kind of attention."

"I hate to admit it, but he's right," Joe said. "There's press parked outside the building right now, waiting for him."

"I don't care how much sense he's making," Elle said. "I don't want him to go."

"There's another reason." Ryan took a deep breath. "I

want a life with Sarah, and she couldn't cope with me working this job."

And again with the explosive opinions.

Megan, especially, was furious. "You can't give up what you love because your girlfriend can't handle it. You'll just resent her in the long run. And she has no right to ask this of you. None!"

"She hasn't asked. She isn't even my girlfriend. She walked away in Paris and has no intention of coming back."

"Then why does she even factor?" Megan demanded.

"Because he loves her," Julia said with an understanding smile.

"Yeah. And I'm going to harass the life out of her until she marries me. The truth is, this is a job for me. I'm good at it, and happy to fit wherever I'm needed, but it isn't my life's passion. I'm not going to miss it. But I will miss all of you. And that's what makes this hard."

"You'll see us," Callum said gruffly. "Look at Rachel—she left and I cannae get her to stop coming back."

Laughter defused the room slightly, but Elle still looked sad, and Ryan hated seeing her like that.

He nudged her with his shoulder. "You can come over whenever you like. I've got the new PlayStation. We could gang up on David and Sarah—if I can get Sarah to play." *Or take him back...*

"So, if she doesn't take you back, does that mean you aren't resigning?" Megan said.

Ryan shook his head. "No, this is it. The end of the road for me at Benson Security. No matter what happens with Sarah, this job is over."

"Well," Harvard drawled when nobody else seemed to know what to say. "A new beginning calls for a party."

That definitely lightened the mood.

A chair scraped and Julia stood, twisting her hands in front of her. "I, we, have news too."

Joe smiled at her as he joined her at her side, wrapping an arm around her shoulder. She looked up at him and nodded.

"We're having a baby," Joe said.

This time the room exploded with congratulations and excitement. All except for Harvard, who was laughing so hard it made everyone else turn quiet.

"Something funny?" Joe asked his lifelong friend.

"Yeah. Rachel's pregnant too."

There was a stunned silence as Rachel smacked her husband's shaved head.

"Don't make a big deal about it," she told everyone else. "I intend to pretend it isn't happening."

"You're pregnant?" Megan seemed to be torn between looking horrified or amused. "Is it human?"

Harvard chuckled as Julia gasped. "Megan, you can't say something like that to a pregnant woman."

Rachel held up her hand and pointed a red talon at Julia. "Save your hearts and flowers for someone who cares. We won't be bonding over baby onesies. And there will be *no* talk of breastfeeding from anyone, do you hear? If I'd had time to plan for this, we would have used a surrogate. Someone suitably lower-class and eager to be paid to endure swollen ankles and childbirth."

"She's joking," Harvard said hurriedly. "About the lower-class part. Probably not about the rest. What can I say? My wife is still a work in progress."

"I knew I shouldn't have married a commoner," Rachel complained as Harvard grinned.

"Well, I think pregnancy is wonderful." Julia practically glowed as she placed a hand reverently over her belly.

Suddenly, a pang of envy hit Ryan, so sharp it made him wince. He wanted what Joe had. The wife, the family, all of it. His days of staying up all night partying with lingerie models were over. And he couldn't have been happier.

Unless Sarah refused to change her mind and admit she wanted him in her life.

Pushing back his chair, he faced his team one last time as a member of Benson Security. "I need to track down Sarah. Let me know when the party is. We've got a lot to celebrate. Now, who's going to create a diversion so I can slip out the back without the press on my tail?"

Everyone except Callum and Rachel put up their hands.

Sarah waved to her neighbor, Mrs. Pinner, as she walked up the path to the door of her South London terrace house.

"Any nibbles yet?" she asked, nodding to the for-sale sign in the front garden.

The old woman sighed as she fluffed her lilac hair. "Nobody appreciates a well-decorated house these days."

Considering Mrs. Pinner's idea of interior design lent itself to chintz and lace, Sarah wasn't that surprised.

"It'll happen." Sarah had even looked up the statistics to back up her claim, in case Mrs. Pinner ever asked.

"It'd better happen soon. I'm not getting any younger, and I want to move to Spain before I die."

With a smile, Sarah unlocked her front door, swung it open, and smelled bacon.

What?

She'd taken two steps into her house when Ryan

appeared in the kitchen doorway, frying pan in his hand and a loopy smile on his face.

Sarah double-checked that she'd opened her house door and not the entrance to another dimension. Definitely her house.

"Ryan, what are you doing here?" she managed to get out as her eyes drank him in.

"Well, I'd planned to sit on your front step until you got home, but then this guy walked past with a T-shirt that had a print of a can of Spam on the front of it. Then I thought, Spam-ham-pork-bacon. Next thing I knew, I was buying bacon from the guy at the corner shop, and now I'm making sandwiches. You want one?"

Nope, none of that made any sense at all. "Couldn't you make a bacon sandwich in your own house?"

"Yeah. But you aren't there." He glanced at the pan. "I need to get this on the heat." And disappeared into her kitchen.

Shutting the door, Sarah wondered if she was experiencing some form of psychosis. A break from reality, perhaps, brought on by thinking about Ryan every minute of every day.

"Stats, get in here," he yelled.

Feeling disoriented, she made her way into the kitchen, where Ryan was frying bacon at her stove. He wore a white T-shirt that stretched over his shoulders and stomach, reminding her of Steve Rogers when he'd just been turned into Captain America. Under it were soft, worn blue jeans that cupped his backside like butter on a hot potato.

"Where's the tomato ketchup?" Ryan asked as he started opening and shutting cupboards.

"I don't have any."

He screeched to a halt and stared at her. "That is so

wrong. How can you not have tomato ketchup? It's a staple."

Sarah pressed her fingers to her temples as she tried to focus. "Ryan, why are you here?"

"I explained," he said as he shoved the bacon on some fluffy white bread that she also hadn't bought.

"Not about the Spam T-shirt. I mean, why are you *here*?"

"Oh." His smile was pure temptation. "Well, I came to tell you that I've quit my job and to ask you to move in with me. But then I realized your house is way nicer than mine, so now I'm asking if I can move in here."

She sat down at the small round table with a thump. "W-what?"

"I know, I'm surprised too. I was going to wait with the whole living together conversation because I was so damn mad at you for the Dear John letter, but then I got hungry and now I don't care so much about the letter." He smiled again. "I might have already eaten a few things to take the edge off."

"Wait, go back. You quit your job?"

"About an hour ago." He brought a plate loaded with cholesterol sandwiches over to the table and sat beside her.

"You can't quit your job," she said, her brain at least two steps behind her mouth. "You love it."

"Ah, but not as much as I love you." He stood. "Forgot my coffee." He strode over to the counter.

Sarah was back to saying, "What?"

"Plus," he said as he sat back down. "I have hand spasms and headaches that make my job hard. And there's a whole bunch of newspaper people who won't leave me alone." He frowned. "Nobody has annoyed you, have they?"

"No." She'd been really grateful that her name had been

kept out of everything and had wondered why Ryan's hadn't.

"Good. An idiot cop let it slip that the guy leading them back into the tunnels was the one who'd escaped the killer. That's how they found out about me. I'm glad we managed to keep the lid on your identity." He took a large bite of the sandwich, which, she had to admit, smelled wonderful.

"Are you talking this much so that I can't get a word in?" she asked while she could.

He swallowed, took a sip of coffee, and stared at her. "Do you have anything sensible to add to this conversation?"

"Ryan." She placed a hand on his arm, which was a huge mistake. Because now all she could think about was how fantastic it was when those arms held her. "I can't live with you resenting me for making you leave your job."

"You didn't. We're good." He shrugged like the topic was over.

"I'm serious. I know how much you love working for Benson Security. You thrive on the adventure and excitement. You won't get that from me and you'll resent me because of it."

He leaned forward in his chair, his eyes never leaving hers. There was such serious intent within them that it made her nervous.

"I'm only going to explain this once, and then this conversation is over forever, okay? I can find adventure and excitement anywhere. I don't need to risk my life to get it. More to the point, I can show *you* how to have excitement and adventure along with me. It wasn't you who changed my direction in life, it was a bullet to the head. All you did was give me a choice for the future that's way better than anything I could have come up with on my own. Whether we spend our lives together or not, I'm not going back to Benson Security. It's done. It's over. And now, I need to find a new way forward. I want that way to be with you. Not to replace my team, but because I love you and I choose you. The question is, do you choose me?"

"I want to believe you," she whispered, holding his gaze. But she'd never had anyone who *chose* her.

"Then get a move on, Stats. I'd rather be doing other things than talking."

Sarah hiccupped out a laugh as tears streamed down her cheeks. "I'm scared."

"You'll be fine. I won't let you get hurt."

"If you do, if you're lying, I'll call Rachel." And Rachel would probably do something they'd all regret.

"I seriously regret introducing you two," he said with a shake of his head. "It's one of life's mysteries that you can even talk to each other, let alone scheme together."

"I mean it," Sarah said. "I couldn't handle it if this was just you being wonderful and thinking of me instead of yourself."

"Trust me, baby, I'm very much thinking of myself. But if it makes you feel happier, sure, keep Rachel on speed dial. I know it will take a while for you to believe me. Until then, I'll just keep telling you that you're my choice and I love you."

Damn it, she was crying hard now. What a sissy! She cleared her throat and flashed him a smile. "So, living together, huh?"

"Too soon?" He caressed the tears off her cheek. "Because that's the toned-down option, I was going to start with proposing but figured it might freak you out completely."

"Good decision." Her stomach did somersaults just at the thought of marrying Ryan Granger.

"So, can we live here?" he asked, reminding her of an eager puppy.

She was standing on a precipice. The drop was too far to comprehend. But Ryan was telling her he'd be her safety net. Did she have the courage to step off the edge? To fly free instead of clinging to the safety of her small, boring life? To believe he'd catch her?

Staring into his eyes, she said the only thing a person could say when they were offered everything. "Yes."

"About bloody time," he muttered before taking her mouth in a kiss that was tender and needy, and tasted of bacon.

When they finally parted, Sarah felt drugged and desperate.

"Is it too soon yet to bring up marriage?" he asked before nodding. "We can talk about that tomorrow. Don't you think you should tell me you love me? I've said it a couple of times now and I'm feeling neglected."

"Stop being a big sissy," she said.

He just cocked an eyebrow at her.

Honestly, he was impossible. Feigning a sigh, she gave in. "Fine, I love you."

"At last. Was that so hard?"

Standing, Ryan took her hand and led her through the kitchen to the stairs up to her bedroom. *Their* bedroom. It was going to take months, maybe years, for her to believe this was real.

"I was thinking," he said as they climbed the stairs. "David and Elle might be interested in the house next door. If they bought it, we could join the attics and turn it into a huge hangout space. What do you think?"

"I think you were alone in here for far too long before I got home." She grinned at his back, which turned to a different kind of look when her eyes slid to his firm rear end. "What are you going to do if you don't work for Benson Security anymore?"

"Well," he flicked her a wicked look over his shoulder that made her trip on the stair. "I thought I'd focus on getting to know you better."

"Uh, huh, and when I'm at work and you can't *get to know me better*, what are you going to do with your life?"

"Oh, I have some ideas," he drawled as he tugged her into the bedroom.

EPILOGUE

Two years later
New York Times

Ryan Granger, the former army specialist who took the literary world by storm when his first thriller was published earlier this year, has sold the movie rights to Tom Cruise's production company. The film of his bestselling novel, Reset, is set for release at the end of next year. There is no word yet as to who will star. In the meantime, Ryan is hard at work on the second book in his series, which revolves around a London security company. Ryan, along with his wife, Sarah, came to the public's attention after they were held captive by the world's most prolific female serial killer. They are her only victims to have survived their fate and his first book was loosely based on their experience. Ryan Granger lives in London with his wife and their fifteen-month-old baby daughter.

ABOUT THE AUTHOR

Janet is a Scot, living in New Zealand and is married to a Dutch man. She writes contemporary romance and romantic suspense with a humorous bent – this is mainly due to the fact that she has an odd sense of humour and can't keep it out of anything she does! If she wasn't a writer, she'd like to be Buffy the Vampire Slayer, or Indiana Jones. Unfortunately, both of these roles have already been filled. Which may be a good thing as Janet has no fighting skills, wouldn't know a precious relic if it hit her in the face, and has an aversion to blood. When she's not living in her head, she's a mother to two kids and several pets.

Janet loves to hang out with her readers. You can chat with her in her Facebook group, which is full of awesome readers. And don't forget to sign up for her newsletter too!